BLUE OUT

CAPE HARMONY

MIRANDA STORM

SIGINT
PUBLICATIONS

First published by SIGINT Publications in 2022

Book cover design by More Visual
Additional artwork by Angelika Lialios & Petros Tsapalis
Copy edit by Kelly Urgan

ISBN: 978-1-8384723-0-6
eISBN: 978-1-8384723-1-3

SIGINT Publications

www.mirandastormbooks.com

To friends and family and all our first readers who supported us with their enthusiasm and love for stories. Thank you!

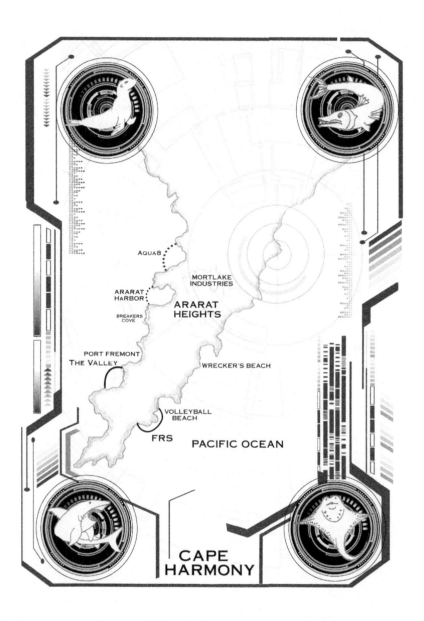

AQUA8

MORTLAKE
INDUSTRIES

ARARAT
HARBOR

ARARAT
HEIGHTS

BREAKERS
COVE

PORT FREMONT
THE VALLEY

WRECKER'S BEACH

VOLLEYBALL
BEACH

FRS

PACIFIC OCEAN

CAPE
HARMONY

CONTENTS

CHAPTER 1

— Flood Warning —

In the distance the sirens wail for Blue Out. A warning that another flood is imminent. I wade through the knee-deep water and the maze of abandoned houses in their murky canals. It's hard to imagine that the Valley was once home to fifteen thousand people. Jagged green lines run along the mossy walls marking the levels of all the previous floods. It was probably a bad idea to come here. Actually I'm pretty sure of it. Not just because of the weather. Since The Valley Flood, the one that washed this whole town away eleven months ago, the area is strictly off limits. No one is allowed in or out of our old neighborhood. I'm risking a one-way ticket to labor camp just by being here, just by sneaking out of the wire fence perimeter of the FRS, the Flood Relief Shelters, while everyone was reinforcing the flood barrier with sand bags. I shut out the image of armed government patrols sploshing through the water in pursuit, megaphones blaring, "Citizen Naya DeLora, you're under arrest for trespassing, suspected terrorism, and vandalism." Because if you're FRS trash, it doesn't matter whether you're a hulky vandal in full battle gear, or a skinny, sixteen-year-old girl, like me. Anyone breaching government regulations is immediately suspected of terrorism.

I push through the derelict front door into what was once a hallway. All that's left of the living room now are a few fragments of wood and a tilted table floating on the boggy water. Whatever furniture there was is mostly gone, destroyed by the floods. A damp, acrid smell fills the room and makes me gag. With an effort I force myself forward. It's difficult to make out anything beneath the muddy surface. Something soft and spongy brushes against my leg, exactly what I don't know. I recoil and keep walking. Mom would probably have a heart attack if she knew what I was doing.

Outside, gray clouds are gathering. Today's storm is meant to hit only the East Coast of Cape Harmony—but you'd have to have seaweed for brains to believe the official weather predictions, no matter how infallible our illustrious Governor claims them to be. And if the storm reaches the West Coast, the Valley where I am now and the surrounding area will be turned into a gigantic saltwater lake. There won't be enough time to run for the grassy hills. I know. I've seen it before. But it's too late to turn back now. Besides, I won't get another chance like this. How often do the storms hit only the eastern side of the headland? How often is the waterline in the Valley only a couple of feet deep? And how often can I get away from the FRS unnoticed? With any luck I'll be out of here before the first raindrops fall. I just need to get what I came for and get out.

I'm passing the window when the vroom of a motor engine cuts through the wail of the sirens. I duck down. I mustn't be seen here. Crouching low, I risk a peek over the rim of the cracked, wooden sill. There's a boat. Three men inside. Government patrol. One of the men gets up and the broad neon-blue stripe on his black wetsuit flashes in the rays of light of the setting sun. My heart skips a beat. This isn't just local search and rescue. They're Aqua8. The government's elite military unit. Being caught by them is a one-way ticket to labor camp—if I'm fortunate enough that they don't shoot on sight.

Drops of sweat drip into my eyes. Just my luck, the one time I sneak into a restricted zone, I have to run into the really bad guys. What are they doing here? The water is barely high enough to navigate a boat. I can only hope they won't conduct any house searches. If they do, I'm a sitting duck.

My clothes stick to me like a second skin. There is no reason for Aqua8 to be here. The whole area has flooded and dried up several times since anyone last lived here. With 75 percent of the Earth's former landmass submerged, coastal floods are a common occurrence. Even with flood barriers protecting our shoreline, the oceans have become so wild that the waves often splash high over the top of the protective dams during storms.

Which is why the government sound the Blue Out warnings. Sirens to inform us that another floodwave is imminent. Ordinary citizens are ordered to remain in their residences at that time—which is kind of what I'm doing. Except that's not how the authorities will see it.

Outside there's a crackle of static from a radio. "Follow . . . Alpha team . . ."

The growl of the engine grows distant. As it fades, I wait before peering out the window. The black motor dinghy is heading into the gray dusk of a gathering storm. I get up and scurry into the hall. I know I should turn back. Aqua8 and the imminent flood. But I'm too close to finding what I came for.

Mud squelches out of my sneakers as I leave the flooded first floor behind and climb the stairs. First door on the left, I pause. Mom's bedroom. The normality of it is both comforting and eerie, as I squeeze down the handle and step inside. The rosy-pink bed sheets unmade, her bathrobe laid on top. I scan the chest of drawers, the closet, the ottoman that Mom always used to bang her knee on but could never bring herself to part with. What I'm looking for is in here somewhere. But where?

I rummage through the drawers. Blouses, sweaters, skirts . . . Mom's treasured silk scarves, nightgowns. My mom's problem is when she hides stuff, even she can't find it anymore. We spent three months looking for a silver coin that was taped to the bottom of a foldout knitting box. All right, no need to panic, it's only my life that's at stake. I throw open the ottoman, breathing in a mixture of mothballs and mold. Pullovers. For a moment I debate taking them with me, but since the polar caps melted, it never really gets that cold, and the thought of lugging bulky clothes two miles through the flooded Valley isn't very inviting. Especially not with Aqua8 around.

I get down on my knees, ignoring the stench of damp that the carpet breathes into my face, and check under the mattress. There's nothing there either. Now I'm getting nervous. I need to be more systematic. I comb through the room from door to window. The shadows of the furniture grow longer in the dwindling daylight. Although I'm turning the whole place upside down, I'm not finding anything.

Where, where, where? I dig my hand through my hair and sit slumped on the bed. Think! Where would she have put it? Beneath me, the quilt is relatively dry. As I stroke the fabric, its familiar soft fibers spark happy memories. I choke back tears at the thought that this was once my home. Mildewed and smelly as it is, it's still paradise compared to the FRS, the Flood Relief Shelters where Mom and I now live.

Of course, we'd known about the danger. For all those too poor to live up on the verdant hills of Ararat, the floods were an ever-present threat. But the Valley was meant to be safe. A place where the middle classes could live in peace. Here, on the West Coast of Cape Harmony, we dwelled, like we were on an island, cut off from the chaos on the mainland by the northern mountain range and the sea. Protected from the ocean by a tall dam that ran the length of our bay. None of us had expected the sudden vehemence of The Valley Flood. The tsunami-like wave that breached the barrier, swallowing the whole Valley in a single day, not one inhabitable house left.

I ball my hands into fists. On the bedside table, the ballerina on Mom's music box stares at me, the same polished smile on her face as always—as if she pities me in my helplessness. I grimace. But in my mind, I can hear the music that plays when the lid opens. A tune from Mozart's *The Magic Flute*. I think of Mom, sitting on this bed, brushing my hair out of my face as we listened to it. We used to love those moments.

Wait! It dawns on me—could it be? I flip open the lid. No music plays. The mechanism that makes the ballerina spin is gone. In its place is what I've been looking for. My breath catches as I pull out a fist-sized golden conch, Mom's most treasured possession, and my reason for coming. There are no traces of damage on it; it's pristine, untouched by the cold and damp that has seeped into the house.

Mom always said, "This shell speaks to you with the voices of the ocean. Listen. If worst comes to worst, this can save us."

But as I cradle it in my palm, doubts creep into my mind. Can a conch really help us with everything that's happened? Mom and me being flooded out, the FRS, the endless lining up for food, never feeling clean, the crushing lack of privacy. Yet, the memory of Mom persists, her eyes hopeful, her whisper low and mysterious as she smiles and holds the conch to my ear. "Listen." And I listen now, even though I've learned that it's only my own blood rushing in my ear when I hold the shell close. I picture the ocean, the white waves washing up on the shore. Then the noise gets louder, tempestuous, roaring—like a warning shout. I tear the conch away. Dark water is washing around the soles of my shoes.

The flood! No, no! How can it have reached the second floor? Today's Blue Out was meant to be harmless. Just a smaller storm. That's why I risked coming here. Leaving the conch on the bed, I run to the window. Dusk is gathering into night. It's much later than I thought. And the still water that had idly covered our front lawn has transformed into a streaming, swirling torrent that now reaches to the bottom of the bedroom window.

Fear twines itself around me like seaweed. How can I have been so distracted that I didn't notice this? Can I get back now? The thought of the two miles between me and the FRS roots me to the spot. I'm no swimmer at the best of times, and as I look outside at the dark torrent of water, my hope fades. This is not like one of the Blue Outs where the storm waves wash over the dam a bit and Mom curses because she comes back from work with wet feet. It looks more like The Valley Flood, when it was as if the barrier that protects the Valley wasn't even there anymore.

I grab the conch. First of all, I need to make sure that it's safe. I look around for somewhere to stow it. Mom's tin box with her spare buttons and sewing thread! With shaking hands, I spill the contents onto the bed, grab a silk scarf and wrap it around the conch then tuck it in the tin. I close the lid, shove the box into the zipper pocket of my windbreaker jacket, and run back to the window.

The water is coming at the house in actual waves, slamming against the window. Outside, lightning forks across the sky. I duck down below the window sill, terror stricken. A boom of thunder roars. The room is momentarily lit up by another flash of lightning, then plunged into an eerie dim gray light. This is a raging storm. And by the sound of it, one that's only just gathering.

Above me, another wave smashes against the window. Then another. The glass vibrates and creaks.

CRASH!

I scream as water and glass rain down on me. The force of the wave throws me to the floor. I spit out water. My hearing has gone all funny, like I've just dived into a pool. A dull bang echoes and the bedroom door is thrown open, streams of swirling seawater pouring inside. I've got to get out of here! The water is already up to my waist. Using the walls to steady myself, I push through the current. My eyes are burning from the salt. The water is streaming in so quickly, it's as if I'm on a sinking ship. I know that if I make it out of here, my mom is going to kill me!

I manage to catch hold of the doorframe and pull myself onto the landing. The attic . . . It's the only place left to go. The current is trying to force me back. Above me there's a red cord that pulls down the hatch for the folding stairs. The water gurgles as I reach for it. Just as my fingers close around it, the next wave throws me back.

AAAH! With a rattle the stairs come down but my head goes underwater. My leg knocks painfully against the doorframe. I grope around, searching for the rungs and pull myself up, spewing water. My soggy shoes slip on the metal. I scramble through the opening and slam the hatch shut behind me.

The darkness of the attic surrounds me, the sound of the rising water distant. I slump to the floor, my breath raspy. Am I safe? Above me, through the slanted skylight, I see the moon growing brighter in a dark sky.

Maybe I can wait out the storm. Curfew is only half an hour away, but I'm sure I can sneak past the apathetic FRS security guards or even talk my way past them if I'm spotted. And this house is well built. After all, it survived The Valley Flood. Living in a world prone to flooding, we had the space below the roof converted into a safe room, like most of our neighbors; we stocked it with bedding, water bottles, and boxes of canned food. There aren't many other things up here, only a few old items of furniture overhung with spiderwebs, but it's enough to get me through the night—even through a few nights—if need be.

But only if the water stops rising. I stare at the attic trap door, willing it to stay shut. But even as I do, the wood begins to push up, letting the first drips spill into the room as the water from beneath gurgles in. I jump up. What's going on? Why isn't this stopping? Even during The Valley Flood, the sea never rose more than a few inches above the bedroom floor. The watermarks on our walls show that.

I rush to the skylight. Can I get to the roof if I have to? Standing in the dark, my clothes dripping wet, I peer out. A strong beam lights up the roofs opposite. Aqua8. I pull back, my heart racing.

Why are they still here? And how will I get away now?

I drop onto a pile of boxes. I wipe a shaking hand over my eyes. Think. I've got to think. I force myself to focus. I have three options: one, I get lucky, the water level stops rising, Aqua8 leaves, and I make my way back to the FRS in the pitch black; two, I'm a little bit lucky, the water stops rising, but Aqua8 don't leave and I stick out the night here. As long as I'm back before community class in the morning, I should be OK. Except there's also option three: the water keeps rising, and with Aqua8 gone or not, I take my pick between drowning right here in our house or out there in the storm.

I hug my arms around my legs. The panic I've been trying to suppress sweeps over me, like the rising flood. What if I don't make it? What if I die here, and Mom wakes up all alone, me gone, only her knitting needles and an empty mattress in our assigned shelter? Never knowing what happened. Never knowing that I was here, washed away with all the memories of our past. I choke back a sob. In the darkness, with just the drumming of my heart, time passes agonizingly slowly.

A sudden motion shakes me from my thoughts. The boxes. They're moving! The floodwaters have risen so high that they are starting to lift the furniture off the floor! I reach for the skylight and give the handle a quick turn. Aqua8 or not, if I don't get out now, I'm dead. I push against the glass pane, but it doesn't budge. Hammering against the skylight, I try to force it open. The water is rising more quickly than ever, lapping around my stomach, my chest. I slap a flat palm up against the glass pane. There has to be a reason why the stupid thing is jammed. A lock? A latch? I run my hands over the weather-worn frame. I can feel bulges on the sides where the wood is all cracked and swollen.

Oh no! It must have warped because of the damp! I push my full body weight into it, but the water is already covering half the pane. Come on! My breath clouds up the glass. I grasp the golden trident pendant that I've worn since birth.

A wavelet splashes into my face. I rub my eyes, clearing away the salt. Only I can save myself right now. In a sudden fit of determination, I grab the edge of my jacket, pull it off, and wrap it around my hand. I can feel the tin box with the conch safely inside. Turning my head away from the window, I slam my fist against it.

WHAM!

The force makes the pane vibrate. I draw my arm back and punch again.

WHAM!

This time the glass shatters. My hand stings as the saltwater touches it. I must have cut myself. Ignoring the pain, I reach through the broken skylight. Jagged glass brushes my hair. I clear away the remaining fragments from the frame, fling my arms out either side, and pull myself through the narrow opening.

Free at last, I collapse onto the roof tiles. The night air, fresh and cold, mixed with drops of rain, caresses my face. Gradually my breathing calms. My hand is still throbbing with pain. Blood is running freely across my right wrist. The cut is deeper than I thought. I press it against my shirt to stop the bleeding.

Then I clamber up toward the ridge. It's completely dark now, the full moon and most of the stars hidden by the storm clouds. No sign of Aqua8. Have they gone? All I can see are triangular shapes, roofs rising out of the water. The only sound, that of the water slapping against the wooden gables.

To the west, rising above the waves, I can make out the concrete top of the crescent-shaped flood barrier. The wild ocean rages beyond. High up and to the right, among the stars, lie the luscious hills of Ararat Heights. At the other end of the

Valley, floodlights illuminate the dilapidated factories that have been commandeered as Flood Relief Shelters. How on earth am I going to swim that distance? The water is swirling around the roofs, full of currents, floating debris, darkness. It's like a wild river, threatening to swallow me whole.

Tentatively, I put my jacket back on, making sure that the box with the conch is safely in the zipper pocket. My hand is still bleeding, but there's nothing I can do about it. I just hope that it won't get infected. What am I waiting for? I've seen people brave all sorts of tides. Even our lame FRS swim champs are the heroes of our school, celebrated, admired—it's just too bad I'm not one of them. My high school team are the Carps and there's a reason why we've been nicknamed "the Craps."

OK, OK, I can do this! I take a cautious step down the tiles. It's lucky that I can see better in the dark than most people. I take another step forward when something moves in the shadows at the edge of the roof. Aqua8! I leap back. But it's only the silver light of the moon briefly breaking through the storm clouds. I exhale, relieved, when the tiles below me shift. I slip, scream, and slide down the roof, hitting the water with a splash.

At once the flood is around me, cold and forceful. Before I can get my bearings it has me in its clutches, dragging me away from the hills, toward the flood barrier. I reach for the nearest roof gable and grab a hold, but the brute force of the waves tears me away. My heart is beating as fast as the wild, aimless current. Helpless, I am swept toward a gap of swirling darkness.

The water's tearing at me, crashing over me, forcing me under. I come up coughing and spluttering, my throat burning from the salt. I vaguely register that the wide stretch of darkness around me must be the main road that runs through the Valley. New Frisco Highway, as the locals nicknamed it. A wooden plank sails past my head. Then I'm blindsided by another wave.

Underwater something soft brushes my arm. Algae? I try to brush it off, but I can't move my left arm. Somehow the material has wrapped itself around me. The more I struggle to free myself the more the water keeps dragging me under. My arm is completely entangled, pinned to my body. I kick my legs, then realize that I no longer know which way is up. A rushing noise fills my ears. The pressure on my lungs is unbearable. Despite the pain in my injured hand, I tear at the rope. No, please. No! I need air! I'm drowning!

CHAPTER 2

— *The Voices of the Ocean* —

The world twists and I'm being pulled forcefully to the surface. I come up spluttering, gasping. The next moment I think I must be hallucinating—what I'm seeing can't be real. Crystal-blue eyes stare at me from under a shock of curly blond hair. I blink away the saltwater. He's the most handsome boy I've ever seen. His face is youthful yet mature with a strong jawline. I'm about to stutter thank you when I see the neon-blue stripe across his black wetsuit. The words die in my mouth. He's Aqua8!

I stare at him in terror as he grasps my bleeding wrist.

"What are you doing here?" His clear blue eyes bore right through me. They are enigmatic.

"I . . . I lost m-my way in the flood," I say through chattering teeth. Even to me that sounds lame, but the coldness of the water is seeping right into my bones.

"Are you out of your mind? Don't you know what happens if you're caught?" Behind his harsh question, I hear concern. But that can't be. Aqua8 are ruthless.

Already, the engine of another boat roars closer. I struggle to get free.

"Stay still!" His grip on my injured arm is so strong that it's painful. A searchlight sweeps his face.

"Lieutenant, found something?" I catch his eyes, pleading with him not to say anything, but of course he will. He's one of them.

He turns into the light, cool, unwavering. "Negative. False alarm," he calls out. "Do one more sweep. Retrace your steps then head back."

"Copy that," comes a reply from the patrol boat. The searchlight turns and the noise of the engine grows distant.

My heart beats frantically. Why did he do that? He could have handed me over. He should have handed me over. Instead, he pulls me out of the water and into the boat.

"Stay down!" he whispers. I lie at his feet in the dank hollow of the stern. He pulls the cord that starts the motor. The front of the dinghy rises into the air as he lets out the throttle. I look up at him, trying to read his face, but his expression is set, his eyes fixed on some point in the distance as he steers with military precision through the watery alleys between the rooftops.

Where is he taking me? If I jump overboard now, he might not be able to stop me. But his quiet determination holds me in place. Is it the naive thought that behind those strong cheekbones I can see no deceit?

Maybe I'm a fool. What if he turns me in after all? Just chauffeurs me to the labor camp so I can start my sentence without delay? I'd be going there like a lamb to the slaughter—relying on my bad instincts and his handsome cheekbones.

His gaze is still facing straight ahead. I sneak a peek over the rim of the boat. At once, I feel his hand on my shoulder, pushing me down.

"I told you to stay down."

I recoil at the harshness in his voice. As we get closer to dry land, the motor slows then stops completely. He leaps out of the boat, pulling it close to the shore. He's scanning the area like a hawk.

"Come on!" He holds out his hand.

I take it and clamber onto the muddy, rocky slope.

Where are we? I stumble and he steadies me, his hand brushing my cheek.

"You're freezing!"

This time I definitely catch concern in his voice.

"That's what happens to you when you've been in the water all evening." I blurt out the words before I can stop them. I bite my tongue.

He gives me a curious glance. "The FRS are over that hill, three quarters of a mile east." He points up the slope to the right. "Keep close to the water until you reach the Valley path. Patrols are weak on the north fence tonight."

"Why are you doing this?" I ask.

He doesn't answer. "Just go. Now!"

With a quick leap he's back in his boat. I hear the engine start. Then he's gone and I'm alone. I watch the dark water, lapping at the rocks. Still shivering, I turn and run along the foot of the hill toward the FRS. My head is spinning with questions. Who is he? Why did he save me? And will I ever see him again?

*

Old Toothless Pete stares at me as I enter our block of the FRS. I ignore his empty, alcohol-filled gaze as he studies me, disheveled and four hours after curfew, and climb up the gray stairs to area L9. Here, on the first floor of the concrete skeleton that was once an old factory, Mom and I, and eighty others, live in makeshift cubicles.

As quietly as I can, I cross the large hall. It stinks, the smell of many people forced to live together in close proximity without sanitation. The security floodlights pour in through the upper windows. Behind the sheets of plastic meant to provide privacy, I see people in rags bundled up on the floor, hear the heavy snoring, the groans of the ill, the whimpering of children with nightmares. The noise and smell are much worse today, with the memories of our old home so fresh in my mind.

I see my mom and all the horrors of the day are washed away. She's sitting in her chair, her frail figure more hunched than usual. She seems calm but somehow distant, as if that last spark of fire that sometimes lights up her eyes is forever gone.

She looks up.

"Naya!" Her knitting needles clatter to the floor as she jumps up and rushes toward me. "I've been worried sick about you!"

For a moment, I'm surrounded by long, brown locks as she throws her arms around me then she looks me in the eyes and I can see all the pain, the fear, the anger.

"Are you all right? Where were you? Why were you gone so long?"

They are more questions than I can answer all at once.

Her hands feel my wet clothes. "You're freezing—let's get you somewhere warm." Quietly, she draws across the plastic that marks the entrance to our cubicle. She guides me to the two moth-eaten mattresses that comprise our sleeping space and helps me out of my wet clothes. As she takes me by the hand and wraps a blanket around me, she stops in horror. "You're covered in blood! Naya, what happened?"

I open my mouth to reply, but all the exhaustion kicks in and I can't get a word out.

"Stay here. I'll get some clean water." She grabs an empty bucket, slips through the plastic curtain, and hurries away. I know she'll only be gone a minute, but loneliness comes crushing down. I want it all back, our peaceful, happy life.

This tiny space is all we've got in the world. Two raggedy, old sleeping mats, two pillows, and a spare change of gray FRS work clothes, each labeled with our names, Nerissa DeLora and Naya DeLora, plus the two or three personal items that we had on us when we left our home.

I still remember the day we were flooded out so clearly. It was windy, gray, and overcast. The Blue Out sirens had been ringing all morning. I'd just got back from school, worrying about the D that I got in community class—I never got the point of the whole "respect the authorities, government devotion" thing that those lessons are all about. Mom was in the kitchen, in her teacher's outfit, making seabass for lunch. Outside, the neighbors were pointing at the darkening sky, complaining about the weather. Suddenly we heard this rumble, like an earthquake and a clap of thunder hitting at the same time. The whole house shook and in a split second, all the windows burst. I've never seen Mom react so quickly. While I was staring at the approaching huge, muddy-brown wave, she had already grabbed my gym bag, snatched up her work bag, and pulled me out the back door.

As we fled across the flooded vegetable patch in our garden, the water was already up to our waists. She told me to run, swim, head for the barren hills that enclosed the Valley. I remember looking back and seeing my friend Rosy's parents frantically stuffing clothes and personal belongings into bags piled onto the brick wall that surrounded the front yard of their house, and Mom shouting at me to keep moving, not to look back. But I did look back once. I caught a flash of Rosy's red hair as she hugged her dog, Shortbread. That was the last time I ever saw her.

Mom and I made it to the hills an hour before dusk. We were among the first to be picked up by the rescue squads. They took us to the abandoned factories above the Valley. We were alive. But our home and our possessions were gone.

At first, it didn't matter that the shelters were grim. They told us it was only temporary. That new homes were being built for us. But Mom was suspicious from the start and her suspicions were well founded: eleven months have passed and it doesn't look like anything is about to change.

"Let me clean that, so it won't get infected."

I jump when Mom returns. She has clean water and some bandages and iodine. It's lucky that she spends so much of her day nursing the sick, helping the wounded. The head of section probably didn't even ask why she needed all these things in the middle of the night.

Her grip on my wrist is firm, yet gentle. She takes a cloth and washes off the dried blood. I flinch as she pours the iodine over the wound. I look at her and not at my hand. I don't see much of myself in her. I certainly don't have her wild, waist-length, dark locks or her deep, almond-shaped eyes. Although I have never met him, it stands to reason that I inherited my father's looks. My hair is a light, sandy brown, and Mom says my eyes are so green that they have the strength of the sea in them.

"What happened? Did you get stuck outside the fence after curfew? Naya?"

It takes me a moment to realize that Mom is talking to me. I shake my head.

"Then why were you gone so long?" She unrolls a length of bandage and deftly cuts it with the scissors. She binds my palm and wrist with the bandage, over and under, over and under.

"I got caught in the Blue Out," I whisper.

My mother pauses. "The Blue Out that was supposed to hit the other side of Cape Harmony?" Suspicion intermixes with concern in her voice. "Naya, you didn't . . ."

"I went back to our old house," I say. "Ow! —"

Mom pulls the bandage tighter than intended. "Are you out of your mind! What were you thinking?" She has trouble keeping her voice down.

I grab my jacket with my bandaged hand and take the tin box out of the zipper pocket. Carefully, I open the lid. "I brought it back for you." I show her the conch inside.

She freezes. For a brief second, she stares at it wistfully then, just as fast, her expression changes. "You went back for this? You risked your life, everything, for a stupid keepsake?" She grabs the conch from its box and furiously holds it up at me. "This . . . this piece of junk?"

I've never seen her like this before. The trance-like wall that she builds around herself when she is knitting has crumbled, and all her frustration at the FRS, all the emotion she buried deep inside herself, is bubbling to the surface.

"I . . ." I falter.

"You what? It's a conch! What good did you think it could do? Naya, I thought you had more sense than this!"

"But . . . you always said it would help us in times of need." I hold back the tears welling up in my eyes.

"Naya." She puts her hands firmly on my shoulders. "Whatever I may have told you as a child, whatever value this may have had in the past, it's useless now."

I shake my head. "No! You said . . . How can it not be important?"

"Oh, Naya, you're the only thing that's important now." She pulls me into a desperate hug. "Don't ever think that any object is more valuable than your life. I couldn't bear the thought of losing you." Her arms are tight around me, like she never wants to let go again. When she finally does, she looks old and frail. The sight of her makes me feel lost. Was I an idiot to believe in some childhood tale?

I open my mouth, a host of questions on my lips, but I see that look in her eyes, and I know that the conversation is over. After pulling on my nightshirt, I slip under my blanket. Mom sits beside me in silence, holding my hand. She strokes my cheek, whispers goodnight and begins to get ready for bed. I pull my blanket around me and sink into my mattress.

"Night, Mom," I say.

I lie on my back. Light is coming in through the high windows and there's the distant sound of the ocean. Absentmindedly I twirl my trident necklace between my index finger and thumb. It's the only remembrance I have of my father. When I was small, I used to tell myself that it would protect me when I'm in danger. That he would hear me and keep me safe, like a guardian angel. So many mysteries shroud my past. Things I can't even begin to comprehend. Is the conch really just a shell? A fake treasure to hear the fake sound of waves?

I know its thin coating of gold wouldn't get us more than a week's double food rations. When I was younger, I used to believe that my father had given it to Mom as a token of his intent to return. I used to picture them together on a sandy beach in the light of a magical sunset. And I imagined him in a white boat, returning to take us away from this place, to an island somewhere far away, where we could live, just the three of us, forever safe. But as the years passed Mom never once talked about him. I don't even know if he's still alive. This image that I had of him is gone. And I don't believe that there was anything magical about their meeting. Not in a world like this.

Next to me, Mom turns in her sleep. Despite her anger and outrage, the tin box is next to her pillow. Her right hand is resting on it protectively. Her expression is peaceful, like it used to be when we still lived in the Valley.

As the months pass with us stuck here in the FRS, talk about the atrocities committed by the Elites is growing stronger. I think of the things my mom told me, repeating what her mom had told her. The Global Flood destroyed our planet 242 years ago. Year Zero—the start of our current calendar, Post Inundationem: the years after the Global Flood. Prior to that the world had been on the brink of war, a huge arms race was building up between the Eurasian and American continents. Then there had been the terrorist attack on the White House; the explosion during the attempted peace talks left three of the world's leaders dead. Suddenly ballistic missiles had started arcing between East and West. But the real tragedy struck in the South, where a submarine of one of the competing powers lay in wait, ready to turn the war nuclear. Ten of its nuclear warheads smashed into Antarctica. They blamed it on faulty guidance systems. Nobody owned up to it. The Americas blamed the Eurasians. The Eurasians blamed each other. Not that it mattered in the end. Because that was the day the world changed. Irreparably. Forever. The day the waters rose.

The war ended there, but the catastrophe had only begun. The southern ice cap was vaporized. Those who had denied the very existence of global warming now saw it happen a hundred times faster than climate-change experts had predicted. The oceans grew wild with hurricanes, sending unstoppable tsunamis to every point on the compass. Sixty-foot waves thrashed the coasts. But it wasn't only islands that sunk. Major capitals were swallowed up by the sea, too. Of the cities most affected by the destruction of war — New York, London, Moscow, Shanghai — nothing remained but charred remnants of skyscrapers, rising from the sea like weird twisted coral.

Attempts were made to stop the waters rising, of course. Flood protection booms were dropped far out at sea, concrete walls were hastily thrown up along the coasts. But the sea tossed aside the booms, gushed over the concrete walls — and people scrambled for high ground.

Anyone rich enough secured properties and construction materials in mountainous areas and built new homes. The rest were forced to fend for themselves in cheap coastal shelters. Society split into the Masses and the Elites. It didn't take long for the dictatorships to follow. There was no place for democracy in a world where only the most powerful survived.

Until that day of destruction, Mom said, everyone had lived on the low-lying plains. Now 90 percent of these inhabited areas were gone. Large swathes of the Americas, of Eurasia, and of Africa were claimed by the oceans; Australia had become nothing more than scattered islands. Factories, airports, industries, power plants, and oil pipelines were all swallowed by the water. Resources ran low and were hoarded by the rich. Although the past and the social divide are forbidden topics, I've heard the hushed whispers circulating behind cupped hands.

Horror stories about the mainland, about Masses being en-slaved, killed due to the lack of resources, even instances of cannibalism.

When I was a child these were just rumors. We were safe in the Valley on Cape Harmony, a headland in the outlying re-gions of the former US West Coast. All the evil from the main-land was far away and unreal. I remember the Blue Outs when Mom and I sat by candlelight. I'd cuddle up close to her be-cause I was scared. She would comfort me and tell me that my father had picked Cape Harmony because it was safe. Because it had strong flood barriers. And because it had resources . . .

The howling wind outside lashes against the thin window panes of the FRS. I try to imagine the lives of the kids up on Ararat Heights and can't even begin to do so. How is it up there, among the trees? How is it to live without the ever-present dirt and filth, without the crushing lack of privacy? How is it to live in safety, above the floodplain?

Defiance wells up inside me. I don't need an absent father to return and make things better. Wherever he is, he obviously didn't want me. Or Mom. He never cared about us. Otherwise he would have taken us with him. I will find a way of getting out of here, of taking matters into my own hands.

But how? My wrist throbs with a dull pain, reminding me how vulnerable I am. I close my eyes. Some problems are best left for the morning. Tonight, I don't mind that my bed feels like somebody has stuffed it full of rocks. In fact, it's almost comfortable. My muscles are breathing a collective sigh of re-lief after their recent exertions.

My thoughts drift back to the conch, Mom's reaction, the aura of mystery surrounding it. For a moment I'm lost again in the dark water, the waves pushing and pulling at me. Dizzi-ness takes me, and it's like I'm falling into an endless pit. Then there's that grip around my wrist and I know I'm about to be pulled to the surface, about to be rescued. Above me shines a bright stream of light. I float toward it as if I'm one with the water, and when I break through the waves he's there, the per-fect image of a hero with his blond hair and blue eyes. My heart is beating wildly in my chest.

"How did you find me?" I ask.

"I will find you anywhere," he says.

I'm safe. He will protect me. "But the water was so dark and murky," I whisper.

He doesn't reply, just smiles softly.

I want to smile back, but his eyes change, growing black as coal, as if dark blood is swallowing up their crystal-blue. The sky turns gray, thunderclouds gather thickly, the sea storms around us, lightning strikes. I freeze. His grip is ice around my wrist. A shiver travels up my arm. I scream and try to break free, but I can't. He's drawing me toward him, closer and closer. The corners of his mouth twist in a mocking grin.

"Let me go!" I scream.

My heart pounds against my ribcage, drowning out all sound. His grin grows unnaturally wide. His mouth is full of razor-sharp teeth, a gaping maw, black as his eyes. He draws me in with his monstrous claws and I know that I'm his prey. And I know that I can't escape. The waves crash over us. Tearing us apart. And I'm lost in the ocean once more, swimming, fighting, drowning.

CHAPTER 3

— *Sand and Sea Fodder* —

"Come on!" Ralph shouts out from the beach as my friends on the Carps swim team and I walk down the winding path from the FRS.

Neal bounces the volleyball along the dirt track. "Hey, what are you doing down there already? There's no *i* in *team*, Ralph. You can't just rush ahead."

"Yeah, weren't you paying attention in community class?" Ethan yells while he helps Neal tug the old fishing net that we use for our game through the hole in the security fence. "'Do your duty, Children of the Flood.' 'Remember, all your work is for The Greater Good.'"

Neal scowls at him. "One day I'm gonna burn those books, I swear."

"You can't," Ethan says. "They're the government's."

Emily shoots a worried glance along the wire fence that surrounds the FRS. "Where's the guard?"

"Who cares?" Neal says, laughing. "We all know how he 'does his duty.'"

"Yeah, you think he snores for The Greater Good?" Ethan steals the ball off Neal. "Come on! Race you to the beach. Last one there is a Mega-Carp!"

They sprint down the sandy slope.

I love Neal and Ethan. The world could be ending and they'd still be cracking jokes. Sometimes I wonder how they ended up on a team of losers. Neal's actually very sporty, but in the water he paddles like a dog. As for Ethan, he doesn't even try. He once dived and retrieved a food token that had accidentally wound up at the bottom of the pool when he was meant to be freediving. Ralph, the tallest and lankiest of us, would probably be a great swimmer, too, if he weren't dead scared of water, and

Jonathan, the youngest, just isn't fast enough yet. Which leaves Emily, the pride of our swim team. The Carps actually made second place once, thanks to her. Black-haired and shy, she's too sweet to be with this wild bunch really.

I smile at her as we follow the others at a more leisurely pace. It's good to be out in the sunshine after school, away from all the misery and oppression. I breathe in the fresh sea air.

The beach is not that big, just a thin stretch of sand in the lee of the FRS flood barrier, which shelters it from the big waves. On the right it curves toward the northern horizon and the open sea, creating an illusion of freedom.

Emily and Jonathan string up the net to the wooden poles that were left abandoned halfway along the beach.

"I . . . I can't reach the top," Jonathan chirps.

"Did you already forget, Johnny? There's no *i* in *team*," Ethan jokes.

"There's no *Ralph* in *team* either," Emily says. "How about you lend us a hand, Ralph? You're not just here for your scrawny looks, you know."

Neal's hazel eyes beam at me cheekily from under his mop of light brown hair as we finish marking out the volleyball pitch in the sand with our feet and our toes touch in the middle. "See, we're all set for the future. We can become professional beach volleyball court designers."

I laugh.

We split into teams. I join Neal and Jonathan while Ethan, Emily, and Ralph gang up on the other side of the net.

"Go on then! Take your serve, Mega-Carp!" Neal calls out.

"Who are you calling a Mega-Carp? I got to the beach before you." Ethan puffs out his chest. "Ladies and gentlemen," he begins one of his favorite impressions of the Governor's video speeches to the FRS refugees. "Cape Harmony's finest beach volleyball match is about to start. Please, finish your swamp soup and take your seats. As sure as my teeth are diamond studded and my bodyguards bog brained, this will be a match to remember!" He flings the ball up into the air and slams it across the net.

"Hey!" Jonathan calls. "Ethan didn't say 'Go!'"

Neal doesn't let this put him off his shot. He grins and immediately pounds the ball back over the net. On the opposite side, Emily keeps it in play and passes to Ethan, who sets the ball for Ralph. Ralph slams it across the net. It's a good shot, heading straight for the front left side. I dive into the sand and knock it back up, and Neal's brown hair defies gravity as he jumps and blasts it into the empty far right corner on the opposite side of the court.

One point to us.

"Nicely done, Naya." Neal gives me a high five. He tosses the ball to Jonathan to take the serve, but Jonathan's barely caught it when the loud vroom of motor engines echoes across the bay. We turn toward the sea. Three Jet Skis are rounding the corner of the bay, making a beeline for the beach.

"Oh man," Ethan groans. "Here come the mountain squatters."

Sure, only the Elites have enough money and gas to zoom around the headland. There are three girls and three boys. I recognize the big, blue Jet Ski in the center.

"It's Duke and his gang," Ralph says.

"Let's just go. We can come back and play later," Jonathan squeaks, already heading up the sandy slope to the FRS.

"No." Neal holds him back. "They'll have seen us by now. If we leave we'll look like cowards."

"Besides, they have plenty of beaches of their own," Ethan says. "No need for them to take ours."

"Yeah, but we're not meant to be here," Emily whines.

It's too late anyway. The Elites have already reached the shore. They make a show of dismounting, and follow Duke across the sand. On land, their height is as noticeable as their flashy Jet Skis. Only Ralph is as tall as the Elite boys, but where he is lanky they are built like rocks. Duke is the bulkiest of them all with black, short-cropped hair, olive skin, a square jaw and a mean streak of a smile. The girl at his side is the perfect blonde. Her shiny hair is pulled back with a pink headband, and she's wearing a fancy pink bikini.

Though I don't know her, it's obvious that she's the Queen Bee. The two black-haired girls wearing matching headbands are like carbon copies of her, one dressed in blue, the other in green. Jonathan nervously shuffles his feet in the sand as they get closer. It strikes me that we must look like the washed-out versions of the bright and shiny Elites.

Duke speaks first. "Well, well, well, look what the tide's washed up. I was wondering why the beach looked so dirty."

The Elites break into a chorus of mocking laughter.

"Nothing compared to the trash that floats around at sea," Neal counters.

Duke holds up a hand to his ear. "Hang on a minute, Jessica," he says to the blonde. "I could have sworn that factory boy just talked back to me."

"That's right!" Ethan chimes in. "Now hit the surf and get off our beach."

"Your beach?" Duke says. "I understand that your education may not be the best, but you should get basic English by now. I told you not to show your faces around here."

"Yeah, Duke, you tell them," one of Duke's henchmen says.

"Wow, so that's the sort of rhetoric they teach up on the Heights," Neal mocks. "Guys, we're really missing out. What vocabulary! What wit!"

Duke takes a step toward Neal. "Got something to say, factory boy?"

OK, this is about to go badly wrong. Duke alone could probably take both Neal and Ethan. And the other two guys are the long-on-muscle, short-on-brains types.

"You want this beach?" I stick out my chin at Duke. "Then you gotta win it. One volleyball match. Winners keepers, losers leavers." My hands are shaking. I have no idea what made me speak up like that.

"It's not for you to set terms, shelter girl," Jessica snaps. "One word to the guard and you'll all be shipped off to labor camp."

"That's right, run to security, airhead," Neal taunts her.

Duke is still holding my gaze. He looks at me in a way that makes me very aware that I'm in a bikini. Not the standard issue FRS bathing suit, but my own, nice bikini that happened to be in my sports bag that Mom grabbed as we fled the Valley.

"Fine, let's have a match—if you enjoy losing so much." Duke's stare turns into contempt and he spins around to his team and shouts. "OK, form up! We're gonna teach these Valley nobodies a lesson they won't forget. You can start, factory scum."

With grim determination, Neal picks up the ball for the serve. Suddenly I feel like an idiot. I just lost us the beach for good! We're nothing but a bunch of scrawny kids fed on "swamp soup." What chance do we have against the tall, broad-shouldered Elites?

But forty minutes in, the score is still twenty-one to twenty-one. What energy the Elite boys and Jessica are wasting on taunting us and showing off, we are using to our advantage. They don't even realize that their goofing around is costing them points. As for the two other Elite girls, they just stand at the back of the court, looking bored.

"Want me to show them the Fist of Thunder?" Duke asks Jessica cockily.

He picks up the ball and pounds it across the net so that it overshoots the baseline by yards. Jonathan runs and gets it. I expect Neal or Ethan to comment something like, "Whoa, fist of blunder!" but they don't. They're fully focused. Neal is back in serving position. I see calm concentration in his eyes.

His first serve is a straight ace. The second one, too. On the third, the Elites somehow manage to keep the ball in play, but then it's over to us again, and Emily sets it for Ethan, who plays it toward the two Elite girls at the back. Neither of them moves as the ball slams into the sand between them.

"What are you doing, you plankton brains?" Duke fires at them.

"This game is stupid," one of them complains. "And it was her ball!"

"No, it wasn't. It was hers."

Duke angrily snatches the ball up and tosses it across the net. "Time to assert our authority!" he hisses. His henchmen nod and grin gleefully.

Neal takes the serve. The Elites play it back to us and Emily fists it over to Ralph. He's by the net, ready to play it straight across. As he jumps for it though, the spiky-haired boy opposite knocks into him from the other side of the net. Ralph's smash turns into a vertical shot, that arcs high into the air.

"Foul!" Neal shouts furiously, but the Elites don't pay attention to him.

I fling myself into a full dive, arms stretched out. The ball zooms down fast. Just as I hit the sand it ricochets off my wrists, and I catch a glimpse of it rising across the net, toward the two Elite girls at the back.

"Out!" Duke shouts.

"Come on, that was in by a foot," Ralph says.

"It was out, beanstalk," cries Jessica.

I get up and brush myself down—then I freeze in horror. My necklace! It's gone. I must have lost it when I dived for the ball. I scan the sand, looking for a glint of gold, but I don't see it anywhere.

"Hey, if cheating's the only way you can win, go right ahead." Neal's shout pulls my attention back to the game. Duke's got the ball on his side of the court and is about to serve. I feel myself burning with fury.

"Like they could win any other way," I say loud enough for everyone to hear. It wipes the smile right off Duke's face.

"What was that, shelter girl?"

"You heard me!" I have no idea how I've got the courage to talk to him like that. He starts walking toward me, the ball clutched under his arm.

"OK, it's your ball . . ." He holds it out toward me. I reach for it, but he pulls it back again and flings it into the air. "If you get it out of the water before me." He pounds his fist against it. "BOOM! The Fist—of—Thunder!" He squawks as it soars far out into the bay.

His henchmen roar with laughter. "Yeeeah, Duke!"

I watch in disgust as they gather round and high-five him. "Hey!" I find my voice again. "You can't just change the rules."

He smirks. "Can't I?"

"Hey, what's this?" Jessica says. She's a few paces away dangling something from her fingers. My necklace.

"Give that back," I shout and make a grab for it.

26

She jumps aside, grinning. "Lost something, shelter girl?"

The other Elite girls giggle.

"Didn't know you could afford pretty jewelry."

"Give it back!" I shout again.

Jessica holds it up in the air, teasingly. "You want it back? You play by our rules."

Neal steps in front of Duke, who stands by grinning. "What's the matter, Duke? Too chicken to race someone your own size?"

"SHUT UP!" Duke fires at him. "She's the one that made the challenge."

"It's OK." I grab Neal's arm. I don't want him to take my place. The waters are dangerous around here. And he paddles like a dog.

I turn and face Duke. "I'll do it."

"Ooooh, she's gonna do it," Duke's minions bray. "Shelter girl's gonna take on Duke. Hey Duke, you up to it, man?"

Duke swaggers down to the shoreline. He has the advantage, and not just in size. The Elites are obsessed with swimming, as a skill and as a sport. They have the best facilities, the best teachers, the best beaches. Half their day is spent in the water. Which means that Duke—or any of his buddies—could outdo me and my friends in less time than it takes to say "Carp."

My chest tightens as I follow Duke through the wet sand. I watch the ball, bobbing on the waves. It's already drifted beyond the rocks that flank the bay. I know that my challenge will be just to stay alive. Only a few months ago a couple of Elites went out for a moonlight swim here and never came back. Riptide got them.

The irony of it strikes me. I almost drowned yesterday and now I'm about to risk my life in the water again. Maybe I'm just meant for a watery demise. Or maybe it's like Neal always says, "We're the Carps. We don't need to worry about labor camp. We'll be the first to drown, anyway."

"GO!" Someone shouts.

Before I have time for any more thoughts, I'm running alongside Duke to the freezing water. I dive headfirst into the upward curl of a wave. I'm not ready for this. Not after yesterday. The current is wild. Already I feel it trying to drag me under.

The burning salty water streams up my nose and into my eyes —but the ocean feels different. I don't know if the storm has cleared away all the seaweed and dirt or if yesterday's ordeal has toughened me up, but the deep, blue waves seem to carry me, effortlessly.

I kick and feel myself shooting forward. It's a smooth, pleasant feeling. Is it my imagination, or is Duke not even that far ahead? I lunge forward. The waves splash into my face. I have no idea how I am doing this, but I'm catching up!

Suddenly, Duke is just a few arm lengths away. It's as if I'm entranced by a powerful rhythm, my body flowing in smooth, synchronized movements, and then I'm level with him. I catch the surprise in his eyes, see him spouting water as he tries to go faster, but he can't keep up with me. Ahead, the white swirl of the volleyball is dancing on the waves. I hurl myself forward, into the deep blue, one more stroke and I'm there, ball safely in my arms. As I turn and make my way back, I catch Duke gaping in disbelief.

I pass him, the sound of the sea in my ears, just like I heard in the conch, but this time it's all around me, like a rhythmic melody. It feels as if I'm one with the ocean. I've never felt so good before! Exhilaration runs through my body—and I'm swimming butterfly! A technique I don't even know.

My eyes are fixed on the beach. Somehow I'm gliding toward the shoreline like a wave. This isn't normal. As I continue flinging the ball in front of me, it dawns on me. I've won! I've really won! The water beneath me is getting shallow. My feet touch algae. With one last mighty flick, I reach the shore.

I toss the ball to Emily, who catches it.

"Yes!!" she squeaks, beaming.

She's the only one. The others are all quiet. The Elites, and my friends—as if they're too surprised to cheer. Jessica's mouth is open as she stares at me.

"Naya, how . . . how did you . . . ?" Neal stutters.

I grasp the hand he offers me. After the weightless ease of the water, my body feels heavy as lead.

I walk up to Jessica. "My necklace," I say and stretch out my hand. "I want it back."

"No!" Jessica jumps back. It's a hectic jump, almost as if she's scared.

"Give it to her," a peremptory voice behind me says.

I spin around. Duke is standing by the shoreline. Of all the people here, he's the last I would have expected to stand up for me. Jessica obviously feels the same way. Her open-mouthed stare changes into plain disbelief. Reluctantly, she holds out my necklace. I snatch it from her. Around me, everyone is still keeping their distance. Duke is looking at me strangely, as if he's seeing me for the first time. It's an expression that makes me more nervous than the shock and fear I see reflected in everyone else's faces. I walk over to my friends.

"We're done here!" Duke says. He leaps onto his Jet Ski.

The other Elites follow suit and vroom away after him.

The beach is ours—but there's no whooping or cheering. Everyone's silent. Silent in a way that makes me wonder if what I did was bad somehow. What happened to me out there? Nobody can put on a sudden burst of speed like that. Can they?

Then Ethan smiles slowly. "Boom! There goes the Fist of Thunder!"

We've moved up the evolutionary scale—from Craps to Carps all in one day.

CHAPTER 4

— *The Scout* —

The sunrise the next day is red and brilliant and the last traces of the storm have subsided. It's the first week of November, the end of the 'calm season'—though 'calmer season' would be a better name for the months of April to November. It's not like the Blue Outs on Cape Harmony ever stop completely. Neal is waiting for me at the stairs of L-block and we walk to school together.

When we were little, people often thought that Neal was my brother. He's a few months younger than me, has the same color hair and is of a similar height. He used to live on my street. In the Valley we were in different classes, but here all the students from the same grade are bunched together. The school building, if you can call it that, is only a stone's throw away, and was a former school that has been revamped for those of us who survived the flood. Like the rest of the FRS, it's part of a failed large-scale infrastructure building project that began only a few years after the Global Flood and was terminated just as quickly. The elevation here simply wasn't considered high enough to provide safety from the floods for the Elites' new project. So Oceanstromium Energies, as they called it, was scrapped. Until The Valley Flood, only vagabonds and hunted rebels sought shelter here.

As we walk into the school, it's strangely quiet. No squeals of kids in the hallways. No students or teachers in sight. What's even stranger is the absence of the Governor's voice. He's not on the video screens giving his daily "Don't give up hope, People of the Flood" speech.

"What's going on?" Neal's voice echoes through the empty hall. At that moment the loudspeakers crackle, "ALL STUDENTS ASSEMBLE IN THE SWIM HALL."

Of course! It's Swim Scout Day. We exchange a glance and hurry to the swim hall. Calling it a "hall" is something of a pomposity. The roof is made of corrugated iron and the mangy concrete pool is filled with saltwater that's pumped up from the shore. Most of us are glad if we can keep out of there. Ethan swears he got stung by a jellyfish once.

"Naya, over here!" Emily calls out and waves as Neal and I enter.

All around the hall are pathetic-looking plastic decorations. Raggedy, makeshift bunting to celebrate the "special day" and posters scribbled with Welcome Ararat. It's all show, to demonstrate our respect for the Elites. Neal and I climb up through rows of seated spectators and sit down with the rest of the high school Carps team.

"Burned those books yet, huh?" Ethan nudges Neal, while the chitchat around us continues.

Neal grins. "Coach Bench seems to be sweating more than normal," he whispers.

We turn our heads in unison to spy Coach Bench. He's by the poolside, grumpy as ever, assembling his top high school swimmers: a couple from the Lobsters, one from the Tunas, a few Turtles. None of the Carps of course. Bench is sporting his best tracksuit and a comb-over in an effort to minimize the sheen of his balding head.

Neal continues to whisper, "Somebody please buy that man a toupee."

We crack up. Our "Bench" jokes are endless. To be fair he isn't even called Coach Bench. His real name is Dench. We just call him Bench because any time he has a Carp in sight, his nostrils flare up and he roars, "You, Carp, bench!"

Not that any of us ever mind sitting out his swim class. Today, Coach Bench is huffing and puffing around the swimmers more than usual. The lower and middle school contestants are already sitting on the team benches. Most of them are messing around, pulling at one another's swimsuits, focusing on anything but the pool.

"Poor old Bench," Emily says. "Another wonderful opportunity to embarrass himself in front of an Elite."

We grin. For me and the Carps, Swim Scout Day is just a nice, relaxing school-free morning. While everyone else is sweating seawater to impress the Elite scout, who comes down from Ararat to see if there is any outstanding swim talent among our students, we get to sit back and watch the whole charade unfold. Really, I'm surprised they bother. No one can remember the last time that someone was chosen.

I scan the hall and notice a tall, thin man in a pristine business suit. That must be him. He's standing at the back of the pool beside Principal Simmonds. Our principal is talking to him with apologetic gestures, but the man neither moves nor acknowledges him in any way.

"I heard they had a problem with one of the high school competitors," Jonathan pipes up. "He didn't show."

"Thinkin' of jumping in for him, Johnny?" Ethan teases, messing up Jonathan's hair.

"What's that? . . . A Carp in the pool?" Neal affects outrage. "Somebody get a life jacket!"

"Quiet!" a voice suddenly calls. We look up, surprised, as our principal picks a microphone off a stand. "The lower school swimmers will hold their races in breaststroke, freestyle, freediving, and butterfly starting in fifteen minutes. The first category is breaststroke and will begin at ten o'clock sharp."

Why is he announcing the race timetable personally? Normally Coach Bench does that. Principal Simmonds just gives his boring, "We take pride in doing our duty," kiss-up speech for the government, which he seems to be skipping this year. I look around the hall. Bench is now right below us, hectically talking to some of the older boys from the Tunas in the front row. One of his hands is flattening his hair. He's trying to keep it as low-key as possible, but in his flashy red tracksuit, he's as conspicuous as a goldfish in a shoal of sardines. Whispers are spreading like wildfire along the benches.

". . . one swimmer down."

"Patrick from the Lobsters . . . didn't show."

". . . need an extra butterfly swimmer."

Butterfly!

Ethan shoots up from his seat. "Coach! You gotta pick Naya!

She's awesome!" he calls out over everyone's heads.

Coach Bench's head takes on the same color as his tracksuit. "Sit down, Wong!" he barks. "There's no time for stupid jokes."

"But he's right," Neal joins in. "She beat an Elite boy at butterfly yesterday."

This is too much for Coach Bench. "If you don't stop wasting my time . . ." He stomps up the steps, ready to explode.

"Please Coach, it's true," Emily calls out.

Coach Bench stops in his tracks. He's used to pranks from Neal and Ethan, but Emily is a different matter.

"So, Naya?" he sputters with impatience.

"I . . . I guess I did," I stutter. I wish Emily hadn't said anything. Everyone around us is staring at me.

"She was awesome," beams Emily. "We just don't know why she didn't show it before."

"Yeah, you could have shared your secret with us, Naya," Neal says.

Ethan gives me a friendly nudge. "Could have saved us from being the Craps third year in a row."

I force a smile. Truthfully, I have no idea what happened. It must have been some freak adrenaline rush, I should ask Mom about it.

"Quiet!" Coach Bench calls. "Naya, get changed. Your race is at twelve thirty." He turns on the steps, muttering. ". . . sure gone crazy. A Carp in the race . . . Somebody ready a life jacket."

I hurry down the stands and into the hallway. My hands tremble as I close the door to the locker rooms. I'm the only one in here, all the other competitors are already in swimwear and warmed up. I pull off my clothes and put on my purple Carp swimsuit from the Valley school. Once again I thank Mom that my gym bag was one of the few items she grabbed when we got flooded out. At least I don't have to wear the horrible standard issue FRS swimsuits. I look at my reflection in the cracked, spotted mirror opposite the showers that don't actually work. I look about as terrified as I feel. It's the first time that I'll be in front of such a big audience. Clutching my trident necklace I wish myself luck then wrap my arms around myself and walk into the swim hall.

I sit down on the plastic seats and watch the little kids flapping through the water in a fast, messy crawl. My mind is in a whirl about the upcoming race. I know there is no way I can repeat yesterday's performance. I can't even swim butterfly. At least they didn't put me forward for freediving. I heard you can black out if you get your breathing technique wrong, and I'm already hyperventilating.

It seems like only minutes have passed when the first high school students line up for their race. The freestylers are followed by the freedivers. The whole point of the freedive is to swim the entire length of the pool underwater using breaststroke, but none of the freedivers manage to complete the twenty-five meters in one breath. Bench waves at me to get ready for the butterfly.

"Remember, Carp, it's a two lap race. That's four lengths. Two laps. Now go!" he hisses.

I walk to the far end of the pool and take position a few steps away from the edge. My stomach is churning so much that I'm worried I might throw up. I look down the lane in front of me like I'm staring down the long barrel of a speargun. I can do this! Nervously I grasp my pendant and step forward with the others until my toes touch the edge of the pool, as I'm waiting for the whistle to sound the start of the race.

"Hey, you, lane four!" It takes me a moment to realize that our assistant coach is addressing me. He motions with his hand to his neck. "Remove your necklace. No jewelry. Competition rules."

No! I stop myself before the word reaches my lips. After almost losing it yesterday I don't want to take off my necklace again. Reluctantly, I unclip the chain. I'm acutely aware of the silence in the hall, everyone's eyes on me.

Where am I supposed to leave it?

Suddenly Emily is by the poolside. "Here, I'll keep it for you."

I give her a grateful smile. "Thank you."

"Hurry up," the assistant coach calls.

What little confidence I had is shattered as I get ready for the dive a second time. In about two minutes, everyone's going to know I'm a fraud, I'm going to be ridiculed in front of the whole school and Coach Bench will never forgive me for making a fool out of him.

FWEET!

The whistle goes and I fall more than dive into the pool, but as soon as I'm in the water, the fear subsides. It's like the crowd, and the silence, and the tension are gone. To my amazement my body knows what it's doing. My legs synchronize automatically. There's no need to think about style and form, I'm moving in perfect rhythm, like yesterday. With no effort at all, I keep pace with the other swimmers. At least I won't have to hide in embarrassment for finishing a whole length behind everyone else. I hope that for once in my life I can get the flipturn right. My fingertips touch the wall at the end of the lane, I dive, spin in a perfect underwater turn, and push off the wall, forcefully. Yes! I did it!

My head breaks the surface. I can't believe it. I'm in the lead! Flinging my arms forward I continue. Despite my lead, I don't dare slow down. The others will surely catch up soon, and yet, I feel power coursing through my body, a wild power that tells me that I cannot lose and that I will leave them far behind, just like I left Duke behind. There is something terrifying about it. I'm no longer in control of my body, like I'm not one with the water but am being consumed by it. In my despair I flipturn and swim even faster. At last, my hand touches the rim of the pool. I cling onto it as if I were drowning. My heart is beating, fast. I look down at my legs. I wiggle my toes, which bend like they should. With a feeling of relief, I clamber out of the pool. The other swimmers have only just reached the finish line. While I wait for my breathing to slow, I see Coach Bench walking toward me, a serious expression on his face.

"Get changed." He throws me a towel. "My office. Now."

I press the towel to my face. Oh no. Does he think I cheated somehow? I hurry along the spectator stands, toward the locker rooms.

"Naya!" Emily runs over and presses my necklace back into my hand. "That was awesome!"

"Thanks," I whisper, but I don't feel awesome at all. I feel like I'm about to get suspended and assigned to labor duty — for winning the race rather than for losing it.

My hands shake worse than they had before the race as I run along the hall to the locker rooms, then to Coach Bench's office.

". . . I sure didn't teach her that!" Bench's voice rings through the closed door. My heart is beating. What on earth could he want? I wait a beat before I knock.

"Enter!"

Inside the office, the smartly dressed Elite scout is standing by Bench's desk. He's even more unpleasant than when I saw him from the stands. His narrow face looks like it got squished between two heavy shelves at some point in his life. The eyes are a watery blue and his hair a pale brown. He flashes me a smile of welcome that reveals a perfect set of white teeth.

"Naya, thank you for joining us. Coach Dench was just filling me in on a few details for which I thank him, as I do for the use of his office while you and I have a little talk." He clears his throat. "A little *private* talk."

It takes Bench a moment to get the message. "Private talk. Yes, of course, sir." He gives me a nasty look, then scrapes his way out of his own office, hissing to me. "You, Carp, listen." The door shuts behind him.

"Good." The scout motions me to the chair in front of Bench's desk. "Now to business. My name is Emilio Bridgewater. I'm sure you are aware of the purpose of my presence here?"

I nod tentatively, not taking my eyes off him as I sit down.

"That's some amazing talent you've got there." Mr. Bridgewater's eyes fixate me with a steely stare. "Why is it that we've never noticed you at the tryouts before?"

"I . . . I guess I hadn't found my style yet."

"But it's safe to say that you have found it now, isn't it?"

I just keep quiet. I don't know what to say.

"What you have is a gift, Naya. It would be a real shame to waste it here, at a third-rate school with decrepit swimming facilities and questionable coaching, don't you think? You deserve better."

"Uh . . ."

A satisfied smile spreads across his face. "I hardly need to explain the importance that swimming has in the world that we live in. It is in my power to offer you a place at Eden Academy.

There, you will receive the best training that Cape Harmony has to offer."

I listen, dumbfounded. Is he saying that I should go to school with the Elites? I have no place there. This is all some very bad joke.

He detects the mistrust painted over my face. "You don't think I'm being serious?"

"I can't train on Ararat," I say. "How would I even get there?"

"To further your training, you will be provided with certain important basics, such as a healthy diet and suitable environment to live in. For that reason, you will be accommodated with a host family of our choice," Mr. Bridgewater explains.

Me, live on Ararat?

"Don't tell me you would rather stay here." I can detect the slight threat in the tone of his voice. "Because, for you, there really is no choice in the matter." Laying both hands on the table, he slowly gets up and crosses the room. "Our society is built on duty. As I'm sure you have been taught, each and every one of us must perform our assigned tasks for the greater good. Your duty to society is to perfect your swimming skills. It is a rewarding task. Many with talent such as yours find themselves drafted into search and rescue teams, working to save lives. Don't you wish to save lives, Naya?"

I swallow down the lump in my throat. "Yes, but . . ." I can't explain what just happened in the pool. I can't explain what happened on the beach. What if I can't repeat today's feat when I'm at the fancy Elite school? The consequences of being found out as a fake are too bad to even think about.

"No arguments, Naya," he says. "All you need to do is keep swimming like today and you will have nothing to worry about. Nothing at all."

This is worse than I thought. The Elites will think I used some kind of trick to con myself into a better life. He takes my silence for acquiescence.

"Good." He gives me a fake smile. "Now that we're finally in agreement, let's consider this the start of your new life. A car will be outside in five minutes to pick you up."

What? Right now? "What about my mom?" I ask.

"We can only accommodate those of exceptional standard,"

he says. "Your mother is no asset to society. But as long as you perform well and integrate into your new surrounding without problems, she will be well looked after in the FRS."

I look at him shocked. "And if I don't?" My voice is shrill.

"You are a smart girl." His cold eyes hold my gaze. "I don't take you for one of those few insurgents who waste their own and their family's lives in a labor camp because they fail to contribute to the benefit of our society. And, naturally, there can be no contact between those on the hill and those in the Flood Relief Shelters."

"But . . ." The thought of a life without Mom makes my throat tight. After all we've been through, I've never once been separated from her. I can feel the tears burning in my eyes.

"I would like to pick up my things," I whisper, in the hope that I can at least say goodbye.

"What things?" he retorts. "You don't have any things."

He motions me out of the office.

I follow, numb, in shock, as if I've been hit by a rogue wave. They can't do this!

We walk out into the blinding sunlight and the car is there waiting, black, fancy, polished. The sun reflects off its windscreen. The driver pulls open the back door for me and a waft of suffocating gasoline hits me. Feeling queasy, my heart in a knot, I bend down to get in.

Then I see her. My mom. Standing in the school yard. Neal is beside her. She raises her hand. She looks sad but somehow composed—not half as surprised as I thought she would be. Neal looks more shocked than she does. I give them a small smile then quickly look away and get in. I don't want to start crying in front of the Elite scout.

The car seats are soft leather. I sit back and hear the muted *thud* of the door shutting. As the car glides away, I look out the back window. I see Mom and Neal standing there, watching. She has his hand tight in hers. A breeze ruffles her dark, wavy hair. Then the car takes a turn and she is gone.

CHAPTER 5

— *Ararat Heights* —

The car purrs along the road winding up to Ararat Heights. Still in shock, I watch as the sea falls away on our right and sheets of luscious greenery speed past. No one from the FRS has ever been up here. It is strictly forbidden; any that venture up the mountain are shot on sight, like stray animals. I find it hard to believe that this won't be my fate as well. Mr. Bridgewater and the driver don't say a word.

The video screen in the backrest of the passenger seat jumps to life.

"Welcome to Ararat Heights, the verdant home of innovation and technological progress," a woman announces in a fake-happy voice, accompanied by calming, serene music.

"Ararat, where dreams become reality, where thoughts become action, where all your wishes come true."

Seriously? They've got their own promotional video? I'm pretty sure I'm the first to see this. The screen fades to a picture of a calm sea, fluffy clouds, and radiant sunshine.

"Ararat Heights is a place of hope, prosperity, justice, security, and peace. Watch and learn how we strive to obtain better, more sustainable resources. Solar power, wind energy, tidal power, and our innovative Red Earth Project."

White-coated figures in a lab appear on the screen, followed by a picture of trucks full of reddish-colored dirt.

"Red Earth is the path to the future. The hope for our children. Found in the soil of Cape Harmony, industrially processed and refined, it is the key to the new energy. Soon all of Cape Harmony will be entering a better, brighter future."

I almost laugh out loud. They're planning on fixing our problems—with dirt?

The woman on the screen smiles with her fake smile. "Ararat, where dreams become reality, where thoughts become action, where all your wishes come true."

The music crescendos and a logo of a golden anchor flashes across the screen. At that moment, the car slows and we pull up in front of a big, white house. It's built like a bunch of boxes piled together in an irregular pattern. The roofs are large sloping planes and it has huge, clear, floor-to-ceiling windows. Leading up to it is a neat, tiled footpath that crosses a pristine lawn with small beds of flowers on either side. I get out of the car and stare. I must look like an idiot, but I can't help it. I don't know what to marvel at first. The green lawn, the red roses, the white house. There's total quiet here, too, only chirping birds. I'm in a dream world far away from all the misery of the gray FRS.

A mechanical voice rings out as Mr. Bridgewater pushes the bell.

"Visitors detected. Citizen ID 1312, Emilio Bridgewater, government official, and—unknown citizen."

The front door opens and a tall, blonde woman in an expensive-looking dress sweeps out. She's slim, poised, and manicured, not a single hair out of place.

"Welcome to Ararat, Naya," she exclaims very loudly, as if I'm deaf. "I'm Adelia Queen. Your new host mom. And this is my daughter, Jessica. I'm sure the two of you will be best friends."

She beckons to a girl in a tightly fitted cream dress with light blonde hair, a white hairband, and a doll's smile.

Oh no, Jessica! The girl from the beach. Duke's little minion who stole my necklace.

"Pleasure," she says, in a honey-sweet voice and extends a white-skinned arm for a handshake, smirking at my discomfort.

"Hi," I breathe nervously.

"Simply adorable!" Mrs. Queen exclaims. "You'll feel right at home here—but look at the state of you, poor thing." She just about stops herself from pulling up her nose at the sight of my clothes and messy hair. "Jessica, please show Naya inside and get her something clean to wear. I have to see to the arrangements for tonight. Goodbye, Mr. Pondwater." She waves at the scout, who gets back into his car with a sour expression.

Jessica gives a demure smile as her mother leaves. "So, Naya, is it? Come on then, I'll show you what a house looks like."

I grimace and follow her inside. The rooms are all big and vast with ostentatious furniture but feel empty. The dining table could seat ten people easily. On it is a silver bowl with fake fruit and on the walls are large paintings with geometric shapes in bright colors. Why do they have all this space if they don't put anything in it?

My old sneakers squeak on the smooth, shiny marble floor. I look down and freeze with terror: dried mud is falling off my shoes onto the floor. Just then a bleep echoes behind me and a little silver box whizzes across the floor, leaving the area it passes sparkling clean.

"That's I-Sak our cleaning bot," Jessica says. "Sorry I-Sak. Your workload is going to triple now that you have FRS trash to clean up after."

She leads me into the kitchen. Bright sunlight reflects off a floor-to-ceiling glass pillar, bang in the middle of the room, filled with water. Inside it, multicolored fish are circling artificial rocks and corals. An array of silvery, sparkly machines are aligned on the kitchen counters. One large, cylindrical one is labeled Nutrigator. Curious, I lean closer.

"Wow, you really haven't been in a house before," Jessica says. "I suppose you'll want something to eat?"

I want to say no, but my stomach betrays me with an angry growl. Jessica hits the orange *snack* button. There's a whirr then a ping as the central cylinder turns and a compartment opens.

"It's called a Nu-tri-ga-tor," Jessica says preachily, as if I can't read the label, and she hands me a plate with a yellowish, rectangular object sitting on it.

I eye it suspiciously.

"We call it a booster bar," Jessica says. "It's full of nutrients, you know, the stuff your body needs."

Tentatively, I take a bite. It's like apple mixed with cashews. Oh my, after eleven months solid on swamp soup, this is a shock to my taste buds.

"Woah, slow down. It's a snack, not a swim race. Nutrigators recharge in, like, seconds. We have everything here, Naya.

Everything you could possibly want. This way."

I follow her into an enormous atrium. Light pours in through a pyramid-shaped glass roof. In the center, a palm tree rises from a small bed of pebbles and to the right an open staircase leads to an upper gallery.

"My father works for Zephyrus, one of our most important companies. They're our wind and tidal energy resource. He's one of their senior executives." Jessica gives me a smug smile. "The other energy companies are Solaris for solar power and Mortlake Industries for coal and oil and of course my father also works on the new Red Earth Project. Without the combined efforts of these companies, life as we know it on Ararat would not be possible—and you guys down in the shelters would be living on rats."

Jessica walks up the stairs and knocks on a door set in an archway.

"Come in," a friendly male voice calls. We stick our heads inside, and a man in his early forties rises from a chair behind a desk.

"Ah, there you are, Naya." He stretches out a hand to me. He has a young face and bright blue eyes. His short brown hair is brushed back in an elegant wave. He's dressed in gray pants and a shirt that has the top three buttons undone.

"So how do you like the Queen residence so far?" he asks with a twinkle of amusement in his eyes.

"It's uh . . ." I look around for Jessica then realize that she didn't follow me into the room. "It's very nice," I say honestly. "Thank you, Mr. Queen."

"Please, call me Jim," he says. "Formalities are just a waste of time. So, I hear you're going to be our new star. All of Ararat is abuzz."

I swallow. *All* of Ararat knows already?

"Don't worry, nobody expects any miracles."

I manage a weak smile. Without a miracle I'll be out of here quicker than I arrived.

He seems to read my thoughts. "It's just government hype. You know, I always found these 'Do your duty' talks a bit excessive."

I look at him, unable to hide my surprise. Isn't everyone on Ararat rule obsessed?

"One time I even missed my coach's speech before my race finals," he says.

"You were a competitor?"

"A freediver, yes, but that was a long time ago. It's up to the new generation to uphold the family tradition." He looks at a framed photo of Jessica on his desk. "We Queens have great potential, but we're late bloomers. Takes us a while to work out what we really want."

For a moment his eyes flicker to a big glass video screen on the wall with a flashing Zephyrus logo. It has a login bar labeled Deputy Director, and there are more screens, too. They look like giant window panes. Some of them display figures, others charts or maps, and on one of the maps a green light flashes.

"What are these?" I ask.

"They're energy consumption charts," he explains. "I work for Zephyrus. One of Ararat's three energy companies. Jessica might have told you. We work in close collaboration with Ararat's research and technology companies, Galileo Tecc, Goldstein Ventures, and the Cape Harmony Research Institute to efficiently harness the energy of the winds and tides."

I watch the chart closest to his desk. It's a map of Ararat. The main settlement, on the mountain peak, slopes down to the west with several more houses scattered around an amphitheater-shaped harbor. I notice that there are percentage bars, some bigger, some smaller on specific houses and areas. The ones that are almost full are red, with an EXCESS warning.

"Is energy assigned?" I ask.

Now he glances at me with surprise. "That's right, Naya. We need to be careful with our resources. They're not unlimited. Without them we'd be forced to make some very difficult decisions." There's a strange look in his eyes. "Very difficult indeed." He turns off the screen. "Well, now you know where I work when I'm home. If there's anything you need just knock. The Queen ladies can be a little overbearing sometimes, but I'm sure you can stand your ground." He winks at me. "I have some work to finish before the party tonight. I will see you later. Welcome to the family."

Slipping out quietly, I walk back into the atrium. Jessica is nowhere to be seen. I wander along the gallery. There's a door next to Jim's study. I try the handle and it opens, revealing a poster on the back wall. It depicts a triangular object, made up of intersecting lines. Like a geometric bird. IKARUS, the title of the poster says and underneath, To Defy is to Deify.

"Are you all right dear?"

I jump. I didn't hear Mrs. Queen come up the stairs. Her eyes flicker to the room behind me.

"Yes," I say. I hope she doesn't think I'm snooping around, but her look of suspicion is already gone, replaced by an immaculate smile.

"Where's Jessica? Hasn't she shown you your room yet?"

"Not yet."

Mrs. Queen tuts and motions for me to follow her to the opposite side of the gallery and down a hallway. "Jessica!" she calls out musically, like she's masking her shouting by singing instead. "Jessica!"

One of the doors opens and Jessica hops out.

"There you are dear. You're completely neglecting your hosting duties. I found this poor girl wandering the atrium utterly lost."

Jessica mutters something under her breath.

"Don't mumble, sweetheart, it's not etiquette. You girls should be getting ready for the evening. The welcome party in Naya's honor starts in three hours. Your father's boss is the host, so we want to look our best."

With that, Mrs. Queen turns on her highly polished heel and walks away. Jessica raises an accusing eyebrow at me. "Great. So, now I'm stuck with you, am I?"

I'm too panicked about what Mrs. Queen just said to reply. A party? In my honor? That's what she and Jim were talking about before?

"Don't just stand there. You've wasted enough of my time already," Jessica says. "Do you have any idea how long it takes to get ready for a party?"

I hurry after her as she struts along the hallway. The light streaming in through the large windows overhead casts geometric boxes onto the floor.

"This is my room," Jessica says as we pass the door she just emerged from. "Needless to say, it's off limits to seaweed-trash."

I catch a glimpse of a pink bedspread covered with hearts and a white teddy bear sitting on it. Her window faces southeast, overlooking the slope of Ararat with all the gigantic villas and its leafy treetops.

"And this is yours." Jessica opens another door. My mouth drops. It's so beautiful. There's a gigantic double bed with snow-white sheets and four fluffy pillows. The ceiling slants above it to create a cozy corner with tiny starlike spotlights. Opposite is a mirrored closet with six doors, and a white desk and a matching chair. The carpet feels soft beneath my feet. I can't believe this is for me and me alone.

Even more breathtaking is the view. I stand there, my mouth agape, and stare at the triangular window that covers the whole wall in front of me. It looks out far across the sea. The sun sparkles on the thin line where the waves and the sky meet. A feeling of freedom and happiness seizes me, a feeling I haven't ever known before.

"Why Mommy had to give you a whole bedroom when we could've put you up in the basement is beyond me. I was using this as my private dressing room."

I turn, surprised. For a second I'd completely forgotten she was there. Wishful thinking, I guess.

"Anyway," Jessica claps her hands at the cupboards and shouts, "Open everything!" All doors snap open and the drawers and clothes racks shoot out at once. At least two of the racks are lined with dresses. Jessica runs a hand along the first one. "Nice, aren't they? Unfortunately they don't fit me anymore. Bust-wise." She points to a drawer. "The underwear is new by the way."

Well, that's a relief. I reach in the drawer and pull out a set of silky, silver pajamas. They're so soft, they flow through my fingers.

"I was going to put the dresses in the trash, but Mommy said I should give them to you. Same thing really, I suppose. But for now . . . time to get ready for tonight, and you can't wear those. They're pajamas."

I roll my eyes but she's already hopped over to the bed. "I guess I'd better give you your present or my parents might kill me." She hands me a parcel with blue wrapping and a purple ribbon. "It's from Daddy. We did a little shopping before you arrived. There wasn't much time—we only found out an hour ago—but we can't let you go to the party looking like a beggar. It would be embarrassing," she shoots me a bitchy smile, "for us, I mean."

I take the parcel.

"It's a dress. Obviously," Jessica says. "You can unwrap it in the bathroom. Now for the shoes. I put out some that go with it." She points to a pair of strappy high heels that are standing beside the open mirrored cabinet. Their greenish-blue leather is the color of the sea.

"They're totally my favorites," Jessica says. "Daddy practically forced me to lend them to you. It's real bad luck that we're the same size."

Does she ever stop talking? It's gonna be a nightmare living with her.

"This is the bathroom." Jessica piles the shoes on top of the present I'm holding and pushes me through an adjoining door. "Nice, isn't it?"

That doesn't quite cover it. I've never seen a bathroom like this. So big, white, and sparkly. Jessica taps a metal pad by the door and a display lights up.

"Interactive," she says.

"*Hello,*" a metallic voice announces. "*My name is Vanilla. I am on full interactive mode. Tell me what you want and it will be done.*"

"Vanilla, start off by giving her a good hose down," Jessica replies. "We don't know where she's been. And make sure you get out all the grime. She's supposed to be the star of the evening. Tall order, I know."

"*What theme?*" the metallic voice inquires.

"Uhm . . ." Jessica scans through the options list. "How about *seashore*? That's where you find seaweed-trash, right?"

"*Seashore is a very nice selection,*" the metallic voice says.

46

"Yeah, whatever." Jessica turns toward the door.

"Wait, what . . . ?" I start.

"Don't tell me you've never showered before," Jessica says, "because that would be gross." She slams the door behind her.

I stare at the shower. It doesn't even have taps. How am I meant to use it? I leave the present and the strappy high heels on a shelf beside the sink, take off my muddy sneakers and step into the shower fully dressed to figure out the mechanism.

"Please remove your dirty socks," the metallic voice says.

"Vanilla, I'm not actually seaweed-trash, you know," I say.

"Anyone would claim that," the metallic voice replies.

I huff, outraged at being insulted by a machine, but before I can say anything a jet of water rains down on me. "Eeew!" I shriek and pull off my wet clothes.

"Say your wish and it will be my command."

"Less . . . water," I splutter.

The water slows to a trickle.

"Very funny. A normal amount of water, please?"

"Define 'Normal.'"

"OK, I get it! You prefer showering Jessica! She knows all the right commands."

"Correction, she thinks she knows all the right commands."

"Well, I'm new here," I say. "So you'll have to choose for me."

"Choose for you?" Vanilla sounds more upbeat than I expected. *"Is that an affirmative confirmed?"*

"Yes!"

"All right!" Vanilla plays a little fanfare. *"Choosing for you is what I am programmed for. Now, let me see what we have here. Multiple pigmentation blemishes, several subdermal contusions, numerous scabs and scars. Start by applying soap. Extra strength. Antibacterial, antimicrobial, anti—"*

The water splashes around me in rainbow colors, trickling off my skin at a nice, mild temperature. I pick up the bottles from a niche in the shower wall and start squeezing various liquids and lotions over my skin and hair. They burn in my eyes and I can't see where I am. Disoriented I take a step back and almost skid on the slippery floor.

"Caution! Lotion, water, and GermAloid detected on shower floor,"

Vanilla warns me. *"Remain motionless until lotion is removed."*
"What?" I splutter.
"Didn't anyone teach you as a child?" Vanilla asks.
"Teach me what?"

Remember to avoid
Mixing lotion, water, and GermAloid.
Lotion makes you pretty, the way you want to be seen,
Water's hygienic, keeps you spotless and clean,
And GermAloid kills,
All bacteria and other ills.
But when mixing the three beware,
or you will wind up on your derriere.

OK, none of that made any sense, but it doesn't matter. The water splashes over me and I'm starting to feel nice and clean.
"Nice necklace," Vanilla comments. *"Would you like display on?"*
A moment later the glass walls of the shower turn into an oceanic display of tropical fish swimming around. Vanilla talks me through everything: makeup, perfumes, nail polish and how to use the automated hair-styler. Then it's time to unwrap the dress. I gasp as I lift it out of the box and let it unfold. Layers and layers of silky satin in different shades of blue cascade down to the floor, one gradually folding over the other. It's as smooth as water. I love it. I carefully pull the straps over my shoulders and tie it at my waist. The bottom unfolds like a waterfall around me. It flutters with the tiniest movement. Never before have I worn anything so delicate.

I hardly recognize the person that's staring back at me from the mirror. My hair is styled up in a fancy knot and has a shiny glow. A few strands fall over the light and dark blue of the dress. And my lips are glossy pale-pink with the lipstick that Vanilla chose. I wish Mom could see me like this, so elegant. Even . . . beautiful?

Timidly, I push the bathroom door open. The room is dimmer than before. I look out to sea where the sun is just setting on the horizon. What is this new world that I am a part of?

CHAPTER 6

— Power and Money —

"You look nice, Naya." Jessica's mom gazes at me approvingly.

"Thank you, Mrs. Queen." I smile back. I struggle not to fall out of the heels that Jessica gave me, but neither Jessica nor her parents notice as we walk to the car that is waiting outside. It is a black government vehicle, like that of the swim scout, and it takes us to a villa, uphill, only a few minutes away. We stop in the circular gravel driveway and the driver opens the doors for us. The sound of voices and clinking glasses carries in the evening air. Jessica and her mother walk up the stairs, all poised and upright. I wobble after them in Jessica's shoes. They're horrible; my feet ache as if I were walking barefoot on a rocky beach.

"Very brave of you, Naya, trying heels on the first evening." Jim offers me his arm.

"But . . . I . . ." Jessica spins around to me and flashes her bitchy smile. Of course, she tricked me—Jim would never have given me these shoes!

I give him a sheepish look. "I . . . just wanted to make sure I didn't embarrass you."

Jim returns a fatherly smile. "You most certainly are not."

Together, we walk across the imposing entrance with white stone columns on either side and double-winged doors that have sun symbols engraved on them. The doors open into a golden reception hall with a big chandelier overhead. A light blue family crest, depicting a fat otter that has caught a fish, is emblazoned on the wall. The chatter gets louder. A crowd of formally dressed people stand together, all with tall glasses in their hands. Metallic machines with flat, square heads and trays on top to serve food and drinks are whizzing around them.

"Welcome, Jim, Adelia, Jessica—and Naya." A blond man in a dark suit strides over and shakes my hand.

He seems smug and wealthy and happy about it.

Jim beams as he introduces us. "Naya, I'd like you to meet my boss at Zephyrus and our host for the evening, Brice Donovan."

"Pleasure." I try to smile naturally as we shake hands. Hopefully, he didn't notice how I nearly fell out of my shoes when he tugged at my hand.

At that moment there's a crackle of static and everyone around us stops talking. Only now do I notice the dais at the far end of the room. Governor Proctor, dressed in a smart suit, is standing there holding a microphone. In person, he looks much more ordinary than in his video speeches, an ungainly man in his sixties. Gray hair frames a receding hairline and he's wearing a striped sash around his shoulder.

"It is with great joy that I take this opportunity to welcome Naya DeLora . . ."

"That's Governor Arcadius Proctor," Jessica leans over and whispers in my ear.

No kidding! I roll my eyes at her.

". . . a young lady whose talent, as I have been told, is nothing short of outstanding. A new competitor for our excellent swim team at Eden Academy, a future recruit of Aqua8, and thereby one of the core elements that allow our society to prosper in this world of water. Water surrounds us. Water is our origin, and, if we fail, it will be our fate . . ."

My gaze wanders to the banner strung above the dais, announcing my arrival: Welcome Naya. This much attention, just for me? I feel myself turning red.

". . . so, fellow citizens, thank you for your attention, and enjoy your evening," the Governor concludes his speech.

As clapping fills the room, everyone's eyes turn to me and, all of a sudden, people swarm toward me like bees to honey, all trying to shake my hand. I find myself nodding, mumbling, and managing to get out the occasional thank you whenever my voice decides to work. What am I supposed to say to them? They're Elites. Am I betraying my friends, simply by standing here, simply by smiling and nodding and doing nothing? The former Valley populace are dying while these people are wasting resources on fancy parties. My head dizzy, I want to disappear, or scream, or run away—not that I could in these shoes.

"Ah, so that's what's at the center of this heap."

I look up at a tall, round-shouldered man with tousled, graying mousy-brown hair and gray eyes who is suddenly standing in front of me. He watches the crowd with quirky bemusement as if he finds it funny how people are falling over themselves to say hello to me.

"Arlo Quinn, councilman for the Cape Harmony Research Institute, delighted to make your acquaintance. Shall I rescue you from this untamed mob?" He beams at me with scholarly refinement and without awaiting an answer takes my hand and leads me away. "Governor Proctor would like to greet you in person."

I give him a half-panicked smile. Now I'm supposed to meet the most powerful man on Cape Harmony? I'm heading from the paddling pool straight into the shark tank.

He smiles back mischievously, clearly in his element. "You'd see a stage of dancing apes if you looked behind the illusion of this dignified extravaganza. Step on a few toes—if you have to. You, young lady, are not here for their entertainment."

As he leads the way through the crowd, I sneak a glance at him.

"Councilman Quinn!" A pigeon-chested man with blow-dried, black hair jumps in our way with the eagerness of a salesman for nonrobotic vacuums.

"Ah, Principal Preen." Arlo stops in his tracks and announces, "The head of your new school."

Principal Preen holds out a smooth hand with manicured nails. "Miss DeLora, a pleasure. We at Eden strive for the best. Academic success and outstanding swimming achievements. You will find no greater opportunity to pursue your career goals—"

"An opportunity Miss DeLora will soon explore for herself, I'm sure, Eugene," Arlo says and whisks me away.

"There, now you've met him. He's all work and no play. Very boring." Arlo spins me around, toward the Governor. Arcadius Proctor is actually midconversation with two important-looking people. The tall, pale man to his right has silver-gray hair and a long straight nose and is very serious. On the Governor's left is a bulky woman of equal stature. The name tag on her chest says CALDER and her black-and-gold uniform is decorated with many ribbons and medals. Her black hair is tied back firmly and her lips are so tight, it looks like she's pulling a pout. Neither she nor the silver-haired man is happy at being interrupted.

Arlo Quinn takes boyish delight in the situation. "Governor Proctor, forgive my intrusion into your Red Earth talks with our esteemed Mortlake CEO, but here's our young guest of honor."

"Aha! So this is the delectable young lady!" The Governor beams at the silver-haired man next to him. "We're all so happy to have you here, aren't we, Kallion?"

The silver-haired man forces a crooked smile. "Ecstatic. If you'll excuse me, I have business to attend to, amidst all these frivolities and sugar-coated cupcakes." He nods stiffly and walks away.

"And I have the sugar-coated cupcakes to attend to," says Arlo Quinn. With a half-playful bow he bids his farewell and disappears into the crowd.

Governor Proctor turns to me. "I hope you enjoyed my little welcome speech?" His shrewd eyes gaze out from under bushy eyebrows.

"Uh . . . very much," I stutter, lost for words. Actually I zoned out during the speech. My face is burning with embarrassment.

Governor Proctor doesn't notice. "Please let me introduce you to General Calder, our distinguished head of Aqua8."

"Welcome to Ararat Heights." As General Calder squishes my hand in a painful handshake, I can't hide my wince, but it's her voice that sends a real shiver down my spine. Somehow it hurts my ears, distorting the chatter and clinking of glasses into a loud ringing of static.

"I hope the uniform didn't put you off." Calder's voice is normal this time, but totally devoid of emotion.

"No . . ." In truth, I find her intimidating. It's like I'm talking to a machine. A perfectly efficient killing machine.

"Aqua8 is the crème de la crème," the Governor jumps in. "Everyone is hand-picked by the General—and myself, of course." He gives a happy chuckle that Calder dismisses with an almost sinister smile. "Always doing their duty to help save lives. As well as defend our shores from . . . from uh, let's say, undesirable elements." He finishes with a nervous cough.

Undesirable elements? What did he mean? Is he speaking about the element of water, the sea? Or the people in the FRS? Or is there something else out there? I look at him bewildered.

Calder steps in. "That's why Aqua8's twin role in patrolling our coasts and training our young cadets in combat is so important."

"Exactly," Governor Proctor says merrily then clears his throat. "Though . . . aren't we doing a little too much combat training, recently?"

"It would be foolish to neglect it. It is a dangerous threat, the Aquatic Other." Calder's lips curl in cold pleasure.

The Governor gulps. "So you see, Naya, to what useful purposes your talents might be put."

At his remark Calder's gaze turns toward me, studying me intently. "Indeed. A girl like you, from a broken home with everything to prove, might well possess the drive that's needed to take you to the top."

Her words curdle my blood. Is this what the Elites have in mind for me? To become like General Calder? Emotionless? Icy?

"There are several talented future officers here this evening, you should become acquainted with," General Calder says.

"But alas . . ." the Governor chimes in, "our most promising young officer, Gallagher, isn't here tonight. I sent him away on a secret miss—" He breaks off and coughs, realizing he said too much. "Anyway, he's not here tonight, alas."

Calder, who apparently lacks enthusiasm for her most promising young officer, gives a thin-lipped smile. "Alternatively, you could meet people who actually are here tonight. Kallion Junior, for instance."

"Yes, an excellent idea," the Governor says. "On that note, General, you remind me that I hadn't finished discussing some urgent business with young Kallion's father. Please excuse me."

Calder holds my gaze for a moment longer. "I'll be watching your progress with a keen eye," she says then turns abruptly and walks away.

As I look around for the future officers that Calder and the Governor suggested I meet, the sudden thought strikes me whether *he's* here. The boy from the Valley. My heart gives a little leap, followed by an immediate frisson of fear that stops my breath. What would he do if he saw me here? He saved my life while I was breaking the law. How would he feel now that I'm in the middle of all these Elites? A rebel, right at the heart of Ararat society? The horrific image from my dream jumps back into my mind. Did I subconsciously perceive him as a threat? Or was my dream just a nightmare? Mom once mentioned that dreams can be prophetic. I wish I could ask her, but she's miles away; I dare not wonder whether I'll ever see her again. And this boy is probably the last person I should meet. I'm insane to even be thinking about him.

I slip through a doorway on the right, brushing past a server bot carrying a tray of drinks. Perhaps it's best if I can find somewhere quiet, where I can blend in until the end of the evening. The hall I enter is smaller than the first, with French windows overlooking a garden. A few people are sitting on couches, engaged in desultory conversation. At the far end is a banquet table set with a fine tablecloth and silver trays stacked with delicacies. Right in the center of the table is a huge, white, cream cake decorated with the words Naya DeLora. I swallow down the lump in my throat. The last time I had cake was on my tenth birthday. I can't even remember what it tastes like.

The Elites apparently can. Huge chunks of the cake are already missing. Why have they already eaten more than half of it when my name is on it? I set my foot on the three steps leading down to the table, but my stiletto slides from under me, my ankle twists and I lurch sideways. Whoah! Great, now I'm greedily flying toward the buffet like a big, human pancake!

Except I don't fall. A strong arm catches me around the waist.

"You know, that dress really makes your eyes sparkle."

"Thank—" My words catch in my throat. It's Duke.

"Well, who'd have thought we'd meet again so soon and on the same side of the court, butterfly girl?" He gives me a suave smile.

Seriously now? Butterfly girl? I pull away from him. He's eyeing me with that uncomfortable stare again.

"Let me introduce myself properly. I'm Duke K—"

"So Naya, taken a shine to something else of mine?" Jessica appears at our side.

Duke quickly takes his hand off my waist. "I was . . . I just . . ."

"You still don't know how to make a decent introduction, son," a voice behind us says. The pale, silver-haired man, who was talking to the Governor earlier, takes my hand and brings it to his lips. "Douglas Kallion, Mortlake Industries."

What? Douglas Kallion is Duke's father? But he and Duke look nothing alike. Douglas's eyes turn to Duke and I notice how small they are, how mean. "So, this is the girl that beat you in the swim race? Perhaps I should thank you, Miss DeLora, for bringing my son down to Earth. He thinks he's Aqua8's finest," Douglas Kallion says, but he doesn't actually look like he wants to thank me. He looks like Duke has disappointed him and I'm the enemy.

"I didn't mean to . . ." I say.

"Of course you didn't." His polite smile sends goosebumps down my back.

Duke doesn't say anything but looks glum. And Jessica glares at me as if I had tried to steal her boyfriend. I wish I had stayed in the main hall with the other Elites, shaking hand after hand. I want to disappear—snap my fingers and vanish.

But it's everyone else that vanishes. In one instance all the lights go out and the whole villa is plunged into darkness. There's a nervous murmur and the sound of guests shuffling their feet. A power cut? On Ararat?

Then the Governor's voice rings though the darkness. "For Oceans' sake, Kallion, is that what you call advancements on the Red Earth Project?"

CHAPTER 7

— In Eden —

"Of course Daddy's work is SO-O crucial to Zephyrus. Oh sure, Donovan's technically his boss, but it's really Daddy who does all the . . . the, you know, the sciency stuff. Of course, Daddy's a genius, everyone says so, even Dr. Planck. He was teaching us something in physics and suddenly he said, 'But of course, we have Jim Queen to thank for that equation.' I was so excited I accidentally deleted the shopping list that I'd been working on for like, ages . . ."

Jessica's EV, "It's short for e-lec-tro-nic vehicle, duh," she said as we got in, purrs softly as she drives toward school. It resembles a rainbow bubble with half-height doors and is smaller and slower than a car. I look at the landscape that flashes past. Jessica continues to chatter faster than any human should be able to.

"Still, I can't expect you to understand what it's like to have a genius for a parent. I guess they don't have geniuses down in the FRS. Else, they wouldn't be down there in the first place, right?"

My blood is nearing boiling point. "Why don't y—"

My reply is cut short as we round a corner and spin toward a building shaped like a gigantic, white sculpture, unfolding in intertwining curves of stone, glass, and metal. The main entrance rises out of the ground like the prow of a ship.

"Eden Academy," Jessica announces.

I stare. If my new school on Ararat Heights looks like a sleek yacht, then my old school in the FRS is a leaking rustbucket in imminent danger of sinking.

"What, you've never seen a school before?" Jessica asks sarcastically. "It's really not that great. Please don't tell me you're a nerd."

I don't say anything. Even the school's parking lot looks glamorous with all the symmetrical bays of bubble-shaped vehicles in their metallic, fluorescent colors. We stop near the entrance and get out.

Jessica walks up to the sliding glass doors and pushes her thumb onto a screen beside them. The screen lights up red.

"Visitor detected. Unknown citizen. Report to security office, level one."

Jessica leads me into the prow-shaped entrance hall, a big, empty space with a model of an old-fashioned sailing ship suspended from the ceiling. I follow her into a sunlit atrium, with six levels rising up around us. The plexiglass railings on each level have different colors: blue, green, pink. The Elites seem to love glass about as much as swimming. It's all display and no privacy. When I look up, I see students walking along the galleries on each level.

"That's Shane Borgman, he's an even bigger creep than you," Jessica says loudly as we sweep past a freckled boy with red, scruffy hair. He looks up with a scowl while Jessica continues, "Please don't embarrass me by hanging out with the total losers. It's bad enough that you're wearing my old clothes. They're sooo last year."

We stop in front of an office labeled Security.

"OK, time to get you tagged." Jessica opens the door.

I glance at the two guys in white uniforms who are sitting in the office. Their expressions are blank, like robots.

One of the guys pushes a glass tablet toward me. "Put your thumb on the screen."

I press down and my photo and name appear, along with the number 7121.

"OK, citizen 7121. This is your ID card. Don't lose it." The guy pushes a small plastic card with my photo toward me.

"Sure," I mumble.

"And here's your e-pad for note taking." The second guard hands me a flat, rectangular see-through piece of plastic. My ID number is imprinted in one corner.

"Don't I get a pen as well?" I ask.

Jessica snorts with laughter. "It's e-lec-tro-nic." She presses a small, white button on the side of the piece of plastic. The e-pad turns white and a neon alphabet appears across the bottom. "You write notes by pressing the letters," Jessica explains, "and you can select your school assignments, homework schedules, and calendar at the top. Today is Wednesday, so you have math, starting in five minutes, followed by politics and English." She hits *math* and a classroom on the fifth floor lights up while an arrow appears, pointing through a 3D map of the school. "If you select the subject, it shows you the room that it's in and the route to get there."

"Thank—" I start, but Jessica continues talking.

"But you have to pick up your things from your locker first." She swipes her finger across the screen and selects a location on the second floor. "Which is here! And by the way, you better hurry. Miss Li really hates it when we're late." With that Jessica spins around and stalks out of the office.

I give the security guys a helpless stare, but they don't even blink. Clasping my new e-pad under my arm I run along the hallway. I reach the second floor in three minutes flat. The lockers are in a U-shaped alcove, a series of square, illuminated compartments with frosted glass doors. Here and there kids are rushing up to them and tapping at the glass. When they do, the frosted glass turns transparent and swings outward. So that's how this works—but which one is mine? I notice the numbers. 4490, 4500. These must be the citizen IDs. I look for 7121 and find it on the left, at waist height. At that moment the bell rings. Groups of chatting students break up midsentence and scatter along the hallway, like shoals of minnows disturbed by a thrown rock.

I press my finger against the thumb-shaped dent in the glass door and at once the contents are revealed in a mellow orange light: a neatly folded red-and-white competition swimsuit, a red swim cap and a pair of white goggles, one shoulder bag, and a red sports bag embroidered with the image of a big, slim, gray fish. Then there's a set of bottles: shampoo, bath gel and the by now familiar GermAloid. According to the blue label it's some kind of antibacterial foot gel. Guess the Elites are paranoid about warts. Quickly, I stow my e-pad in the shoulder bag, then scoop all other items into my sports bag. By the time the glass of my locker has frosted over again, I'm three minutes late. I sprint to the math room.

"Miss DeLora, I presume." A petite woman in a short-sleeved, black blazer, her dark hair done up in a bun with two black sticks stuck through it, welcomes me with a disapproving expression. "You missed one-tenth of this class!"

I feel the blood rushing to my face as everyone in the room stares at me. Flustered, I slip into a seat in the front row. There are no desks, only weird wire stands attached to the right armrest of each chair. I look around the class and see that the other students are all tapping their e-pads, set onto the stands in front of them.

"Problem, Miss DeLora?" Miss Li is standing over me with a frown.

"No, no." I fish my e-pad out of my bag, switch it on and search for the equations that everyone else has open. Miss Li gives an exasperated sigh, takes the e-pad from my hands, taps a few icons and puts it down on the stand in front of me. In the top corner of the screen is a live video of our classroom and of Miss Li glaring at me.

Are they recording this?

"Ignore the video. It's for home revision purposes," Miss Li says. "You need to be looking at this." She taps a section that says *matrices*. "This is just a quick refresher for the exam."

I look up at her. I've never done anything like this before. We only got taught basic arithmetic in the FRS and the Valley.

Miss Li shakes her head, muttering under her breath. "Career exams a month away. What in seas' sake is Principal Preen thinking, sending me an FRS student now . . ."

Five minutes before the bell, Miss Li returns and snatches up my e-pad. "Four out of fifteen exercises correct. Well, I expected zero."

With a shock I realize that this is probably the closest thing I'm gonna get to a compliment.

I hurry after Jessica and the crowd of students from my class, heading along the flashing route that my e-pad has mapped toward the politics room. And then I see him. Diagonally ahead of me. The boy from the Valley. My heart makes an involuntary leap. Blond locks hide his face from the side. He's taller than most of the students and stands out in his white shirt. In his left ear he's wearing an earring. A silver shark's-tooth-shaped stud. It has a pattern of cut out triangles. I wait for him to turn, to notice me, to meet my gaze. Will he recognize me? What will he say? My feelings are tumbling one over the other. The elation at seeing him, the fear of what will happen now. But he doesn't look back even once, he just walks through the crowd as if the rest of the students didn't exist.

I hear a giggle behind me. "No chance there, lover girl," Jessica sneers. "That's Ararat's golden boy, GG. The Governor's squeaky-clean protégé. The only thing he's in love with is holding officer rank in Aqua8. Don't even know why he's here. It's not like he shows up to class or anything."

I turn my face to the ground to hide my blush. Last thing I want is for Jessica to know that she's right. But can it really be? Can the boy who rescued me from the Valley be the talented young officer who Governor Proctor wanted me to meet?

Keeping my head down, I follow Jessica to the third floor. Politics is followed by English and marine biology. The teachers all react pretty much the same as Miss Li, but each class is even worse than math—if that's even possible. As for the students—nobody talks to me. By the end of marine biology I catch some girls staring at me and giggling. I'm sure I have Jessica to thank for that. When the bell rings for lunch I can't get out of the classroom fast enough.

"Hey, FRS! Who let you out of your aquarium? Lab fish over there." A guy with a mop of black hair deliberately steps in my way so that I bump into him. He smirks and points at a glass tank by the window. "See the uncanny resemblance?"

I knock my elbow into his side as I push past him and hurry from the room, a sick feeling in my stomach. I hope they don't actually experiment on animals here!

In the lunch hall Jessica sits down with the two girls from the volleyball beach. They're both wearing pastel yellow, like her. Halfheartedly, I turn to their table.

"Na-ah," Jessica says. "Don't even think about it! This is an Elites-only table. So scoot."

"Why are you sending her away?" one of the girls from the beach asks. "Isn't she like your new—"

"My new what, Kayla? Adopted stray? House invader? Yeah, she's my house invader." Jessica waves her hand at me. "Scram!"

I turn and find a quiet table for myself, finish the meal from the school Nutrigators, then hurry out of the lunch hall. I just want to be alone somewhere.

Jessica's voice echoes in my mind. *Ararat's golden boy* . . . So why did he save me? An FRS-girl breaking the law? And what will he think when he finds out why I'm here? The drowning girl that he fished out of the Valley—at Eden Academy as the future swimming sensation. He'll know there's something wrong. He'll know I'm a fraud. What if he tells someone . . . ?

Wham!

I knock right into someone.

"I'm so sorry . . ." I begin but then my heart stops. It's him. It's GG.

He blinks, as if he's gazing into a bright light. We stand frozen, our eyes locked. I can see him fight to hide his emotions as the recognition kicks in. In his eyes there is shock . . . joy . . . also worry.

"I'm Naya." I hold out my hand. I have to say something to break the silence.

In a flash his frozen expression is a replaced with a polite smile. "Gillan, welcome to Ararat."

He is literally the first student to have said that. He shakes my hand briefly. The touch sends a nervous tingle through my body. He's even more handsome than I remember him. Boyish cute, with strength and confidence that lend him maturity.

Footsteps behind me break my trance.

"Scouting out the competition, Gallagher?" Duke steps into the hallway. Behind him are Kayla and the other girl that Jessica was sitting with.

Gillan gives a reconciliatory shrug. "Just introducing myself to Ararat's newest member."

"Yeah, well, back off. She's on our team."

Does he mean swim team? What! I'm on a team with Duke and Jessica's minions? How . . . ? Why . . . ?

Gillan shoots me a quick look. Did he not know either?

"Guess your team needs the help more than mine," he says to Duke.

"Guess we'll find out now. If you actually stick around for class," Duke says.

Gillan gives him a short nod and turns to an exit marked Swim Halls, but before he leaves he holds my gaze for a second. His eyes are as they were when we first met, drawing me in and locking me out at the same time.

"Come on, we've got twenty minutes for a game of Frisbee," Duke says. He and the two girls walk off, leaving me alone in the empty school hallway. Some "team" they are. I walk through a glass door on my left labeled Study Area and cuddle up in an egg chair. I haven't been there long when my e-pad gives an emotionless chime and flashes a notification: *Lunch time ending. Next class: Swim class.* Five minutes until my first swim class. The one I've been trying not to think about. The one that might be my last on Ararat. Or as a free citizen. I stare at the e-pad and chew on a fingernail. I guess it won't matter whose team I'm on. I'm already shark fodder.

The bell rings. I take a deep breath. I walk across a pristine lawn to a gigantic complex of outdoor and indoor pools. Now I feel truly abandoned—here on Ararat, the verdant, hostile home of the Elites.

The chatter of the high school girls in the locker room rings like a wordless buzz in my head. There's a lump in my throat and an odd drumming in my ears. I take my red swimsuit out of my sports bag and pull it on. It's completely new, no stretchy, see-through patches, no worn elastic, but I'm too nervous to admire it. My heart drops to my feet as I follow the others into a bright hall with vast floor-to-ceiling windows. The filtered pool water is sparkling, crystal-clear. Along the inner wall run perfectly parallel spectator stands. Squishy plastic mats cover the floor to prevent anyone from slipping. The starting blocks are all a different color. A scoreboard and plaques with the images of the four team logos hang on the wall opposite. The team logos are repeated in the four lanes, on the turquoise tiles at the bottom of the pool. A shark in lane one, then a barracuda, then a seal and finally a ray. Up here the swim teams actually have cool names, not names of stuff you eat for dinner. Above the scoreboard is the crest of Eden Academy: a compass and a star, above the waves of the ocean.

"Listen up, team." The voice of Eden Academy's head swim coach echoes through the hall. Somehow I expected a classier, equally grumpy version of Coach Dench, but the sporty young woman who just walked in couldn't be more different. She's got blue eyes and blonde, chin-length, straight hair, and is dressed in a blue, shorty wetsuit, emblazoned with the school crest.

"We're five weeks from the first stage of the swim tournament. Captains, take your teams and join Coach Milkins and the noncompetition squad in hall two for warm-up, then lead training in hall three. I've got our new champion to attend to."

"Yes, Coach Janson!" the students call and plod out of the hall. I notice that she's not much taller than I am. She steps toward me shaking her head. "Look at that, our new champ. Still thinks she got dropped off here by accident. Well, don't look so shocked. The government doesn't make mistakes—or have you been skipping your FRS community classes?" I stand there, my mouth agape. She continues. "Yes, I know what goes on down there, but it's a totally different ball game here."

Her eyes flicker to the crest of Eden Academy. *Omnia vincam,* the motto says.

"I will conquer all," Janson explains. "It's Latin. The forgotten language. Makes you wonder what place it has in a society where talk of history is forbidden. But let's not worry about that. For now all you need to know is how the knockout tournament works—and how to stay in it. Has anyone told you the basics so we can get you straight in the water?"

I shake my head, waiting for the expected reprimand, but Janson looks like she expected that answer.

"Typical, they want you to check all their boxes, but they won't tell you how. So let's get you up to speed." She walks up to a row of screens on the wall below the spectator stands that display information about the races. "We have three stages to our swim tournament, one at the end of each academic term," she explains. "The Initials, the Midterms and the Finals. The singles categories are the ones you know: breaststroke, freed-iving, butterfly, and freestyle. Boys and girls compete in separate categories. The race distance decreases with each tournament stage. That's four hundred meters for the Initials, two hundred meters for the Midterms and one hundred meters for the Finals. Excluding freediving, which is always a one hundred meter race. The tournament is knockout. That means one competitor gets cut in every stage. So in the first stage we have four swimmers per race, in the second stage three and in the final stage only two. All clear?"

Yeah, crystal. I won't make it past stage one.

Janson goes on. "We also have a mixed relay. It's a team race, two girls, two boys, every participant swims fifty meters of a different style. The team that comes last is cut from the relay, same as for the other categories. Nice and easy, right?"

I nod.

Janson turns around to the starting blocks of the Sharks, Barracudas, Seals, and Rays, which are arranged in the order green, red, black, and yellow. "You'll be swimming in the same lane, lane two, for all competitions."

So I guess I'm a Barracuda. Duke's on the red team. Figures. He's pretty hot-headed.

But why do I have to be with them? I look at the team photos on the wall. Everyone who crashed the volleyball game at the beach is a Barracuda. Jessica, Kayla Sommers, Mia Coote —Jessica's other minion—and the two black-haired guys from the volleyball beach, Marlo Carter and spiky-haired Ezekiel Wright. Duke is team captain of course. I look at the photos of the other teams. I would literally rather be with anyone else. The team captain of the Sharks is a black-haired girl, called So-raya Diaz. The Rays have Shane Borgman, the red-haired boy with freckles, who Jessica insulted in the entrance hall. And the Seals—

"Ah, you spotted your competition," Janson says. "Gillan Gallagher. He used to be my best student. Swept up all the medals. Now he's in Aqua8 so much, I hardly see him."

I suppress a nervous flutter of my heart. "Don't all top swimmers join Aqua8?" I ask.

"Get drafted, more like," Janson corrects. "But Gillan got called up earlier than the rest after he lost his family. He's an officer already. Youngest of his rank."

My heart stings when I realize that Gillan is an orphan. What kind of ruthless system takes advantage of such a cruel circumstance to conscript early?

"Training will be in hall three every afternoon at one thirty," Janson continues. "You can do extra training during your free periods, any time you want in any of the indoor or outdoor pools and—did you get your bottle of GermAloid?"

I nod.

"Make sure you apply it every day," Janson says. "It's an antibacterial gel that keeps your feet clean. Any questions?"

I wiggle my toes. "Do I have to be a Barracuda?"

Janson raises an eyebrow. "Now there's a question I hadn't expected so soon. Already picked your sides?"

I shrug.

"School rules dictate 'no family rivalry'," she explains. "You're in the Queen household, so Principal Preen decided that you'll be in the Barracudas, same as Jessica. Now, let's get you in the water, before they have both our asses."

Did she just say *asses*?

I climb onto the red starting block and pull my new goggles over my eyes. They steam up instantly, blurring my vision.

"Ready?" Janson calls. "Dive!"

I jump and hit the water squarely. The added height of the block didn't do me any good. My chest stings. Disoriented, I reach for the floating lane divider.

"So let's put your technique to the test and see if you're the butterfly prodigy they promised me," Janson calls. "Who knows? The last genius they sent me as a freediver turned out to be a freestyler."

I'm too nervous to laugh. This is the moment of truth. I want to grab my necklace for support, but it's stashed away in my sports bag in the locker. After Jessica almost stole it on the volleyball beach, I didn't want to draw any more attention to it. I won't be allowed to wear it on the day of the competition anyway. Better get used to it.

"We'll start with breaststroke," Janson calls out to me. "Four lengths. We're in the competition hall, so there are touchpads at the end of each lane. Make sure you tap your hand to them after each lap for the timer."

I nod, swallow water and push myself into a forward stroke. It isn't working at all. Halfway through the pool I'm still paddling uselessly, like a drowning duckling. I try not to panic. I'm no swimmer. I never was.

"Stop! Stop!" Relief and resignation take over when Janson calls out to me. "Who taught you breaststroke, kiddo? You swim like a sinking canoe. Split the water with your arms — like a frog." She mimics. "There now, that's better."

The next stroke carries me forward half a body length. I swim on until the end of the lane.

"Nothing that a bit of training can't fix," Janson calls. "Let me see your freestyle."

I kick off the wall and hurl myself forward. Water splashes around me. Left arm, right arm, left arm . . . I'm churning up the water too wildly, but just as I want to pause, to check where I am, my hand hits the touchpad for the fourth time. Janson looks at the competition display board. "Not bad. Definitely not bad. You could qualify with that. Now freediving."

I wish she'd asked for butterfly. I don't want another failure.

She sees my hesitation, walks to the poolside, and sits down. "Calm your breathing. When you feel ready take two more breaths. Exhalations longer than the inhalations. Then fill your lungs with air and dive. Don't worry if you don't make it very far, most students can't do more than a quarter length. OK?"

I nod and take my time to steady my breathing. The water closes around me as I dive. I see the turquoise pool, the Barracuda logo below me. I push on in underwater breaststroke until the longing for air kicks in. Maybe I can make that quarter length. But the excitement raises my heart rate and suddenly that's it.

I surface and see Coach Janson staring at the display board. "Impressive," she calls out. She's standing well past the halfway point. It can't be . . . I did more than half a pool length?

"That was almost fourteen and a half meters, wouldn't you say?" she asks.

I nod, unsure. There are numbers written on the side of the pool, but she's standing on the closest one. If that's the number fifteen, I did more than fifteen meters—but something in her expression prevents me from saying anything.

"Now show me that butterfly," Janson says.

I'm no longer scared. The freediving boosted my confidence. Water rushes around me as I kick off. Suddenly the old thrill is back, the one I felt when I swam against Duke at the beach. The pool doesn't seem twenty-five meters long anymore. It's just a tiny pool. I dolphin kick, sweep both arms out of the water simultaneously and slap my hand against the touchpad for the final length.

Janson smiles at me. "Our school champ has some serious competition coming up, kiddo. We'll wait to see how tomorrow's training goes, but I think I'll enter you for the butterfly singles and the mixed relay qualifiers. The government want to see victories, so let's give them victories."

I nod as I get out of the pool. I feel an odd buzz of excitement. I'm gonna stay here on Ararat. I didn't fail. I didn't embarrass myself. I didn't put my friends or family in danger.

But as I shower off at the end of class I wonder how things will go from now on. I hate being a Barracuda, I hate being on a team with the bullies who have been tormenting me and my friends for months. And I might not understand why Gillan saved my life in the Valley, but I don't want to be on a team with his rivals. That way I'll never find out.

Deep in thought I walk out of the swim hall. The sun reflects off the various EV roofs as I walk across the parking lot. Green, blue . . . but in the space where Jessica's EV was is a gap. She must have taken off without me. I'm figuring out how to get back to the Queens without her when I feel a tap on my shoulder.

"Naya DeLora?"

I spin around and my euphoria disappears. Behind me stands a young guy in a blue camouflage battle dress uniform, a handgun in his waist belt and a rifle slung over his shoulder.

I see him and I know it's all over. Gillan must have told them. About the Valley, about everything. That explains his shock when he saw me. Maybe that's why he wasn't at swim class. He just wanted to tell them where to find me. And now they have.

CHAPTER 8

— A8C —

"Thought I was gonna arrest you, didn't you?" The straight face of the brown-haired guy in front of me pulls into a smile. "I'm here to take you to your first day of training."

I stare at him.

"For Aqua8."

Suddenly I'm breathing again. Of course, Governor Proctor mentioned I might be a part of that if I were good enough, but I didn't realize they'd test me on the first day.

"I'm Lieutenant Williams, follow me." He leads me to the first of two large EVs, with about fifty students already inside, a lot more boys than girls, all a bit younger than me. They peer at me as we get on. I grab the frontmost seat while Lieutenant Williams jumps in the driver's seat.

"You're gonna be part of the A8C, the squad for our new recruits. C stands for 'candidates'. Normally you'd have joined at the age of fourteen and would have already progressed to the next level. The first two months in the A8C are a trial period, to determine whether you're fit for a military career. If chosen, you stay in the A8C for a maximum of two years until your superiors decide which role you are best suited for, within Aqua8," he tells me as we drive along. "You've missed the two initiation years, so you'll have plenty to catch up on."

"Seems to be the motto of my day."

Williams laughs.

The Aqua8 military base, one bay north of Ararat Harbor, stretches down the hills to the coast, its perimeter fence encased in barbed wire. We pass through a guarded gate then pull up in front of a squat, concrete building which looks like barracks and officers' quarters. Across from it is a long, rectangular structure with a barrel-shaped roof. In the center of the compound is a square training ground of sand and dirt. A solitary uniformed figure stands there, waiting.

My stomach turns as I get out of the vehicle.

"The initial training's tough," Williams says, "but once you pass this, you're ready for anything." He indicates for me to follow the others to the training ground. The waiting drill instructor turns to me with a serious expression.

"Name and purpose of visit?" he bellows.

I stare at him confused. Don't they know that already?

"Naya DeLora," I reply. "I was told to, uhm, turn up for —"

The drill instructor doesn't let me finish. "Naya DeLora, sir. Reporting for Aqua8 duty, sir. Do you understand, recruit?"

"I do," I say then quickly add, "Sir."

The drill instructor remains expressionless. "Recruit DeLora, pick up your uniform in unit one and report back here for training. You have five minutes."

I turn and look at the building with the barrel-shaped roof. Is that it? I dare not ask.

"Yes, sir!" Quickly I run toward it.

"A hundred and eighty degree turn, recruit!" the drill instructor bellows.

I spin around and run to the squat, concrete building instead.

The blue-and-gray camouflage battle dress uniform, or BDU, they give me is new and stiff and a bit too big. It flaps around my arms and legs as I rush back to the training grounds. The drill instructor gives me a quick look. Without any explanations, he nods at the other recruits and shouts, "Fall in!" I start jogging after the recruits who arrived in the EV with me. They are chanting a song.

Come on, come on A8C,
Time to learn our abcs.
Runnin,' swimmin' day and night,
That's how re-cruits win the fight,
Through storm and surf we will prevail,
We're A8C we'll never fail.

I try to keep up with the pace, and to chant along, but the dust from the training grounds gets into my nose and throat making me cough. I hate this.

"Line up!" the drill instructor shouts and all the recruits run to the end of the square forming a straight line. I get there last, huffing and puffing. A lot of catching up? Williams must've been kidding. There's no way I'll EVER catch up with these guys. At another shout the recruits drop to the ground and start push-ups in perfect synchronization. I try to copy them, but once I've bent my arms I can't get back up. The moment I finally manage one they all leap up for squats then drop again for sit-ups. Whatever they do I'm always behind and out of rhythm. My breath is coming in short rasps and my muscles are screaming with pain. The second I drop to the ground the drill instructor is on my case like wildfire.

"You call that exercising? I've seen better crunches from a piece of seaweed."

For the rest of the training session, he stands over me, his beads of sweat dropping at my feet while shouting insults. Just when I'm certain that my head will explode, a honk rings from an approaching black-and-blue EV and we stop. I roll over onto my back, breathing heavily.

Was this it? Are we done? I hope they've decided that I'm not military material. Then I recognize General Calder in the EV. Quickly I get up, brushing dust off.

"Recruits, line up!" the drill instructor barks. "Follow General Calder to the beach for battle training. Move it, NOW."

The EV takes off and the recruits fall in line behind it. The chant resumes. "Come on, come on A8C . . ." Will they even notice if I don't manage to keep up? Everyone is facing straight ahead and I'm last in line.

The EV disappears down a slope. Just as I'm sure I'm gonna lose them, the ground gets sandy beneath my feet and I can hear the sound of waves. We stop in a small inlet with dark-brown cliffs rising to a low height on either side. Stones jut out of the sand and the water looks too shallow for anything bigger than a motor dinghy.

"Attention recruits!" Calder's voice is amplified into a nasty screech by a megaphone. I look up. Her EV has stopped on top of the right-hand cliffs. I didn't expect her to personally oversee recruit training. The boy next to me looks equally confused.

"Welcome to battle simulation arena two," Calder shouts. "In a moment, targets will start to appear behind the rocks surrounding you. Your objective is to hit all these targets. A combat team is hiding in the rocks around you. They will begin firing on you as soon as the targets appear. If you're hit, you're out. Every recruit for themselves. Gear up."

I fall in line behind the others, who snatch up gear from metal racks that have been set up along the path to the beach. Thick, protective, black helmets and vests are lying ready and I strap on one of each then pick up a rifle. I'm not sure what to do with it. I have no idea how to fire a gun. Gingerly, I lean it against my shoulder, like the others do and hope that I won't shoot anyone by accident.

"Exercise commencing in fifteen seconds," Calder shouts.

A few of the recruits glance at the surrounding rocks. You can't see anyone—or anything moving.

"Take your positions."

Around me the recruits break up and take cover. I spin left and right, but there aren't enough rocks to hide behind. I'm still in the middle of the beach when Calder shouts, "Fire!"

Something swishes past my ear. It's coming from the rocks opposite the sea. I break into a run. At that moment there's a mechanic whirr and a silhouette cutout of a soldier snaps up ahead. Instinctively, I raise my gun and fire. The cardboard soldier gets splattered in red paint.

At least now I know the bullets aren't real. Reassured, I whirl around at the next target—and miss. Or did I? The gun just clicked as I fired. Is it jammed? A shot whizzes past me. I dive behind a small rock by the water. A shower of pellets rains over me. They must've realized I'm a sitting duck. I fiddle with the gun until I find a latch. Don't guns have some sort of safety mechanism? I flip the latch, but it doesn't change anything.

To my left and right two other recruits have taken cover. The boy on my left mouths, "Blocked?"

"What do I do?" I call to him, but he's already leaped up and jumped toward a target.

A shot rings and a voice calls. "OUT!"

More pellets rain down around me. They've got more time to focus on me now, because the other recruits are getting kicked out of the game fast. I peer around the side of the rock. Someone's fallen gun is lying in the sand. I drop mine and quickly run toward it, snatching it up as I go. A target pops up and I fire—then I duck and fire again. Only me and four boys are left. We spin around, back-to-back. Clap! Another target shoots up and I turn to fire, but freeze midaction. This target is a civilian, not a soldier like the others. A pellet hits me in the arm.

"OUT."

Someone calls, "Exercise over. Mission failed."

"Recruit DeLora!" Calder's voice cuts through the silence. It doesn't sound like I'm about to get any compliments.

"You are supposed to be Aqua8's shining new talent. This was the most pathetic attempt that I have ever seen. You think you can spend your soldiering time hiding behind a rock? The A8C is not a sunbathing squad!"

"My . . . my gun blocked," I say.

"Then elbow someone in the face and take theirs."

"B—"

"This is an 'every recruit for themselves' exercise!" Calder shouts. "Did I not make myself clear?"

"Yes, sir!" The other recruits shout.

Calder isn't done yet. "One more thing, Recruit DeLora. You had a clear shot on your last target. I ordered hits on ALL targets. Your team failed this exercise because of you."

"But General Calder," the boy who was hiding behind the rock next to me jumps to my rescue. "Lieutenant Gallagher told us not to hit civilian targets."

"I give orders here. Not Gallagher!" Calder shouts. She holds my gaze. "My most promising officer let me down. Don't be the next." She turns and walks off. "Dismissed! And someone tell Gallagher to report to my office immediately."

Anger overwhelms me at the unfairness of all this. Nobody even showed me how to handle a gun. I managed four out of four hits and still I'm getting singled out. And somehow I managed to drag Gillan into all of this, too. The idea of having to report to Calder's office with her in this mood gives me the shivers. And it's my fault he got in trouble.

*

"Naya!" Jim Queen is standing by a large silver car as I walk out past the sentries. He's in his business suit and tie and there's a smile on his face.

"So, how was your first training session?" he asks when we are in the car and pulling out of the compound.

"It was . . . it was . . ." I huff. I'm so glad Jim picked me up and I want to pretend it was all OK, but I can't. "It was terrible!"

Jim laughs. "What went wrong?"

Everything, I want to say. I tell him about the training exercise on the beach and Calder. "She failed me," I blurt out. "She failed everyone—all because I didn't shoot a civilian—"

"A civilian-shaped cutout," Jim corrects, laughing. "Even General Calder wouldn't make you shoot at a real civilian." Seeing my worried expression he adds, "Military institutions are meant to intimidate. The three *i*s, I call it: intimidate, instruct, indoctrinate. But don't let it worry you. You won't lose your place on Ararat because of this."

"Are you sure?" I ask.

"Certain. Anyway, as your new foster father I might have a word or two to say about that."

I give him a grateful smile. "I think General Calder hates me."

Jim seems to read my mind. "General Calder can't send you away, even if she wanted to. Not with your swimming talent."

I take a deep breath. Good thing that my swim session shaped out OK. We pull up in front of the Queen residence. An electronic voice rings out as we enter. *"New resident detected: Citizen ID 7121."*

Jim smiles at me. "Welcome home. From now on you can go in and out as you please without special announcements."

Jessica stares at us, mouth dropping as we walk into the living room together. "Daddy? You're home . . . early?"

"Just taking a little afternoon break," Jim says.

"But . . . you . . . never . . ."

"Aren't you going to say hi to Naya?"

"Hi, Naya," says Jessica, uninterested. Then, in an excited chatter she continues. "Oceans alive, Daddy, it's sooo good you're here. I need to tell you something really important!" And she drags him into the kitchen. I hear her explaining something to Jim about this dress that she MUST have, otherwise she'll, like, DIE.

"Naya." Mrs. Queen wrinkles her nose when she finds me alone in the living room in my muddy uniform. "You look like you've been battered by a sea squall. Don't they have showers at Aqua8? Go and get changed."

I sigh and walk through the empty atrium. Once I'm in the large room that I have all to myself a wave of loneliness grips me. I miss my friends, my mom. I wonder what they are doing right now. At least I didn't get them into any trouble.

My muscles shaking, a low buzz in my ears, I watch the sun sparkling golden on the waves of the sea. And what about Gillan? The name still sounds new and strange as I think about it. Is he OK? Today's the second time I thought he'd turn me in and he didn't. But why didn't he say anything when we met in the hallway? There are so many things I don't understand in this new place. So many things that worry me. Yet how long can I stay worried when I'm cuddled up on a fluffy, white bed with soft pillows under my head? No sooner do I lie down than I can feel myself drifting to sleep.

*

"Dr. Planck?" Jessica's hand shoots up.

"Yes, Miss Queen?"

"What if you had a really, really stupid student slowing the class down?"

Oh, no. Not again. I sink down in my chair. I actually like Dr. Planck, our hydrostatics and physics teacher. He's funny, with a cool Afro and a permanently good-humored expression. And he's the only one who didn't single me out first thing as I walked into his class. Obviously Jessica is about to change that.

"Aren't you worried about our grades?"

Dr. Planck raises an eyebrow. "I don't follow, Miss Queen."

"We're, like, a few weeks before our career exams." Jessica puts on an innocent smile. "Is it really necessary to have a new element disturbing the 'stable equilibrium' of our learning environment?"

"Oh. I see." Dr. Planck turns to me. "Well, speaking from a hydrostatic perspective, the element I'm most familiar with is water. And you can trust water to always find its own level. Unless of course you're worried about your own grades, Miss Queen? Perhaps you would like to enter the hydrostatic pressure equation into our display screen?" He winks at me. I return a smile.

I find his class fascinating—learning how water behaves at rest, the pressure it exerts on an object, and how its surface is always perpendicular to the direction of gravity . . .

When the bell rings for lunch a few hours later, I pick up my e-pad and head downstairs, following the route marked on the screen to an area named Study Garden. Maybe I can have a quiet lunch there.

"Going somewhere, newbie?" A girl in a varsity jacket with the words Underwater Hockey and two preppy guys in navy-blue blazers block the doorway.

"Just . . . outside." I try to squeeze past them.

"Nah-ah, Valley hobo." The girl crosses her arms. "It's Elites only beyond this point—unless you're a servant bot."

The guys at her side guffaw.

I want to lash out with a witty comeback, like Neal and Ethan, but I can't get out a word.

"You . . . you . . ."

They break into snorts of laughter.

"Oh boo hoo, frickin' barn girl. Can't even speak properly. I'm gonna make this real simple." The taller guy casually drops an empty can of VitaLize on the floor. "If-you-pick-up-the-trash-you-can-go-outside."

I stare at him.

He grabs my shoulder. "You heard me! Pick up the trash."

"No!" I shrink back. I wish Gillan were here to help me.

At that moment the tall guy is lifted off his feet and thrown against the wall.

"Barn girl?" a voice asks.

I spin, and with a start recognize Duke. Kayla and Mia are

standing behind him, making calming gestures—to no effect.

"Hmm, interesting, Peterson," Duke growls. "Last time Dad went over to your folks' place he said it reminded him of a pigsty. Like where they used to keep farm animals back in the past. You should be the last person to talk about barns."

"Elites only out there, right Duke?" the boy stutters, from beneath his collar, which is pushed up to his chin. "Just wanted to make sure we keep up standards around here."

"You wanna keep up standards? Take a hike yourself." Duke releases Peterson. "For seas' sake, you're pathetic. Already feeling threatened and races haven't even started yet," he scoffs.

Peterson scrambles to his feet, but when he's at a safe distance, he draws himself up and shouts at Duke, "Maybe if you cared more about standards, Kallion, you'd be a full Aqua8 member. Like Gallagher."

"You're an idiot, Peterson," Kayla shouts. "Duke, don't—"

But Duke's already springing after Peterson, his face flushed with anger. In his frenzy, he drops his bag and his e-pad bounces to the floor. The fall must have activated some kind of teacher's audio feedback, because the voice of Dr. Meier, the chemistry teacher suddenly rings across the hallway.

"This is the worst PIECE OF DRECK homework that I've had the great MISFORTUNE of grading in my fifteen years at EDEN . . ."

Duke forgets Peterson and hurries to retrieve the e-pad.

". . . unless you sit your LAZY BUTT down and start reading some chemical formulas you and your TINY PEA-BRAIN won't pass a single theoretical paper . . ."

Duke frantically stabs his finger at the screen, but he's hitting it so wildly that the tablet doesn't respond. Peterson and his cronies peek back around the corner of the hallway, cracking up.

". . . don't even THINK of attempting any PRACTICAL ASSIGNMENTS, or our lab is gonna look like it got hit by a TORPEDO . . ."

A small crowd has gathered and is laughing at Duke, who finally gets the tablet to stop. He barges down the hall, knocking into people.

"What was all that about?" I ask Kayla and Mia as we walk back to the lunch hall and wait in line for the Nutrigators.

Kayla sighs. "Duke's been in competition with GG since first grade. They're both team captains, both top-notch swimmers, both sons of big businessmen with seats on the council."

"The council?" I repeat.

"The Governing Council that helps the Governor rule," Kayla explains. "It's comprised of representatives from all the big research, technology, and energy companies, as well as the head of Aqua8. Douglas Kallion represents Mortlake, whereas GG's gonna inherit his father's seat for Galileo Tecc when he turns eighteen in August. But Duke doesn't care about politics. GG's won the championship for the Seals every single year since middle school and that's what sets Duke off."

"And what's worse, GG got into Aqua8," Mia adds.

"But Duke's Aqua8, too, isn't he?" I ask.

"Yes, but GG's an officer. Duke's only a Junior Cadet," Kayla says. "Duke's father wanted him to make the officer ranks ahead of time, too, but he didn't pass the written test."

We find a table and sit down. With a twinge of excitement I realize that this is my first casual conversation with anyone at Eden.

"Is that bad?" I ask, scooping up a spoonful of combograin.

"Not really," Kayla says. "It's fairly standard to become a Junior Cadet at sixteen. Students don't normally join the officer ranks until they graduate, because they'd miss too many classes otherwise. But GG had to become a full Aqua8 member, to avoid foster care, and now Duke's dad thinks that Duke should already be an officer, like GG."

"Duke's father's been on his case since, like, forever. Duke's mom died when he was just four," Mia adds.

Kayla shrugs. "Duke shouldn't be so pissed, he can retake the exams. GG's just . . . exceptional."

"Nobody's exceptional," says a voice behind us. Duke slams his tray on the table and sits down.

"And this year, with Naya on the team, we're gonna beat the Seals." His look is so threatening that I choke on my combograin. Too many expectations are resting on me.

*

"Look alive, teams!" Coach Janson calls as we walk into the swim hall after lunch. Training hall three is almost identical to the competition hall, but the pool is wider, with eight lanes and two sets of team starting blocks, and there are fewer rows of spectator stands. There are no timers and no displays.

While the competition teams sit down on the team benches, I stand to the side, tugging at the tight elastic straps of my new red-and-white swimsuit. Jessica and Duke are sitting together, laughing. On the next bench, Shane, in the yellow-and-white of the Rays is adjusting his goggles. Further along, Soraya, tall, long-legged and drop-dead-gorgeous, is joking with the boys in green-and-black on the Sharks' team. The Seals in black-and-white are sitting on the bench next to her. Their squad is made up of lots of tall guys, but leaderless, just like yesterday.

"Team captains, lead the warm-up, then practice your swim styles. Lanes two to eight. Torres take over for Gillan," Coach Janson calls. "Naya." She turns to me. "You're with me. Lane one. We're gonna work on your technique."

Technique? What does she mean? Yesterday she told me that three out of four of my swim styles were excellent.

Coach Janson looks at me as if she has the uncanny ability to read thoughts. "What, you think you don't need that? Then up on the starting block and show me a proper front dive. Or were you planning on falling into the pool like a log on the day of the competition?"

Twenty front dives later, I'm splashing through the water in a disastrous breaststroke.

"Again, synchronize your arms and legs, you can do better," Coach Janson calls. Why she has me practicing the only technique I can't do is beyond me. I'm pretty sure we've established that I'm no hidden breaststroke talent. I speed up as I near the end of the pool, reach for the rim and look up at Coach Janson, but her gaze is directed across the hall, to the entrance of the boys' locker rooms.

"Gallagher!"

My heart leaps. Gillan is walking into the swim hall in a casual stroll. In the black-and-white jammers of the Seals he looks taller and younger. I can't help staring at his evenly toned body.

"You think this is some kind of beach resort, Gallagher?" Coach Janson greets him. "I don't care if the Governor's given you special permission to stay dumb. As long as you're part of my swim squad, you show up for training."

"Good to see you, too, Coach." He gives her a cheeky grin.

"Lose that smirk," she fires at him. "Your team needs you. The Seals have new competition—in case you haven't noticed."

He glances at me briefly. "She doesn't look like much, Coach." He gives Janson a teasing smile as he gets onto the Barracuda starting block then dives into the pool in a perfect front dive. In smooth strokes he swims freestyle to the end of the lane and surfaces right beside me.

"Naya DeLora. I'm not sure red suits you."

I hold my breath as we are face to face. How can he act so casual? He's Aqua8's idol. I'm on the rival team and he's treading water almost a hair's width away, cracking jokes. Is he crazy?

Around us there's an excited murmur.

"Make them race," somebody shouts out. "Coach, make them race!" More students chime in.

I swallow. The new FRS miracle versus their all-time champion. Of course they want to see what happens.

"Come on, Coach Janson, we know you want to see it too!"

"Quiet!" Janson blows her whistle. "Nothing like the adrenaline kick of a race to bring out your personal best," she tells me. "You up for it, kiddo?"

I glance at Gillan. He's grinning. Does he want me to say yes?

"OK."

"All right, then," Janson says.

A cheer erupts from the students. Gillan dives into the Seals' lane.

"Two lengths butterfly, on my whistle."

I try to focus on the wavering water in front me, taking quick breaths. I'm racing against Gillan! No, if I think about that I stand no chance—

Janson's whistle blows and I kick off the pool wall. Gillan and I are shoulder to shoulder, right from the start. Water splashes as we swim like dolphins in a pod. Gillan gets slightly ahead of me and I speed up. By the time we reach the end of the pool, we're side by side again. We flippturn in almost perfect synchronization. Underwater, I glance at Gillan and catch him looking at me. He points his index and middle finger to himself, then to me, then back to himself. "I want to see you?" Is that what he's saying? But why not just tell me? Why is he signaling underwater? In my surprise, I almost forget to surface. Quickly I lift my head out of the water and grab a breath. Gillan's barely ahead of me, as if he were waiting for me to catch up. Is he letting me win now? The questions are nagging at me and I can hardly concentrate on the lap. A noise above the surface reaches my ears and I realize that the other students are cheering us on, shouting his name, and mine. Then my hand slaps against the pool rim. That's it. We finished.

I glance at up at Janson—then at Gillan. Did he win? Did I win?

"Naya, you win. One second faster than your time yesterday." Janson raises an eyebrow as she looks at us. "And Gillan, two seconds slower than your last race." She drops her stopwatch decisively. "That's it, Gallagher you're not missing any more of my swim classes."

Did he just let me win? The other students don't notice anything, they're just whooping.

Janson spins around to them. "What are you lot so happy about? You wanted one-on-one races. You got 'em. Pairs of two, lanes three to eight. Line up. Pronto!"

Shouts erupt. "What? No! Come on, Coach!"

Janson turns to me and Gillan, hiding a smile. "Gillan, lane two, all styles. And you, Naya—back to breaststroke."

*

"So, how was your swim training today?" Jessica asks in her honey-sweet voice at the dinner table.

I groan. I did so many front dives that I feel like I hit my head against a brick wall.

"Naya, quit making these terrible sounds. They're not ladylike," Mrs. Queen reprimands me. "You need etiquette lessons."

"Why don't we all have dinner at the Aeon Club this week-end?" Jim suggests. "I will make reservations."

"A marvelous idea!" Mrs. Queen says, and she and Jessica break into an excited chatter about what to wear and which table has the better sunset view.

As soon as we've finished our meal, I slink off to my room. My thoughts wander, but there's only one place where they really want to linger. Swim class. Gillan. What was his signal? Was it about the night in the Valley? About the swim teams? I keep picturing him walking into swim class, half an hour late, completely nonchalant. I can't explain why, but I feel connected to him. Does he feel the same? He seems so different from me; so self-secure, so independent . . . but now I know that he has to be. He has to make all important decisions himself. I wonder how he lost his parents. Or what it is like, living in the world of the Elites, without them. At least I never knew my father— but what about Mom? I don't know if the Elites will ever let me talk to her again. I roll under the bedsheets and cuddle up. I miss her.

CHAPTER 9

— Storm Warning —

"NAYA DELORA! DO YOU UNDERSTAND?"

I blink as Calder's words distort over the storm. The wind is pulling at my ponytail. The weather has been like this for a week, gray clouds moving fast through the sky, and right now Calder's head looms above me, like a bad weather beacon.

"IF YOU CAN'T Krrrrcheeeep RED AND GREEEEEN APART YOU'RE GOING TO CRrrrreeeeeASsssh EVERY BOAT YOU EVER DRIVE!"

I swear her voice sounds just like static noise. Don't the others notice?

"YOU'VE BEEN HERE TWO WEEKS AND YOUR PERFORMANCE STILL ISN'T WORTH SHIT!"

OK, this bit I heard. Loud and clear. I stare dead ahead and try not to move a muscle as military protocol demands.

"MY MOST PROMISING OFFICER FAILED ME. DON'T BE THE NEXT. SQUAD DISMISSED!"

I hit the showers, letting the hot water splash over me. Harpoon practice, pistols, combiguns and endless sessions dismantling and reassembling standard issue rifles and spearguns. I hate all these exercises designed for killing. They told me I'd be training to become a rescuer, not an assassin. And in today's exercise my combigun somehow switched from shoot to stun, all by itself. I must be subconsciously rebelling.

As I hurry across the Aqua8 yard, the wind billows up my sweater. Gillan has missed school the whole past week, out on Aqua8 shore patrol duty. With this weather they send boats out every day to make sure the flood barriers hold. I'm not sure why. Ararat's flood defenses are high tech submersible colossi that, when raised to their full height, cast a small shadow over the western hillside. It's a needless risk to send anyone out there.

And now Gillan and I are even farther apart, just when I was hoping to get to know him. His underwater signal has been nagging at me but I can't figure out what it was about. I haven't had much time to think about it either. Everyone's all worried about the upcoming exams that will determine their career options and subject areas for their senior year. I don't really have that choice. I'll either excel in Aqua8 and the swim tournaments to become some mini-Calder or I'm taking a trip from Ararat to labor camp, never mind my As in math and hydrostatics.

"Hi recruit, how'd the beach battle go?" Jim waves from his usual parking spot. "Killed any more cardboard civilians today?"

"Not today." I smile.

"Adelia's been wanting me to hire a gardener," Jim tells me on the way home. "Do you think one of those cardboard guys would do?" I burst into laughter and Jim joins in. We're still chuckling as we enter the house.

"Yeeeaay, you're back!" Jessica puts down her nail varnish and jumps up from the couch to pull off her new "Daddy you're home" act. "Finally! I've been totally waiting for like, ages." She throws her arms around him, holding her hands out so that she doesn't ruin her nail polish.

"Hi, hun." Jim frowns. "I'm hearing some rumors from Eden that Naya hasn't been made to feel fully welcome. Don't you think it's up to you to change that?"

Jessica scowls. "How?"

"Well, Naya's been here two weeks and she's still wearing your old clothes. I think a shopping trip is in order."

Jessica's eyes brighten. "Really, Daddy? I've seen this killer dress—"

Jim holds up a finger. "Sky's the limit, *as long as* you make Naya look like a star."

Jessica rolls her eyes and mutters, "Tall order . . ."

Jim clears his throat.

"OK, we'll go tomorrow after school," Jessica says quickly.

As far as I'm concerned, we could have waited a little while. Tuesday morning is even stormier than Monday afternoon. Walking across the school parking lot I feel like I'm going to be blown away. December's usually the worst but this year somehow the windy season seems to have started early. It's the end of November and this week's storms are crazy. From the lighthouse above the harbor, a blue beam circles over Ararat Heights, sweeping the landscape in its eerie glow.

"It's a pre-Blue Out," Kayla explains, catching my confused look, as we huddle together in the entrance hall. "A weather warning that a Blue Out might be approaching."

This beacon is the blue light that we used to see from the Valley and always wondered what it was. Why do they get *pre*-warnings up here, when the FRS on the low plain, with nothing but a shabby, generations-old flood barrier to protect them, get barely a warning?

Above us, the ship hanging in the entrance hall creaks ominously. I shiver. I want to cower away in a corner, like Rosy's dog Shortbread during a lightning storm.

"Don't worry," Kayla says. "Nine out of ten times it's a false alarm. And it's not a proper warning until they ring the sirens."

But by break time the sirens have started howling. Kayla takes me to sit at the lunch table with Jessica, Mia, and Duke. Jessica scowls, but Kayla ignores it. I pick at my food. It's not like I could eat today, when my mom and my friends might get washed away while I'm sitting safely on the hilltop.

"Looks like we won't see GG before the Initials," Kayla remarks.

"No fun swimming without competition," Duke grumbles. His mood has been darkening with the weather.

"What can Aqua8 do during these storms, anyway?" I whisper to Kayla.

Jessica glares at me for daring to speak at her table.

"It's not just the storms," Kayla replies, and the glare's passed on to her for answering my question. "It's what gets washed up on the shore. Some people fear that the tidal surges bring in the genetic variants."

"Genetic variants?" It's the first time I've heard this term mentioned. "What are they?"

"Some kind of sea monster," Kayla replies. "But that's just a rumor. I don't think they actually exist."

"We don't know that!" Mia squeaks.

"All I know is that we like, moved on to a reeeally boring topic," Jessica scoffs.

The lights flicker.

Mia whips around, scared. "The gale stopped the wind turbines from working. That's a bad sign."

"Yes, but that's why we have the Red Earth alternative energy source now." Jessica seems to be the only one enjoying her meal.

"Can you really get energy out of earth?" I ask.

Jessica shoots me a killer look. "Yes, of course. Mortlake and Zephyrus are developing it together. Daddy left early this morning to check on its progress." She flips her empty lunch tray to Kayla and gets up. "OK, pretty girls, gossip session, let's go."

A clear message that I should leave. I grab my bag and slink off, my mind spinning with new questions. Are genetic variants the same as the mysterious Aquatic Other that Governor Proctor and General Calder mentioned at my welcome party? It seems likely.

The sky clouds over so much after lunch time that it's almost like dusk. For the first time I really don't want to get in the pool. Although I know that the wind and storm can't reach me in the indoor hall, I feel I'm at the mercy of the elements. I switch to butterfly one lap too early, but Janson doesn't notice. Her eyes keep wandering to the floor-to-ceiling windows and the gray weather front.

If I thought the bad weather might deter Jessica from shopping though, I was wrong.

"Mall trip, come on, hurry up, we only have four hours before dinnertime," she calls to me in the locker room.

The storm drags our little EV left and right, but Jessica bends low over the steering wheel and drives like a raging fury. As the road climbs higher we get a view of the harbor. Dark and ominous, the white-crested waves wash over Ararat's flood barrier, almost reaching the lowest houses.

The EV's route planner indicates that it's only a five-minute drive to the mall, but in this weather it takes us fifteen. While thunder roars above us, I wonder what "the mall" even is. Is it the name of a shop? Do the Elites shop at only one place? And, if yes, how big would that shop have to be to fit everything?

Turns out, it's jaw-droppingly big. About three times the size of Eden Academy with twice as much space for EV parking. I crane my neck as I look up at the facade. It has the same glossy white, sculpture-like structure as Eden Academy, except that high on top, like a giant banner, is a massive aquarium. There are all sorts of animals inside: turtles, rays, even sharks. I feel a bit strange, walking through the entrance, with that thing looming above me.

Jessica pulls me along to the second level. "There are over two hundred stores in here," she explains excitedly. "And you are in total luck, because I've got customer cards to all of them."

She drags me into a store called Jades.

Before I can say "glittery dress," I have seven hangers in my hand and Jessica is pushing me toward the changing rooms.

"Here, try these on."

The changing rooms are built like a shower cubicle, with glass walls that frost over as soon as I press the *close door* button. I've got two tops, four skirts, and one turquoise piece of clothing—which could be anything, I'm not even sure which way is up. I struggle to put it on then peek at myself in the mirror. It wraps strangely around me, showing flesh at the hips and belly and thighs. Wow that's revealing! I'm glad it's just Jessica outside.

"Eeeeh, you made it! Awesome!" A squeak from Jessica, and the chatter and laughter of Kayla and Mia shatter my illusion.

"Of course we did."

"Wouldn't miss a shopping trip for the world."

Of course, Jessica wouldn't go anywhere without her little clones.

"Naya, are you ready?" she calls. "My style squad has arrived. And they've been given strict orders to help transform you from the hopeless, homeless shelter girl to something that screams popular."

"Great." I try to sound upbeat as I open the door.

"Hiiii!!!" Both girls wave at me enthusiastically.

Jessica claps. "Perfect. That dress is coming with us. Bag it up! Now try on the tops."

I return to the changing rooms and put on the dark blue one. I touch its fluffy sleeve to my cheek. It's cuddly and comfy, with golden, glittery stars. I love it!

Jessica looks at me critically when I step outside. "That's a no, I think. Style squad?"

Kayla and Mia wrinkle their noses like they smelled something bad.

"Ditch it! OK, Naya, let's move on to the next store." Ignoring the remaining items in the changing room, Jessica drags us to a machine by the exit. There's no person in sight, but Jessica presses her thumb to a screen. It pings and a green light appears.

"What's that?" I ask.

"Aw, so cute," Mia says, giggling.

"It's a biometric thumb reader," Jessica explains. "It's linked to Daddy's bank account for today—and Oceans, he *has* put a generous limit on it."

Not long after I'm walking through the mall with ten shopping bags in each hand. I have no idea what the items inside cost, but my bet is: more than Mom and I ever owned.

"Let's drop these off for delivery and get some ice cream!" Jessica announces. "We've earned a treat."

*

The ice cream shop is on the roof terrace, covered by a glass dome that blocks the wind. The view is of the entire northwest side of Ararat, down to the harbor, across the green hilltops and all the way to the lighthouse, which sits at the peak on the cliffs above the harbor. On top of the mountains to the north, I see the cables of a huge cable car running up the hill. I trace them with my eyes to see where they lead, but the cable car station is hidden by the mountain slopes.

"What are you staring at?" Mia follows my gaze.

"Have any of you ever been up that cable car?" I ask.

Jessica and Mia crack up.

"We're not allowed," Kayla says. "It's government property."

"Where does it go?" I ask.

Jessica shrugs, bored. "Don't know. Just ends in the bushes below Mortlake somewhere, right?"

Mia nods and giggles.

It beats me what's so funny about not knowing where the cable goes that runs straight over our heads. But that's Jessica all over: if it doesn't have a price tag and label on it, she doesn't care about it.

Jessica shakes back her hair theatrically and collects a tray laden with four bowls of ice cream off the head of an approaching server bot. "A well-deserved break, style sisters. Keeping up with fashion trends can be so exhausting."

Kayla and Mia nod sympathetically and chorus, "So-oh true." They dig into their ice cream while a reef shark makes its rounds in the aquarium behind them.

I scoop up a mouthful too—and swallow it whole. Whoa, this is so good! And sooo cold . . . I scrape my spoon along the bottom of the bowl. "It's incredible!" I exclaim.

"Really, Naya, I would never have guessed."

I look up to see them all giggling. They've only taken a few spoonfuls in the time it has taken me to eat the whole thing.

"It's hotter down in the Valley," I stutter, "you . . . you've got to eat it quick before it melts."

Jessica, Mia, and Kayla dissolve in laughter.

"Before-it-me-lts," Jessica wheezes. "Naya, you slay me!"

*

On our way home from the mall, lightning illuminates the sky. The thunderous storm rages on overnight. I pull my pillow over my head to shut out the flashing lights that are followed instantaneously by loud, ominous growls. By break time the next day, my nerves are jangling and I just can't take the stress anymore. I keep picturing the water storming into the FRS, swallowing it up in the same way that it swallowed up the Valley. I seek refuge in the lunch hall, but as I enter, the announcement screens spring to life with a video of a dinghy tossed about by whitecapped, gray waves.

The caption AQUA8 WANTS YOU!!! flashes up while the screen changes to an image of a sea-sprayed Gillan in his blue-and-gray BDUs. Apparently Ararat's elite military unit are using the storm for a bit of advertising. Gillan grins and points his harpoon gun at me. JOIN US AND CONQUER. I stare at him with an odd mix of longing and dejectedness. Is the only way I'll see him now on a video screen?

A close up of Calder takes his place. BRAVE THE STORM, TAME THE WINDS. It's like she's screaming at me with her screechy voice. Like I don't get enough of that in training every second day after school.

Leaving my lunch tray on the table I hurry to the sixth floor study area. Outside, black storm clouds shroud the view. With every burst of lightning, the lights in the hallway flicker. I cower on the plushy, blue couches. Maybe I shouldn't have picked the sixth floor as my hideout—but then again all of Eden is made of glass.

"Hey there." I look up, surprised, as Duke enters. He's the last person I'd expect to see here. He walks over to the window and stands there, staring outside. "Wish I was out there."

"I'm fairly happy in here."

Duke turns and notices the e-pad trembling in my hands.

"Sorry, I . . ." he trails off. "Blinds," he says.

At once the panoramic window pane turns black, shutting out the view to the sea. The lights flicker, dipping the room in and out of darkness. Duke walks to the door and fiddles with the electronic touchpad.

"*Teacher overrid— Access denie— Access den—*" says a mechanical voice.

Duke punches buttons in quick sequence.

"*Access granted. Energy rerouting.*"

The room grows bright and the lights stop flickering. Duke grins at me and steps back. "Not too bad for a dumb guy, right? Though it might be a little dark in Preen's office now."

I laugh, then weighing up whether he'll mistake it as flirting if I say something, I add, "You're not dumb, Duke."

He hands me his e-pad showing me his hydrostatics homework full of red highlights and the letter F in a big circle. "Recent assessments say otherwise."

I glance at the equations. "Your calculations aren't wrong.

You're just using the wrong formula. Here, see. You need to use p equals mv."

"You serious?" He leans over.

"Yeah, let me show you." I open the examples page.

"You know my dad would kill me if he knew I'm letting you help me with my homework."

"Well maybe you can help me with economics in return, 'cause I don't get a word," I say, then I bite my tongue. Did I just offer to do study sessions with Duke? I've got half a mind to hurry out of the room, but Duke has already started the first equation. I keep my focus strictly on the e-pad. He concentrates on the calculations, too, but after half an hour's work I see him smiling at me.

"You know, I think I'm finally getting this." He reaches for my hand. I quickly pull it away. "Let's just stick to hydrostatics, OK? So you take the numerator—"

"So that's what you're up to," Jessica's voice rings out.

Duke almost drops his e-pad. "Jess, I—"

"Oh, look at the two of you." Her eyes flicker between me and him. "Real cozy."

"We're studying," Duke says.

"Studying! Oceans alive, Duke. How dumb do you think I am? It's more likely to be raining jellyfish than for you to pick up your e-pad to study."

"It's true, Jessica, I'm just helping Duke with—"

"You, zip it! You don't talk to my friends. You don't sit at my table and start boring variant conversations, and you don't study with Duke! You're . . . you're . . . FRS! You're supposed to be stupid!" She stomps off.

Duke grimaces awkwardly at me.

I pick up my e-pad. "Let's just get to swim class."

*

The students' voices echo in the swim hall as I enter. Jessica's sitting at the far end of the Barracudas' bench scowling at Duke. Duke is scowling too, but not at Jessica. His gaze is directed across the hall to the starting blocks, where Gillan, in his Aqua8 uniform instead of his black-and-white jammers, is talking to Janson and a younger girl from the Seals.

I slow down and catch a few words of what they're saying.

"It's just a precaution, Alba." Janson hands her a small medical packet. "Take it easy over the next days . . . and don't let it stress you. When you get nervous, try to focus on your swimming rhythm to calm your breathing. Any time you need a break just let me know."

"Thanks, Coach."

Gillan's e-pad chimes. He gives a worried nod to Janson, pats Alba on the back and walks out the door.

I watch him leave as I sit down on the Barracuda's bench. Next to me Duke scoffs and grumbles, "Why's he even here if he's not gonna swim, the self-important blowfish?"

Zeke sniggers. "Maybe he's getting soft you know, can't deal without the moral support of his team."

"Captains, Torres, let's go," Janson calls across the swim hall. "The competition qualifiers are next Thursday. No more goofing around."

The swim session turns into something of a catastrophe. Jessica resurfaces twice during freediving then loses her one-on-one race to the Sharks' freediver, and Duke and Zeke almost collide during our team relay practice. Jessica doesn't speak a word to me on the way home. The next day I avoid her and Duke and sit down alone at an empty table in the lunch hall — but of course Mia and Kayla spot me and sit down beside me. A moment later Jessica and Duke slump down into the two free seats, midconversation.

"It's not just flick-a-switch and the whole Red Earth project works, Jess," Duke grumbles.

"Yeah, OK, whatever." Jessica glares at him.

"See, that's your problem!" Duke fires at her. "You don't take anything seriously. And what was up with that swim session yesterday?"

"It wasn't that bad," Jessica protests, "I came pretty close to beating Chastity."

"Pretty close!" Duke explodes. "Do you know what *close to winning* means?" He stares at us. "It means LOSING." He crushes his VitaLize can in his fist.

Kayla edges away from him. "Just chill, Duke."

Duke's face turns red in fury. "NO!" He pounds the table with his fist. "That-was-the-worst-team-swim-session-EVER."

Behind Jessica, the Aqua8 recruitment advert with Gillan in his blue-and-gray BDUs flashes up. JOIN AQ—

Duke's face curls up and with a snarl he hurls the remains of his drinking can at the announcement screen. "Oceans curse you, Gallagher! Why would you even smile like that if you're doing a hundred push-ups a day?"

The thin glass screen cracks, a wide gash running down the middle.

Immediately an alarm starts blaring. *"Disturbance detected in area o-eleven,"* a voice announces over the speakers. *"Room in lock-down."* All the doors slide shut and the daylight is locked out as metal shields descend in front of the windows.

"Oh, great!" Jessica huffs and drops her fork into her com-bograin. "Now, we're stuck here."

Duke glares left and right, confused, as if he can't quite comprehend that he caused this. The doors open and white-uni-formed guards storm in armed with guns and stun batons.

"It's OK, it's OK. I'm calm!" Duke holds up his hands in a pacifying motion. The guards stare him down for a moment.

"Area secure," one of them radios. The doors open and Dr. Meier steps into the room. "Students, go back to lunch. Kallion, report to my office for detention. DeLora, Queen, Coote, Sommers fill out eyewitness forms in the admin office after your final class."

Mia, Kayla, and Jessica groan.

"Thanks a million, Duke," Mia grumbles.

The form that admin uploads to our e-pads after school is four pages long: a three page checklist, followed by a blank page with the heading: Please outline the event in detail. Today's date: November 29, 242.

I start filling it out when a boy in BDUs runs into the office. "Are you Naya? Lieutenant Williams said to tell you that we've got A8C theory classes on Thursdays, stating today. The bus is leaving in ten minutes."

I type up a hurried paragraph and race for the Aqua8 EV, making it just in time.

The first lieutenant who is waiting for us at the gate in a formal black-and-white Aqua8 uniform with one thick and one thin golden stripe on its sleeve takes us straight to a conference room in the squat, concrete building.

"Recruits, today you will be learning navigation theory."

The boys roll their eyes as he switches on a screen and begins to explain how to set a course and calculate distance and location at sea. I breathe a sigh of relief. It's a welcome change to crawling through the sand and mud—even though the wind and rain have abated a little today.

As we leave the classroom, I hear two boys whispering.

"They'll be picking out recruits starting at the end of this term. The ones that excel academically will join the Junior Cadets for leadership training. The others will stay in the A8C for another year or continue as Sea Warriors and become Officer Combatants."

"I heard it's insanely difficult to get into the Junior Cadets," another boy chimes in. "They only picked three last year. Besides, everyone knows Calder favors girls over boys."

I raise an eyebrow. If that's true, she's sure got a funny way of showing it.

"Yeah—everyone says Calder's been looking for a new girl to train as her second-in-command since the last one got kicked out." The boys continue their chatter.

"I didn't know you can get kicked out of Aqua8 after you passed initiation training."

"Sure you can. Calder's flying into a rage about it all the time. You know: 'My most promising officer let me down . . .'"

That was a girl? I always figured Calder meant Gillan.

"I heard she told Calder to go and . . . you know . . . herself."

"I heard she deliberately sank Calder's flagship. With Calder on it."

I snigger. About half the rumors going around the A8C aren't true, but picturing Calder, pouting on the prow of her ship, while it sinks beneath her, is pretty funny.

"Man, can you imagine what Calder would do to you?" the boys chatter on, then turn to me. "Hey, Naya's got a pretty good chance. She aced navigation today."

"Yeah, and it's not like there's a huge crop of fresh recruits on Ararat—"

I laugh and shake my head. They'd never pick someone from the FRS for leadership training. Besides, Calder hates me.

*

As Jim and I arrive home, Mrs. Queen emerges from the door followed by a brand new green garden bot. "Oh lovely, there you are. Just in time for dinner." She beams at the sight of my clean uniform. "And Naya, you're not dirty, how refreshing. Why don't you join us right away?"

I take a seat at the table, beside Jim.

"So four sessions of A8C a week now, I marvel at how you're keeping up with your school work." Jim winks at me. "Well done on yesterday's homework, by the way. Dr. Planck told me you've developed a skill for hydrostatics."

Jessica shoots me a hostile expression. She's not hiding the fact that she thinks I'm stealing her father away from her. And Duke as well.

I stare at my plate. "Thank you."

As soon as dinner is done I escape to my room. I lower the blinds to shut out the storm outside, dig out my e-pad, and start my homework.

The Governing Council assists the Governor in his decision making. It is comprised of eight members: three seats for the leading energy companies: Zephyrus, Solaris, and Mortlake Industries; two seats for the commercial enterprises, Galileo Tecc and Goldstein Ventures, one seat for the head of the military defense force Aqua8, and two seats for the Cape Harmony Research Institute. The Governor may call a session whenever he deems it necessary and has the deciding vote and the power of veto. Sitting members include: Brice Donovan, Samantha Driscoll, Douglas Kallion, Rhidian Cho, Magnus Goldstein, General Helena Calder, Arlo Quinn and Lucia Roth.

So this is the council Kayla mentioned. I scroll through the politics notes. Our teachers made it sound as if the council were some grand, constitutional force that makes Ararat more democratic, but from what I gather, the Governor technically has the power to overrule them all on important decisions.

"An F, Jessica!" Jim's voice from downstairs tears me away from my reading, "An F! And in physics, no less! Oceans' sake, girl, I'll be the laughing stock of Ararat!"

"But Daddy, it's not my fault. It's just the one paper. I had an off day. Besides, I'm fine with physics. I'm averaging a C, in fact."

"Oh, you're averaging a C. You say that like it's some sort of achievement. Well, let me run this by you to see how it flies. The daughter of Ararat's most eminent physicist is averaging a C in physics."

"Daddy, that's not fair. You know how hard I try. I'm always meeting Kayla and Mia for study sessions. And after school, Daddy. On top of all my other responsibilities."

"Browsing the latest fashion with your friends and varnishing your nails is not a study session! You should take a leaf out of Naya's book. The girl's been at Eden a few weeks and she's already scoring As in some of her assignments."

"Daddy, I'm trying my —"

"You're trying my patience, is what, Jessica. No more hanging out with Kayla and Mia on school nights, no more shopping trips to the mall. Until I see some major improvement in these grades, you're grounded."

I hear him grumble as he leaves the room. "For Oceans' sake, an F. In physics. My own daughter."

Jessica storms past my room. I duck my head. Why did he have to do this? Tomorrow Jessica will be unbearable. Two splotches drip onto my e-pad. It takes me a moment to realize I'm crying. I'm all alone here, away from Mom, my friends . . . and Jim's the only one who's made me feel at home, the only one who's made me feel safe. I don't want Jessica to ruin that. I curl up on my bed and listen to the rain splash against my window. Once again I wish I were far away from here.

*

When I go outside the next morning, Jessica's EV is gone. I can't believe it. She ditched me. Jim's already at work and Mrs. Queen left to organize some event at the Aeon Club. I glance down the empty road. How far is it to school? The thunderstorm rages in the distance, ominously lighting up the clouds above the mountains in the hazy, misty morning light. At least it's not raining.

I walk quickly along the concrete track. After some time the road forks. A sudden whirring fills the air. I look up and see a small, black drone hovering in front of me. *Citizen ID 7121 registered* flashes across its display screen. Then it soars off again. I walk on, taking the road to the right that winds around the foot of the barren northern mountain slope. The solitary Mortlake Industries building sits high on the peak above me. I'm hoping to run into someone who can give me a lift, but the road remains empty, lined with only bushes and trees. I'm going to be late. I quicken my pace, careful not to trip over any loose stones by the roadside. Lightning strikes again.

Suddenly, I see a pair of eyes staring at me from the bushes. I freeze on the spot, heart pounding. What was that? Who was that? Spurred on by fright I dart along the road as fast as I can. My school bag knocks against my hip, the wind blows my hair into my eyes and mouth, but I don't slow down. Get away! It's all I can think. Only when I'm so winded that I can't run anymore do I stop. There are houses on my left again. Resting my hands on my thighs, I glance back. No one is behind me. I hear no footsteps either. Gasping, I straighten up and continue walking. Why would anyone hide out in the bushes in the wilderness? The Elites never walk. They go everywhere in their little EVs. Unless someone from the FRS snuck up and hid here? But the patrols between Ararat and the low regions are so tight. And if it was an animal . . . no, no animal has a face that human. But who else is up here? I think of the variants that Kayla mentioned. Could this have been one of them? Could it have washed ashore in the storm and made its way up into the mountains? I glance back the way I came from curious, terrified, but the road behind me is still empty. Did I imagine this? Maybe I'm losing it.

I walk on, telling myself to relax when a clutter of stones and the almost silent hum of an EV on the mountain slope above makes me jump. A black-and-blue military vehicle with three men and one woman in mountain pattern, khaki-and-beige camouflage BDUs is speeding across the rocky outcrops. They look like they're on active service, rifles slung around their sides. I duck down. They haven't seen me yet. But why are they heading up the mountain? The flood barrier and the harbor are down below. Do Aqua8 have another base there? Or are Aqua8 hunting whatever it is I might have seen? The thought makes me shiver. I hurry on.

The rain comes down just as I reach the school. A proper downpour. By the time I place my thumb on the electronic reader beside the entrance, I'm soaked. My hair clings to my face like wet seaweed as I walk through the foyer. I hurry to my locker to get my swim towel and at least dry off my hair before class, but as I get there, I hear the sound of irate voices.

"So you're spending what should be our together-time with her instead? Is that like a date, or something?"

I'd know Jessica's voice anywhere.

"For the last time, if I don't ST-UDY, I'm gonna fail my exams!" Duke shouts. "You want me to get demoted to Officer Combatant and become a hill patrol guard?"

I freeze in the hallway. This is one fight I don't want to interrupt. But Duke's already seen me.

Jessica rants on, "I'd rather . . . Can you at least look at me when I'm speaking to you? You're so RUDE, someti—"

"SHUT UP!" Duke fires at her. He's looking at my wet clothes, my wet hair. "You made her WALK? In this weather? Don't you know how dangerous it is to be on an open road when there's lightning? Oceans' sake, you're so irresponsible."

Jessica pulls an angry pout. "Go on, defend your new crush. No surprise there."

"Naya is helping me!" Duke howls. The bell rings, but he doesn't even register it. "We've got one week to career exams and I've got to pass. If you want to spend your life repairing cleaning bots be my guest, but I've got to show my father that I'm Aqua8 officer *and* management material—"

"I don't care if you—" Jessica begins.

"Ahem." Dr. Meier clears his throat behind her. "Whenever you're done, perhaps we can start the class?" He points to the third floor. "Unless, of course, you've given up on the idea of a career, already?"

By lunch time I've convinced myself that helping Duke is the worst mistake I've ever made. I'm just looking for a way to tell him as he sits down in the study area when Jessica busts in, a typhoon of pink and blonde.

"Fine!" She slams down her bag on the table. "Fine! You want to study, we study." She pulls out her e-pad like it's some kind of weapon.

Duke stares at her with an I-can't-quite-believe-it smirk. "Jess, I —"

"Save it! Let's just get started, shall we? Naya, show us how this revision stuff is done."

I give her a nod. Of all the things I expected to happen, this was most definitely not it.

CHAPTER 10

— *Team Rivals* —

"So . . . everybody loves Elijah Goldstein. He used to date So-raya Diaz, but they broke up a month ago, and Daphne Vansart, who heard it from Ayumi Tanaka, said that he's now dating Alba Williams from the year below us, totally uncool."

The EV buzzes along to Jessica's rant. I'm wondering if it was nicer when she wasn't talking to me. It's like I've released some verbal waterfall.

"And yesterday Zeke asked out Soraya and now he's super pissed, because she said no, which is totally stupid, because, she, like, always says no since she broke up with Elijah . . ."

Jessica plonks her EV diagonally between a bright blue EV and a green one.

"Hey, forget your glasses or something?" an irate brunette with gigantic, round glasses shouts and gets out of the blue EV next to us.

"Problem, Sloane?" Jessica drawls as she steps into view.

"Uh, no, no problem." The girl backs off in a fluster. "Sorry, Jessica. Didn't see you there." She hurries toward the school entrance.

"Sloane van Buren," Jessica confides, "otherwise known as Sloane van Snoren, the most boring girl at Eden. Stick with me, Naya, and I'll make sure you only get to know the people worth knowing."

I force a smile. Only last Friday I was on the receiving end of Jessica's taunts. A part of me recoils at the way that she treats people, but another part is very aware that my life was misery without her on my side.

Jessica leads the way into the entrance hall. "And that girl over there is Chastity Kelly, Eden's resident skank."

She gives a glossy smile to the Shark's freediver, who stands there surrounded by a group of boys. "Hi, Chastity!"

A few students look up in surprise as we walk through the hallway together.

Jessica flips open her locker and pulls out a tube of lip gloss. "Teachers can open these, worse luck. Spot checks. So don't keep anything incriminating in there."

Before I can ask what she means by *incriminating*, she waves to Kayla. "Hey Kayla, joining us for study session today?"

By lunch time it's not just Kayla, but Mia as well.

"So if this purse is reduced by like 20 percent and then further reduced by 10 percent, does that mean it costs only twenty-five credits?" Jessica asks. She likes to use shopping examples for math.

"Yeah." I nod.

"Bargain," Mia whispers.

Jessica swipes away her math revision page and makes a note on her shopping list.

It's a strange new feeling being at the center of their group, but at least it takes Duke's attention off me.

The news that Jessica and I are hanging out together rushes through the school like a tsunami. By Wednesday, the snippets of conversation that I hear in the hallway are very different from the ones I heard in my first week.

"Maybe ask the FRS-girl."

"Shhh! Don't call her that. She's Jess's friend!"

"Hey Naya, like my new top?" a sophomore girl calls out.

"Sure," I answer uncertainly. What in the world is going on? It's like I've moved from outcast to trendsetter. It's not exactly what I wanted—although it's nice not being picked on anymore.

"Go Kallion!"

"Go Wright!" the team shouts as I enter the swim hall.

Duke and Zeke are using the Barracudas' starting block for an arm wrestling competition while the whole team is watching and cheering them on.

"Place your bet, Naya," Marlo greets me.

"No thanks," I mutter and sit down on the empty Barracudas' bench.

Two boys on the Rays' bench next to me are whispering.

"Do you think there'll be an Irons this year?"

"Nah, Naya'd have to be, like, a super freediver, and Janson's hardly got us training in all the strokes, so I don't think she is."

"Couldn't that just be because—"

"Teams, warm-up, get moving!" Janson calls as she enters. "We've got the qualifiers tomorrow. Naya, with me."

I get up and join her by the poolside while everyone else lines up with their teams.

"Let me see your progress. Breaststroke, freestyle then butterfly."

I dive in with a smooth front dive and the lesson begins.

*

When I exit the locker rooms an hour and a half later, Jessica, Duke, Marlo, and Zeke are hanging around, waiting for me. I'm about to tell them that I don't need a welcome committee everywhere I go when I realize that they're huddled together, whispering. They're up to something.

"All set." Jessica hands something to Duke with a gleeful grin. He nods, gloating. What have they got planned now?

"Hey, Williams." Duke beckons to Alba Williams, who exits the girls' locker rooms after me.

She rolls her eyes. "What do you want, Duke?"

"Question is, what do you want, Williams?" He holds up an inhaler.

"How did you get—" Alba opens her bag and rummages frantically.

Jessica bursts into a fit of giggles. "You should take better care of your stuff, Williams."

"Shut up, you big, pink, flamingo-float!" Alba turns and tries to snatch the inhaler from Duke's hand.

"OK, OK, relax." Duke pretends to give it to her, feints and tosses it to Marlo instead. "Think this is the end of the Seals. Next thing they'll be swimming with water wings."

"That's not funny," Alba shouts. "It's for emergencies, don't break it, it's government issued." She runs toward Marlo but he throws it to Zeke.

"Aw, no need to get all choked up," Duke says, grinning.

"Marlo, go long!" Zeke shouts and throws it to Marlo, who catches it and pitches it over to Jessica.

"Naya, catch!" Jessica screams and suddenly the gray, plastic tube is arcing toward me. I catch instinctively, then freeze as Alba stops opposite me and holds out her hand.

"Naya!" Jessica sees my hesitation and waves both arms.

"Naya, here!" Zeke shouts.

I shoot Alba an agonized look. I just want to hand it to her, but instead I halfheartedly toss it over to Marlo. Except it doesn't get there because out of nowhere someone else grabs it.

"Think sudden, unexplained medical symptoms are funny, Duke?" Gillan's face is calm, but his eyes are spitting fire.

"Come on, man, it was just a game," Duke sniggers.

"Life and death matters are not *games*," Gillan snaps. He looks like he wants to grab Duke and punch him. "I know you're a real jerk Kallion, but I never thought that the Barracudas would sink so low as to prey on the weaknesses of others."

He puts his arm around Alba and leads her away. Before he turns, he glances at me and for the first time I can read something in his blue eyes. Disappointment. I feel like I've let him down, no worse, like I've betrayed him. In the deepest way possible. And in that moment I turn and bolt back into the locker rooms. I pull my swimsuit back on and race to the outdoor pools. Somehow I want to be in the water. Away, just away.

I close my eyes and shut out Jessica's voice that still resounds in my head after I left her behind. She probably drove home without me. Or to the mall. I heard her mutter something about Blue Wednesday pre-vacation sales.

I sit on the pool's edge and dangle my feet in the water while the cool December breeze casts ripples across the surface. I'm exhausted from swim class but it doesn't cover the nervousness I feel. It's all too much. The training, Aqua8, Gillan, not knowing what's going on. And now he hates me and I'm one of the popular girls. The center of attention when all I wanna do is hide, just bury my head in the water. I take a deep breath and dive into the pool. The water closes softly above me, numbing my senses. It's so quiet. So peaceful. Almost healing. I swim underwater, in breaststroke. Without goggles the blur of turquoise shimmers around me in all directions. Then the shape of the tiles comes into focus, as if I can see better without the goggles than with them. I hardly want to surface but suddenly there's a wall in front of me. I break through the water and rub my eyes. Wow! Did I swim in a circle or did I really just dive to the other end of the pool? That felt like nothing.

"Naya!" This time the shout is real. "What got into you? Did you forget that you have A8C training?" Jessica is standing by the poolside. "I know we've got the qualifiers tomorrow, but it's not like *you* need to freak out about them."

I brush a hand over my face. "Uh . . . I . . ." Doesn't she feel the slightest bit guilty about what we did to Alba?

"Grab a towel and let's go." Jessica taps her foot. "Lieutenant Williams just, like, totally bossed me around to get you to the EV on time. And I don't think he's waiting for you to have another twenty-minute shower."

She stalks off. She isn't giving this a second thought. It does not even cross her mind. Head bowed, I dry off and follow her.

*

The next morning Gillan's in school. I know, even before I look around the chemistry room and see him sitting in the front row. The class feels different somehow, like there's this electric current in the air. I search for something to say to him but he's surrounded by his team members, and actually I've never seen a Barracuda have a conversation with a Seal—at least not one that wasn't laced with insults. It feels like the school might implode if I break this unspoken rule. Gillan's looking straight ahead, keen, observant as if he's only waiting for Dr. Meier to start the class, so that he can get out of here again. I pause for a minute as I'm about to pass his desk. I owe him an apology at least, but someone pushes me along.

"All right, Naya?" Kayla asks. I nod and take my seat next to Jessica.

"Hydrophilic versus hydrophobic substances," Dr. Meier begins. The classes today drag on forever until we finally reach lunch break. I want to go to the swim hall to prepare somehow, but Mia and Kayla drag me off to our new hangout in the study garden. Jessica likes it, because it's the place where she's least likely to be seen. I haven't bothered asking whether she means *seen with me* or *seen studying*.

"A hydrophilic molecule is one which is capable of forming a hydrogen or an ionic bond with the water molecule," Mia reads slowly from her e-pad, "as opposed to a hydrophobic molecule, which is a non-polar molecule with an observed tendency to aggregate in an aqueous solution—"

Jessica groans. "Why can't they say that in proper English?"

"Is hydrophilic a forgotten language word?" Mia asks.

I don't reply. Gillan is sitting at the table across from us. I watch him, as he taps his pencil onto his notebook. He's the first person at Eden I've seen who's not using an e-pad. When he gets to a difficult bit, he furrows his brows and twirls his pencil in smooth figures of eight around the blond locks of his hair. But he doesn't look up. It's like he's broken the connection between us and we have become the rivals that the Elites wanted us to be. My chest tightens. I did nothing to stop Duke from bullying Alba out of fear of being an outsider again and now I've lost Gillan. Without ever knowing whether his underwater signal was an attempt to talk to me, or to warn me. And now I feel as though he no longer cares. And that scares me.

"Naya?"

I look up.

"Do you get this?" Mia asks.

"Uh, it just means that some substances repel water, whereas others bond with it," I say. "*Phobos* is fear and *philos* is friend. The e-pad notes say that it comes from a language called Greek, that they once spoke on the Eurasian continent."

Kayla grumbles, "I'm sure Meier just made up difficult terms on purpose, the old sadist."

I'm expecting some comment from Duke, but he seems even more distracted than me. In fact he missed our past two study sessions. I thought that his reading efforts would redouble, with the exams looming ahead, but if anything, he's less focused, constantly on the alert, always on the edge of the seat. The others haven't noticed, they're so preoccupied with themselves.

"Let's try Naya's memory strategy for learning the phrases," Kayla suggests.

"Yeah, like . . . like hydrophobic repels water, so—" Mia begins.

"I know, I know!" Jessica shouts, "Peterson's socks! Ayumi Tanaka once caught a whiff of them and fainted on the spot. So Peterson steers clear of water—Peterson's hydrophobic!"

Mia lets out a burst of infectious laughter, but as we're giggling, tears in our eyes, I see Gillan looking over at me. His face is blank and the laughter dies right on my lips.

When the bell rings at last, I tag along quietly behind the others to the swim hall. Gillan's look was like a wake-up call. I'm goofing around with Jessica and Duke when my focus should be on the imminent swim qualifiers. If anything goes wrong, and I don't make it today, they'll send me and Mom straight to labor camp. I shudder as the old fear resurfaces. It's the seventh of December. If I get arrested today, I'll have lasted exactly one month on Ararat.

In the competition hall the atmosphere is quiet and tense. Some students are already warming up and all the other Eden coaches from the noncompetition squads and lower years are assembled at the end of the pool. I don't know why I believed Janson when she said the swim qualifiers wouldn't be daunting. They feel pretty intense to me. I watch Gillan talking to Torres on the Seals' bench. Unlike me he doesn't look nervous at all. I guess he's done this a billion times.

The whistle blows and Janson calls, "Team captains, lead a general warm-up. Contestants, your categories will be called up, one after the other, ending with the relay. This is not a competition so focus on yourselves, not on the person next to you. You'll get your chance at a race next week on Sunday."

The first category to be called is boy's freestyle. Janson's announcement went right past Duke; he races through the pool like a, well, I guess like a Barracuda, constantly tilting his head in the direction of Gillan in the lane next to him. They're shoulder to shoulder for most of the sixteen pool lengths, but somehow Gillan still touches the pressure pad first. Duke pounds the water. Even from this distance I could swear Janson is rolling her eyes.

Girl's butterfly is fifth.

"Go get 'em, Naya," Duke bellows.

I ignore him as I get on the Barracuda starting block. Does he have to be so rowdy? I wonder what it's like to have Gillan as a captain. Quiet, calm, supportive . . . But this is not the time for distractions. I zone in on my lane. The whistle goes. I dive.

I make my time with fifty seconds to spare, but it's no great achievement. At the end of the day there isn't a single person who didn't meet the minimum time required to qualify in the race. I hit the showers and let the hot water splash over me. If a few extra coaches get me this nervous, how am I ever gonna swim in front of the whole school? I slowly wash off the chlorine, until the steam clouds up the entire shower room. I dry off and put on my hoodie and take a deep breath before I step outside. My hands are all wrinkly from the water and the wind feels cool as it ruffles through my tangled, wet hair. The parking lot is busy with students getting ready to leave. I walk across the lawn and lean against one of the trees that line the teachers' parking zone while I wait for the Aqua8 bus to pull up. Around me the eager chatter of the students' voices blends into the quiet buzz of EV engines. Somewhere there's a familiar voice talking quietly. Then another, barely audible over the rustle of the wind through the leaves.

"Will you be in class tomorrow?" That's Janson.

I peak around the tree trunk. She's standing next to a blue EV, talking to Gillan. His blond hair is wet, but he has already changed into his BDUs.

"It's going to be another stormy week. Calder's got everyone on double shifts," he says.

"Be careful out there," Janson replies.

"Always am." He grins, but then he turns serious. "What's got you worried?"

Janson huffs out a breath. "She's getting good too fast. She has a lot of . . . talent."

"I told you she would," Gillan says. "First her, now Alba. It's the same pattern as before."

Can they be talking about me? But why would Janson be worried about me being good? It's only a problem if I'm *not* good.

"You think she's like Aidan?" Janson whispers.

"I think she's stronger than Aidan," Gillan says.

"Preen's been breathing down my neck for weeks." Janson frowns.

"Don't worry, we've had the qualifiers, nothing can happen now," Gillan says.

"You think I should talk to her?"

"Be cautious." Gillan's voice is stern. "She might be more Barracuda than I thought."

Janson lets out a sarcastic laugh. "If there's one thing I know, that girl's no Barracuda!" She pauses. "But what if I can't help her? How do I teach her?"

"Just do exactly what you did with me. There's time before the race. We can talk strategy."

Janson nods slowly.

"I have to go." Gillan jumps into the EV next to hers. "Hang tough."

"Always do." Janson smiles grimly.

They must have been talking about me. Who else in my class developed their swimming skills super fast? But who is Aidan? How am I like him? And why are Gillan and Janson worried about me? With a sudden chill, I think of the day when the swim scout came to the FRS and I first discovered my swimming skills. When I swim it's like my body moves by itself, like it's the most natural thing in the world—and in butterfly my legs feel in sync, like they are one. I've gotten so used to it that it feels normal, but there's nothing normal about it. I didn't beat just anyone in that race that day on the volleyball beach —I beat one of the Elites' top champions. A seventeen-year-old boy, who is taller than me, stronger than me, and one of Aqua8's most promising cadets. How was this even possible?

*

Jim picks me up after the navigation theory class and drives me home. Mrs. Queen has arranged for a special dinner with a fruit salad for dessert. "Fresh from our greenhouses," she says. "I heard you both passed the qualifiers. Well done."

Jessica wrinkles her nose in disgust and mumbles something about having to watch her figure.

I dig in. I can't even remember the taste of fresh fruit.

"Jess, sweetie you know the family rules. No getting up from the dinner table unless you've finished what's on your plate," Mrs. Queen scolds.

"But Mother, you know I can't think on a full stomach—and we still have revision exercises for tomorrow," Jessica complains. "Don't you think it's unfair that we have our career exams right before the Initials?"

"Not at all sweetie, you'll have to manage multiple tasks in your day to day working life all the time after you graduate," Mrs. Queen says. "But I suppose we can make an exception about dinner today, for the benefit of your studies."

"Thank you!" Jessica gives her mom a glossy smile and pulls me along by the arm.

Once we get to my room, she turns on the light with a snap of her fingers. I pick up the e-pad that's lying on my bed.

"So are we starting with math, or physics?"

Jessica giggles. "You didn't buy that little act for Mommy, did you?" She grabs the e-pad out of my hand and tosses it aside. "Who cares about homework! We are going to celebrate."

"Celebrate? Celebrate what? We're not even allowed out during the week."

"You wanna be a Barracuda?" She smirks. "You gotta break the rules like a Barracuda."

What does she mean *wanna be*? I never got to pick my team.

"What about the exams?"

Jessica rolls her eyes. "Ever heard of stress relief? Before a test you need to chillax—Open everything!" she shouts and pulls various tops out of my closet. "I think you should wear turquoise. It goes with your eyes—oooh and it's gonna look sexy!" She throws a range of items at me.

"What, no." I protest.

"Oh come on already, you officially qualified, you goody-two-shoes. We gotta party." She swaps the top for the dress that we bought at the mall, with the gaps at the hips and waist and one shoulder free. "Hurry up, I'll show you how to put Vanilla into fast styling mode."

Before I can protest I've got my head under the hair-styler while Jessica argues with Vanilla about eyeliners, eyeshadows, and mascara. Fifteen minutes later I'm standing in front of the mirror looking at a provocatively dressed girl with flawless red lipstick, tightly curled hair, and a skintight dress. Oh, no. No, no. That's not me at all!

"Wow!" Jessica's reflection mouths in the mirror next me. "You're ready to rock." She runs from the room. Ten minutes later she's back, dressed and styled in a pink-and-white sequin dress that matches her white-blonde, dead-straight hair. I bet she decided on that outfit days ago. There's no way she put it together that quickly.

"This is so cool, we're totally like sisters now." She hooks her arm through mine. "I am officially the queen of makeovers. Now come on, don't make any noise in the atrium." She drags me along the hallway which, in the evening light, has a pattern of alternating light and dark stripes.

With our high heels in our hands, we tiptoe down the stairs. Jessica leads the way through the kitchen and to the backdoor. It has a nightlock across it and a touchscreen. Jessica keys in 1-1-1 to open it. "That was the temp code," she whispers. "Daddy has no idea that I know that he never changed it. He thinks the Queen curfew's never been broken. The bolt locks again, automatically after three minutes, so we'll need this remote to get back in." She pulls a glass stick from her handbag and lets it disappear again while we creep along the side of the house. "This way, hurry!" She waves me to a gap in the garden hedge, through trees and brush, down a slope until we reach the winding street. About ten yards away a parked car flashes its headlights.

"Duke!" Jessica waves excitedly.

"Ladies." Duke, in a gray silk shirt, flings open the door. His eyes pop at the dress I'm wearing. I hug my arms around the side slits, feeling not just half, but fully naked.

"Are you ready for the most badass club on Ararat?" Duke gives us a wolfish grin as we slide into the sporty convertible.

"Idiot," Jessica giggles from the front seat. "Nice wheels, by the way."

"Compliments of my father. At least there would be, if he'd known I've taken it." Duke floors it. The tires scream and I'm pushed back against the seat. My hand shoots to my necklace. The prongs of the trident pendant dig into my palm while trees and rocks flash past as the car speeds through the dusk.

The nightclub is on the edge of Ararat, jutting out over the cliffs. The building is so dark that it melts into the night sky. Only the neon-colored stripes proclaiming the name The Net shine out against the black. Jessica and Duke lead me past the line of people queuing at the door. The doorman gives Duke a quick nod and we walk in. A wave of sound hits me like a boulder. For a moment I can't even tell that it's music. Who *listens* to this stuff? A hostess in a shiny black leather dress greets us and escorts us to the upper gallery of the club where it is quieter and a section of tables is roped off.

A sign marks this area as VIP Guests Only. The elite of the Elites? Mia and Kayla are already sitting under dim lighting on the wine-red banquettes. Next to them are the bulky shapes of Marlo and Zeke.

"Here are the champs!" they roar as they see me and Duke.

"Welcome to the Barracudas, Naya." Zeke raises his glass at me. "Qualifiers passed! You're officially one of us now."

I force a smile as Jessica and I take a seat.

"Isn't it great?!" Jessica nudges me. "I love this song!"

I nod. This whole buzzy atmosphere is so strange . . . unnerving . . . and yet making me hyper. I feel the itch to move . . . to get that energy out of my body . . . although I don't wanna be on the dance floor.

Jessica hands me an orange drink and blows a playful kiss at the guys. The boys laugh.

I take a sip. The liquid is strange, all dry and heavy on my tongue. I splutter, "Jessica, is this—alcohol?"

Jessica laughs. "What did you think we'd drink? Guava juice? You don't want to join team nerd, trust me. Drink up!"

"To the Barracudas," Duke hollers.

"The Barracudas!" his teammates bawl, and clink glasses. I hesitate, then follow suit and down my shot.

"Another?" Marlo asks.

He pours one before I can answer. Whatever this is, it tastes miserable. I wish that I weren't so shy, that I were one of those people who would just get up and figure out a way to leave, to escape all this. Duke pours another round, then another and another. One drink is bright red, one neon-green, the other dark purple. Each tastes as horrible as the first. A few more rounds and I feel all woozy and happy.

"We're gonna win because we're the best!" Duke glares at his teammates, daring them to disagree. "Anyone who races against us is going to wish they'd never been born. And that includes Gallagher! BARRACUDAS!" He raises his glass.

Marlo and Zeke cheer and shout, "BARRACUDAS!" Our table is the only one so noisy and roguish.

"Come on, let's hit the dance floor!" Jessica jumps up and drags me along. We descend the stairs and the crowd parts like a wave before us as we move to the center of the dance floor. I throw my arms up to the music and spin and twirl around. The brightly colored lights swirl above me. The ground is shaking, pumping the beat of the music through my body. Why did I not want to do this? Dancing is great!

Jessica raises her eyebrows at me and grins. "Naya, you're so totally my new clubbing partner," she shouts in my ear over the music. She takes my hand and we dance together. Spinning around each other. Swaying together, back-to-back, lowering ourselves to the floor.

"Whooop!" The crowd around us whistles and shouts. Jessica giggles as a few boys edge nearer and one of them takes her arm and draws her close. I can feel somebody's arms surround me, pulling me closer. I do what Jessica does, making my dancing more provocative, letting him guide my movements.

There are more shouts, more people watching. The music becomes a dull thud, the dance floor flashes with blinding lights. Suddenly I feel claustrophobic. There are so many bodies around me, pushing against me. I feel dizzy.

"Barracuda girl!" Zeke brawls and I realize that both he and Marlo are right beside me. Groggily I register someone's hand on my thigh and someone's hand on my chest and they're not the same person's.

"I need some air," I shout out and shove my way through the crowd. I stumble toward the green exit sign, but it's so packed I can't move. I bump into someone.

"Oh, sorry," I giggle, embarrassed. I push off his chest, feeling the round edges of the shirt buttons under my fingers. Black shirt . . . nice shirt . . . Nice chest!

I look up. Oh, crap, that's Gillan. His curly hair is slicked back, making the silver shark's-tooth-shaped stud earring in his left ear stand out. His blue eyes are fixed on me, strong jaw set and there's something very sobering in his look. I try to speak, but my throat is parched and my mouth just won't open. We stare at each other for a few seconds. I can feel the heat rising to my face. Then he turns and walks out of the club.

"Wait!" I shout.

Someone pushes into me, almost knocking me over. I wriggle through the crowd to the exit. He is standing outside, next to a sporty black motorbike.

"Wow, cool," I splutter. How come I've never seen Gillan on it before?

"Huh," Gillan gives a hollow laugh as I nearly topple over. "You sure seem to be enjoying yourself. Almost didn't recognize you there."

His blue eyes bore into mine and I'm frozen, rooted to the ground, dizzy from the alcohol. "I . . . I . . . that wasn't . . . me." Thoughts are forming slowly in my mind.

"Oh really? Who was it?" He raises an eyebrow at me then swings himself onto his motorbike.

"I've never been to a club before," I slur.

"Could've fooled me. Looked like you fit in just fine with your new gang." For a brief second his eyes meet mine again. Then he revs the throttle and roars away into the darkness.

"Gillan!" I want to cry out, but my voice is gone and so is the bike. I choke back a sob. Why is he acting so strange? If he doesn't want me to be with Duke and Jessica, why doesn't he do something about it? Is he worried he might incriminate himself if he speaks to me? Because he saved my life when he shouldn't have?

The music blasts out from inside the club in muffled thuds.

I hear a familiar giggle behind me. "Did you just hit on GG? Wow, are you so drunk you're chatting up the competition?" Jessica staggers over in her heels. "Zeke is *in* the club!" I groan and follow her back inside.

Hours later when I'm in bed, numb from the alcohol, half-deaf from the music, the reality of it starts to sink in. In the back of my mind I can hear Gillan's voice, "She might be more Barracuda than I thought." I bury my face in my pillow, drinking in the darkness. What am I becoming?

Suddenly, even with my eyes closed, a ray of light appears. I blink. My reflection stares back at me from an infinite multitude of dark windows in the Eden hallway. I'm alone. I know Gillan is somewhere and that I have to find him. I hurry along, but other students appear, crowding around me, pointing their fingers at me, laughing.

"You're not an Elite!" They're not speaking but I can hear their thoughts.

"Get out of here, FRS."

I spin around—and then I see Gillan, walking away from me. I try to run after him, but the other students crowd tighter around me, knocking into me, suffocating me. Thunder growls and lightning strikes, and all at once the crowd disperses and General Calder appears. She points out of the window at gray storm clouds and a whirling sea. "GET OUT THERE," she shouts. "STOP THE STORM." I turn and see that the waves have split into a swirling whirlpool. Gillan is out there, fighting against the torrent. I want to move, to help him, but I'm rooted to the spot. The whirlpool drags Gillan into its midst and swallows him up. I scream, but my voice is drowned out by Calder's laugh. It rings shriller and shriller until the ground reverberates. Suddenly all the glass of Eden's windows bursts. Shards reflecting my face rain down on me. I scream and cover my head with my arms—

And wake with a start. My forehead is covered in sweat and my breath is coming in short bursts. Outside my room the moon reflects silver on the calm ocean waves. It was a dream. Just a dream.

CHAPTER 11

— *The Iron Teens* —

"Wake up, NAYA!"

I groan. My head feels like I front dived into a pool of concrete.

"NA-YA!" It sounds like Jessica's speaking through one of those megaphones that the Aqua8 instructors use. I open one eye and immediately shut it again.

"Wow, you've really never gotten drunk before! Aw, cute. Anyway we need to get ready, we've got our economics and politics exams today, but what's waaay more important: after last night you're like *the* most popular girl at school. Elijah might, you know, consider 'hanging out' with you, and Marlo said that Zeke totally likes your moves . . ."

Oh no! I was hoping that was just a bad dream. Did I really do all that stuff? Who was I dancing with? Marlo? Zeke?

"Our social calendar just got so BOOKED!" Jessica screams in excitement. "I mean you could at least have given me a heads-up. One moment you wouldn't say hoot to a minnow, and the next you're like a firecracker, but anyway, let's have breakfast before Mommy throws a fit!"

I'm kind of relieved when we're finally in school and Jessica has to shut up because the exams are starting.

"Guaaah, economics is a total snoozefest." Duke yawns as we sit down for our first test of the day.

"Yeah, right?" Jessica grins.

I say nothing. It's not like I have a career choice. I might as well be doodling on the test screen.

In between the exams we have longer breaks than usual. Extra time to study or relax or clear our heads. Before the politics test I go to the study garden to read through some notes. Even though my career with Aqua8 is set and I probably won't ever need the grades, everyone's tension is getting to me. I sit at our usual desk. Gillan is alone at the table across from me, but this time he doesn't look up. Still feeling a bit queasy from last night, I scroll through the notes of my previous revision session.

At last the bell rings and I get up to leave. I'm halfway out the door when I realize that I left my bag on the bench. I go back to get it. When I turn around I'm standing right in front of Gillan. He gives me the cold shoulder. Something in me snaps.

"First you save me, now you hate me. Why?"

He freezes. "Naya, not here!"

"You could just have let me drown. What was the point? Tell me!"

"Shhh, stop it!" he whispers. His face is inches from mine, brows furrowed, blue eyes begging me to be quiet. Suddenly I hear my own heart beating so loudly, I can't think anymore.

He clears his throat and takes a step back again. "Uh, don't forget you bag." He picks it up from the bench and hands it to me. Then he's out the door.

I sigh. I didn't even realize that I was holding my breath. He didn't answer any of my questions. What does he mean *not here*? What am I missing? It's like everyone on Ararat is either crazy or talking in riddles. And why is Gillan sending me underwater signals one day, and angry with me for being on the Barracuda team the next? What secret does he think I am hiding? Why did he speak to Janson about me? And how can I possibly concentrate on my exams after a moment like this?

*

As soon as we finish our politics test we head to swim class. Duke is fidgety and stressed as we walk across the lawn to the competition hall. With Gillan back in school, an odd sort of tension is building up. Today might be the first day in a long time that Gillan is actually going to attend swim class. Somehow it's rattled Duke completely. A line of sweat runs across his forehead and he used the break between economics and politics to rush away rather than spending "quality time" with Jessica. She looked just as mystified as everyone else when he burst into the politics exam room five minutes late.

"So you're back, coward Gallagher," Duke mutters under his breath.

He seems to have taken Gillan's absences as a personal offense. As if Gillan missed the past weeks' classes on purpose, so that they don't have to face each other in training. I puzzle over it while I put on my swimsuit.

Janson is already addressing the class when I step out of the girls' locker room. "Listen up, I know this is a tough year, because the career exams are right before the Initials, but I need you to stay on the ball. You know which race you're competing in, and what your strengths are. The touchpads and competition board are activated, so get in the pool and let me see some top times. Any questions?"

"Yeah, Coach, I got one," Peterson from the Rays calls out. "Shouldn't we be practicing CPR? You know, with the Valley's track record on Ararat." The Rays burst into laughter like they have been waiting for this joke. Some of the Sharks and Barracudas giggle too.

"You think that's funny, Peterson?" Janson whips around. "Get in the pool and give me fifty extra laps after training. You want to save lives? Make sure you've got the muscle to pull somebody out the water."

"But Coach, I can't after school. We've got Junior Cade—"

"You should have thought about that earlier. Anybody else got any smart comments?" Janson looks as if she's going to kill the first person who answers.

There's total silence, the kind that makes you want to fidget with your pencil or notebook if you have one.

"Then start your warm-up." With that Janson storms out of the hall.

Wow, Peterson really pushed her buttons. Under the sheepish glances of the class, I walk to the warm-up area when I realize I forgot to put GermAloid on my feet. Better not skip that today. I turn back to the locker rooms—and almost get knocked off my feet.

"Hey, watch where you're going!" I shout at the figure bowling past me then realize that it's Duke. He's running along the edge of the pool in mad, jerky movements. A boy ahead of him

116

leaps out of his way. Then Duke barges straight into Theo Kingsley from the Seals, knocking him into the pool.

Theo hits the water, motionless. His head disappears slowly below the surface. It takes me a second to realize that Duke's flailing fist must have knocked him unconscious and another to realize that no one is doing anything. I spring forward and dive off the pool's edge. Below me, Theo is sinking toward the bottom. Two strokes bring me to him. I grab his arms and tug but he's six foot, athletic, and weighs a ton. Even with my Aqua8 training it feels like someone attached dumbbells to my wrists. I kick and struggle and still his weight drags me down. So I hold my breath and wait until we sink to the bottom. When I feel the smooth tiles of the pool beneath my feet, I push off. It takes me two goes to lift him up and above me. My lungs scream for air then we break through the surface. My ears clear of the water and suddenly I can hear the students shouting and jumping into the pool and pulling Theo out.

"What's going on here?" Coach Janson's voice cuts through the turmoil.

A blur of voices fills the air while I hoist myself out of the pool.

"Theo . . . accident!"

"Naya saved . . ."

"Duke . . . running . . ."

Janson's face turns red. "How many times have I told you not to run around the pool! Six classes to the tournament and you're behaving like a colony of storm-lashed seagulls!" She tosses aside her stopwatch and kneels down beside Theo, who sits up, coughing up water. "Theo, can you hear me? Look left and right for me." She holds up her index finger for an eye tracking test, then fires at the rest of the group, "And why was Naya the only one trying to save him?"

There's an embarrassed murmur.

At that moment a sharp voice rings through the hall. "Coach Janson!"

I follow Janson's gaze to the spectator stands. Principal Preen is standing there, dressed in a navy suit, his black hair slicked back. He's holding a stopwatch in his hand and he's got a weird expression, like he's both angry and elated at the same time.

"Coach Janson, what is this girl's freediving time?"

What? Why does he care about *that* right now? Why is he even here? And does he mean *my* freediving time?

I glance at Janson confused, but her face has drained of color, like she knows exactly what Preen is talking about. "I have an injured student to attend to." She turns back to Theo abruptly.

"Coach Janson, I asked you a question." Preen steps off the spectator stands. "A word, NOW."

Janson draws in a sharp breath. "Torres, take your teammate to the nurse." She gets up and stands in front of Preen like she's facing off against an opponent.

"What is Miss DeLora's freediving time?" Preen repeats.

"She didn't qualify. She swam less than the required distance when I tested her."

They *are* talking about me. I draw a sharp breath. But why does my freediving time matter?

Principal Preen's face has taken on a red hue. "Didn't qualify! How is that possible? Miss DeLora just held her breath for one minute and twenty seconds. ONE MINUTE AND TWEN-TY SECONDS!" He holds the stopwatch up in Janson's face. "Can you imagine my surprise when I stopped by to see how the competition training is going and discovered this—*by chance*!"

Janson clenches her fists. "Extreme situations push us to our limits. This is not her usual time."

"Coach Janson, we have rules at this school." Preen's expression is stern. "These rules demand that every student be tested for the Iron Teens, if eligible. Give me one good reason why you have not entered Miss DeLora?"

Janson looks cornered, but her reply is loud and clear. "She didn't qualify. And she can barely do breaststroke."

"Breaststroke?" Preen explodes. "I don't give a flying fish's ass about breaststroke! Freediving is the determining category and you know it. The Barracudas have been unable to put forward a champion for six years—and for six years everyone has been out for my blood. The Governor wants to see a race. The council want to see a race." He jabs a finger at Janson. "And guess what, Coach? This year, we're giving them a race. We're holding the qualifiers right now."

"No!" Janson steps in his way. "If you put her in the Irons now, you risk getting her cut in the first stage—"

"Coach Janson, it was not a request." Principal Preen holds her gaze. "I am going to overlook the fact that you *forgot* to test this girl properly, but you are entering her for the competition. Insubordination is not a highly regarded quality on Ararat. You'd do well to remember that." He turns to us. "Swimmers to your starting blocks."

Janson hesitates one second then blows her whistle. "OK, you heard the principal! Diaz for the Sharks." She waves over Soraya, who gets up and walks to her block. "Borgman for the Rays."

Shane Borgman looks up and shakes his head. "No, I can't, Coach, please."

"You're good enough, off to your block," Janson says.

I can feel my cheeks burning as she turns to the Barracudas. It's me. Somehow I'm the reason this is happening.

"Naya." Janson puts a hand on my shoulder. "You're gonna swim breaststroke, freediving, butterfly, freestyle, in that order, all in one go, OK? Four laps of each style, two laps of freediving. Take your time before the freedive for a quick breath to calm your breathing. Then you do one lap, resurface, and complete the second lap. Got it?"

I nod and swallow. I still don't know what's going on. The Iron Teens—I don't even know what they are; only that Coach Janson didn't want me to compete in them for some reason—and that she just stuck out her neck for me.

"Take your marks," Principal Preen calls out, the stopwatch still in his hand, although the competition board is on. I suppress the dull throb at the back of my head. Oceans, I wish I hadn't had all that alcohol last night. Soraya, Shane, and I step onto our starting blocks in unison. The black block beside me is still empty. There's a murmur on the benches.

Preen calls, "Ready, set—"

"Wait, Coach Janson, the Seals don't have a candidate," someone shouts.

Janson looks around. In all the confusion she's obviously forgotten. "Torres!" She calls for the substitute captain of the Seals.

"You told him to take Theo to the nurse, Coach," a boy replies.

"Oh, right." Janson scans the Seals' bench at a loss.

A soft set of footsteps sounds behind us. The room goes quiet as Principal Preen's and everyone's gaze turns to the boys' locker room entrance.

"Did I miss something?" Gillan asks.

Janson walks over and in a few hushed words fills him in. Gillan listens, nods then he puts his hand on her shoulder. For a second a worried look flickers across his face, but it's gone again as he steps to the pool's edge. Our eyes meet as he steps onto his starting block. He gives me an almost invisible nod, then turns to the lane in front of him. The whistle sounds and we dive in, in sync.

Water laps around me as I glide through the pool in breast-stroke. No matter what Janson told Preen, she actually has been coaching me in all four techniques. Still, the other three shoot ahead quickly. I spur myself on, forgetting all about pace and breathing techniques. What will happen if I fail? The fear makes me weak and I fall even further behind.

It takes me until the end of the fourth lap to finally focus. I have to freedive next; I can't do that when I'm hyperventilating. Joining the others, who have lined up at the end of the pool, I take a brief moment to calm my breathing. Gillan dives first. Then Soraya and Shane almost simultaneously. I force myself to stay back and allow myself more time. One breath . . . two . . . now. The blue of the pool closes around me. I've never even tried to freedive a whole fifty meters before. But I know that this time I will—because I have to. It's the same as saving Theo: either I make it, or I die trying. I flipturn. The sting in my chest gets stronger. I can see the wall ahead of me. I stretch out an arm, push my hand against the touchpad and come up coughing. I made it—I made it.

And now I know that I can do it again. I don't focus on the others, I just dive and swim. Then it's butterfly. Although I can barely catch my breath, I fling myself right into it. Water splash-es, my chest is close to exploding, and suddenly an odd sensa-tion grips me—like my legs are glued together. All I can do is try to keep up with Shane and Soraya. Switching from butterfly to freestyle is painful, as if I pulled a ligament. My eyes tear up. My body refuses to obey my command and for a moment I feel like someone's draining the air from my lungs. With panicked, choking breaths I complete one lap, flipturn and complete the next three. Ears buzzing, I slap my hand against the touchpad. Gillan, Soraya, and Shane all finish ahead of me. I look up at Principal Preen. I barely have the strength to tread water, but I need to know . . . I need to know if I passed.

"Contestants, out of the water," Preen calls. I reach for the outstretched arm above me. It's only after he's helped me, that I register it's Gillan. I'm too tired to decide how I feel about that. Black blotches are dancing in front of my eyes.

"Are you all right?" Janson grips my arm.

I nod. But is she? From the tone in Preen's voice, I worry that she is one step away from getting arrested.

Preen glances from the competition display to his stopwatch. "All champions qualified—by a tenth of a second," he calls out as if he is neither proud nor impressed but simply obliged to do this. "The Iron Teens championship will commence next Sunday at the Initials as the last race of the day. Participants will be allowed to compete in addition to their maximum of two races." He slaps the stopwatch into Janson's hand. "Coach, you have five days to teach this girl a *proper* breaststroke. Let's hope for both your sakes that she does better on the day of the race." He turns and strides toward the exit of the hall.

*

". . . first race in six years!"

"And the Barracudas have a real shot at winning."

The excited chatter around us crescendos as Jessica, Kayla, Mia and I leave the swim hall.

"I don't get it. Why's everyone acting like this?" I ask.

"Oceans alive, Naya! Have you never watched an Iron Teens race before?" Jessica exclaims. "It's like totally insane. Only the best of the best can compete."

"Where would she have seen one?" Mia asks. "FRS people can like, barely swim." She cuts an apologetic face at me. "Sorry."

"The Iron Teens are special, because the race only happens if each team's champion passes the qualifiers," Kayla explains. "They're insanely difficult, because you have to be really good in all styles. And most people can't freedive well enough. That's why anyone who can do a full pool length is automatically put forward."

Mia nods. "The Barracudas haven't been able to put forward a contestant for six years—and it's made us look really bad."

"But what about Jess . . ." I start.

Kayla shakes her head. "Didn't make the time. You have to beat the clock in the qualifiers. It's really rare for one person to meet the physical challenge of doing all four styles within the time limit."

Jessica puts on an aloof I-don't-care smile.

"Still Preen didn't have to be so assy with Janson," Mia says.

Kayla looks worried. "He could have done a lot worse. Janson's been in trouble with the authorities before and breaking the rules on something as important as the Iron Teens is kind of the same as breaking the law."

"But if Naya didn't pass the freediving in the tryouts on her first day, Janson didn't have to put her forward," Mia says.

"True, you need to pass the fifteen meter marker . . ." Kayla still sounds concerned. "I guess she'll be OK."

I bite my lip. Janson had her foot on the marker that day.

"It's stupid anyway," Kayla continues. "We should have bots for measuring distance. We use touchpads for timing, right?"

Jessica puts on a glossy smile. "Who cares, this year's gonna be epic!"

Marlo and Zeke suddenly appear behind us and throw their arms around our shoulders. "You betcha!"

"Barracudas forever," Zeke says, grinning.

Jessica recoils and wrinkles her nose at their rowdy behavior. "Chill, OK, Ezekiel!"

*

"Good day at school, girls?" Jim asks while I spear a piece of swordfish with my fork at dinner.

"It was OK," I mumble. "How about work?"

"Very productive, thank you Naya." He beams. "So, I've heard some rumors about the Iron Teens happening this year."

I say nothing, but Jessica's practically bouncing on her chair. "Daddy, it was super cool! Theo knocked his head and was so totally drowning and then Naya jumped in and saved him and Preen saw it and called for the qualifiers right away."

"And Naya passed," Jim finishes for her. "Douglas dropped in at work and told me."

I swallow. Of course Douglas Kallion would be the first to spread the news. I bet he's only waiting for me to fail and get sent away from Ararat.

"I only passed by a tenth of a second," I say.

Jim smiles. "Are you being modest, as usual, Naya? Don't worry, champ. With that butterfly of yours, you'll ace it."

I wish I had his confidence.

"Perhaps we should make plans for a celebratory dinner for the day after the race?" Mrs. Queen suggests.

I suppress a sigh. Yet another fancy dinner, but does it even matter? In eight days I might not be at Eden anymore. In eight days it might all be over.

*

As the sun sets across the vast stretch of the horizon, I sit on my bed and hug my arms around my knees. It's not just the race that worries me, but that weird thing that happened with my legs. I almost didn't manage to switch to freestyle. If that happens in the Initials, it could cost me the race. What if there's something wrong with me? That medical thing Gillan and Janson were talking about . . . When I was swimming butterfly it felt like my legs had merged together. And what if that actually showed? What if somebody *saw*?

I wish there was some way to check. Wait—what if there is? I climb over my bed and dig my e-pad out of my bag. All our classes are recorded for revision purposes. Maybe our swim class is recorded, too.

I flick through the menu and select *swimming*. There are some notes for me on training. Janson must have uploaded them. And there is a camera symbol. I tap on it. Today's swim session is the first video that comes up. There I am, diving into the pool to save Theo. Preen is already standing in the spectator stands. I forward to where I change from butterfly to freestyle and watch all the lengths until the finish line. Everything looks normal. My legs are moving fast, producing a lot of foam, which covers them almost entirely. I sigh with relief—when the video skips to the next frame. It's the same race, recorded from the other side of the hall. I scroll through. Again there's nothing—but now the screen switches to a top view of the pool. How many of these are there? I flick back to the list of videos. It shows five recordings, all from different angles. I knew the Elites were obsessed with swimming, but this is taking things a little far. It's more like surveillance.

Then it hits me . . . That's exactly what it is! I scroll through the rows of videos. There's a section called *study*, *halls*, *parking lot*, and even *after hours*. The entire school is recorded 24-7.

And suddenly it all makes sense, why Gillan acted so weird. Why he and Janson talked in the parking lot while the wind drowned out their voices. Why Janson had her foot on the fifteen meter marker even though we were alone in the swim hall. They were evading the cameras, and—oh, no, what did I say to Gillan when I saw him today in the study area?

Hands trembling, I select the video of him and me in the study garden. I watch as I get up to leave, go to the door, turn, and walk back. "Don't forget your bag," Gillan says politely, handing it to me. I scroll back. Is there a glitch? The video replays the exact same sequence. "Don't forget your bag." Somehow nothing of what I said to him is recorded. I watch it a third time. There's a tiny jump in our movement, almost unnoticeable, like someone's erased our conversation. Did Gillan do this? How? He'd have had to hack the system. Then I remember Duke fiddling with the control screen in the study area during the Blue Out. OK, so overriding security is possible . . .

But what is really going on here? I thought the Elites were free. That they had everything on their "verdant heights"—but it's just an illusion. Their lives are more controlled and monitored than ours in the FRS ever were. Sure, we had the armed guards in every section, the fence, the patrol guards, but no one ever bothered to watch our every step.

I dig a shaky hand through my hair. So Gillan gave me the underwater signal, because he wanted to talk in private without surveillance. To tip me off probably. About the cameras, and maybe about the Iron Teens, too. If only Preen hadn't seen me rescuing Theo . . . Wait! Preen can't have been there by chance either. He already had a stopwatch in his hand. And he didn't seem very surprised about my freediving time. The conversation between Gillan and Janson jumps to my mind. Janson said that Preen had been breathing down her neck. Had somebody tipped him off? But how? Even if someone was constantly monitoring my swimming videos, I never did a full pool length underwater in class. Except—my heart jolts—except I did do one *after* class. On the day before the qualifiers, when Duke and the Barracudas picked on Alba—the same day that the boy from the Rays said something about me and the Irons!

Preen must have found out and that's why he dropped in on our training session today. And I played right into his hands when I saved Theo. But how is it all about me? Am I in some kind of danger? Or a danger to Gillan and Janson? Why were they trying to prevent the Iron Teens from happening? And is all that connected to that boy Janson mentioned, Aidan? Questions are burning in my mind. And what's worse, I can't ask any of them.

School feels different on Monday, with my knowledge that everything is under surveillance. I'm constantly on edge and I feel watched wherever I go. For all I know they could even be monitoring the bathrooms. It's hard to fight the urge to glance around for the cameras. And without rhyme or reason I can't shake the feeling that I will be arrested if I look at them. They might think I'm up to something. I'm weirdly longing to get to swim class, to be around Gillan and Janson, but when I get there I feel hollow, disconnected. I can't do anything and everyone is behaving so *normally*.

"Line up at your starting blocks for competition practice. Coach Milkins and Coach Almeida will oversee your training today," Janson calls then walks to the end of lane one with me. "Principal Preen's explanation last Friday was a bit short, you must be wondering what the Iron Teens are—"

"It's OK," I say quickly. "The others already explained."
The less we say, the better. I already got us into enough trouble.

"All right." She studies me with a curious frown. "Then do
your warm-up and let's get started."

I do terribly. Not matter how hard I try to go faster, my arms
and legs part the water at a snail's speed. I don't even want to
look at Janson when she checks the timer on the competition
display. I wanna scream or cry. This whole time I felt certain
that I had a chance at winning and now everything rests on
the one style I can't do. I'm back to square one. Only this time
it's worse. Preen's threat was clear. And it was meant for both
of us. The guilt nags at me, for being the blundering fool that I
was, blurting out things I shouldn't have said, drawing attention to myself when others were covering for me.

"You're doing good," Janson calls to me as I finish my lap.
I meet her eyes, the confusion and tension plain on my face.

"It's OK, Naya." Janson sits down by the pool's edge. She's
being nice but I can tell she's just as tense as I am. "Your focus
is key now. You're a natural swimmer. Don't try to go fast, just
trust in what you know. You don't want to overexert yourself
before you get to butterfly. That will be your chance to catch
up. You need to play to your strengths now. Soraya and Shane
are freedivers and freestylers so you need to save enough energy to keep up with them in the final laps. Don't even look at
Gillan. And if you can, try to hold back in the butterfly singles.
So far you beat the others with a full length's head start. You
can afford to cut it a little closer."

"What if I don't make it?" My voice trembles.

"Leave that to me. Besides, if I can teach Duke and Marlo
an elegant butterfly, I can teach you a regular old breaststroke.
Now, this time, pitch your hands down and keep your elbows
high. Strengthen your kicks and turn your feet out. Never point
your toes. Let's go."

*

By Thursday I've pretty much mastered the breaststroke
technique, but that's no guarantee that I'll be able to keep up
with the others. I walk to the parking lot with Kayla, Mia, and

Jessica, who all waited around for me after training. The sub-aqua hockey team knock their bats together as they walk past.

"Yeah, let's play octopush!!"

They're almost at the swim hall, when the girl who hangs out with Peterson calls to me, "Get ready to drown, FRS."

"Bye, bye!" Peterson waves to me in an exaggerated gesture. He and the rest of the team crack up, bawling and laughing.

"Hey, go drown yourself! Idiot!" Mia calls after them.

"What was that all about?" I ask.

Kayla waves it off. "Oh, don't worry, they're just going on about that accident."

"What accident?" I ask.

"Around fifteen or so years ago, one of the Iron Teens high school contestants, Aidan Fynn, had a seizure and drowned in the race," Kayla explains.

A cold shiver runs down my spine. Aidan? The same Aidan that Gillan and Janson mentioned?

Kayla continues, "They say it happened because of overexertion. He was around our age."

Jessica scoffs. "Why you'd push yourself beyond your limits is, like . . . beyond me. Overexertion is bad for the skin. Gives you wrinkles and stuff. Eeugh!"

"Yeah, and what's this got to do with Naya?" Mia asks. "It's just a load of sea tangle."

Kayla stays serious. "It's because of Naya's background," she says. "The boy who drowned, the one that Peterson and Cadence were talking about, he wasn't born on Ararat. He was from the Valley, like Naya."

CHAPTER 12

— The Initials —

The spectators cheer as we walk into the decked out competition hall.

"GO Seals!"

"GO Barracudas!"

There are banners and bunting, and a big wreath hangs off the banister behind which Principal Preen is sitting. Gathered around Preen are all the parents and teachers. They are as hyped as the students, shouting and waving. Some are even wearing team colors. The Queens are sitting in the front row, along with Douglas Kallion. I also recognize some familiar faces from Brice Donovan's party, like the nice, quirky guy called Arlo Quinn. More than ever, I wish that Mom were here, too.

With a thumping heart, I follow the rest of the Barracudas to our warm-up area. I was worried before — but after what Kayla told me I'm terrified. What if there's something seriously wrong with me? The same thing that was wrong with Aidan? Maybe growing up in the Valley made our bodies too weak to support this swimming ability that we developed out of the blue. In the qualifiers I already had difficulty breathing. What if my heart just gives out today?

The boy's freestyle is called up first, and the chitchat and shouting around us dies down as the competitors take their places on the blocks. They're in the same order as always: Sharks, Barracudas, Seals, Rays.

Duke and Gillan get into starting position: Duke is fidgety, switching his stance from a track start to a grab start and back again; Gillan is calm and still, his eyes focused on the water. On the green and yellow blocks of the outer lanes are Elijah Goldstein and Silas Ramsay from the year above ours. Janson is standing on the poolside opposite us along with the other swim coaches. Like them, she is dressed in a turquoise Eden polo shirt and white shorts.

Coach Almeida starts off the race. "Ready, take your marks, Go!" His whistle goes.

"Gghhhhmww!"

I spin around and see a red-faced Peterson, who pretends to choke as he is parading in front of us in the yellow jammers of the Rays. "Hey, FRS-girl, no way they'll keep you on Ararat when you lose this race. Even if you survive. Worried?"

"No," I say with a smile. It's true. I'm not worried. I'm freaked out. My stomach is so tight that I can't breathe.

"What's the matter, Peterson? Can't tell yellow from red? Your bench is that way." Kayla rolls her eyes at me and slumps down next to me.

In the pool Gillan and Duke are neck and neck. The water splashes up so wildly that it looks like they're surrounded by a hoard of hungry piranhas. The words FINAL LAP light up on the display at the end of the hall where the timer is running in big yellow digits. Shouts echo as the spectators cheer the swimmers on. Gillan shoots ahead. SEAL VICTORY: GILLAN GALLAGHER flashes across the display board. Duke slams his fist into the water.

"Girl's breaststroke," Coach Almeida calls.

Four more races, then I'm up. I wriggle my foot as Mia makes a good start in the race. Duke sits down next to me, dripping wet and looking a little worse for wear, but he's got that determined look in his eyes. He's hungry for the next race.

"All right, Naya?"

I nod and shuffle to the side. I don't like being so close to him in just my swimsuit.

On the scoreboard an announcement flashes: BARRACUDA VICTORY: MIA COOTE.

I get up and walk around the pool to warm up, slapping my legs to get the blood flowing. I tighten my googles just a little more, then walk to the starting block. I miss who wins the boy's butterfly race. Far too quickly, the whistle goes. Although my legs are like jelly, my front dive is OK. A smooth dip into the water. The panic wears off and I easily take the lead. I follow

Janson's advice and hold back in the singles, but nonetheless, the others still have half a length to go, when my name lights up the scoreboard. Applause erupts from the stadium. Are they cheering for me?

Dazed, I get out of the swimming pool. With all the adrenaline the four hundred meter race felt like it was over in seconds. Duke, Jessica, and Zeke crowd around me. Apparently I've broken the high school record with my first singles race. A time bonus of one point gets added, so now we're one point behind the Seals with only freediving and the relay left. After that come the Iron Teens.

In the fifteen minute break between the singles and the relay, Duke huddles us together. "Right Barracudas! You know what we have to do. You saw Naya today. She's unstoppable, un-fricking-stoppable. So what are we gonna do today? WE'RE GONNA WIN!" He's so excited, he's foaming at the mouth. The others don't seem to care, they're completely infected by his enthusiasm. Marlo and Zeke clap and cheer and then we put our hands together and shout, "Barracudas!"

We line up behind the starting block for the relay, Zeke and Jessica in front of me, Duke behind. Coach Almeida blows his whistle and the race begins. By the time I enter the pool, the Barracudas are second. I feel a huge surge of power flow through me. On the first length I bring us level with the Seals. I flip-turn and zoom through the water, my legs feeling like silk. When I reach the rim this time I haven't just made up the gap, I bought us a quarter of a length. Duke dives into the pool with a good head start over Gillan, but it's not like he needs the advantage. This must be the fastest I've ever seen him swim. He's churning up the water like a motorboat. When he finishes he's still a yard ahead of Gillan.

With a roar of triumph he pulls himself out of the water, leaping onto the pool's edge and punches the air. "Yeeeah! You see that Gallagher? You LOSE!"

BARRACUDA VICTORY: RELAY TEAM

I turn away. I don't want to watch Duke taunting Gillan. Besides, for me this was just the warm-up. My big race is still to come. While the stadium erupts into cheers and the spectators get up for snacks during the thirty minute interval, I return to the team bench and do some more stretches.

Soraya sweeps past me to the locker rooms. The Elites like washing off before and after any time they swim. Hygiene is an obsession here. During the singles it was a constant coming and going.

"It's gonna be OK." Kayla shows up next to me.

I nod and twist my toe around the plastic of the turquoise floor mats.

Then I freeze. The GermAloid! I'm supposed to reapply that before every race. Not that there's a way anyone could notice, but for the Iron Teens they're super strict about routine. Janson reminded me about fifteen times. And of course I forgot.

As fast as I dare run with wet feet, I hurry back to the locker rooms. Hands trembling, I get the bottle out of my locker and unscrew the lid. I'm about to pour some of the GermAloid into my palm when the bottle just slips from my grasp. Oh, no! I watch as the thick, antiseptic liquid spreads across the tiles.

"Take some of mine." Soraya holds out her bottle to me.

"I—thanks," I say.

We're about to compete in the most anticipated race of the year, and she did not hesitate one second to help me.

"Don't mention it." She steps across the transparent puddle of spilled GermAloid. It's five minutes to the race. I don't know how she's managing to be so calm.

I walk back to the swim hall, my knees trembling.

". . . DIAZ for the Sharks. NAYA DELORA for the Barracudas. GILLAN GALLAGHER for the Seals, and SHANE BORGMAN for the Rays!" Principal Preen calls into the microphone.

The strength of the cheer that follows surpasses that of any previous race. Jim waves at me from the audience. I give him a weak smile. I bet he's the only one here to support me, probably most of the other spectators are hoping that I'll lose. Next to Jim, Douglas Kallion is sitting with a sour face. Duke is the only team captain not competing in the Irons. Douglas must be livid.

"And with this ladies and gentlemen," Preen finishes his announcement, "I give you the FIRST IRON TEENS RACE OF OUR HIGH SCHOOL CHAMPIONS IN SIX YEARS!"

I can barely breathe—and the race hasn't even started. All the contestants are now lined up.

READY

The word flashes up on the scoreboard opposite us while Coach Almeida calls it out.

TAKE YOUR MARKS

I reach down and grab the edge of the block.

GO! The whistle blows.

As I dive into the pool, I hear a yelp and a splash to my right. Something happened to Soraya—but the false start whistle doesn't sound, so I resist the temptation to turn my head, and lunge into breaststroke. Even so, I can tell that there's nobody in the outer lane next to me. I try not to let it distract me and push on. Gillan and Shane have already completed their laps by the time I finish my breaststroke. As I calm my breath for the freedive I see Soraya swimming toward me in lane one. I dive just as her hand touches the pool's rim. Something really must have gone wrong with her start. I suppress a guilty, nervous tension. With her this far behind, my chances of making it to the Midterms have just doubled. This time my lungs aren't burning for air as I complete the first lap of freediving. Not being hung over definitely helps. I take a deep breath and dive again—but when I finish the second lap, Soraya has almost caught up with me. Panicking, I fling myself into butterfly. This is where I have to win ground. The race is between me and Soraya now, Gillan and Shane are too far ahead. I dive-surface-breathe, dive-surface-breathe, dive-breathe-surface . . . I gasp. Wait. What? Did I just *inhale* underwater? No way, then I'd be choking. It must have been my imagination. Don't stop, keep going.

I flipturn and almost forget to change to freestyle. And then it happens again. My legs are glued together. I kick wildly, but they won't separate. Using all my strength, I push them in opposite directions. A sting of pain sears through them as they rip apart. I break into freestyle, but still it's like there's a magnetic pull, trying to fuse my calves together. Am I hallucinating? My muscles are burning from the effort of keeping ahead of Soraya. I'm getting a cramp. My vision blurs.

"Bar — cuda — Go! — Naya — Go!"

The shouts of the audience reach my ears every time I surface. I force myself to swim faster. My hand hits the touchpad just an arm's length before Soraya. I take a gasping breath that stings like ice in my lungs.

SEAL VICTORY: GILLAN GALLAGHER flashes across the scoreboard. Gillan won. But I made it. I came in third. I didn't get cut.

After all the panic and worrying the relief is almost sedating. I'm half-aware of the Barracuda team crowding around me, cheering, clapping me on the back, as I get out of the pool. On the scoreboard the numbers are spinning while the computer calculates the overall scores.

"It's not fair!" Soraya's voice rises. "Somebody messed with my block."

A few heads turn her way.

Coach Janson shakes her head. "Soraya, that's not possible. The blocks get cleaned by bots. And no one's allowed in the hall before the race."

"You know I've never done a bad dive in my life!" Soraya is still trembling from the effort of the race, but her face is heated. "Something made me slip."

Janson looks apprehensive.

Principal Preen walks over with a frown.

"Why wasn't the race stopped?" Soraya asks him.

"Iron Teens don't get stopped for anything," Preen says then hisses under his breath, "Coach, get your student in line, she's making a scene."

I squiggle out of the Barracuda team hug. "Coach! Coach, Soraya's right, it's not fair that she lost just because she fell." I'm shooting myself in the foot if there's a rematch, but Soraya helped me before the race and I only won because of her bad start. I can't just leave her hanging.

Soraya looks at me surprised.

"Naya." Janson sounds conflicted. "I don't think —"

Soraya interrupts her. "Principal Preen, somebody sabotaged me. I want this investigated."

"Whoa, what are you saying?" Shane Borgman joins us. "We can't have a rematch just because you tripped. It's not fair for everyone else."

"There won't be a rematch." Preen's voice cuts across the chatter. "Miss Diaz fell. The race is over. Seals won."

Soraya glares at him. At that moment the whole hall breaks into wild applause as the scores are being calculated on the display board. There are one, two, and three points for the third, second, and first places in the singles; one, three, and five points for the relay; and three, five, and seven points for the Iron Teens, plus time bonuses, which leaves us with:

```
SEALS: 23 POINTS
BARRACUDAS: 21 POINTS
SHARKS: 18 POINTS
RAYS: 15 POINTS
```

"Barracudas!"

"We almost tied with the Seals," Zeke roars.

Across the pool, I catch a glimpse of Gillan and the Seals high fiving, before I'm pulled into a rough group hug. "We're gonna win! This year we're gonna win!"

After showering, we join the rest of the school at a buffet set up on the lawn. I wrap myself into my team hoodie. The storm is picking up again, with screaming winds and dark clouds. The beacon from the lighthouse is lit, but no one is paying any attention to it. So what if the black victory banner of the Seals is swaying violently in the wind? The Elites won't miss a chance to party.

"Congratulations, Naya," a voice behind me says. I turn to find Arlo Quinn studying me with the same bemused smile as when I first met him. "We all knew you'd do well."

"Thank you." I glance at his black-and-white tie. Those are the team colors of the Seals, but there is no student with the surname Quinn.

"Who are you supporting?" I ask, curious.

"I'm Gillan's guardian." He beams at me.

"Right." Why does everyone who's nice have to be on the rival team? "Are you sure you won't start some barbecue brawl just by talking to me?" I ask.

He chuckles. "When the competition's so stunning, who can be patriotic? Besides, Gillan never minds a challenge. Good competition only makes us stronger."

I look over at Gillan sitting at a table, laughing with his team mates. There's a painful longing in my chest to be part of that. They look so relaxed compared to the brawling Barracudas. It's fitting that Arlo is Gillan's guardian. They have the same humor, the same nonchalance.

"Well done, Alexis." Arlo has a mischievous twinkle in his eyes as he catches Coach Janson striding past. "I don't know how you do it, these competitions always have me at the edge of my seat."

Janson gives him a grim smile. "Anything to get you out of the research institute for a few hours, Arlo." She goes to talk to some parents.

Of course, I'd completely forgotten that Arlo is on the council as one of the research institute representatives. I read about it in my school politics notes.

"What do you do at the research institute?" I ask.

"It's biology basically, genetics, anything that helps our species survive in the current world."

"How does biology help us survive? Are some people more resilient to our environment than others?" I ask.

Arlo raises his brows. "You seem to share Gillan's passion for science. Unfortunately, Cape Harmony's research projects are highly confidential."

I sigh. Figures! Everything that's connected to Gillan is one big riddle. Another thought strikes me. Genetic differences . . . Can it be that Arlo's research has something to do with genetic variants? No one on Ararat knows much about them, so it would make sense that they are part of Ararat's highly confidential research. I want to pry for more information, but a tall, businessy-looking guy pulls Arlo into a conversation about Galileo Tecc.

I glance at the Barracudas, who are hanging out on the lawn with drinks, cheering and whooping.

"Hey, guys, who am I?" Zeke leaps up and mimics a front dive then makes himself go cross-eyed and collapses onto Marlo.

Marlo cracks up. "What do you call a shark with vertigo? Soraya Diaz!"

My cheeks blush. My team are the only ones embarrassing themselves and making fun of her. Only Duke is hanging back, oddly quiet and sulky. I wonder what's up with him.

"You have to try this!" Kayla pops up at my side and hands me a plate with a burger that has a slice of something with charcoal stripes on it.

"What is it?" I ask.

"Mahimahi. Grilled fish," Kayla explains and with a grin she adds, "and below that there's cheese and lettuce —"

"Oh shut up!" I shoot her a smile. I take a bite from the burger. I'm starving after the race.

"Wow! Oh that's —"

Kayla gives a knowing nod. "Good, huh?"

I've barely finished eating when the boys suddenly leap up.

"This place blows," Duke grumbles. "Let's go play some volleyball."

The gale is howling as we take the EVs down the hill slope to the less inhabited, windward side of Ararat. I cling onto the side of the vehicle. On this bouncy, pebbly road Jessica's driving is super shifty. The waves that wash into the bay below us have whitecaps. Duke rounds the final curves and parks his EV by an abandoned-looking stone hut. There's a combination padlock on the door. Duke enters the code and flings the door open to reveal three Jet Skis. One is big and blue, the other two are red-and-white. They're the same Jet Skis that Duke and his gang had when I got into the volleyball competition with them.

The wind on the beach is strong, pulling at my clothes, whipping grains of sand into my face.

Jessica looks worried as she holds up a hand to protect her eyes. "Duke, we can't go!" she calls over the storm. "It's a pre-Blue Out."

"Who cares?" Duke glares at the blue glow of the lighthouse beacon that's just about visible from the other side of the hill. "We've had stupid false alarms all month!"

"So? How do you know this one's false, too?" Jessica shouts back.

Duke ignores her. "You're not scared of the storm, are you Naya? A true Barracuda is never scared."

"I . . . uh . . ." Why is he putting me in the middle of this?

"See, Jess, it's just you chickening out." Duke pulls the first Jet Ski across the sand. Zeke and Marlo get the other two.

Jessica's eyes are ice as she glares at me and Duke. "You're insane. Have you seen the sea!? They don't call this Wrecker's Beach for nothing!"

"You do what you want! We're going." Duke starts the engine.

"Fine!" Jessica snaps. "Fine!" She marches back to her EV. Everyone watches, but no one follows.

"Well, what's the matter?" Duke growls. "Let's go."

Kayla and Mia get on the back of Marlo and Zeke's Jet Skis which are already in the water. Duke pulls his into the sea too.

"Naya, you're with me." Duke holds out a hand to me. The last thing I want to do right now is get on the back of his Jet Ski, but if I try to back out, too, Duke will probably flip.

"OK," I say and climb on. The engine yowls and water erupts on either side of the Jet Ski as Duke shoots off in a curve out to sea. We speed right into the midst of the choppy water. I suppress a scream as the Jet Ski is flung up into the air. Duke is attacking the waves so aggressively I'm scared we'll both get thrown off. I cling onto him, not caring that I'm hugging his bare chest — I just don't want to die.

The headwind gets stronger as we round the promontory to the volleyball beach, whipping my hair into my face so that I can't even see. I turn away, cowering behind Duke, glancing back at the hostile gray horizon. At last I hear sand scraping under the base of the Jet Ski. I jump off and onto the beach.

Then my relief turns into terror. We're not alone. Neal, Ethan, Emily, Ralph, Johnny, they're all here. And although I want to run up to them, tell them about Ararat and the Iron Teens, and how scared I've been today, and how much I've missed them, a hollow feeling spreads in the pit of my stomach as I realize what's about to happen.

"Off the beach, losers!" Duke's shout makes me jump.

"What are you doing here?" Neal marches up to him. "We won the beach fair and square."

"OOOooohhh," Zeke and Marlo chorus in the background. "*You* won the beach, did you, squirt?"

Neal juts out his chin at Duke. "Naya can stay, the rest of you can get lost."

Duke towers over him, like a charging bull. "Wrong, losers!" He puffs up. "Naya won the beach. And Naya's one of us now!"

I give Neal a warning glance. Duke's bad tempered on a normal day, but after the tension of today's tournament, it won't take much to send him over the edge.

Neal is too worked up to notice. "That should be Naya's call then, shouldn't it?"

I avoid his glance. More than ever he and the others look like young boys. Neal with his floppy hair, Johnny with his lost puppy eyes.

"Naya?" Neal asks.

I continue staring at the sand. Doesn't he know that if I agree with him now, Duke will tear them up in a rage?

"I see, well look who's become their new Queen Bee," Neal says bitterly. "Come on then guys, let's go." They're already up the hill slope, when he turns and calls over his shoulder. "We'll pass on your regards to your mother, Naya."

I bite my lip to suppress the tears. Does he know how much that stings? Here I am, stuck on the worst team there is, unable to talk to my old friends, unable to make new friends, unable to talk to my mom . . . as if I'm nothing more than a little minion of Duke and the others. But I'm not like them! I'm me . . . I just have to fit in—that's all.

"Everything OK, Naya?" Mia asks.

"Sure, Mia." I give her a polished smile. "Everything's great." But inside, I'm crumbling. Who am I? What have I become?

CHAPTER 13

— Moonlight on the Waves —

A ray of blue light flashes across my face, illuminating the bedroom. Then it's gone again, plunging the room into semidarkness. I don't know how Jessica and her parents can sleep. For me the pre-Blue Out rekindles all the old fears. The Valley, The Valley Flood . . . While the whole hill is sound asleep, I stare wide-eyed at the ceiling. Neal's words ring in my ears. "We'll pass on your regards to your mother!" How did I get so distracted to stop thinking about her every day? What if I never see her again?

Again the beam from the lighthouse passes. Under my breath, I count the seconds until it returns: one—two—three—now! Fear nags at me worse than guilt. It's December, the stormiest month of the year and the FRS are not much higher up than the Valley . . . My hands are shaky as I push back my blanket and walk to the window in the hallway. My bare feet touch the glass pane. I look across the mountain. Down the slope the lights of Ararat form a twinkling circle. To my left, the peaks of black hilltops conceal the eastern shore. Somewhere in the darkness behind those hills lie the FRS. I look that way, a painful feeling forming in my chest.

A wail cuts through the silence of the night. The sirens. They are ringing a Blue Out warning. My mind is made up. I have to find a way to the FRS, whatever it takes, whatever the cost.

I tiptoe back to the bedroom and pull out my socks from under the bed. For a second, I consider waking Jim and asking him to drive me, but I quickly discard that idea. The scout who recruited me made it clear that I am not to communicate with anyone in the FRS. No doubt even Jim, with his dislike for rules, has to obey these orders.

The neon light of my bedside clock shows 4:30. That should be enough time to get there and back unnoticed. Determined, I put on my bikini, then my clothes. I won't be able to use the main road. It's watched by cameras that are set up in a wide perimeter halfway up the hill, and there are patrol guards with dogs, who make their rounds. There is another way, but it's dangerous, kind of insane actually, with a Blue Out imminent.

My palms are wet with sweat as I toss a towel and a flashlight into my school bag. I sneak from my room, carrying my shoes in my hand. My bare feet tread silently down the marble stairs of the atrium. I make my way to the back door when one of my sandals slips from my hand and lands on the floor with a slap. I freeze, terrified and listen for movements from above, but Jessica and her parents seem to be sound sleepers. Nothing stirs. Relieved, I key in the combination 1-1-1 for the temp lock to open the back door. Good thing Jessica showed me the code when we snuck out to the club.

The trees surrounding the Queen property are momentarily lit by the blue flash from the lighthouse as I slip outside. Crouching low, I squeeze through the bushes at the back of the garden and get to the roadside. Jessica mentioned there's a path to the windward shore around here somewhere. After a short search I find it and strike out. It's quite overgrown, with thick branches of brambles that cut my legs as I hurry on. It only occurs to me now that I can't turn on my flashlight. Someone might see the light. Thankfully, the blue beam of the lighthouse illuminates my way every few seconds. I climb down the hill, taking care so I don't slip on the loose stones. I'm listening for drones, hoping that I will hear them over the wailing wind.

After what seems like ages, the path takes a turn and peters out just above the pebbly road that we used when we drove to Wrecker's Beach with the EVs. The waves crash loudly on the shore. To the right, I make out the stone hut. It would be so much simpler if I could just borrow one of the Jet Skis, but I don't know the combination to the lock.

With a final glance around, I undress down to my swimwear. The cold wind and whirling grains of sand sting my naked skin. I hurriedly stuff my clothes into my school bag, so the storm won't take them. Then I leave the bag on one of the rocks that surround the beach, weighing it down with two big stones. On my return I will head straight to Eden. If anyone asks, I'll just say that I went for early swim training.

The sand is cold and wet beneath my feet. I walk down the beach and look out to the dark and stormy sea. The waves that crash on the shore are twice my height. I must be insane to think that I can do this. It's everyone's worst nightmare, caught in a gale at sea in the pitch-dark, but the pull of Mom is too strong.

I grab my necklace for reassurance. I'm a champion swimmer of Eden and a member of the A8C. Who's to say that I can't face a storm like this? At a run, I dive into the curl of the largest wave. At once the sea is dragging me under, pulling at my legs, tossing me this way and that. The current is too strong! I can't put in a single stroke. All my swim skills are failing me. A new wave crashes over my head, forcing me down. I surface, sputtering water. "Help!" Waves hit me in the face, choking me. I'm at the mercy of the sea—even more so than on the night when I almost drowned in the Valley. "Help!" But who's gonna hear me? Although I don't have the strength, I fight for dry land. By some miracle, I'm caught in the swirl of the next wave and washed up on the shore. I drag myself onto the sand, coughing, shaking. No . . . ! How . . . ?

I look back at the dark water. My heart is thumping wildly. I clutch my necklace to soothe my nerves. Why could I swim well in training this whole time? What is different now? I lie back on the sand and let my breathing calm.

If it were simply a fear of the ocean, then I couldn't have won my first race against Duke after Jessica stole my necklace. I was in the sea then, too. Granted, it was nowhere near as wild as today but it wasn't calm either. And if anything, I was more in tune with myself then than I was during all the swim races on Ararat.

So what is it then? In the Valley I almost drowned. On Swim Scout Day in the FRS only two days later I could swim really well. And that was also the first time that I felt all funny during a race. Pensive, I brush my index finger over the golden prongs of my necklace. Funny, how nervous I got when our FRS coach told me to take it off for the race. I never worried about it much since . . .

I freeze. What if that's it? I wasn't wearing my necklace. All the days on which I could swim well had that in common. But how is that possible? Can my necklace have an influence on my swimming ability?

I take it off and stare at the small golden object in my palm. The necklace is the only thing that I inherited from my father. My only memory of him. I've worn it since birth. Every single day. Every single night. The day on the volleyball beach with Duke and Jessica was the first day ever that it wasn't around my neck.

I feel lightheaded. I walk to the rocks where I stashed my bag and stow my necklace inside. Half-excited, half-terrified, I head down to the shore once more. The waves loom over me, big and frightening. Is this another naive childhood fantasy, like the one about the conch? If I'm wrong, the sea will swallow me up, drag me down to its depths. Still shaky from nearly drowning, I plunge forward and dive straight into the incoming wave. But instead of fear I feel ecstasy. It's like I've lost my mind, like I'm about to die, but I'm thrilled about it. Again the water roars around me. I can feel its force, its strength, but this time it's not pulling me under. I kick and I'm out of the bay, in the open sea, swimming in the direction of the wind. My forward stroke is effortless, like I'm carried on the waves. I whoop, all fear of the storm and darkness gone.

The water feels wonderful, cold but refreshing. My eyesight was always good in the dark, but tonight I can make out the details of the rock formations. I can see every crack in the jagged cliffs between Wrecker's Beach and the volleyball beach. I dive and resurface, keeping close to the shore. Duke completed this trip in ten minutes on the Jet Ski. I suspect I will need around half an hour if I swim without stopping along the way. But as I glide through the wild waves, I hear the soft growl of a motorboat engine.

It's distant at first, but approaching quickly—and it's heading straight toward me. Instinctively, I dive down. They probably can't see me, but they could hit me in the semidarkness and the storm. A few strokes take me to the bottom of the seabed. For a terrified moment, I'm worried that in the darkness I will lose track of the surface, but against all reason I can still see. There are shapes below me: an old ladder and a kind of iron ring, attached to a piece of concrete. I hold on to the iron ring, to keep me from drifting. It's rusty.

I try to still my heartbeat, like I do in freediving, to make the air in my lungs last longer. Above, the motorboat draws a circle. I wait and watch the dark hull. What are they doing so close to the shore? There are barely any houses on this stretch of the coast. No jetties or ports either. The only place to patrol would be the FRS flood barrier—and what are the chances of finding an FRS escapee in this weather? Or a drowning Elite for that matter—me excluded?

At last the motorboat turns away. I'm about to let go of the ring when an invisible force hits me. I'm pushed toward the rocky ground. A muffled thunder rings through the water. It makes the whole seabed tremble. I hear the sound of rocks breaking. It's like . . . an explosion, like the dynamite they test near the Aqua8 compound sometimes. Was that motorboat doing impact tests?

I twist for the surface, but a sharp pain sears through my right foot. I glance down. The concrete block with the iron ring has shifted and trapped my leg. I grit my teeth. My movement must have made the block sink down further, because it feels like all the bones in my foot are being crushed. I wince and push for the surface but the block won't move. My heart thuds in my ears, my chest is getting tighter and tighter. Desperate, I try to tear free, ignoring the nauseating pain that shoots up my leg. My vision blackens, my lungs feel the air being squeezed out of them. I gag to hold in the last breath—when unexpectedly the pressure lifts. The constricted feeling is gone, and the sea around me feels light as air. I must be losing consciousness . . .

Suddenly everything is bright and beautiful! A blue-green sheen emanates from my feet. Am I hallucinating? I stop struggling and allow my body to sway with the motion of the waves . . . and I feel an incredible rush! It's running through me like an electric current, like I'm one with the ocean, strong, and powerful. With an effortless kick I toss the concrete block aside. I am free! I make for the surface when I see bubbles escape from my mouth. How . . . ? I'm breathing underwater! How . . . is this possible?

I extend my arm toward the tiny spheres of air and with a wobbly kick I follow them as they rise up. My leg no longer hurts, but it feels funny, like it's all muscle and no bone. I look down and—my heart stops. There's a long, shimmering blue-green tail where my legs used to be. It's covered in scales that meld into the skin at my waist. WHAT? I must be going crazy.

Frightened, I kick for the surface—and shoot out of the ocean like a rocket.

"AAAAH!"

Water splashes as my head bursts through the sea's surface. I draw in a deep breath. It feels unnecessary, like I'm hyperventilating. I brush my hair out of my eyes, feel the cold night air on my arms and face. No, this can't be real. I paddle with my arms. Then I flip my feet out of the water. There's a fin there! Light, transparent, blue-and-white, like the wings of a butterfly. For a frightened beat, I think my heart is going to stop. I reach out and pinch the blue-and-white fin. OUCH! OK, yes, this is definitely real! I'm alive. Not dead. And I think . . . I think . . . I'm a MERMAID!

My heart beats at double its normal rate. Mermaids aren't real! They're legends. Legends that we are not even allowed to talk about, from before the global flooding, from before-before times no one can even remember. If Mom had not told me all those bedtime stories I wouldn't know about them. In some, the mermaids were good; in some, they were bad. Sometimes they could talk to the creatures of the sea, while in other stories they would lure sailors to their death with enchanting songs. The benevolent mermaids could give humans the ability to breathe underwater with their touch, the bad ones thirsted for human blood. They had sharpened senses, supernatural strength . . . and some even knew magic!

Is this part of what I am? Do I know magic? Elation grips me. I'm a mermaid! This isn't scary, this is fun! Flipping around, I dip my head into an oncoming wave and spin through the water as if I were part of the storm that is churning up the ocean. Whooo-hoooo! I dive under, somersault, and come up spouting like an elegant fountain. A swarm of silver-white fish scatters as I dive under again. I can see them, as clearly as if it were day. Yeeees! I swim on and watch my lower body, totally at ease, totally in my element. No wonder I could swim butterfly so well.

For the first time in my life I feel free. There are no restrictions, no one to suppress me. I can be as silly, as careless as I want. I can—whoa, wait . . . does Mom know? Did the necklace stop me transforming? And what does the conch do? I gotta go ask her!

I zoom straight toward the FRS. The water rushes through my hair and tugs at my bikini top as I propel myself forward. Fish scatter on either side of me. I must be going as fast as the Jet Skis! It's amazing. When I surface, I'm at the promontory that flanks the volleyball beach.

The waves lap around me, the gray flood barrier of the FRS looms before me. Spotlights illuminate it and the patrol guard who is making his rounds. The breaking waves splash water over his feet.

BANG!

I hear a noise like an explosion followed by a roar of water.

BANG!

I whip around. Gunshots! I dive quickly. Where are they coming from? And how did they see me? The sky is still dark and grayish. I dart toward the darker blue of the sea. Oceans, I hope they didn't see my tail! They might think I'm a variant. Hang on—could that be what the genetic variants are? Mermaids?

More shots ring out. I push myself to swim faster—and that is much faster than I expected. Whoa! Flipping head over tail, I tumble toward the ocean floor. Sand whirls up. I catch myself and, hovering over the seabed, I look back up.

Bullets swish through the water, but their deadly lines only extend down a few feet before they lose their momentum. Anxiously I hold my breath, but their trajectory isn't aimed at me. It's pointing away from me, toward the wall of the FRS. I follow the bubbly lines and see a person drifting upright in the water.

It's a young guy in swim shorts. A red cloud of blood streams from his shoulder. The current is brushing his hair down, so that I can't see his face. Above, a boat keeps drawing its circles. They must be searching for him. But what's he doing here at the crack of dawn? He's not from the FRS, he's too tall, too toned, too fair-skinned and unblemished . . . I swim toward him. I have to help. As I get closer, the current brushes back the blond hair from his face.

It's . . . Gillan!

A few bubbles escape my mouth. His eyes are closed. He's unconscious. Why is he here? Why are they shooting at him? Another bullet rips through the water. I have to get him out of here. I swim toward him, grabbing him around the waist. My lips tremble. How much time do I have to get him to the shore? His lungs will already be full of water. His body is heavy as I try to pull him with me, but I'm stronger than I was as a human. I whip my fin as hard as I can. My ears crackle—and suddenly I'm zooming through the water. The reefs, the fish, the sandy seabed all turn into a bubbly blur. I feel Gillan's muscles beneath my arms. I cling onto him, scared that he will be ripped from my grasp, but already the dark of the ocean turns to a lighter blue. The water loses its chill. Algae brush my shoulders. A mortifying thought hits me. What if I don't transform back? Gillan will see me as a mermaid. And what if I can't transform at all?

I feel sand below me. Without even planning to, my fin whips down and like a dolphin I leap out of the water, onto the shore. I let go of Gillan, gasping for air.

I . . . can't breathe. I . . . can't . . . My lungs won't take in any air. I choke, then with one gasp, the block lifts and I draw in the fresh morning air.

I roll around and feel grains of sand digging painfully into my knees. Knees! A deep sigh of relief escapes me. I'm human again.

Outside of the bay, the engine of the motorboat grows distant. I jump up and rush over to Gillan. His body is still. He's not breathing. I kneel beside him and draw in a breath. OK, this isn't quite how I imagined my first kiss. Slowly I place my mouth against his. I try to ignore the butterflies that flutter in my stomach. His lips are soft and salty and sandy. I blow in a breath, then I place my hands onto his chest, one on top of the other, and push down at intervals.

"Come on, Gillan!" I shout.

I continue the compressions. Still he's not moving a muscle. Again I breathe air into his lungs. I draw back and wait for a second, ready to thump my hands onto his chest again. He comes to, sputtering, choking, and spitting out water. I collapse into the sand beside him. Above us the sky glows orange with the first light of dawn.

I glance at the FRS fence on the rocks above us. It's too late to see Mom now.

Gillan blinks, a grin spreading across his face. "Why do I feel like somebody just kissed me?"

For some reason, his grin infuriates me. "You should be grateful you're alive!"

"Guess I was just born lucky." He gingerly hoists himself onto an elbow and looks at me, dazed.

His expression changes as recognition dawns on him. "Naya!" He sits up with a jerk. Immediately, he clutches his shoulder, groaning. "How . . . ? What are you doing here?"

I flinch. I can't tell him that I was gonna visit my mom, but my gaze has wandered back to the FRS fence unintentionally.

"I was just . . . lost," I say.

He raises an eyebrow. "Again?"

"You know I have a bad sense of direction."

He glances at me, grimly. "You should work on your excuses."

I grimace. At least we're in it together this time. Whatever he was doing, he wasn't meant to be here either, otherwise he wouldn't have gotten shot.

He brushes sand off his cheek and looks out to the sea. "Did you get me out of the water? Alone?"

"Hey, I just won the Barracudas a new time record—in case you didn't notice."

He gives me a crooked smile.

I bite my lip. I didn't want to rub that in, but it's not like I can say, "Hey, I grew a fishtail and carried you to the shore."

He gets up. "Right, thanks for the rescue, but I have somewhere else to be." He sways and almost falls up the hill slope.

"Hey, wait!" I leap after him. "Why were those guys shooting at you?"

"Guess they thought I was from the FRS."

"But weren't they Aqua8 . . . like you? Didn't they recognize you?"

He turns and frowns. "Why do you care all of a sudden?"

Heat rises to my cheeks. "What do you mean?"

"You just wanna party and have a good time, like everyone else," he scoffs. "You don't ask any questions. You don't look into things."

"That's not true!" I burst out. "I got your underwater signal, I just didn't know what it meant. I'd been at Eden for less than two days. How was I supposed to know that the whole school is under surveillance? And what was so urgent that you had to tell me?"

Gillan rolls his eyes. "It doesn't matter now."

"Yes, it does! You're blaming me, when you're the one who took off and disappeared for weeks."

"Yeah, well, didn't take you too long to find new company, did it?"

I feel a stab of pain in my heart. "Hey, I didn't choose Duke and Jessica! I didn't choose any of this. Nobody asked me! They just shipped me up to Ararat and stuffed me on the Barracuda team."

"You always have a choice." He walks away, toward the road.

"Yeah, maybe when you're born on Ararat," I fire back at him.

"You think I'm proud of that?" His blue eyes are cold. "At least I don't lounge in the lap of luxury. You seem to be just made for the jet set."

"So why did you save my life then? That night in the Valley?"

"I thought you were . . . different. Willing to search for the truth, regardless of the risk. Obviously I was wrong. You just take things for granted. Ararat Heights, the FRS . . ." He turns and pushes his motorbike out from behind some nearby bushes.

"I bet you never even wondered where that big cable car goes that runs straight over the hills."

"Actually, I have," I shout back defiantly.

He stops pushing his motorbike onto the road and gives me a curious look. "Right, but you never bothered to check it out."

I swear he looks almost bemused as he says it. OK, now I just want to slap him. "I'm new here. I don't know anything about . . . anything. I've never seen a Nutrigator before, that doesn't mean I go sticking my head inside to check how it works."

"Well, maybe you should. After all, you're eating the stuff that comes out of it."

I glare at him. Gillan shrugs. The engine jumps to life with a muted EV-like purr. It would be easier to be angry with him if his frown didn't look so annoyingly cute. He lifts himself onto his motorbike. I watch him drive off into the sunrise.

Why did we have to end up arguing? I did what everyone wanted me to do. I made it into the Iron Teens. I won the butterfly race. So why are all the people I care about so disappointed in me all of a sudden?

CHAPTER 14

— The Winter Solstice —

"Naya, where have you been?" Jessica asks as I sneak through the study garden of the school to the classrooms.

I groan inwardly. I mean, what are the odds? Jessica, in the study garden, before first period.

I put on my best attempt at a smile. "Just got up early." I hope she doesn't notice the salty rim that my wet hair left on my top.

"Ugh." Jessica slams her math book shut. "You could at least, like, have told me. I was waiting in the EV for you—for like, forever."

I hide a smirk, despite my nervousness. *Forever* in Jessica's vocabulary means two minutes max.

Jessica rants all the way to hydrostatics, then slumps into her usual seat in the middle of the classroom. "And what's with the wet hair?"

"Oh, I went for early morning practice in the pool." I wave it off.

Jessica's eyebrows rise up as she gives me a pitying look. Then she breaks into laughter. "Way to go, champ! That's hard core. I mean, not even Duke was in the pool this morning." She turns, grinning, and hollers for the whole class to hear, "OK, that's it guys. The championship is ours. This girl has been up since the crack of dawn, training for the end of year trophy when we just aced the Initials. Barracudas rule!"

"Go Barracudas!" Marlo and Zeke shout.

Everyone laughs. I smile absentmindedly. My mind is still sifting through this morning's events. I totally panicked when I realized that I might not get back in time. But no matter how hard I tried, I couldn't transform back into mermaid shape. My head is racing with questions. Why have I got this strange power?

Has it got something to do with my father? Was he like me? Is that why he left us? I vaguely notice Dr. Planck start the class while I try to recall the stories that my mother told me as a child. She never said who my father was or where he was from. Not even his name. I think of her, standing outside the school as the Elite scout took me away. Sad, but not surprised. Like she knew.

But do the Elites know? My heart lurches. If mermaids are genetic variants, then the Elites hunt them. They must never find out what I am. But what if the transformation happens again? Right in the middle of the school pool? I think of the time when I inhaled underwater in the Iron Teens qualifiers. I didn't imagine that. Oceans, I was probably close to turning into a mermaid! How am I ever going to get back into the pool? How am I going to stop myself from turning into a mermaid in front of the entire school? Wow, that sounds so weird.

"Naya, can you help us here?" Dr. Planck asks. "How many volts do you get when you solve this equation?"

"Uh . . . thirty." I look at the blank screen of my e-pad.

He sighs. "What's the matter with all of you, today? The race is over, so you think you're on vacation? Gillan? How about you?"

Surprised, I look up. I didn't even notice him enter the classroom.

"Forty point five," he says.

Dr. Planck nods and gives me a telling glance.

I force myself not to care. Neither about Dr. Planck . . . nor about Gillan. He shouldn't even be here today. He got shot in the shoulder—although he puts on a very good act of pretending he's all right. I don't think that anyone has noticed the paleness of his face.

By all rights, I should be the one angry at him! I rescued him. And he left me on that beach with the patrols on full alert. It's because of him that I didn't get to see my mom. But the truth is that he is right: I have become friends with the wrong people. I saw how Jessica and Duke treated others, and I chose to ignore it. Two months ago, I lay in the old factory building of the FRS, listening to the howling wind outside, wishing that

I had the power to make a difference. Now, I've been given all the privileges of the Elites, but instead of making the most of them, I've let this new life lull me into a false sense of security and comfort.

"Your homework, for the Winter Solstice break—" Dr. Planck calls out.

At that moment the door flies open and two school security guards in white uniforms walk in. I sit up. In front of me Gillan tenses in his seat. Are they here for him? For me?

"Class, I want everyone's attention," one of the guards demands.

My heart races. What happens to you if you break the law as an Elite? I always figured that citizens of Ararat were free from government prosecution, but—judging by the way Preen talked to Janson—I'm not so sure anymore. And why would they have the school under surveillance if not for government control? Suddenly, I'm more scared for Gillan than I am for myself. I doubt the Elites have luxury versions of labor camp.

"Following a sighting earlier this morning, the government has issued a warning of increased variant activity," the security guard reads out. "Governor Proctor has issued temporary security measures for all citizens. A strict curfew has been imposed from twenty-one hundred hours to zero seven hundred hours. Students are not to venture out after dark and must be accompanied by an adult at all times during the day. All beaches and coastal areas are off limits to civilians. That means no beach parties, no Jet Ski excursions, and strictly no swim practice in the sea."

A murmur of protest runs through the class.

The security guard continues, "Given the circumstances, the Winter Solstice celebration on December 22 has been canceled."

Shouts of "What?" and "No!" ring out.

"This is ridiculous!" Jessica exclaims. "The Winter Solstice is like the biggest festival on Ararat. After the Water Festival, of course. We don't even know if variants exist. Like, get real guys."

Duke, who is sitting diagonally in front of her, shoots her a warning glance.

"Miss Queen!" Dr. Planck cautions her. "The variant threat is not—"

"No, I mean, come on, Dr. Planck," Jessica interrupts. "You're gonna close the beaches because of made up sea monsters? When's the last time anyone saw a genuine variant? Like NEVER!"

The school security guards exchange dark looks and take a step forward.

"DETENTION," Dr. Planck barks. "I will not have you questioning the authorities, Miss Queen!"

"Oh, but . . ." Jessica gives him a fake smile. "I wasn't . . ."

"Detentions will be deferred until next term," says the security guard who read out the orders. Turning to the class he adds, "The new regulations are effective immediately. This is the last class of the day. The Winter Solstice vacation will start two days early. Teachers will upload extra revision footage to your e-pads. Those of you living on the windward coast, do not attempt to leave school alone: wait for your parents. Class dismissed." The guards turn in unison and leave.

The whole class breaks into wild chatter, but I can feel a chill running down my spine. The windward coast, that's where Wrecker's Beach and the FRS are, where Gillan and I were this morning—where I transformed. Variant, something that *varies*, that changes shape. The fear that clutches at my heart becomes colder and colder. I was right. I *am* one of the sea monsters.

Next to me Jessica huffs and snatches up her bag. "This is ridiculous! No Winter Solstice AND detention. Just wait till I tell Daddy."

"Be glad it's just school detention, Jess," Duke tells her. "If Dr. Planck hadn't—"

"Awww, look who's all concerned all of a sudden!" Jessica makes a face at him. "I don't need your safety talk, Mr. I'll-ditch-you-on-Wrecker's-Beach."

"Class, you heard the security team," Dr. Planck interrupts. "Pack your things and leave the school building in an orderly fashion. I don't want any incidents in the hall. It's under grim circumstances that I say, 'Happy Winter Solstice.'"

The students get up in a bustle of movement and pack their bags.

Gillan is walking ahead of us as we leave the room. I catch myself flinching as he casually swings his backpack onto his left shoulder. What was he up to? Was it him or me that set the authorities on high alert? I'm still not sure. He obviously only came to class to erase any suspicion that he might have been the person who Aqua8 shot this morning. But were they even Aqua8? I didn't see a blue stripe on the motorboat. Who else has access to motorboats, without breaking any government regulations? I can only think of the FRS patrols. But they're not normally so trigger-happy. In any case, I should be relieved that we both got away OK.

*

"Ugh, I can't believe they're locking us in for the vacations, that's just cruel." Jessica holds up her e-pad while we're driving home. "And have you seen our school calendar for next term? The Midterms are on Saturday, March 30, and we have like zero days to recover from the race. They used to give us at least Monday off before spring term starts."

"I feel bad for Soraya," I say, trying to act normal and steer the conversation in a different direction. "I wonder what made her slip."

Jessica gives me a weird look. "Who cares, it—OCEANS ALIVE!" She slams on the brakes so hard I almost fly against the front windscreen.

"Can't you look out wh—" I yell, but then see the white van blocking the road ahead of us. People in plastic suits are rolling a stretcher toward the loading bay. It's covered by a white cloth that is concealing a human shape. They're transporting a dead body?

"Oh no!" Jessica hand flies to her mouth. "I hope it's not one of the ladies from the clothes design department. Their office is on the top floor of the mall and this road leads straight there."

One of the medics waves her through. I glance at the stretcher. I think I can put Jessica's mind at ease. The body hidden by the cloth looks too tall and broad-shouldered to be female. I'm about to mention it to Jessica, when I notice a gun strapped to the belt of one of the medics. What kind of doctor needs to be armed? Only Aqua8 carry weapons. That moment the stretcher bounces over a rock and a hand flops out from beneath the cloth. I gasp. It is more tanned than most people's on Ararat and the fingernails are covered in reddish dust while the knuckles bear the marks of hard labor.

I think of the man's face that I saw in the bushes. I wonder if he was an escaped labor camp worker, but there are no labor camps up here. Or are there? I wish that the guys in the plastic suits had not seen us. I already feel like I know too much.

*

"Daddy, Daddy you won't believe—" Jessica shouts as she bursts into the house.

Jim silences her with a stern look. "I got notified that you caused a disturbance at school. A talk. My study. Now."

Mrs. Queen is pacing the living room as if armed Aqua8 guards are about to storm the Queen family home. I quickly disappear into my room.

In all my time on Ararat I have never been home this early. If I weren't freaking out, I'd actually enjoy the chance to just lie on my fluffy bed, not doing laps in the pool or crawling through the mud at the Aqua8 compound. I tell myself to relax. The Elites don't know what I am, otherwise they would have either arrested me already, or shot me on the spot. And thanks to the curfew, I now have a two and a half week vacation, without A8C training or school, to figure out how to ensure that I don't also end up getting carried off under a plastic sheet by Aqua8 soldiers disguised as medics.

Why haven't I transformed in the pool? Maybe it has something to do with the chlorinated water. Or with anxiety. After all, I only changed shape when I was close to dying. That would basically mean I can't get nervous in swim class or I might transform. Which is making me fairly nervous!

Then again, what if it's connected to the weather? And I transform more easily on stormy days? It's a ridiculous thought, but so is turning into a mermaid. What I do know is that I have no control over the changes. So what I really need is to get in the water and practice how *not* to transform. But how can I do that when we're not allowed to go outside unsupervised and are totally banned from all beaches while Aqua8 are out hunting for variants? It really is ironic that they are searching for them out in the sea, while I'm sitting right here, in the Queen residence, on top of Ararat hill.

I wish I could talk to someone. I wonder what Gillan would do? Whether he knows anything about all this. Arlo works at the research institute—the place where they possibly research variants, and he might have told Gillan what goes on there. And Janson knows something, too. Otherwise she wouldn't have talked to Gillan about me. But why did she and Gillan try to keep me out of the Iron Teens? I'm in the water either way. So maybe whatever secret they're discussing has nothing to do with me being a variant. Either way, it's too dangerous to assume that they will help me if they find out what I am.

*

Over the following days, Mrs. Queen keeps us busy with a strict schedule of studying and house chores. Somehow I end up doing most of them. Jessica spends most of her time whining about the sabotaged Solstice celebrations, although after the tirade from Jim, she no longer blames the government for it. I find it hard to sympathize with her about the missed opportunity to party. I didn't even know anything about the Elite's Winter Solstice celebration until the day it got canceled.

"Daddy, Daddy, are they making any progress with the variant searches?" Jessica asks at breakfast, four days into our vacation. "I haven't seen my friends in, like, ages. I'm starting to feel socially deprived, I mean, we're practically incarcerated."

Jim sighs. "Jessica, honey, you know I'm not allowed to discuss government topics at home. Just make sure you and Naya stay safe." He kisses Mrs. Queen on the cheek. "Have a good day, sweetheart." Then he heads out to work.

I wish I had Jessica's problems. I keep racking my brain for ways to sneak out of the Queen house and to the beach unseen, but whenever I have a minute to spare Mrs. Queen pops up with a broken cleaning bot that needs resetting, or an aquarium filter that needs changing. It's amazing how many chores she can find in a fully automated household. It's not like I can just go to the school pool either. They have full surveillance, 24-7. Any attempt to practice controlling my transformations could easily backfire. At least Jim doesn't ask any questions when I decline every one of his offers to take me to the pool for personal practice.

On the eve of the Solstice, I sit down on the living room couch for some light revision, but Jessica parades in and starts pacing about with her e-pad. She has switched from complaining about the Solstice to complaining about her "useless boyfriend" who is officially "missing in action."

"Seriously, like, where is he? I mean, he's the *guy*. He should be coming over to see me. He can hardly expect me to go outside in the these *dangerous* times."

"Duke can't leave the house either. He'd need to get his father to escort him," I say.

Jessica scoffs. "Seahorse crap, he's an Aqua8 Junior Cadet, not a civilian. He doesn't need an adult supervisor. Besides, I wouldn't expect you to understand. You had three guys pining for you and you snubbed them all. What's up with that? You'll end up dating seaweed some day."

I cut a face at her and go back to my studies. I'm perfectly happy that I don't have some seaweed-brain drooling over me.

Evening falls as Mrs. Queen sets the table on the terrace for a candlelit dinner. She has prepared a gigantic lobster which she serves on a silver platter. The candles shine golden and flicker in the wind. I try to smile and pretend that I'm enjoying this. In truth, the lobster tastes little better than the swamp soup from the FRS. I don't get how Jessica and Jim can eat it with so much enthusiasm.

After the meal we all go onto the lawn.

"Normally we would be on the beach tonight to celebrate," Jim says. "The Winter Solstice is a festival of hope and remembrance. All the families of Ararat gather together and each family member lights a lantern and sends it into the sky. We do so in remembrance of all those lost at sea and as a signal to sailors searching for safe shores. We all like to believe that there may still be civilized life out there other than ourselves. The lights on the water. They're how Adelia, Jess, and I first found Ararat, ten years ago." Jim lights four big floating lanterns and Jessica releases them into the air. We watch them soar away.

"You're not from here?" I ask.

"We came from far away on a wooden sailing boat," Jim says. "Unfortunately, resources ran out where we lived, and we had no choice but to attempt an overseas journey."

"But I thought that travel by boat across the ocean became impossible years and years ago because of the storms," I whisper.

"That's true," Jim says. "We were very lucky to acquire a vessel. And we didn't make it very far. By the time we got to Cape Harmony our ship was no longer seaworthy and most of the crew had died. We were fortunate to be taken in by the people here and to be assigned a home." Jim wraps an arm around me as I shiver in the cool night breeze. "You see, you don't have to be from Ararat to belong here."

I shoot him a grateful smile. For the first time since arriving here, I feel a little more at home.

*

The last three days of the vacation approach all too quickly. The curfew continues. As night falls on December 31, I sit on my bed chewing my fingernails. I *have to* get to the beach. Oceans knows what will happen if I don't manage to get a grip on my transformations. In a sudden fit of determination, I set my alarm for five o'clock. Tomorrow's weather is meant to be calmer than recent days have been. Perhaps there will be fewer patrol guards on the shore.

In the early hours of the morning, I slide out of bed and slip on the red swimsuit of the Barracudas. If anyone catches me, maybe I can talk myself out of it by saying I needed to practice for the Midterms. I tiptoe down the stairs and out the back entrance, then hurry along the footpath to Wrecker's Beach. The walk is faster than I remembered. A fresh, salty breeze blows from the sea. I stay hidden in the bushes around the beach, glancing around for Aqua8 patrols, but there's no one in sight. Quickly, I pull off my tank top and shorts and leave them hidden in the bushes then step barefoot across the sand.

The locked door of the Jet Ski hut creaks softly in the wind. I glance that way—then freeze. Someone has tossed clothes into the sand next to the hut. I sneak closer. They are blue-and-gray BDUs. Who has left those here? I look out to the waves. Dawn is just breaking. There's no one out there.

I turn and catch a movement from the corner of my eye— just in time to see the butt of a rifle heading for my temple. My arm snaps up in a block. Before I can marvel at the effect that Aqua8 training has had on my reflexes, my attacker pulls the rifle around my neck in a stranglehold. I thrust back an elbow and squiggle free. The wind is blowing from behind me, whipping my hair into my face. Blindly, I throw a punch in the direction of my assailant. Whoever I'm fighting grabs my wrist and tries to force me into an armlock. I free myself with a front flip and roll across the sand. A long leg hits me in the stomach. I fall back. A rifle clicks as it's cocked.

"Naya?" The girl in the black bikini opposite me lowers her gun.

"Soraya?" I stare at her, equally surprised.

"Couldn't keep out of the water either, huh?" Soraya grabs her BDUs, brushes back her long, wet hair then flings on her pants. "Sorry I attacked you—I thought you were a variant."

I am a variant. Probably. I don't say that.

"Let's get you out of here before my commanding officer sees us." Soraya pulls me into the bushes.

When I stare at her military clothes, uncomprehending, she adds, "I'm a Junior Cadet. I'm meant to be on patrol duty."

"Oh, right," I say. "I was just—"

"You don't have to make any excuses." Soraya looks at me with a frown. "I don't break government rules either, but it's totally unfair, right? I gotta wait for one of my moms to escort me to the school pool for personal practice while Borgman and Gallagher and all the Seals have private pools to practice in. How are we meant to perform as well as them in the upcoming race? If I don't make the freestyle singles, the Sharks are out."

I hurry to nod. "Yeah, that's right."

She hands me my clothes. "You better get out of here now. Patrols are about to change. I'm on duty again tomorrow at thirteen hundred hours—if you can get away."

"Thanks," I whisper.

"No, thank you, for standing up for me in the Initials."

I shrug. "I meant what I said. If you hadn't fallen, you'd have beaten me."

"Don't be silly, Naya. You did great." Soraya looks at me like she's sizing me up. "Listen, something was weird that day. After the race I checked my starting block. There was soapy liquid on it. Someone messed with it. The starting blocks get cleaned after every race—and not with soap. There's no way that liquid got there unless someone put it there. Just take care in the Midterms OK?"

"OK," I say. "Thank—"

She holds up a hand to stop me at the sound of a motorboat engine. "GO!"

I run up the hilly slope while Soraya flings on her jacket. With shaky knees I tread over the rocks. Sabotage in the race. As if I don't have enough to worry about already. And with Wrecker's Beach under permanent surveillance, how am I ever going to get into the water?

CHAPTER 15

— Rebels and Red Earth —

"Sooo good to finally see you!" Kayla flings her arms around our necks in the school entrance hall.

"Never thought I'd miss school so much!" Mia joins the group hug.

Kayla wriggles out of the group hug and holds up her e-pad. "And the exam results are in. Mia and I both got the grades we needed for our number one choices. And I heard Duke passed, too. Now we've just got to keep those grades until graduation."

Jessica checks her e-pad and lets out an excited squeak. "I got a B in physics, look!"

I wish I could share their happiness. I'm almost as tense as when I first arrived on Ararat. All I can think of is the next swim class. I didn't get the chance to go back to Wrecker's Beach — and that means I will have no idea what happens when I get into the water.

"I think I'm even happy to see Miss Li," Mia exclaims.

I sneak a peek at my grades. They're all As and Bs. While I look at them, my e-pad chimes. I tap on notifications. Janson's drawn up a personal swim timetable for me for the next twelve weeks until the Midterms. Thirty minutes of extra practice before the start of school on Tuesdays and Thursdays.

"You kiddin'?" Jessica exclaims, looking over my shoulder. "What am I supposed to do for that half hour?"

"Study?" I suggest.

Jessica glares at me.

She's still glaring when we walk into the pool hall in the afternoon. I sit down on the bench with the others and stare at the still, turquoise surface. I'm minutes away from finding out whether I'll grow a fishtail or not . . . Relax. I've been swimming in the pool for two months without my necklace and I haven't transformed—so far. I look across to the Seals' bench and meet Gillan's eyes. He holds my gaze with a tiny frown. Did he notice my shaking hands? I wish so badly that I could speak to him. Although I'm still kind of angry with him.

"Begin with four laps of warm-up then go straight into competition training," Janson calls. "Gallagher, meet me after class for a team strategy talk."

I line up with the others, making sure I'm last to the starting block. The water splashes as I dive in and moves smoothly around my legs as I glide through the pool. I switch to freestyle, relief coursing through me with every kick. If anything, swimming feels easier, having recuperated over winter break. At the end of every lap I glance down at my legs, but there's no sign that they are fusing together. I hold my breath and freedive the last lap. If panic is the trigger, I'm done for, but everything goes smoothly.

"Duke, Soraya, Shane, Theo, let's start with a freestyle race, fifty meters," Janson calls after the warm-up. The four students walk to their starting blocks. With the exception of Theo, they're all potential candidates for the freestyle laps of the mixed relay. I've discovered that swimmers don't have to compete in the same category for the Midterms as they did in the Initials. Marlo got knocked out of the boy's four hundred meter butterfly singles in the Initials but is now competing in the freediving singles, whereas Kayla has become my sub for the girl's two hundred meter butterfly race.

On the starting blocks, Theo Kingsley is adjusting his goggles. I wonder why Janson is holding back Gillan's usual sub, Torres. Duke steps from one foot to the other. He must have spent most of the vacation working out. His chest and upper arms are more pumped up than ever.

"Ready, take your marks, GO!" Janson's whistle blows and the four competitors dive. They resurface and the water foams white around them as the race begins. Soraya is only half a body length behind Duke, despite her worries about the lack of training hours. Shane is trailing close behind while Theo, who stepped in for Gillan, is last. The gaps widen as they flip-turn into the final length. Duke propels himself forward with almost superhuman strength then slaps his hand down on the rim of the pool, like he's trying to tear out a fistful of concrete.

"Yes!" He punches his fist into the air with a crazed grin. "I'm Emperor of the Ocean! Sultan of the Sea!" he roars.

"All right then, Sultan." Janson studies him with a frown as he pulls himself out of the water. "Cool off and make space for the freedivers."

Instead Duke squats down at the edge of the pool and taps Soraya on the forehead with his index finger. "When you mess with the best, you lose like the rest!"

"OK, that's enough!" Janson snaps.

Duke starts parading along the edge of the swimming pool, arms stretched out wide. "The Seals suck! Gallagher is toast! Barracudas rule!"

"ENOUGH!" Janson stands in front of him, her arms folded. "In this school we respect our opponents. Go walk it off outside."

Duke stares at her with bloodshot eyes, his chest heaving, like he's struggling to breathe. A strange expression comes over his face and all color drains from it. He lurches out of the swim hall, running for the locker rooms. Janson shakes her head.

"Wow, somebody needs to chill," Kayla says.

"You think the imposed isolation had psychological effects on him?" Mia ask.

We turn to Jessica, but she is just staring in disbelief as Duke bolts off. After him ghosting her for two weeks, this is the icing on the cake.

*

In the following days, the halls are awash with whispers about Duke's strange behavior. He's tense, erratic, sleep deprived, and keeps rushing out of classes. He'd probably be in a heap of trouble if he weren't Douglas Kallion's son.

Soraya jokes, "I bet he's skipping classes to get in extra training. I think he's trying to grow fins."

Jessica scowls.

Duke still hasn't spoken to her by next Monday, and she practically assaults him in the hallway. "Hey, Duke! Where've you been during the vacation?"

"I had to study," Duke says gruffly and turns away.

"Study, that's what made your biceps pop, really?" Jessica scoffs. "You could at least have visited, once! You know how I spent the Winter Solstice? At home. With Naya! Nice and romantic, isn't it?"

Duke shoots her such a dark look that she falls quiet on the spot.

"Whatever," Jessica whispers to me under her breath, but at lunch break she pulls me, Kayla, and Mia into the study garden. "All right, style squad, Duke's acting weird and I need to find out why. I mean, seriously, where's he going all the time?" She taps her e-pad. "First it was just lunch times, now he's even missing class—and did I tell you how he ghosted me?"

"Yeah. Twice," Kayla says.

Mia holds up four fingers and mouths, "Four times."

Jessica ignores her. "I tried to tell him this super cute story and he just walked right out the room, halfway through."

"Do you think it's the stress of the race?" Kayla asks.

Mia shakes her head. "Nobody can get that stressed out over a race."

I don't say anything. Duke's temper scared me right from the start . . . the week before the exams he already seemed jumpier than usual. It's just gotten worse.

The next day, though, Duke shows up wearing a neat, white shirt and holding a bouquet of red roses and walks right up to Jessica's desk. "I'm sorry I didn't come to see you. My dad had me on this special vacation training program—you know he can get pretty intense. Can you forgive me, Queen of my heart?"

Jessica huffs and tries to stay angry, but the whole class is aww-ing so she theatrically shakes back her hair and puts both arms on his shoulders. "Sure, I forgive you, you sexy studmuffin."

Things go back to normal, at least for everyone else. I no longer feel part of the group. A little because of what Gillan said to me, but mostly because I now know what I am. Every day that I get into the pool my stomach twists with anxiety. I'm dreading my swim classes more than my A8C training—which has actually let up a bit, since Calder is away, out at sea most of the time, leading the variant patrol. As the windy days pass and the Midterms get closer, my nervousness grows. We're practicing intensively for the Iron Teens now and twice the transformation nearly kicked in. Each time it happens, my heart freezes as my whole body is gripped in fear. It's just a matter of time before I turn into a mermaid, in public, by accident.

I want to do something, anything, to win back Gillan's trust, to get him to at least look at me again, but I don't know how. There's no way that I can go investigating, like he told me to, while a partial lockdown continues. If I were a Junior Cadet, I'd at least be allowed out on patrol duty, but the A8C never leave the military base during training. And if the chances of talking to Gillan were bad before, they're less than zero now. Since the Initials, the tension between the Barracudas and the Seals has increased. Although Gillan is in class more often, he is either studying or in the pool and almost always surrounded by his team. Normally I would be scared that the renewed team spirit of the Seals would provoke Duke into fits of aggression, but that doesn't happen. He still occasionally disappears at lunch time but he's gotten more discreet about it. Now that he and Jessica have patched things up, she no longer cares. She, Mia, and Kayla have resumed our lunch time "study" sessions without Duke, except that with the exams done, they are more like shopping sessions.

" . . . and the top is backless," Mia chatters one afternoon in March. "They have some at Lucy Love Lux in the mall. We can go after school and—"

"Hold it, girls, Duke hasn't even asked me to the Water Festival yet," Jessica interrupts.

"Why would he?" Kayla raises her brows. "That's not until the Summer Solstice. We're barely out of the windy season."

"Yeah, but no harm in asking early, right, Naya?" Jessica asks.

"Huh?" I look up. "I was thinking about swim practice."

Jessica scoffs.

I grab my sports bag. "Actually, I'm gonna hit the pool for extra training," I say and leave.

I've developed the habit of going to the pool during lunch break, ahead of the others. That way I can check that my legs are

OK before class. Since we're now midtournament, we have all our Tuesday and Thursday training sessions in the competition hall. As usual, as I walk along the side of the pool my eyes wander to Gillan's picture on the display boards that show each team's contestants. Today, for the first time, I notice the row of victory plaques next to them. They list the winners of the Iron Teens from previous years. Aidan's name jumps out at me from a green victory plaque of the Sharks that reads: Iron Teens Middle School Winner, 225 PI. I run my finger over the edges. Can it be that Aidan was like me? A variant?

I search the display and find his name again two years later, among the high school winners. It's followed by the black victory plaque of the Seals: Alexis Janson, 228 PI. I raise my brows. She and Aidan competed together?

"So, I guess someone mentioned your predecessor to you?" I look up and find Janson standing right next to me.

"Y . . . yes" I say, then glance back at the plaque. "Aidan was really from the Valley, like me?"

Janson nods. "They discovered his swim talent at an earlier age. He was seven when he first came to Ararat."

"Did you know him well?" I ask.

"He was in my year," Janson replies. "Star swimmer, but they never let him forget where he was from. Calder was in charge of the A8C training. She always gave him a hard time, pushed him to his limits."

"Kayla told me he drowned because he overexerted himself."

"That's what the medic on site said."

I try to read Janson's expression. Is she implying that there's more to it? I can't ask her. We're in the swim hall. Conversations are recorded.

"Did they try CPR?" I ask.

"They did. Aidan's girlfriend was swimming in the race with him. She tried to save him, but he was dead by the time she got him out of the pool."

"Oh. Right." I swallow.

Janson puts a hand on my shoulder. "Don't let anything the other students say bother you. This happened years ago. It was an accident. You're gonna do fine."

I force a smile. If Aidan really was a variant, what if his power was the reason he died? The reason he overexerted himself? He discovered his swim skills at an early age; I found out about mine only now and have had zero time to get used to them. What will happen in the Midterms?

The first students walk in and I join them, although my knees are shaking. I remember what Janson said to Gillan in the conversation I overheard. "She's stronger than Aidan . . ." What did they mean? I want to think that she and Gillan *know*. That they will help me somehow. But they were also talking about Alba . . . And Janson gave her an inhaler. Probably they think it's just a medical condition. After all, most of Ararat believes that variants are sea monsters. Why should Gillan and Janson think any different?

When the class is done, I do two more lengths of freediving. As usual, it helps clear my head a little, but my thoughts are still spinning as I round the corner to the locker rooms. Whoa —I stop in my tracks. These are the boys' locker rooms! I was walking along the spectator side of the pool. I take a quick step back. I'm trying so much not to look around that it takes me a second to register that Duke is the only one in there and that he is already dressed. Oh boy, he's the last person I want to walk in on. Quietly, I take another step back. Then I freeze in the doorway. Duke is holding a needle to his arm.

As he presses the plunger down, a blue liquid flows into his vein. He closes his fist and cringes as the liquid discolors his blood vessels. What is he doing? Is he sick? No, that can't be, then he wouldn't be acing the races. I think of his mood swings, his bolting from class. Maybe he's taking something to make his swim times better? Something to do with adrenaline? Mom once administered an adrenaline shot to my friend Johnny when he went into anaphylactic shock after he got bitten by a snake. She said adrenaline's for extreme cases, because it can have all sorts of side effects: breathing problems, pale skin, sweating, anxiety . . . Wouldn't that explain why Duke seems to be losing his self-control?

Duke puts down the needle and picks up his bag. Very quietly I duck out of the room. What now? He's obviously been keeping this a secret. But is this something bad? Could he get disqualified for it? I can't tell Janson. I have no idea how to talk to her outside of school surveillance. And I definitely don't want to confront Duke about it. So who can I trust with this?

*

"No, I doubt anyone has realized . . ."

The door to Jim's office is slightly ajar. I pause, wondering for the hundredth time if I'm doing the right thing.

"Nope, not even she herself . . ." I can hear him speaking, although there's no one else in his room. I realize that he must be on the phone. Access to the small telecommunications system on Ararat is one of the privileges that Jim enjoys as the deputy director of Zephyrus.

"Sure, that should be fine . . . OK . . . Understood . . . We'll talk later, Douglas."

Douglas? Duke's father! How could I be so stupid to forget! He and Jim are business partners in the Red Earth Project. I can't tell him about Duke now. If Jim tells Douglas, Duke will be in worse trouble than if the school finds out. I turn to leave, but my shoe scrapes against the door.

"Naya?" Jim leans over his desk. "There you are, birthday girl!"

Birthday girl? Is it March 20 already? Jim gets up and takes a small, gift-wrapped package out from his desk. "Happy seventeenth." He pulls me into a hug. "This is for you."

I tear open the blue wrapping paper decorated with orange seahorses, revealing a black velvet box. Inside is the most incredible watch from Galileo Tecc, stainless steel with a thin metal wristband and a clear blue face.

"This watch, Naya, is one of a kind. I personally made some adjustments to improve its features. It's waterproof to four thousand meters, withstands corrosion, shock, geo-magnetic pressures, and it functions as a depth-gauge. The dial can be read in the dark." He laughs at my puzzled look. "Horology—watchmaking—is just one of my many hobbies."

"Wow, thank you, this is so cool!" I hug him. With the exception of my trident necklace this is the best thing anyone has ever given to me.

168

He beams happily. "It's my pleasure, Naya. If you advance in Aqua8 as I think you will, it might come in useful."

He sits back at his desk. I notice that where his e-pad was there is now a small model of wooden sticks and white linen. It looks like the triangular shape I saw on the poster in the room next to his study. I carefully turn it around. There's writing on the side. *To Defy is to Deify.*

"It's a hang glider," Jim explains to me. "This little model is all that's left of one of my terminated projects for Zephyrus. Project Ikarus." He shoots me a shrewd glance. "I believe you might have seen the logo in the room next to my study?"

I blush. I opened that door by mistake on the day I arrived. "I'm sorry . . . I didn't mean to pry."

Jim smiles. "Curiosity is not a flaw. It is a virtue." He holds out the model in front of him. "Take this small model here for instance. If properly developed, it would have been able to fly, ascend to the skies and let us see the world from above. Imagine what secrets of mineral wealth we might have unearthed if we had been able to conduct an airborne geo-magnetic survey? But unfortunately the government saw no use for an invention of this nature. As you know, resources are limited; they can't be risked on a wildcat venture into the unknown." Jim sighs and places the model back on the desk. "Let the government hope that its lack of curiosity will not be its downfall one day." He winks at me. "Now, unless I'm very much mistaken, Adelia has organized a birthday cake!"

*

"No, I don't know the name of your 'favorite long one,' Dr. Pescatori!" Duke snarls at our marine biology teacher the next morning.

There's a giggle among the students.

Dr. Pescatori, who is pointing to an identification chart of the ten deadliest fish in our oceans, frowns. "The needlefish is considered by some more dangerous than sharks, Mr. Kallion, because of its ability to jump out of the water at thirty-seven miles per hour. Its sharp beak can be like a spear and has caused fatalities in humans. You'd do well to take this information seriously."

Duke scoffs and wriggles his feet under the table. I bet he's about to rush off again. Sure enough, Dr. Pescatori has barely turned his back when Duke snatches up his bag and bolts out of the classroom.

On the spur of the moment, I pocket my own e-pad and raise my hand. "Dr. Pescatori, could I go to the nurse please? I've got a headache."

Dr. Pescatori glances at me briefly. "Of course, Naya."

"Thank you." I get up and hurry out of the classroom. If I can't tell anyone about Duke, then I'll have to find out by myself what's going on. After all, as Jim said: curiosity is not a flaw, it's a virtue. I hurry down the hall after Duke as he's taking the elevator to the first floor. He's leaving the school? That's why none of us can ever find him. He's not on school premises. He's probably on the way to his EV right now. I hurry along the fourth floor. There's another elevator near the back entrance. If I'm quick, maybe I can beat him to it. Duke always parks at the edge of the parking lot, near the trees by the back exit.

The elevator door dings and I jump outside. *"Warning: state your reason for leaving the premises outside of permitted hours,"* a robotic voice rings out as I press my thumb against the scanner by the exit. I key in 1 for medical reasons and say, "I need fresh air." The door opens while a new message flashes across the screen: *checking air filters for possible malfunction.* I ignore it and go outside. Duke has stopped, a few yards away, and is fishing around his bag for his keystick. Using the EVs for cover, I sneak around to his usual parking spot then crouch down behind his blue-and-turquoise vehicle. What now? My eyes wander to the trunk. I hesitate for one moment. What am I getting myself into?

I ease the trunk open and slip inside. It clicks shut as I pull it down behind me. Oceans, I hope it opens from the inside! And what will school surveillance think of me hiding in the trunk of a car? Will they send someone after me?

The EV wobbles as Duke gets in and starts up the engine. With screeching tires, we speed out of the parking lot. The vehicle glides along smoothly. Then suddenly it jolts and gravel scrapes under the wheels. A moment later, the whole EV tilts diagonally and I know we're going uphill. Where in the world —Ow! My head connects with the lid of the trunk as we bump over a big rock. I suppress a shout of pain. A minute later we hit another, bigger one. With a muffled grunt, I rub my head. This had better be worth it. I push my feet out forcefully, against the rim of the trunk. I don't want to crash against the lid, it might open and then I'll go flying. At last the road evens out. I breathe a sigh of relief as we pull to a halt.

Now I just hope that Duke won't dump his bag in the trunk. I hold my breath while I hear the driver's door open and close, but the crunch of Duke's footsteps quickly distances itself from the vehicle. Fumbling for the lock, I find a latch and it clicks open.

I gasp. We're outside Ararat, on a small mountain plateau. A few green shrubs are blocking my view. I climb out of the trunk and shut it behind me, then crouching by the wheel arch, I peer around the blue-and-turquoise EV.

Duke is standing beside a black SUV parked on the rocky slope, his back turned. There is a second person with him. Douglas Kallion. And behind them . . . is the cable car station! Duke took me straight to it. A thousand feet or so above us lies Mortlake Industries. And down below runs the street that I was walking along when I saw the face in the bushes. Suddenly I wonder if it's all connected: Mortlake, the cable car, the dead body . . .

"You're cutting it close!" Douglas Kallion sounds very angry. "You know we need to keep to the exact timing. An error at this stage could be catastrophic."

"I don't care!" Duke shouts, his voice quavering. "The effects are getting too strong. I . . . I can't control them."

"Quit whining," his father cuts across him.

"No!" Duke suppresses a sob. "I'm through with this."

"You're through with nothing!" Douglas Kallion snaps. "If you want to continue in Aqua8 . . ."

I strain my ears to hear more, but their voices become fainter as they move away, toward the stony platform of the cable car station, perched on the mountain edge. I sidle around the bushes that dot the mountainside, trying not to make a sound as I follow them.

". . . you don't understand. I could hurt someone . . ." Duke's voice breaks.

"Then make it Gallagher," Douglas Kallion sneers. "Remember, you let a little FRS-girl get the better of you in a swim contest . . ."

My chest tightens. Suddenly I feel bad for Duke. Whatever this injection is, his father is the one pressuring him into taking it—and I might have made it worse.

The crunching of Douglas's and Duke's footsteps turns into solid thuds. They have moved into the cable car station. I hurry along the rocky surface and flatten myself against the concrete wall.

"Needed to proceed smoothly . . . Operation Neptune . . ." Douglas Kallion's voice is cut off by a mechanical whirr. Total silence follows. Did they get onto the cable car?

I risk a glance around the open door of the station. No. No cabin is passing by. And the station is empty, too. Only the unmanned controls, operating the cable car, are inside. Duke and Douglas are gone. It's like the earth swallowed them up. I run to the edge of the embarkation platform. There's no other way off it. And the cabins floating down the mountain are all empty.

I quickly step back. If Jessica is right and this leads to a government site I can't be seen here. Pondering what to do, I glance down the steep mountainside when I notice a container passing by about two hundred feet below, in a gorge with rock walls on either side. It's followed by another, and another. They're on a kind of conveyor belt and filled to the top with rusty soil. The conveyor belt does a U-turn right here, below me. When the containers reach that spot, they are pushed one by one onto a turning disk, which empties them into waiting trucks. The empty containers then continue their path back down the mountain, while the trucks drive up a winding dirt track that leads out of the gorge, toward Mortlake. A trail of dusty earth is left behind them. I marvel at its unusual reddish hue. Then it hits me . . . Red Earth! This must be the new energy resource that everyone on Ararat is talking about. But where does it come from? I look down the slope to follow the track of the conveyor belt, but the gorge is too narrow and steep for me to see anything.

Has the government got some sort of secret facility there? I should get out of here. But I'm right at the place that Gillan told me to investigate . . . I won't easily get another chance like this . . .

I look down the slope, to the empty Red Earth containers, rattling along on the conveyor belt. An idea forms in my head. I clamber down the mountain side, whirling up dust and pebbles as I skitter down the slope. Casting one look around to make sure I'm alone, I rush to the conveyor belt. Just as the next container stops in front of me, I jump onto the belt and pull myself over the rim and into the empty container. Red dust rains down on me as I crouch inside. The container rattles on, down the mountainside. Above me, on either side, the rocky slopes of the northern mountains pass by. The container tilts at every bend, so much that I'm scared it will topple over. With a jolt it comes to a stop, snaps another two feet or so forward, and drops onto some kind of metal surface.

"Hey, get these into the loading area, quickly!" a voice right above me shouts. I look up at a uniformed guard in khaki-and-beige BDUs. I squeeze deeper into the container. If the guard turns around, he will see me either way, but his gaze is fixed on a point in the distance. Metal scrapes and with a jerk the container moves forward again. I hear the sound of hacking, digging, and metal hitting rocks. All around voices echo.

How am I gonna get out unseen? The hacking and digging gets louder. There must be about a hundred spades and pickaxes at work all at once.

Am I in a labor camp? The one place I've been dreading? But why would Gillan act as if they were a big secret? Besides, I know people who got sent to labor camps. They were made to work in factories, not up in the mountains. So what is this place?

A scream rings out, followed by a thunderous clatter of metal and angry shouting.

"Careful, you idiots!"

Hasty footsteps pound from all directions. I peak over the rim of the container. Men and women in ragged clothes are running toward a stack of metal pipes that has fallen over. Around them, armed guards are barking orders. I leap out of the container and dash past piles of Red Earth, hiding behind some rusty machinery. While everyone's attention is still on the accident, I take a closer look at my surroundings.

I'm on some sort of mining site. Guards and workers and piles of earth are everywhere. The enormous canyon base that we're in is surrounded on all sides by steep, rocky mountains that form a natural enclosure. Pacing up and down a semicircular footpath, ten feet above, are armed guards with submachine guns. I check behind me, but it's all clear. The footpath doesn't run along the higher, northern side of the canyon.

"Back to work!" a guard shouts. At once the men and women who rushed to the site of the accident fall in line and file into one of the tunnels that open into the canyon. They're not alone. There are more tunnels. And more men and women—even children. They are staggering along numbly, their clothes torn, their faces worn and weathered from the heat. All are covered from head to toe in the reddish dust that is mined here. Their skin is tanned from the sun, like the face I saw in the bushes. I draw a sharp breath.

The man hiding there must have been one of the workmen who are forced to mine the Red Earth. He must have escaped and the Ararat border patrol shot him. But who are these people? There isn't a single familiar face. No one I know from the FRS or the Valley. And some of the children here don't look older than ten. No one ever got taken at that young of an age. An old woman staggers and a guard raises a whip and brings it down on her shoulders. I wince. Jim works on the Red Earth Project. Does he know what's going on here? Does anyone outside the military know what is going on here?

"Move!" The guard shouts. He raises his whip at a little boy with smudges of dirt on his face and Red Earth in his blond hair. The boy stumbles, holding up a long column of workers who are carrying baskets out of the nearest tunnel entrance.

"I said, *move!*" The guard brings down his whip on the boy's back. The boy tries to hurry ahead but falls down, spilling Red Earth everywhere.

"You lazy brat . . ." The guard snarls in disgust. He whips the boy—again and again—until blood starts seeping through the boy's torn shirt. The rest of the prisoners move along, their faces expressionless.

"That's what you get for your clumsiness," the guard barks.

The kid spits a mouthful of blood at him. "Go to the depth of the ocean, saltlicker!"

The guard rips a pistol from his belt.

"NO!" I shout and leap in between the kid and the guard.

A shot snaps into the ground as I skid to a halt, whirling up a fine cloud of dust.

"STOP! State your name and prisoner number." The guard points his gun to my chest, confused.

I don't even dare to breathe. What have I just done? I must look just like one of the prisoners, in my dusty clothes. My heartbeat pounds like a wave through my head.

"Answer!" the guard shouts.

I close my eyes. This is where I die.

"Cadet!" The guard freezes at the shout from my left. So do I. I know that voice. My lips tremble with relief, but I don't dare move.

"There you are. I was wondering where you'd run off to."

I feel a clap on my shoulder as Gillan appears next to me. I stare at him, wide-eyed. He's in khaki-and-beige BDUs, a gun strapped to his side. He gives me a tiny smile, then barks, "What kind of attire is this, Cadet? Where's your uniform? You realize you almost got shot in that outfit?"

"Sorry . . . sir," I spit out.

He waves at the guard. "Newby. Saltwater for brains."

The guard lowers his gun and looks at the other patrols. "Don't bother training this one, Lieutenant. She ain't gonna be around for long."

They crack up in raucous laughter.

Gillan gives them a placatory smile, then he guides me away across the canyon. "You gotta be out of your mind," he mutters under his breath.

"That boy," I gasp. "He was gonna kill him . . ."

"I know," Gillan says grimly.

"Can't you do someth —" I start.

"Better than what you just tried?" Gillan walks along briskly, eyes straight ahead as he ushers me toward the cable car. "You nearly got yourself killed in his place. What are you even doing here?"

"Investigating. Like you told me to."

"I told you to ask questions, not to get yourself shot," Gillan hisses. He takes in my dusty clothing. "Did you get here in the transport containers?"

"How else?" I whisper. "What is this place?"

"Not now," Gillan whispers back. Checking that none of the guards are in earshot, he adds, "Meet me at Breakers Cove, the second bay left of Ararat Harbor, during Marlo's birthday party, on the day of the Midterms. Seven o'clock. Bring a swimsuit. And don't walk. The main streets are watched by drones."

"Yeah, I noticed."

He escorts me past the guards at the cable car entrance and opens the barrier. "Back to base, Cadet. I catch you in civilian clothing again, it's the brig. You look like a sewer rat! It's a wonder you're still alive."

"Guess I was born lucky." I look back at him. Then the cabin tilts and I am pulled back up the mountain, toward Duke's EV that might or might not still be there.

CHAPTER 16

— The Midterms —

"Hey, Dr. Pescatori, who would win in a fight between a seal and a barracuda?" Marlo calls out in marine biology.

Everyone breaks into nervous laughter. Tensions are running high with only one day to go until the Midterms.

In the hallway after class, Kayla asks, "Naya, are you coming to Marlo's party after the competition?"

"Sure, I love birthday parties!" I say.

Jessica looks like I slipped a big piece of eel into her combo-grain. She puts on her glossy smile. "Why wouldn't she, Kayla? She's 'Fun Naya' now . . ."

"How did you know it was Marlo's birthday?" Mia asks.

"Oh, he —" I begin.

"Yo, Borgman!"

We're interrupted by a sudden shout. Duke's cornered Shane Borgman by the lockers. "Coach said you dropped out of the relay. What's the matter? Scared of a little competition?"

Shane shrinks back. "Just doing what's best for my team."

Kayla and I exchange a worried glance.

"What's going on?" Mia whispers.

"Shane told Janson yesterday that he wanted to pull out of the freestyle leg of the relay, because three races are too much for him," Kayla whispers back, hurriedly. "He just wants to focus on the Iron Teens and the freediving singles."

"Think you're gonna help your team by running, Borgman?" Duke grabs Shane and lifts him up by the collar, pushing him against the lockers. "You a coward, like Gallagher, Borgman? You a coward?"

Shane gasps. "Just . . . let it . . . be . . ."

"Huh, Borgman? I can't hear you, Borgman." The blue veins in Duke's neck begin to show.

Jessica's hand has flown up in front of her mouth. It's one of the few times that I've witnessed her be quiet for more than thirty consecutive seconds.

"All right there, Shane?" Gillan casually walks over to the lockers. "Looking a bit run off your feet."

Duke spins around, eyes popping. "Gallagher!" He flings Shane aside. "What rock did you climb out from under?"

Gillan gives a funny little smile that I've noticed when he has to deal with teenage stuff. "*Mariners Reef Two*, our shore patrol boat."

Duke's face takes on a deeper hue of red. "Sure as saltchuck, Mr. Wit would throw a joke before a punch!"

"You should try it, too, some day," Gillan says. "It's very stress relieving."

"Oh, that's real convenient," Duke hisses. "Gallagher the hero, Gallagher the defender of Ararat. What a bucket of bilge water! Gallagher the coward, more like. Gallagher-I-better-not-turn-up-to-swim-training-cos-Duke's-gonna-whip-my-ass-and-hand-it-to-me-on-a-PLATE! Yeah, that's the REAL Gallagher, all right."

Gillan cocks an eyebrow. "We done here, Duke?" He turns to walk off.

Duke grabs him by the shirt and pulls him back round. "No, we're not done, Gallagher. You, me, swim hall, now."

"Not gonna happen," Gillan says.

Duke's knuckles turn white. "How'd you think your daddy would feel if he saw the coward you've become?"

Flushes of red appear on Gillan's cheeks. "You really wanna do this now?"

Duke spits out, "Janson only favors you because you're a washed-up whelp without a mother!"

Gillan draws a sharp breath. He would look calm if it weren't for his right hand, which is clenched into a fist and shaking. For a second, his eyes wander to me and I feel like he's controlling his temper just for me—which is stupid, because I'm standing here with his rivals and he doesn't care about me at all.

"You should worry about your own family, Kallion." Gillan brushes Duke's hand off and turns away.

Fuming, Duke bounces on the balls of his feet and with a sudden burst of fury he lunges at Gillan.

"Look out!" I shout, but nobody hears it, because Gillan has already stepped aside.

Glass shatters as Duke's fist collides with the lockers at full force. Duke holds his bleeding fist under Gillan's face. "This isn't over."

"Careful," Gillan says. "Junior Cadets are training in the sea this afternoon. Blood attracts sharks!" He turns and walks off while around us, alarms start blaring.

"Disturbance detected in area fifteen . . . hallway in lockdown."

"DU-UKE!" Jessica and Mia moan in chorus.

Duke is still watching Gillan walk away, muttering, "Next time, Gallagher. You can't hide behind Aqua8 forever."

I shiver. I think there's nothing Duke wouldn't do to win against Gillan.

*

The gray clouds of another pre-Blue Out crown the sky on the morning of the Midterms. This black weather gives me the creeps. Even the cheers of the audience seem subdued as we exit the locker rooms. I take my place on the bench and glance around at the other teams. I don't see Gillan anywhere. Where is he? He can't be late? Tournament rules are very strict, and he is the captain of the Seals . . .

Next to me Duke wriggles his foot. "Come on, Gallagher," he mutters.

Someone emerges through the spectator entrance. Duke tenses, but it's only Coach Milkins who walks in, a whistle around his neck.

"Contestants for the boy's freestyle, line up!" he calls.

Elijah Goldstein gets off the Sharks' bench while Theo Kingsley gets up from Seals', and they walk to the starting blocks.

"Are you kiddin' me!" Duke jumps up. "I'm not competing if Gallagher isn't!" Before anyone can stop him, he rushes to Coach Milkins. "I'm not swimming against a SUB!"

"Mr. Kallion, go back to your starting block." Coach Milkins points to the red block of the Barracudas.

"NO!"

I'm worried Duke will lift him up and toss him into the pool.

"Go, find Gallagher, or get out of my way!"

Coach Janson rushes over. "Snap out of it, Kallion, the Seals can put forward whomever they want."

Duke's eyes are bulging. "Funny how they're holding back their *team captain*!"

Janson cuts him off with military strictness. "On your starting block. Now!"

Duke falls quiet and lines up with the others. I breathe a sigh of relief when Coach Milkins blows the whistle for the start of the race.

While Duke, Theo, and Elijah churn up the water in the pool, I enter the locker rooms to prepare for my own race. A quick shower . . . rearrange my swim cap . . . tighten my goggles . . . GermAloid . . . I'm so nervous, I check everything twice.

"Contestants for the boy's butterfly!" The announcement rings from the hall.

My turn is coming up. I stow my necklace in my locker. With one last nervous tug at the straps of my swimsuit I walk back into the competition hall. My foot slides across the plastic, turquoise floor mats. Whoa . . . ! I almost slipped. I tell myself to relax. If I'm like this during the butterfly singles, I'm gonna risk dropping an easy victory.

At the far end of the hall the result of the boy's butterfly race flashes up on the scoreboard.

RAY VICTORY: LESLIE PETERSON

I walk up to the pool. On the last step my foot slips and I kick the starting block. Ouch . . . ! OK, focus.

"Competitors take your places," Coach Milkins calls out. "READY, TAKE YOUR MARKS, GO."

He blows his whistle. I jump—but it's like someone has pulled the floor away from under my feet. The swim hall spins, and I plummet toward the pool in a front flip. Water splashes as if I cannonballed, and I'm underwater, surrounded by bubbles. My knee connects with something solid. Right by my face I see the turquoise tiles of the pool wall. I twist and force myself to the surface. As my ears clear, I hear three sharp blasts of a whistle, the signal that the race has been called off.

Then the pain kicks in. I must have hit my knee against the wall—only it felt rubbery, jellylike . . . Oh, no! No, no! Don't panic! I look down in the blue water, where the bubbles are clearing and see a bluish-turquoise shimmer.

"Naya . . . Naya, are you OK?" The boys who have already lined up for the breaststroke race stretch out their arms to pull me out.

"No, no, wait!" I scream. I stare at my legs and breathe a sigh of relief. Their skin color is normal.

"Stand back." Coach Janson pushes her way past the boys. "Naya, what happened? Are you all right?"

"I d-don't know . . . My knee. I knocked my knee." My voice is trembling from the shock.

Coach Janson makes me stretch out my leg. "How did this happen?"

"I guess I lost my concentration . . . my feet felt all slippery— you always did say I hit the water like a log."

Janson looks like she would laugh if the situation wasn't so serious. Cautiously, she feels the area around my kneecap. "How's that?"

I wince. "Not too bad."

It doesn't hurt as much as I expected. My legs must have transformed slightly on impact.

A crowd of students has gathered around me.

Kayla shakes her head. "It looked like you were gonna break your neck. You're insanely lucky."

Marlo nods. "Yeah, that was proper kamikaze."

"I . . . just slipped," I whisper, feeling incredibly stupid.

Janson frowns. "If that was a slip, I'll eat my swim cap. You went into the pool head over heels." She looks at Soraya, who has joined the crowd around me. "Something isn't right . . ."

She brushes her hand over the red starting block of the Barracudas. It comes away covered in soapy liquid. The students around us let out a murmur of surprise.

Janson turns to me directly. "Naya, what did you put on your feet?"

"Just GermAloid," I say.

"Could you have confused it with soap?" Mia asks.

"NO!" I burst out. "I'm not stupid."

"Quiet, quiet," Janson interrupts. "Kayla, take my keycard and get Naya's GermAloid from her locker."

Kayla nods and runs off.

I vaguely register Coach Milkins making an announcement to the audience. "Ladies and Gentlemen, please excuse the slight delay. We will continue the race in just a moment."

Kayla returns with the bottle of GermAloid from my locker. Janson takes it and pours some into her hand. It shines like a rainbow and as she rubs her fingers together, it pulls soapy strings between them. There's a burst of outrage among the Barracuda team.

"Sabotage!"

"Someone swapped the gel!"

"It must have been a girl . . . from another team."

"GALLAGHER!"

I jump as Duke bawls out the name. Duke's head snaps around to the locker rooms.

"Duke, GG can't—" Mia starts.

But Duke isn't listening. "It's Seals' SABOTAGE!" He hurtles toward the girls' locker rooms.

"KALLION, STOP!" Janson jumps up. "If you go anywhere near the girls' locker rooms, I will have you removed from the swim squad for . . . for gross indecency."

Duke halts in his tracks.

"Gillan isn't even in school today," Janson snaps. "He's at an Aqua8 officers' meeting. He told me weeks in advance. The Seals had to rearrange their whole team and get special permission to allow a sub to swim in the Iron Teens." Janson is fuming, though whether about Duke or about General Calder messing up her race day I'm not quite sure. "Now pull yourself together. You're team captain and one of your swimmers is injured."

Duke slouches over to where I'm sitting. "Sorry," he huffs. "How are you?"

"Hurt," I say through gritted teeth.

"I don't think that your knee's broken," Janson says, "but we should ice it. And you're not swimming the butterfly singles, that's for sure." She waves over Kayla. "Sommers, you're up.

I'll talk to the principal. With two of three Iron Teens swimmers out, I'll tell him to move the race." She walks past Coach Milkins, who is putting a cleaning bot onto the Barracuda starting block.

"No!" I push myself off the floor. "You know he won't do it. I can swim the race!" My knee is pounding from the effort of standing up, but I ignore it. I don't want Janson to get in trouble because of me again.

She scrutinizes me for a moment. "We'll let the doctors decide," she says at last. "Duke, rearrange your relay team."

I let Zeke put my arm around his shoulder and hobble to the Barracudas' bench with his help. Kayla steps onto the starting block while Mia wraps an icepack around my knee.

"Kayla's got this," Zeke says. "She's a total allrounder."

I still don't dare to look at the pool as the whistle blows. What will happen to me if I don't stay in the butterfly singles? I don't even want to think about it. I listen to the splashing water.

"Seven seas, Naya, look, she's not last," Mia squeaks. I peek up and indeed Kayla is right behind Ayumi Tanaka. There are only three swimmers, of course, because we are in the second stage of the knockout tournament, but Alba Williams from the Seals is coughing and clutching her chest in between strokes and doesn't look like she is gonna catch up.

"Look, Jess! She's not losing!!" Mia shouts, but Jessica is standing by the window of the hall, alone, looking away. Is she worried that me not swimming the relay will put more pressure on her?

SHARK VICTORY: AYUMI TANAKA flashes up on the scoreboard.

The medic comes over and holds some kind of device over my knee. It bleeps and flashes up the word *Scanning*. I hold my breath that it won't come up with any fractures—or with anything unusual in the bone structure, but before I can read the results, he rips it away and heads over to Janson. I see them gesturing furiously. The medic returns.

"You're all good. No serious injury detected." He hands me a fresh bottle of GermAloid. "Make sure you apply this before you enter the pool, contestant." He walks off.

"All good, my ass!" Janson rips the bottle of GermAloid from my hands. She looks as if she'd like to throw it at the medic. "DON'T put that on your feet."

"It's . . . OK." I lift my legs off the bench and get up gingerly. "I . . . think I can actually do the relay."

"Forget about the relay," Janson says. "We need you fit for the Irons." She puts a hand on my shoulder. "Rest a bit more, then do a few warm-ups, but nothing that strains the knee too heavily. We have one hour until the race. Let's make the best of it."

I nod and wait for a moment then begin my exercises. As I glance at the audience I catch a glimpse of Arlo. He is looking my way. I shoot him a shy smile. Somehow seeing him boosts my confidence. Then I wonder why he's here. Gillan isn't competing today.

"COOTE, QUEEN, CARTER, KALLION," Coach Milkins calls up the names for the relay. I keep my focus on my stretches. The race begins. I let the splashing water and the shouts of the audience blur into background noise. One left stretch, one right stretch. At last clapping erupts and I look up at the scoreboard.

SEAL VICTORY: RELAY TEAM

My heart turns to ice. Are we still in? Did we come second or did the Sharks beat us?

Duke pulls himself out of the pool. His skin is bright red, muscles bulging. "Course they'd win!" I hear him mutter, as he walks past me to our bench. "With Gallagher cheating!"

"Stop, already!" Shane Borgman jumps in his way. "You know it wasn't Gillan who swapped Naya's footgel."

Duke rounds on him. "Who was it, then? Someone from your team?" He pokes his index finger at Shane's chest. "Or you? Was it you?"

"No!" Shane takes a step back.

I hold my breath, hoping that they won't start a fight now, but Duke just stares Shane down then marches on. I glance at the audience. A few people are cheering and holding up Shark banners.

"How did we do?" I call to Mia, as she passes.

"We're second. All good," she smiles at me.

"Thank Oceans!" I close my eyes and try to shut out everything around me. Twenty minutes to the race. I sit down again and try to relax. I open my eyes just as Principal Preen gets up and makes a special announcement. Something about Torres stepping in for Gillan, doing your duty and Aqua8. Then Coach Milkins calls out our names. "DELORA for the BARRACUDAS, TORRES for the SEALS, BORGMAN for the RAYS."

My knees are shaking like leaves as I walk to the starting block—both of them, not just the injured one. Next to me, Shane looks equally rattled. I think the confrontation with Duke was the final straw for his nerves. Banishing that thought from my mind, I step onto the starting block. My leg wobbles as I bend my knees. It will have to be a quick dive. I only hope that I won't half-transform again.

"READY, TAKE YOUR MARKS, GO." The whistle sounds. I front dive into the water. As soon as I start swimming, I almost scream from the pain. This silly frog-style angle is killing my knee. I hate breaststroke! Gritting my teeth, I kick out and continue. Maybe it is the adrenaline or the cool water but slowly my pain is numbed and I can bend my leg more easily. Oceans, I hope I'm not covered in blue scales. Just before the freediving my stroke feels almost normal—but I finish a quarter length behind Torres and Shane. I take two hurried breaths, inhalations longer than exhalations, and dive seconds after them.

For a moment I'm worried that I rushed the breathe-up and will run out of air or black out, but the stillness of the water calms my mind and my confidence returns. I press my palm against the touchpad, resurface, draw two deep breaths and dive again. It's almost as if I didn't need the stop. I look around for Torres and Shane, but there is only one shape to my right now. Did Torres get so far ahead that it's just between me and Shane? I struggle to the end of the lane, my lungs bursting from fright—I shouldn't have looked. But as I resurface, I catch a glimpse of Shane, treading water at the twenty meter marker. There's a defeated expression on his face. He didn't make the freedive! But . . . he's really good at freediving. Duke must have unnerved him so much that he messed up his breathe-up.

To my left, a huge splash spurs me into action as Torres begins the butterfly. I fling myself into the stroke. It was him next to me, not Shane. He's so close, I've actually got a chance at catching up. Suddenly the thrill of the race takes over. It's only on the flipturn that I realize I don't have to do this. Shane is out. Torres and I have already made it to the Finals.

But I'm ahead. Head spinning, muscles aching, I finish the butterfly laps. My knee screams in pain as I switch to freestyle. I know what I'm doing is crazy. I could turn. I'm straining my injured leg without reason, but I swim on and make the first flipturn ahead of Torres.

"Go! Go!" Garbled shouts from the crowd reach my ears. Torres is catching up again. He's faster than I am in freestyle. My breath almost catches in my lungs from the effort of staying in the lead. I cough and choke in the splashing water.

"What . . . you doing!" I hear Janson shout. ". . . slow down!"

But the temptation is too big. I can win this!

In the last quarter length of the race, Torres almost draws level with me. I remember Duke's freestyle races and hurl myself forward in my final stroke. My hand slaps down on the touchpad just as Torres pulls his arm around.

BARRACUDA VICTORY: NAYA DELORA flashes up on the scoreboard.

I can't believe it. My name is up there. I won. I won an Iron Teens race!

Janson runs up to the poolside as I climb out. "You're crazy, kid! Totally crazy."

Next to her Duke leaps into the air, throwing his fists up. "BARRACUDAS!! WE WON!!! BARRACUDAS RULE!!!"

Marlo and Zeke high-five and shout, "Barracud-errrs!" And it's clear from the points on the scoreboard.

BARRACUDAS: 34
SEALS: 32
SHARKS: 28
RAYS: 20

We have taken the lead over the Seals!

As the shouting finally dies down Janson pulls me aside.

"Wrap up in something warm and make sure you rest that leg." Then she claps me on the shoulder. "Well done, Naya!"

I smile as I head to the locker rooms. It's surprising how little I feel the pain. It must be the adrenaline. I shower, get dressed and walk onto the lawn in a slight daze. The school has organized a barbecue, like after the first race, only this time the decorations are red. A huge banner reads CONGRATULATIONS BARRACUDAS! Principal Preen is getting ready to make a speech. I look around for the others, but there are only adults, parents, and middle school students around.

"Congratulations, Naya, quite remarkable, your victory," an icy voice says. I find myself face to face with Douglas Kallion. "You have the whole mountain rooting for you—including my brainless son." I can almost feel his breath, his face is so close to mine. His little beady eyes are full of malice. "But you can't fool me—"

"Naya!"

I jump as Kayla rushes up to me. "What are you doing here? Come on, we're going to Marlo's! You don't wanna hang with the grown-ups. Mr. Kallion, excuse us!" She drags me toward the parking lot.

I throw a glance back at Duke's father. What did he mean by, "You can't fool me"? Does he know about me?

Jessica pulls a face as we arrive at her EV. She hasn't said a word since the race—which is more than unusual. "Let's go, Naya, you're with me, the guys have already left." She gets into the driver's seat.

"Jess, is everything all right?" I ask.

"Never better!" She gives me her fake smile. Together we take off toward Marlo's.

"Check out the Fists—of—Thu-u-u-nnnder!!" Marlo's voice rings out over the party noise as we arrive at his house, which is perched on a bend in the road just a little north of the Queen house. Duke is doing a keg stand on the lawn, balancing on two fists, guzzling beer through a tube. Marlo and Zeke and most of the Barracudas are cheering him on. Jessica follows my gaze with a mixture of pride and disgust. She parks on the road, in a row of identical looking, blue, green, and pink EVs and starts climbing the thirty foot grassy slope that leads up to the house.

"Eugh." She wrinkles her nose. "Walking!" It's the first thing she's said since we left the parking lot.

"Here's the champ!" Mia exclaims and throws her arms around my neck. "Oh, this is so wonderful. I wish we could celebrate on the beach like we normally do, but the curfew's still on. Hey, where's Kayla?"

"On her way," I say, then whisper, "What's up with Jess?"

"Nothing. Why?" Mia glances at Jessica and Duke, who are now standing apart from the others.

"Don't know. She was just . . ." I trail off. By the look on Jessica's face anyone would have thought that the Barracudas just suffered the defeat of the century. ". . . very quiet," I finish.

Jessica picks that exact moment to raise her voice so loudly that all of us hear it. "You just can't enjoy anything anymore, can you? It's all 'the race' and 'training' and 'swimming.'"

Mia raises an eyebrow at me.

"You spend more time with Naya than you do with me—and now you stop kissing me because you need to talk to Marlo about the stupid 'sabotage?'" Jessica draws sneer quotes in the air with her fingers. "Naya put soap on her feet. Get over it!"

"You're wrong!" Duke fires back at her. "Naya's footgel had a weird rainbow color—and why would Naya put soap on her feet?"

"Because she's from the F-R-S!" Jessica cries out. "They're stupid!"

A few people look from me to her. I try not to sound offended as I say, "Actually, I learned the difference between soap and GermAloid on my first day here, from that Ararat rhyme."

"What rhyme?" Marlo asks.

"The one that the automated showers sing," I reply. "You know, 'Remember to avoid mixing lotion, water, and GermAloid. Lotion makes you pretty, the way you want to be seen . . .'"

I break off, because the guys are staring at me, as though I've lost my mind. "Don't you know it?"

"What . . . pretty and . . . No!" Duke exclaims. "That's a girl's rhyme!"

"Yeah, my shower doesn't say that," Zeke agrees.

"So what are the substances you shouldn't mix?" Marlo asks.

Kayla groans. "Marlo, you grew up here."

"So what? Doesn't mean—" Marlo begins.

"Hey, guys!" Mia exclaims. "That's it. The liquid in Naya's bottle *was* GermAloid and lotion. When she stepped on the wet floor, it mixed with the water, and then it became hydro . . . hydrophilic." She beams at me as she remembers the word. "And that's why Naya slipped."

"Yeah, but who could have tampered with Naya's stuff?" Zeke asks. "The locker rooms are busy during the tournament and training. And after, Naya would have locked her things away or taken them home."

"Will you all STOP!" Jessica exclaims. "It was an accident, OK?"

"Taken them *home* . . ." Duke stares at her and his face suddenly drains of color. "Oceans alive, Jess. It was you."

Jessica gives an innocent smile. "I don't know what you—"

"Lotion, water, and GermAloid," Duke exclaims. "You got the idea from your shower. You put that mixture in Naya's bottle!"

Jessica backs off with a shrill laugh. "No!"

"What was the idea, huh?" Duke grabs her by the arm. "Injure Naya so bad that she wouldn't be able to swim anymore? Get her kicked out of Ararat? Is that what you wanted?"

I walk up to Jessica, shaking in anger. "Is that true?"

"Of course it's true!" Jessica spits the words out. "You FRS —dirt! You show up here, wear my clothes, steal my time with Daddy and with Duke, and you really think I'd like you? You gotta have seaweed for brains!"

"You envious little bitch!" Duke slaps her. "Sacrificing the Barracudas' chances of winning for your own personal revenge!"

Jessica takes a step back, scared, but still furious. "However long she spends in the water, Duke, doesn't get rid of the FRS dirt."

"SHUT UP!" Duke roars. "You almost ruined our chances of winning by taking out YOUR OWN TEAMMATE!"

An awkward silence descends. Duke's chest is heaving. Everyone is glaring at Jessica. She glares back. For a moment she looks like she'll claw at my face with her nails. Then she turns and struts off. "Fine! If that's what you want. You'll see I was right one day!"

I sink onto a nearby deck chair. I feel sick. I clutch a hand around my swollen knee. All of this, my accident, my near transformation in the pool, was Jessica's fault. Her stupid jealousy! All this time she was pretending to be my friend, when really she couldn't wait to get rid of me. This whole term . . . No, the past two terms! She must have tried the same trick before. In the Initials. But I dropped my bottle of GermAloid, Soraya stepped in it, and Jessica took out Soraya instead of me.

Marlo groans. "You think Preen *will* make us repeat the races now? If he finds out—"

Kayla cuts him off. "He can't find out. Think what will happen to Jess if any of the staff discover that she tried to sabotage Naya."

The rest of the Barracudas throw anxious glances around, to check if anyone overheard us—not all that unlikely considering the volume of Duke's voice—but all I catch are a few whispers.

"Duke's really losing it . . ."

"Are they breaking up?"

Duke glares at us as if daring anyone to speak. "You're right, this stays within the team!"

I suppress the burning tears in my eyes. I just want to get away, from the party, from everyone. Gillan was right, these people aren't my friends.

"Hey, it's OK . . ." Zeke walks over.

"No, it isn't!" I hiss. "Your mom won't get dragged into labor camp if you lose a race." I swallow down the lump in my throat. More than ever I want to see Gillan. To run away. But how exactly am I going to do that when everyone on the team is staring at me?

CHAPTER 17

— Port Fremont —

"Naya, brighten up, you take life waay too seriously." Mia drags me into the midst of bawling laughter and high-pitched yells. "This party is so wild and awesome!"

Has she already forgotten that Jessica just tried to knock me out of the race? Well, I guess she has, but then everyone around me looks pretty drunk.

Chastity suddenly hooks her arms through ours. "GG could totally throw parties like this. He's got that big place, all to himself. But he's all work, work, Aqua8, work. Booooring."

I force a nervous smile. Where did she pop up from? And why is she talking about Gillan of all people?

Chastity continues, "Is that Ayumi over there with Elijah . . . ? I wonder how Soraya is taking it . . . Ooh, Daphne looks fat in that top."

Mia giggles.

They're so hammered they wouldn't notice if General Calder walked in and joined the dancing. I try to free my arm from Mia when someone shouts,

"He's gonna do a double flip!"

Everybody rushes outside and stares up at Marlo, who leaps off a balcony into the swimming pool.

"Whooo!" A fountain of water explodes as Marlo hits the pool's surface, and everyone cheers.

OK, this is my chance. I dive through the crowd and hurry through the entrance hall and down the winding slope to the line of parked EVs on the road. Half of them still have their key-sticks in. Great! I jump into a baby-blue one, next to Jessica's and press the starter button. It's probably Kayla's, I'm sure she won't mind if I borrow it. Not that I have any idea how to drive, but if Jessica can do this, how hard can it be? I push down the right foot pedal. The EV gives a jolt and rattles backward toward the mountain edge. Whoa, brakes, brakes! OK, I move the lever between the seats from R to D and step on the pedal again. Slowly the EV starts moving again, downhill this time.

I've managed three wonky bends when I notice a pungent smell behind me. Eugh . . . it's like something died in the trunk. I brake and glance over my shoulder. A pair of dirty socks is stuffed between the backrest of my seat and the trunk lid. Kayla, seriously? Then I notice the name tag dangling off the keystick. PETERSON. Oh no, this belongs to my least favorite person from the Rays! I think about turning back, but decide that it's actually quite funny. I'm only borrowing his EV after all.

After two wrong turns, I find the road that takes me to the southern hilltop that overlooks Ararat Harbor. Gillan said Breakers Cove is the second bay to the south. Driving as fast as I dare, I zoom past the last houses into a forested area. A dirt track splits off the main road, winding its way downhill toward the sea and I take it. The EV does a little jump as I hit the gravel. Whoa, the steering on this thing is funny. I slalom around the trees, trying not to crash. A note flashes up on the front display screen: *Off-route alert. Deviation from cleared pre-registered itinerary detected. Please contact EV Control Center, Citizen ID 3892.* Oh no, I hope they can't trace the EV. I don't want Aqua8 guards chasing me down. I search for a way to turn the screen off, but the EV does another jolt and suddenly I'm heading for a cliff and the blue ocean. I hit the brakes. The EV skitters to a halt right on the edge of the cliffs. Phew! I jump out, anxious to put some distance between myself and this deadly vehicle — not to mention Peterson's socks.

"Hey there!" Gillan waves at me from a small motorboat as I climb down the slope. He's wearing a loose, white shirt and swim trunks.

"Got away easily?" He raises a curious brow at the vehicle.

"Just something I borrowed," I call back, clambering over the rocks in the bay.

He gives me a *nicely done* smile and holds out a hand to help me on board. The motorboat is completely white, no Aqua8 colors.

"Where did you get this?" I ask.

"Family collection." He casts a look at the rocky outcrops that hide the view to Ararat Harbor. The flood barrier is all the way down, but there are no other boats in sight.

"Let's get out of here." Gillan unties the mooring rope and turns on the engine. The motor roars to life and we glide out into the smooth, blue ocean. Away from the Elites, away from society, away from rules and regulations . . .

The wind ruffles Gillan's hair as the boat skips across the sea. In that moment he looks so independent, so outside the system, as if nothing on Ararat could touch him.

"How was the race?" he asks.

"OK," I say. I don't want to tell him about Jessica, or mention the fact that I beat the Seals in the Iron Teens. "How was your officers' meeting?"

"Boring." He grins.

I smile at him, uncertain. From the moment I arrived on Ararat, no, from the moment he rescued me in the Valley, there's been a part of me that wanted nothing more than to be with him. But now that we are here, heading across the open sea, I don't really know what to say. I sit back and let the wind tug at my clothes while we speed along the West Coast of Cape Harmony, toward the cape. In the distance a lonely seabird draws its circles in the afternoon sky. I draw in a breath of salty air, and it feels like a fresh breath of freedom.

How can I ask all the questions burning in my mind now that we are alone together? Does he know what I am? Can I trust him with it?

"You all right?" he shouts to me.

"Fine!" I shout back.

Gillan steers closer to land and eases off the throttle. The engine chugs and comes to a rest. We are just outside a bay, somewhere between Ararat and the Valley. The hills on the shore are gently sloping and covered in bracken and gorse. There is no sound now, just the sea lapping against the boat. The rays of the sun shimmer golden on the deep water. Gillan's eyes are bluer than the sea in the dimming light, like he is part of it all, the ocean, the waves. Is it me or is he looking at me really intensely?

I wish he would take me in his arms and kiss me. I wish this moment could last forever.

Then the waves turn the boat and spin us toward the gray shadows lengthening on the shore. I shiver. I can sense more than see the gloom that hovers here until I notice the remains of buildings, dotted here and there in the undergrowth. Rows of collapsed walls, crumbling gray facades, peeled and blistered by the sun. There are telltale scorch marks on them. More than that, I can feel the eerie silence. Whatever fire or destruction was at work here left more than visual marks.

"What is this place?" I ask.

"Port Fremont," Gillan says in a voice of reverence. "It was a coastal town, a settlement built by people who wanted to escape the confines of Ararat. They lived here in peace—until Governor Proctor ordered Aqua8 to burn it down and had every last man, woman, and child taken prisoner."

"Why?" I whisper.

"The people here allegedly provided refuge and assistance to genetic variants." Gillan's gaze rests on the destroyed houses.

The darkness of the town seeps into my heart. Variants? People like me? A whole town was eradicated because of them? How would Gillan feel if he knew that I was one of them?

"What are genetic variants?" I ask.

"Most on Ararat believe that they are sea monsters," Gillan says. "Lizards that live in the depths of the ocean."

"Are they?" I ask.

"No." Gillan gives me a small smile. "They're humans, whose lower part of the body has the shape of a sea creature. Mermaids, if you will."

I can feel the hairs on my arms rising. So it's true. This really is what I am.

"Where do they come from?" I whisper.

"Some people in Port Fremont believed that they have always lived in the sea, unbeknownst to us land dwellers. The more likely theory, which agrees with the findings of the Cape Harmony Research Institute, is that they evolved. That humans began to adapt to the watery environment and developed the ability to transform at will. According to this theory, humans developed a new gene. The variant gene. It spread and got passed on, dormant in some, activated during adolescence in others. Hence the term *genetic variant*."

"And . . . the Governor hunts them?" I ask.

"The Governor refuses to believe in the evolutionary theory," Gillan says. "He has stopped the Cape Harmony Research Institute from carrying out any further investigations and forbids all talk of it. His greatest fear is that one day the floodwaters will rise and Ararat will be conquered and destroyed by the Aquatic Other. He will stop at nothing to have every last genetic variant exterminated."

"But . . ." I start, "What if they're harmless?"

Gillan gives me a grim smile. "The head of Aqua8 decides what's harmless and what is not."

Enough said. I shudder as I think of Calder in her black uniform, asking me to shoot the cutouts of civilians. Aqua8—the military force that is supposed to save lives—destroyed a whole town.

I think of the boy in the mines, the boy who almost got killed right before my eyes. "Those people in the mountains . . ." I begin.

"Were the former inhabitants of this place," Gillan says. "The mere association with variants earned them lifetime imprisonment. They're slaves now, laboring for what the Governor calls 'The Greater Good.'"

"Do the people of Ararat know?" I ask, shocked.

"Some do, most don't." Gillan gives me a telling glance. "It is not common, as you may have noticed, for those with wealth and power to ask questions."

I look at my hands, silently. Now I understand why Gillan was so infuriated with me. He's seen how the whole mechanism inside of Ararat works.

"Did those people actually help variants?" I ask.

"The people of Fremont had great insight into the mysteries of our world, but there was never any proof of variants living in their community. A sighting was made a few months before the destruction of their town, but Aqua8 shot the creature instead of capturing it. The body sank before it could be retrieved. They never found out where it came from. There certainly weren't any variants in Port Fremont when Aqua8 burned it down."

"She could have had them shot," I whisper. "Calder could have had all these people shot."

Gillan gives a bitter laugh. "Yes, but then who would mine the Red Earth that is supposed to be the answer to our limited energy resources? No, the Governor didn't allow that."

"Why do you support the Governor?" I ask. "If he allows all these terrible things to happen?"

"He's the best of the worst," Gillan says. "The Governor may hate genetic variants, but he does not hate the people in the FRS, the former people of the Valley. Not everyone on Ararat shares his opinion."

Gillan starts the boat engine again and we glide past the barren shore. The ocean turns a deeper blue again and we leave the shadowy bay behind us. My heart jumps as we approach the Valley. Then the huge, gray structure of the flood barrier towers out of the water — the barrier that I used to stare at as a child on my way to school, the barrier that kept me safe throughout most of my life. It's strange to see it from the other side. Gillan slows the boat as we near it, steers closer to the shallows near the north section, and drops anchor. There are two metal gates in the abandoned concrete structure. High above is a pulley system and a crane.

"They're hatches to get the patrol boats to the other side," Gillan says, following my gaze. "Mostly intended for the search and rescue teams."

"Oh." I glance at them. I never even wondered how the Aqua8 patrol boats got from one side of the flood barrier to the other.

Gillan grabs two scuba tanks from a tank rack inside the boat. "We're gonna go for a short dive."

"OK." My reply is more breathless than intended.

Gillan looks up at me while assembling the gear. "You've never dived before, have you?"

I shake my head.

"Don't worry, it's easy." He talks me through the basics. "The mouthpiece that you breathe from is called the regulator and connects to your air tank, the BCD vest that holds the tank can be deflated or inflated and functions like a life jacket when you're on the surface."

When Gillan is sure that I've understood everything, he takes off his shirt and puts on his own gear. I strip down to my bikini, feeling very self-conscious. Even though we've had swim training together tons of times, Gillan is so close to me, and it is just the two of us this time. His hand brushes my chin as he helps me into the vest with the tank. I let him fasten the buckles and adjust the straps for me.

"All set?"

I nod. His eyes linger on mine. There's that intense look again. I think of the touch of his lips, soft, salty . . . I swallow.

He clears his throat and hands me a diving mask. "Check if the strap's right."

Maybe he doesn't feel the same way about me. I hope I'm not blushing again. I keep my head down as I put on my fins. Then I think of my necklace. Will he notice if I don't take it off? It's kind of odd not to, but I can't risk turning into a mermaid with him around. Not after all that I've just learned about variants. And if emotions play a role in my transformations, let's just say mine aren't exactly stable at the moment. I fiddle with the straps of my buoyancy control device, or BCD as Gillan called it, until I notice that he's still wearing his silver shark's-tooth earring, too. OK, if he keeps that on, he might not wonder about my necklace.

Gillan sits down on the side of the boat, gives me a thumbs up, and lets himself fall backward into the water. I do the same. The heavy tank pulls me down beneath the surface. I turn in an underwater somersault until the air in the vest makes me float up again. Inhaling through the mouthpiece, I listen to the amplified rattle of my breath. Next to me, Gillan releases the air from his vest and disappears beneath the surface. I copy him and sink down slowly. The air reaches my lungs reluctantly as I breathe only through my mouth. It's a scary feeling . . . like suffocating. I want to throw away the regulator and inhale the water, like I did when I transformed, but I'm pretty sure that with my necklace on it would kill me. So I do what Gillan told me to do and relax, taking calm, deep breaths. I feel a tap on my arm and see him on my right. He motions to dive toward the barrier. With a flick of my flippers I follow.

The pressure in my ears increases as we descend toward the seabed. The ocean is oddly quiet around me. There were so many voices and sounds when I was a mermaid. Where have they gone? It's as if I'm deaf all of a sudden and like we're moving in slow motion.

I flick out my flippers to swim faster. Gillan is ahead, close to the reinforced concrete flood barrier. I look at its dark structure rising vertically upward. I wonder where he's taking me. We're close to the middle of the barrier, where it's at its thickest. Gillan scans the wall searching for something, then stops. I look to where his outstretched arm is pointing and choke into my regulator. There's a huge, circular hole in the flood barrier wall. The edges are jagged, surrounded by thin, spider web-like cracks. Gillan waves me on and I see another breach, like the first, and another, until we get to a gigantic hole several yards wide. A whole whale could fit through here. The wall next to the missing sections is covered in black marks. Scorch marks.

Somebody sabotaged the flood barrier! I suppress a sob as the images of the destruction that The Valley Flood wreaked rush to my mind like a torrent of wild water. People screaming, crying in despair, bodies floating on the waves. All those deaths, the destruction of our homes, wasn't an accident. The flooding of the Valley, it all happened because somebody planned it. I cradle myself in my arms to shut out the world. My knees touch sand and stone. I must have sunk down to the seabed. I feel a touch on my shoulder. Gillan gently puts his arm around me and motions for me to surface. I nod and let him guide me back up.

"Who did that? W-What was that?" I stutter as soon as we surface.

"That is exactly what it looks like. Sabotage," Gillan says grimly.

"But . . . why . . . ?" I can barely get the words out.

"The flood barrier was rigged from the start. If ever resources ran low, Aqua8 would have received orders to set off the explosives and kill everyone in the Valley."

"What!" I burst out. "No! — NO — "

" — but resources didn't run low," Gillan says while he adds air to my BCD to keep me afloat. "Naya, listen, the Governor did not authorize this attack. Somebody else did — "

"Do you think I care!" I shout. Water splashes in his face as I pound the surface with my hands. "My mother brought us to Cape Harmony to be safe! But it was all a lie . . . all the years we lived in the Valley . . . all the — "

"Naya, listen to me." Gillan grabs my arms. "We have to — "

"No!" I push him away. "The Governor put those explosives there in the first place. He would have killed us all if he had needed to!"

"Yes, he would have." Gillan's calmness is sobering. He brushes my wet hair out of my face. "Believe me, if I could, I would overthrow it all. The Governor, the council, the whole of Elite society." A fire burns in his eyes.

I swallow, suddenly realizing why he brought me here.

"Sorry," I whisper. "I just . . ." My voice breaks.

"I know." He pulls me into a hug. For a moment I sob into his shoulder. We swim back to the boat. Gillan takes off his scuba gear, helps me with mine, and pulls me on board.

He holds my hand. "I know this isn't easy for you, but we need to stick together. Governor Proctor thinks there's some kind of conspiracy brewing. A struggle for resources among the upper ranks. Naya, I'm risking everything by telling you this."

I feel a lump in my throat. "You're saying all my friends died because someone on Ararat can't get rich enough?"

He nods, slowly.

"Who?"

"I don't know — yet," Gillan says. "There are those of an extreme mindset on the council, like Kallion and Calder, who believe that the people in the FRS deserve to die. At the moment, Proctor controls Cape Harmony's solar power, one third of our natural energy sources. If someone were to seize control of Solaris, they could overthrow him. I need to stop this."

"Is that why you were near the FRS that morning?" I whisper. "To find answers?"

He nods. "I was following a boat that was carrying and testing explosives. I wanted to see what they were doing with them, but they spotted me and fired. That's when you found me."

"Why are you telling me this?" I whisper.

"Because you're one of the only people I can trust. You're not from Ararat. And you're brave. And have cause enough to help."

I clench my fists. After what I saw today I certainly do. Except . . . I'm not sure that's what Gillan meant. He was looking for answers near the FRS. Underwater. And the men who shot him were testing explosives. On the East Coast . . .

"The FRS flood barrier is rigged, too, isn't it?" I whisper.

Gillan's expression is grim. "There are not enough explosives in place to blow it yet, but it will only be a matter of time. . . . Naya, I have to know that you won't do anything rash."

I nod curtly and hold back the tears that threaten to come once more as I think of the danger that my mother is in. "I'll help you, even if it means breaking into Calder's office myself."

A smile plays around the corner of his mouth. "So you *are* the rebel I thought you were when I pulled you out of the Valley."

In spite of everything I smile back.

"Don't worry, I don't want you to break into Calder's office," Gillan says. "I just want you to keep your eyes and ears open. You're on the Barracuda team. With Duke Kallion. If he lets anything about his father's work slip, let me know. Any time you need to talk, just blink at me twice as you pass me in the hall. I'll arrange the rest. And remember, Jim and Douglas are business partners. You're perfectly placed in the Queen household. Anything Jim says about work could be useful."

"You want me to spy on Jim?"

"Only to get to Kallion." Gillan hesitates. "I know it's a lot to ask, since you and Jessica are friends . . ."

"Less than you might think," I say.

In the sudden silence, I notice that the sun has dipped below the horizon, casting a coat of many colors over the sky. I hear a wave break on a rock. It's later than I realized, not long until nightfall now.

"We should go." Gillan pulls up the anchor chain and lets the engine roar to a start. He turns the boat back toward Ararat.

"What about you? Why do you care?" I call over the engine noise.

"Call it family legacy," he calls back.

"I thought you didn't have any family." The words blubber out before I can stop them.

He stares at the coast up ahead. "My parents died when I was thirteen."

"I'm sorry," I whisper.

"I learned to look after myself."

"You live alone?"

"It took me a couple of months to get rid of the lackey that the authorities appointed for me. Fortunately, I have a few connections on the council. There are some benefits to being the sole heir to Galileo Tecc. Arlo is my official guardian now."

We fall quiet again. It's much chillier with the sun gone. Shivering from the cold, I pull my crop top over my bikini. I wish Jessica had bought me some proper clothes, not these skimpy, fashionable bits of fabric. The wind is blowing from the north and our boat bumps over the choppy waves, but Gillan keeps up the fast speed. We leave the old town of Port Fremont behind us. I wonder how Marlo's party is going. Have people started leaving? Has anyone noticed my absence or Peterson's missing EV? I can just make out the wind turbines of Zephyrus on the mountain tops north of Ararat Harbor in the near darkness.

Gillan eases off the throttle and keeps the lights of the boat off. "Almost there." He navigates around the rocky outcrops of Ararat Harbor. Breakers Cove must be nearby. I scan the shore to spy Peterson's EV from the distance, but I can't see it.

Gillan kills the engine. A wavelet splashes against the hull. The boat jolts then sits still. Gillan is standing behind the wheel, frozen, peering into the dark. I follow his gaze to the black cliffs on the north side of the harbor.

"What's going on?" I whisper.

"There are some men on a boat," Gillan whispers back.

It takes a while for my eyes to adjust to the total darkness. Then I see movement and the silhouettes of five men. They're lowering some kind of gigantic, metal device into the water. The man in the middle is tall, gray-haired and thin.

"That's Douglas Kallion," I whisper and then I kick myself. What if it's only because of my variant nature that I can see in the dark? In all my life I've never needed a flashlight even with my necklace on.

"Yes, I recognize him, too." Gillan's voice breaks through my thoughts. "The Governor has had an eye on him for some time. Kallion's been using up a lot more energy than his assigned quota. I wonder —"

Something zings through the air around us. Gillan turns on the motor and wheels the boat around. I feel a rush of wind as something whizzes past my ear. Shots! They're shooting at us.

"Stay low," Gillan hisses. I duck down to avoid the flying missiles. We haven't yet completed the turn when a sudden hiss and clang of metal ring out. The engine shudders, and slows. They've hit the outboard motor.

"What do we do?" I look at Gillan.

A straight line of bubbles shoots through the water, creating fast-moving ripples, as something zooms toward us. They fired a torpedo.

"Jump!" Gillan shouts. We leap into the water. A few *pops* are the last thing I hear as the boat's hull blocks the bullets aimed at us. Then we fly down through the water like arrows. Above us, the surface of the ocean erupts into an orange blaze. An invisible force propels me forward as the explosion rings through the water. I sense more than see Gillan's body next to me.

We freedive toward the shore. I hope the necklace won't stop me from holding my breath. Breakers Cove can't be far now. I fight the suffocating feeling in my chest. The lack of air brings a veil to my eyes, blurring my vision. Just as I can bear it no longer, I feel jagged rocks beneath my palms. I glide to the surface. Gillan appears at my side almost at the same time. He motions for me to stay still and silent. Douglas Kallion's boat is circling the remains of our motorboat. His men are still firing shots into the debris, though judging by the scattered pattern of the bullets, they have no idea at what. Gillan and I clamber to the shore, quietly. We are several yards beyond the perimeter of Douglas Kallion's searchlight. One of Kallion's men leans over the railing and shouts something.

We watch, wet shirts clinging to our backs, shivering in the breeze, as the boat draws several more circles then roars off toward Ararat Harbor.

"I think we got away." Gillan straights up.

I nod.

"You should get home and fast!" He takes my hand and pulls me along. "Kallion's friends with the Queens. If they notice you're missing . . ."

"You're right." I stumble after him up the slope then see the empty spot where I left Peterson's EV.

"Where's the EV?" Gillan asks.

I scan the hill in panic. "I left it right there, on that slope."

We're both thinking the same thing. Has someone found it? Are they waiting for us in the trees? I half expect armed guards to jump out and arrest us.

"You put the handbrake on, right?" Gillan asks.

I stare at him, dumbfounded. "What's a handbrake?"

Gillan raises an eyebrow. "You've never driven an EV before?"

"No!"

"Well, you gotta put the break on to lock the wheels," Gillan says, "otherwise . . ." We look at each other, then down the slope that leads to the sea. Underneath the cliffs, the waves are splashing against the rocks like a black monster digesting its latest meal.

"Oh, no," I whisper.

We cannot help it—we both break out laughing.

"I hope you borrowed that off of someone you don't like," Gillan says. Still smiling, he pulls out his motorbike from behind a large oak tree. "Hop on, I think I can handle one extra passenger."

We speed through the night. The motorbike doesn't have anywhere to hold onto, so after the first bumpy curve I fling my arms around Gillan. He turns his head a little and I can almost imagine that small smile flash across his face. The evening wind rushes through my wet hair. I dreamily rest my head against

Gillan's back. I wish we were driving somewhere far away from here. Away from the Elites and Ararat and all the terrible things I've learned today.

"We're here." Gillan stops the bike. I look up, torn from my thoughts. Just visible above the road bend is the Queen house. It's all dark, no lights on behind any of the gigantic glass windows. Is Jessica still out? Are her parents asleep? I climb off the motorbike.

Gillan looks wary, as if he doesn't trust the quiet.

"Don't look at the house." He sweeps an arm around my waist. "Act normal."

His gaze is on me all of a sudden. Not worried, not scared, but taking in every part of my face, my eyes, my cheeks, my lips. Even in the dark where I can hardly see them, his eyes are drawing me in.

"Don't slap me," he whispers. Then he brushes a hand over my cheek and suddenly his lips are on mine and in that moment there is only us and the stars sparkling in the evening sky.

But just as quickly, he steps away, leaving me breathless.

"If this was just an act," I hear myself say, "I will slap you." I'm pretty sure I can see his bemused smile. He leaps on his motorbike and zooms away into the night.

I watch him ride away, my heart beating with elation and tension. He kissed me! My fingertips are tingling. I pinch my lips together. I want to remember this feeling . . . But did the Queens see? Are they awake, like Gillan thought?

The entrance hall is empty when I tiptoe through it. No lights are on anywhere. They must be asleep already. Relieved I hurry toward the atrium then I skid to a stop, my heart skipping a beat. All three Queens are sitting at the dimly lit kitchen table, hands folded on the surface, looking at me, their faces masks.

"Naya, where have you been?" Jim asks.

CHAPTER 18

— *Out of Air* —

I stare at them all, in shock.

"I was . . . out," I stutter, "with . . . a boy." For the first time in my life I'm glad that I have a tendency to go red when I'm put on the spot.

"WHAT?" Jessica yells. "She's so totally lying —!"

"Jessica, quiet. I want to hear this from Naya," Jim interrupts. He takes in my wet clothes, wet hair, wet shoes. "Why are you soaked to the skin, Naya?"

"We . . . kind of . . . sort of, ended up in a swimming pool."

"Daddy, that's so not true!" Jessica points at me in outrage. "The guys did a team pyramid in the pool. Marlo did a double flip off the top. I know she wasn't there!"

I stare at my shoes. "I didn't say it was Marlo's swimming pool."

"Oh, as if!" Jessica flares up.

"JESSICA!" Jim cuts her off. "Whose swimming pool was it, Naya?"

"I . . . I don't want the whole school to know," I say.

"It's after ten o'clock in the evening, Naya." Jim's expression is stern. "The ban on accessing the beaches is still active, and I've just been informed that there was a shooting in a bay down the coast from Ararat Harbor. We are on continued variant alert. Naya, were you anywhere near that bay?"

Am I imagining the glint of suspicion in his eyes? Was Gillan right? Did Douglas Kallion warn the Queens?

"No." I shake my head. "It's true we were on the coast, but on the eastern shore."

Jessica jumps up from her seat. "She broke the curfew! Punish her, Daddy. Punish her!"

Jim stares at her, annoyed.

"Please, Jim . . ." I whisper. "I've never been out with a boy before. This was the first time we . . . kissed."

"And so you thought you'd sneak in and no one would notice?" Jim asks.

"I didn't think you'd still be up." Oh, no. I can't believe I just said that.

To my surprise Jim suppresses a smile. He looks from Jessica to me and shakes his head. "I will let you sort out your personal differences yourselves. Naya, I've given you a lot of leeway so far, more than the authorities would have wanted me to, considering your background, but my bending of the rules stops here. No more trips out with boys at night and no more curfew breaking. You're my foster daughter, I want you to be safe."

He picks up an e-pad from the table. "As it is, I won't punish you. Not this time. General Calder has just informed me that your academic standards are high enough to qualify for Aqua8 leadership training. As of tomorrow you will join the Junior Cadets in training." He puts a hand on my shoulder. "I'm very proud of you, Naya. You surpassed everyone's expectations, including mine."

I smile at him. "Thank you." But I feel a shiver run through me. Leadership training? This is so much bigger than I thought. Bigger even than winning swim races while trying not to transform into a mermaid. And I thought I had my plate full already.

*

"Spill! C'mon, you gotta tell me! I'm like dying here," Jessica exclaims on the way to school.

That makes two of us, I think, as she narrowly swerves away from the grass verge running along the edge of the cliff road. I wish that she hadn't started talking to me again so soon, but probably she'd be torturing herself more than me by not asking about Saturday night.

"Was it Ramsay? No, wait. Harriman."

"What, Harriman, the senior? Are you kidding me?" I ask. There's a reason why Harriman is known as Hairy Man.

Jessica stifles a scream of nervous laughter. "No, no, you're right. Hang on. Borgman, no, wait, not Borgman—Peterson!"

"Peterson? Are you nuts—" I begin, but then I notice that Jessica isn't looking at me. She's craning her neck out the open side of the EV. We swerve dangerously.

"PE-TER-SON!" She points, choking with laughter, just about managing to get the word out. "WALKING!"

I look out the rear of the EV as the forlorn figure of Peterson recedes into the distance. We zoom along the school driveway. Jessica's obviously eager to serve up the latest gossip while it's good and hot. When we get there, however, a crowd of students has already gathered in the parking lot. Jessica slams the EV diagonally into a bay and leaps out as fast as her stilettos allow her to see who or what stole her thunder. As we rush over, a bedraggled object covered in barnacles and seaweed is being set down from a tow truck surrounded by pointing and laughing students.

"Eew, what's that?" Jessica wrinkles her nose.

I shrug, feigning ignorance. Unfortunately I have a pretty good idea what "that" is.

A moment later Jessica gets it, too. "EV!" she squeaks. "Peterson's EV! It looks like a drowned duck!"

"Wow, Galileo Tecc have come up with an EV submarine!" Marlo roars.

The laughter dies down and the crowd parts to allow Peterson's scurrying figure, followed by a drone, to the front. His expression changes from confusion to wide-eyed panic.

"Back off," he shouts at the crowd. "Get away!" He lets out a strange whimper, and hugs the seaweed-covered hood of his EV, then pulls open the driver's door. A wave of water splashes over his shoes, followed by a flapping parrotfish.

"Yo, check it out," Zeke calls, "Peterson's got a new pet!"

A roar of laughter erupts. I look around nervously. Really, I wish the ground would swallow me up.

Once in class, Jessica thankfully goes back to ignoring me, while the rest of the Barracudas ignore her, so there isn't much of a chance for uncomfortable questions. Despite her eagerness for news in the car, Jessica's now decided to give *me* the cold shoulder. It really should be the other way around, but clearly, according to her, it must be my fault that the whole Barracuda team is angry with her. I'm already dreading the drive home, but as I leave the building, Duke's EV shoots up in reverse and pulls to a halt in front of me.

"Need a lift?"

I take a step back. OK, I know he's pretty much broken up with Jessica, but he could be a bit more subtle in his advances.

"Thanks, I'm OK."

Duke smirks. "You sure about that? It's a long way to the base and there's no school shuttle for Junior Cadets."

"Oh . . ." I completely forgot about my new training. Not to mention the fact that Duke and I are in the same group now.

"You don't wanna be late today, trust me," Duke says. "Calder oversees the Monday sessions herself."

"Uh . . . OK." I climb into his EV. At least I'm not in the trunk this time. "What happened to the shuttle?" I ask.

"That's for the A8C recruits. Junior Cadets all have their own driver's licenses and EVs." Duke grins, pushes it in gear and we speed off.

As we arrive at the base I'm actually glad that he's with me. There's no drill instructor waiting for me this time, and where I'd have needed to go would have been anyone's guess. Duke marches toward the concrete building with the barrel-shaped roof and shows me where to get my new uniforms. They give me a whole stack of different clothes. Khaki-and-beige BDUs, blue-and-gray BDUs, a formal black-and-white dress uniform with a thin, golden stripe on the sleeves, and a black neoprene wetsuit with a blue stripe. I put on the wetsuit as Duke told me to and hurry to the training hall, which is at the back of the building, a vast swim hall, gray and dimly lit. There are no windows, only artificial lighting with a blue hue. The massive swimming pool looks dark and foreboding in the sparse light, like water in a cave. It's so deep, I can't even see the bottom of it. Overlooking the pool is a big, glass-fronted control booth, the window of which fills the upper half of the wall opposite us. Inside, General Calder is standing in her usual, rigid pose.

"Cadets, take a scuba kit and gear up," shouts our drill instructor, a Major with the name tag Hope. I grab a BCD off the equipment stand at the end of the pool. I'm grateful that

Gillan showed me how to use scuba gear, but I still struggle to put it on while Major Hope keeps up an uninterrupted flow of motivational speech.

"Cadets, I have seen a shoal of blubber-fish move faster than you! You have one minute." He bends down and shouts into the ear of Elijah Goldstein, who's fumbling with his oxygen tank, "ONE MINUTE!"

I follow the other cadets into the pool and let the half-inflated BCD keep me afloat. The water laps around my chin and mouth. It has a salty taste to it. Sea water! So far all my transformations happened out in the ocean. I reach for the trident necklace, concealed beneath my full-body wetsuit. I'm glad that I kept it on. It would be pretty inconvenient if I accidentally transformed right here in the pool, surrounded by a squad of soldiers with rifles at the ready.

"Attention, Cadets!" Calder's voice, devoid of any emotion, rings from the loudspeakers in the corners of the hall. It's accompanied by the usual weird screech of static. I shiver. Somehow it seems to make the temperature in the swim hall fall by about twenty degrees.

"Your exercise is as follows: You will crawl along the bottom of the pool. You must complete four lengths without resurfacing. As you exit the pool, you must take out the targets that await you there. This exercise is called Out of Air."

I glance up at the big glass-fronted control booth. It is dark now, but I can imagine Calder's solitary figure observing us. The thought alone chills me to the bone. Sometimes I wonder whether General Calder is human at all. Shaking off the chill, I let the air out of my BCD jacket and sink to the bottom of the pool. As soon as my hands touch the floor, I start to crawl along the slippery tiles. I've made two lengths, when a hollow clunk echoes next to me. I see two figures struggling, twisting around each other, then a huge eruption of bubbles. Is someone attacking us? I hurry on to the end of the pool. I should have known that Calder would add a catch to the exercise. Drawing a breath from my regulator I begin my fourth length.

Suddenly I'm jerked back and pulled off the floor of the pool. My air tank is forcefully pulled upwards. I roll over and try to twist out of the clutches of my attacker, but he loosens the straps of my tank and drags it off. I take a huge breath of air before my mouthpiece is yanked away. Turning around I see my assailant disconnect the breathing tubes and tie them into a triple knot. Then he swims away. I try to undo the knots, but they are hard as rocks, I can't even begin to see which one to pull at first. There's no way I can hold my breath long enough to finish the extra pool length while I've got my necklace on. With my lungs bursting for air, I swim for the surface.

"Cadet DeLora!" Calder's voice echoes through the hall. "You have failed this exercise."

I swim over to the side and haul myself out of the pool, to join the line of dejected-looking cadets who got out before me. I've barely made two steps when someone grabs me from behind and slides a plastic knife along my throat.

"Congratulations, Cadet DeLora, you have now failed this exercise twice!" Calder shouts.

What—but . . . ? Didn't Calder say to take out the targets after completing the exercise?

I look at the ten combatants, armed, dressed in black, lined up around the pool, between five plastic dummies.

"Your instructions were clear," Calder calls. "Take out the targets as you exit the pool. You exited the pool, Cadet DeLora, did you not?"

I clench my hands into fists. Is it all tricks and word games with her?

At that moment the heads of the seven remaining successful cadets bob up by the rim of the pool. Duke is one of them. He leaps out of the water and throws himself at the combatant who attacks him.

Calder's voice rings through the loudspeaker. "The failure rate for this exercise is 76.7—" She breaks off as one of the remaining cadets gets "stabbed" in the side. "Correction, 80 percent. Those of you who passed the test, part one of today's training is done. Move on to the next exercise! As for the ones who failed me, twenty lengths punishment drill! And thirty—"
I'm suddenly blinded by a spotlight beam that hits my face,

"for those who have failed me twice. Cadet DeLora you have barely begun your training and already—"

"AAAAAH!"

A shout of rage interrupts her. Calder's searchlight sweeps over the pool and in its milky beam I see Duke stabbing his knife into a plastic dummy in wild rage—again and again and again. The plastic figure is in shreds. Calder clears her throat over the loudspeaker, but it's not like she'd tell anyone off for excessive violence. "I think you got him, Kallion." Then she calls out, "Exercise over. Commence punishment laps."

By the time I hit the showers I can hardly walk. Duke is waiting for me outside. His eyes are more bloodshot than ever and the skin of his upper body has taken on a reddish hue. With all that's been going on I've completely forgotten about his injections. The effects have gotten worse. But what can I do about it? There's something fishy going on, no doubt, but if this is a Kallion family secret, getting involved might be just as dangerous as it would be to move against the government. Besides, I have no idea what is contained in the blue liquid. I don't even know why Duke keeps driving up to the cable car . . . unless he's injecting Red Earth into himself, which I highly doubt.

*

Over the next few days, I make it my mission to quiz Kayla and Mia about Duke and Douglas Kallion, but with Jessica acting weird, and Duke and Jessica looking daggers at each other, it's impossible to talk to the style sisters about anything but the latest gossip. I finally get my chance one afternoon when Kayla announces that she got a C¬ in her latest hydrostatics paper. "Great, the only job I'm gonna get is in retail, serving slushies."

"I love slushies!" Mia says.

I laugh. "Oh, come on, it's not that bad. Though I guess it'd be nice if we all had our own companies, like Duke's dad."

Kayla grimaces. "I think I prefer serving slushies to having Douglas as my father. He might be high and mighty now, but without Céline he'd never have had the social connections for Mortlake—"

"Céline?" I ask.

"Duke's mom," Kayla says. "My parents told me she had real grace. Even when her illness got bad—" she breaks off at the sight of Jessica and Duke, just outside the lunch hall. The three of us stop, a few feet away, as Jessica flashes Duke her best flirty smile.

"Hey Duke, quit scowling at me already and take me out to dinner, you mean, old grumpus!"

"Don't you get it?" Duke is so tense that his T-shirt looks like it's gonna rip. "When you stabbed Naya in the back, you sabotaged the whole team!"

"Big deal. One stupid race. Why in Oceans are you stressing so much? Like, so uncool." Jessica runs a glossy pink fingernail over his bulging bicep. "Anyway, she was stealing your thunder, you're the Barracudas' big hero, hun."

Duke brushes her hand off. "One stupid race, huh? That's all this is to you? We're in the lead over the Seals, for the first time in THREE YEARS! Nobody gives a flapping flounder about your pathetic little feuds. We care about Naya. We care about winning!"

Marlo and Zeke suddenly appear at his side.

"Yeah, don't you care about Naya, at all?" Zeke asks.

"It's not like anything would have happened to her!" Jessica scoffs.

"Yeah, if she loses, they'll just send her back to the FRS, and she probably feels more at home there anyway," Mia jumps in to back her.

Kayla gapes at them. "Oceans, you're so naive and stupid. Do you actually believe that?"

"Have you never heard about the labor camps?" Marlo asks.

I back away as Duke, Marlo, Zeke, and Kayla glare at Jessica and Mia. This is the first time I've seen the team divided like this. And over me.

Jessica breaks into a fake laugh. "Seriously, all this shouting is bad for your vocal cords. And it gives you wrinkles. Why don't we all just get some ice cream at the mall and, like, chill. GO BARRACUDAS, right?" she shouts.

"Forget it, Jess." Duke scowls at her. "We're not going for ice cream. And as for the two of us, we're over."

"What?? Seriously?" Jessica's smile vanishes.

"Yes. Through. Done. Get it? And here's a shocker for you: you're not the only girlfriend material at Eden." Duke glances at me while he says it. I quickly look away.

Jessica hoists herself up onto her tiptoes, and shouts, her voice shrill, "NOBODY dumps me! You're gonna regret this, Duke. Take a good look, so you remember what you're throwing away. THIS—" she motions at her body, "—isn't available to just anyone." She stamps her foot and whirls around to stomp away but runs straight into Harriman, who is walking along the hallway in front of Gillan and Torres. "Eugh, gross!" She pushes him off and storms away. Mia waits a beat, then rushes after her.

Gillan and Torres have stopped and are looking at us, trying to work out what just happened.

"You all right, Naya?" Duke asks.

I nod, but keep my distance.

Gillan's eyes wander from him to me. There's a worried look on his face. "Gonna get the hall locked down again, Duke?" he asks.

Duke puffs up his chest. "Not if you keep walking, poster boy."

Gillan shoots me a glance to make sure I'm OK, then walks into the lunch hall with Torres. I draw a breath. I hope Gillan and Duke won't start fighting over me now.

By the end of the day I'm feverishly thinking of alternative ways of getting to Aqua8 other than a lift with a super-hormonal Duke, but as I meet him at the parking lot, he doesn't say a word. He jumps into his EV and motions for me to get in. We drive toward the base in silence. And my second session of Junior Cadet training begins.

When I get home that evening I'm so tired, I don't care that Jessica's slinking around the house, not talking to me. But as we sit down for dinner I see another chance for finding out more about Douglas Kallion.

"In hydrostatics, Dr. Planck mentioned that Zephyrus is one of the most efficient wind power installations ever designed," I tell Jim.

Jim nods. "That is correct. The load factor that's achieved by Zephyrus—"

"Dr. Planck's my favorite teacher, Daddy," Jessica butts in. "He said I'm really good at hydrostatics-y stuff, like, uh, equations and . . ."

While Jessica is trying to think of another scientific term I jump in. "So that made me think how companies on Cape Harmony, such as Zephyrus and Mortlake, pool resources to develop new technologies. Doesn't Douglas Kallion play a key role in—"

"Dr. Planck's also a super great judge of character!" Jessica interrupts again. "He said that my new friend Sloane van Buren is really clever, too."

"Yes, yes, that's nice." Jim frowns and turns back to me. "You're right, Douglas's background makes him perfectly suited to a number of new energy projects, notably the Red Earth Project—"

"You know why Sloane is my new best friend, Daddy?" Jessica asks.

Something in me snaps. "Will you shut up already! Nobody cares about Sloane van Buren! You said she's the most boring girl at Eden."

"Manners, Naya!" Mrs. Queen exclaims.

Jim throws us a perplexed look. "What's up with you two? Sort out your differences. I won't tolerate fighting in this household."

Jessica scowls.

I pinch my lips, then mutter, "Sorry, Jim."

*

To administer the coup de grâce to an already bad week, on Friday General Calder appears at our outdoor Aqua8 session. I'm not sure what earned me the special honor of her overseeing a second training day, but I could do without it.

"Targets ready. Fire!" Major Hope shouts.

I grab my speargun and run across the rocks, shooting at the paper disks that snap up to my left and right. Since I got the hang of switching my combigun from stun darts to bullets, I've discovered that I'm actually a pretty good shot. No matter what I do though, I'm never fast enough or violent enough for Calder.

"Cadet DeLora, two meager stabs to the ribs don't take out a target. On the battlefield those dummies will not wait for you to decide whether they're civilians or not. My most promising officer let me down! Don't be the next."

Major Hope follows up by planting his boot on my back as I'm doing punishment push-ups. I grunt. Whoever that last officer was, she and Calder obviously have some unresolved issues.

While we're gearing up for another exercise, blue lights begin flashing and the sirens on the buildings behind us start to howl.

"Variant Alert Level One! All Junior Cadets gear up and report to mooring station one!" The voice on the loudspeakers rings out across the Aqua8 compound. "Flood barrier to remain down, I repeat, flood barrier to remain down."

Already equipped with weapons for the exercise, we run to the next bay. Calder speeds alongside us in her black EV.

"Attention! Combatants and cadets. There has been a variant sighting in Ararat Harbor. Your orders are to capture or kill and bring it back to base. Do not disappoint me."

My stomach twists itself into a knot. A sighting? Can it be true? And how is it that ever since I arrived on Ararat, I'm always on the wrong side? If there's a fight, I should be in the water with the variant. After all that's what I am too.

"Cadets!" Major Hope shouts. "Grab a boat with one of the Officer Combatants or graduating Junior Cadets. Three people per boat."

I notice a boy with a crew cut among the Junior Cadets. He gives me a quick nod. Does he want me to join him?

"MOVE IT!" The Major yells.

In unison, the other cadets and I jog to the black dinghies with the flashy blue stripe that have been pulled up onto the sand. Calder's small gray flagship is already in the water. Her stiff figure crowns the bow, facing out to sea, a pair of binoculars in hand. While the Junior Cadets and Officer Combatants are pulling their boats into the water, I turn around to the crewcut boy, but he's not there anymore.

"Keep to starboard!" the Major shouts from a dinghy that's just leaving and my heart jumps. I'm the only one who got left on the beach. I stare at the boats heading into the waves. Knowing Calder, she will probably give me punishment lengths if I remain behind. I yank the last dinghy free of the sand and drag it into the waves at a run. As I jump into the boat and start the engine, the other dinghies have already reached Calder's flagship. They've spread out around it, harpoons at the ready. I steer toward them, hoping that nobody notices that I'm alone, without an Officer Combatant. My dinghy bounces and bumps over the waves as I speed up; it is easier to operate than I thought it would be. I'll have to remember this, in case I ever want to get away from Ararat with Mom.

Soon I'm in the middle of all the mayhem. People shouting, one boat occasionally bumping into another and Calder barking orders.

I'm still trying to figure out what we're meant to do, exactly, when a voice in the water close to me calls out, "Found one!"

My heart skips a beat. Oh no! But, hang on . . . I know that voice.

"Sorry, false alarm! Help me!" Gillan grabs onto my dinghy and hauls himself in.

"Who told you to get in the water, Lieutenant?" Major Hope barks from a dinghy near us.

I grab Gillan's arm and help him on board.

"Hi, Naya." He grins at me, water dripping from his hair and Aqua8 wetsuit.

Where did he come from? Did he jump from his boat to find me? But I didn't see him on the beach. Does he even know what's going on? In any case, I smile, because he's here by my side.

"Whoa!" Gillan exclaims as the dinghy twists wildly. Oops, did I lean against the rudder while staring at him? He motions me to the front and takes charge of the steering.

When we're out of earshot of the others, he leans over and looks me in the eyes. "Finally, caught you in a quiet place."

"Gillan, there's a variant!" I blurt out.

"I know. Naya—"

"But Calder's gonna kill it."

216

Gillan grins. "Something tells me it isn't here anymore."

I stare at him. And then I get it. We're on the north side of the harbor, near the spot where we saw Douglas Kallion. Chances are the variant alert was triggered by Kallion's men who returned to finish whatever job they were doing; or more likely, by Gillan himself, trying to sneak a look at whatever Kallion's men were putting in the water that night. That would explain why he was in the sea . . . and why I didn't see him on the beach when we launched the boats.

"I don't have any news," I stutter. "It's only been a week, I didn't get a chance to find out anything about Kallion."

"Never mind," he whispers. "Naya, we need to talk."

"How?" I point to the badge on my new Aqua8 wetsuit. "I'm a Junior Cadet now, they're making me train all the time."

"I know," he says grimly. "I'll take care of it. Next Thursday, after school —"

"VARIANT!!"

Gillan and I spin around at the shout. There's a splash in the water and one of the cadets from the dinghy to our left fires his stun gun. His two crew mates throw out a big net, which pulls tight at once. I hold my breath.

"We've caught it. It's here," a cadet shouts.

"Attention, all cadets!" Calder's boat is already speeding toward us.

I look at Gillan, concerned. At that moment the cadets who are hauling in their quarry scream and jump back. In the net, a dusky shark is yapping and snapping at them wildly.

"AAAH!"

"Throw it back in the water!"

BANG!

A shot strikes through the air. Calder's towering figure leans over the edge of her boat, a semiautomatic pistol in her outstretched hand. The shark shudders and, with a twitch, is still.

"Pay attention, you idiots." Calder yanks the loudspeaker from the hand of the officer standing next to her. "Variant hunt dismissed. You have failed. Return to base."

"Poor shark," I say.

Gillan grimaces. "Rather him than me."

As we head back, the wind picks up. The whitecaps of the waves are running diagonally across the rocky bay. Gillan looks unfazed as he steers the boat in spite of the current. I'm struck again by how different he is to anyone I've ever met before. I don't take my eyes off him. He doesn't look away either, but once we're back on shore his "perfect soldier" facade is up again. We pretend to ignore each other as he lines up with the Officer Combatants, and I line up with the Junior Cadets to jog back to the training area.

"Lieutenant Gallagher!"

I jump when General Calder shouts into her microphone. "I said all *cadets* to the beach. You are a ranking officer."

"I thought you could use the help."

"My office. Right now!"

I glance over my shoulder while Gillan walks up to the building with the barrel-shaped roof. He's playing a dangerous game. And I'm a part of it, too, now.

CHAPTER 19

— Conspirators' Council —

DETENTION. The word pops up in red on my e-pad on Thursday afternoon, after swim training. I stare at it in disbelief. Oh no, what have I done now?

"Oooh, you got a detention!" Jessica cranes over my shoulder, gleeful. "When I got detention, we had to clean out the fish tanks in the marine biology classroom. Really gross."

It's pretty annoying, how she only speaks to me when she wants to taunt me.

"Sorry, Jess, gotta go." I stuff my e-pad into my school bag. "The fish tank calls." I run down the hall, my heart racing. I'm supposed to meet Gillan today.

As I halt in front of the security office, the door swings open and the boy with the crew cut from Junior Cadets steps outside. What is it with him popping up everywhere? Did he overhear me and Gillan somehow? For a second I'm scared that he's taking me to Calder, but he just says, "Cadet DeLora, as a member of Aqua8, you've been assigned to the coastal remediation detention detail. Pick up a boiler suit and come with me."

I take one of the dirty, navy-blue rags that are stacked in the corner of the security office along with a pair of goggles, and follow him outside.

He motions me into a four-seater EV and drives along the road that leads to the Aqua8 dry docks. I want to get out as the vehicle stops but he holds me back. The door behind me opens and a person of my height and build, wearing a boiler suit with a hood and goggles identical to the ones I just picked up from school, steps outside. Was he or she there the whole time? I didn't notice anyone on the backseat. The boy with the crew cut makes a U-turn and heads back toward the south road at high speed. I hold onto the dashboard.

"Where are you taking me?"

He doesn't reply. We scale the southern slope of the hill and approach a huge, white house with tinted floor-to-ceiling windows. It is set apart from the neighboring houses, perched high on the hill, overlooking the bay and Ararat Harbor. Floating steps lead from the first to the second floor and a rectangular infinity pool, of a very light turquoise color, covers most of the terrace below the overhanging top floor.

"What's going on? Why did you bring me here?" I demand of the cadet.

He stares dead ahead, as if I had not spoken.

"I guess I'm meant to get out?"

No answer.

"Fine!" I snatch up my overalls and goggles and leap out of the EV.

He shakes his head, as if I had done something stupid, then speeds away. I walk up to the house. The doorway is open.

"Visitor detected: Citizen ID 1334, Rhidian Cho, Galileo Tecc," an electronic voice drones from a control panel beside the door.

I spin around, searching for another person, but I'm definitely alone. Why did the control panel just announce me as Rhidian Cho? I step inside, hesitantly.

"Hello?"

No answer. I look around and see a crest-like family plaque in the entrance hallway with a wave and three dolphins that says GALLAGHER. My heart thumps. I'm at Gillan's house.

And suddenly it all makes sense. The guy with the crew cut is arranging Gillan's meetings. He left me behind on the beach, so that I'd take a dinghy alone . . . and now he brought me here.

I cross from the white marble entrance hall into the living room. It's glass fronted and it's as if I'm on a big observation platform from which there is a bird's-eye view of the whole harbor, and the white mansions on the hill slope opposite. One mansion stands out in particular, with its huge, terraced garden and triangular portico. It's perched above the mouth of the harbor, right on the edge of the northern hill, where the cliffs are at their steepest.

I turn back to the living room and notice how curious all the furnishings are: shiny and modern, yet antique. The whole back wall of the room is covered in bookshelves full of ancient books. Shelf after shelf of heavy leather tomes, unlike any I've ever seen before, with titles in dull gold on the spines. They're a far cry from the dog-eared textbooks that we had in the FRS.

"Fascinating, aren't they? Like so many of the things forbidden to us." I whirl around to see Arlo Quinn.

"Arlo!"

He smiles, delighted. "And about high time that we saw you here. Gillan has been . . . more than reluctant."

I blush and turn my attention back to the books. "Where are these from?"

"Oh, they're . . . Gillan's family heirlooms." Arlo adjusts his glasses and squints at the nearest title. "Hundreds of years old. The Governing Council could actually learn something if they read them; not that they would. *World War II*, *Ivanhoe*, *On the Origin of Species*. Ah . . . and *The Tempest*. You've never read these, have you?"

I shake my head. "Should I have?"

"For your own safety, no." Arlo smiles mischievously. "If anyone knew these existed they would burn them, and arrest Gillan for owning them."

I look at him, shocked.

"Don't worry," Arlo reassures me. "Gillan learned to tread carefully a long time ago."

"Arlo, why did Gillan get drafted into Aqua8 ahead of everyone else?" I ask.

Arlo frowns. "It was a deal he made with General Calder after he was orphaned. Junior Cadets receive certain privileges normally granted only to adults. General Calder promised that she would get rid of Gillan's government-appointed guardian if Gillan joined the military immediately."

"But . . . Calder hates Gillan. Why would she give him an early promotion?"

"A well-played move by Gillan." Arlo smiles. "Gillan holds a very special standing as future head of Galileo Tecc. His mother and father were on the council, among Ararat's most influential members of society—and Calder's strongest opponents. Gillan suspected that Calder might attempt to win him over. It would

have suited her just right to mold Gillan into her personal pup-
pet, thereby gaining control over the production of EVs, marine transportation, e-pads."

"So she hates him so much because her plan didn't work."

"Precisely," Arlo replies.

"Arlo . . ." I hesitate. "What happened to Gillan's parents?"

"They died in a boating accident. Their sailing-yacht cap-
sized in a storm that came out of nowhere. That was nearly five
years ago, Gillan was thirteen. Some members of the government were certainly glad to see them go. Gillan's parents' lib-
eral-minded politics were a thorn in many people's sides."

"How do you mean?"

"Well, they . . . ah, there you are."

I turn to see Gillan come into the room in a white shirt and
loose cotton pants. His blond hair is still wet, brushed back
neatly and just beginning to curl behind the ears.

"Naya, you're here!" He steps toward me with a smile, as if
to hug me, but halts with a look at Arlo and falters. "Good you
made it."

Arlo hides a smirk. "So, what are the latest developments?"

"Mortlake's energy use is off the scale again," Gillan says.
"Massively. And there are no signs that they're exceeding their
agreed quota, so it's obvious they're using more energy than is
available."

"Hence, the Red Earth Project is already in operation, although they're claiming that it's still in its testing phase," Arlo
concludes.

I glance from one to the other, confused. "But . . . isn't Jim
working on that, too?"

Arlo looks pensive. "It's possible that Kallion is pulling the
strings alone. Energy usage is skyrocketing at Mortlake, not at
Zephyrus."

"I don't trust him." Gillan strides across the room. "Queen
and Kallion have been business partners for years. It's unlikely
that Kallion could have the Red Earth Project up and running
without Jim Queen knowing. And it's an odd coincidence that
Naya got pulled into Junior Cadets on the same evening that

we observed Kallion lowering that device into the water. It's like someone's deliberately trying to keep her busy."

"How do you know I got pulled in that same evening?" I ask surprised.

Gillan shoots me a cheeky smile. "Oh, Aqua8's a big compound, it's easy to uh . . . get lost and accidentally end up in the main office where the files are kept."

Arlo clears his throat. "In any case, Naya getting recruited was bound to happen sooner or later. There's no evidence that it was an intentional move, nor that Zephyrus or Queen are involved. Brice Donovan has never sided against the Governor on council matters so far, and Queen has not voiced any opinions against Proctor either. The real question is what is all that energy at Mortlake being used for?"

Gillan glances at the sea. "I guess we can rule out an escape plan? Kallion trying to get away from here in style?"

"Almost definitely," Arlo agrees. "You've combed every inch of this coastline. We found no evidence of a secret dockyard. Besides, there's no reason for Kallion to leave. He is one of the most powerful members of the council."

"Then Proctor is right," Gillan says. "It's about energy and seizing power."

Arlo nods. "The Red Earth Project is meant to benefit all of Ararat. If Kallion disguises his progress, claims it doesn't work, the state might lose interest and he can surreptitiously develop it and privatize it. United, Red Earth and Mortlake will be more powerful than the Governor's energy company, Solaris. Even if Proctor and Donovan merged, which is unlikely, Solaris and Zephyrus would still be dwarfed by the combined size of Kallion's coal and Red Earth resources."

"So what is he waiting for?" Gillan asks. "If the Red Earth Project is fully operational, why didn't Douglas Kallion set his coup d'état in motion, overthrow Proctor, blow the FRS barrier, and gain control of the Governing Council and all of Ararat's energy resources?"

"Perhaps it's a matter of timing." Arlo rubs his chin. "He could be waiting for some event in the future that provides the ideal circumstance for him to strike his blow."

"The Water Festival?" Gillan asks.

"It would seem the obvious choice since it's held at the Governor's mansion, which is just above the location in the port where the two of you saw that device being lowered into the water," Arlo muses.

Gillan stares at the large white house with the triangular portico perched on the opposite cliff.

"Is that where he lives?" I ask.

"Indeed," Arlo says. "And it is also where the Water Festival, Ararat's annual celebration of its victory over the element of Water, takes place on June 21, the day of the Summer Solstice. It will include a giant display of illuminated fountains. All of Ararat will be invited."

"Then what if that device is some kind of bomb designed to kill the Governor in front of the assembled Elites?" I ask.

Arlo wriggles his brows in scholarly thought. "A bomb's blast wouldn't reach high enough. The rock foundations are too strong. Not to mention that the Governor has his own personal bodyguards who patrol the shore with scanners designed to detect explosives. Any sign of foul play and they would evacuate him in a second."

Gillan's expression darkens. "I think Calder's also involved in Kallion's plans. I tried again to get a look at the device this afternoon. It's being guarded underwater by Aqua8 divers."

"Oh, is it?" Arlo smiles grimly. "This just keeps getting better and better. Now you're accusing the head of the armed forces? Some might consider that treason."

Gillan gives him a smirk. "Everything we do is considered treason."

"Rightly so," Arlo says. "Which reminds me: have you mentioned any of this to our esteemed Governor?"

"Only the explosives on the FRS flood barrier," Gillan says. "I can't bring up Kallion's name unless I have proof."

"But what about the device below the Governor's house?" I burst out. "Shouldn't he know?"

"Governor Proctor is a nervous man," Arlo replies. "He may jump to the wrong conclusion and hasten his own demise."

"And ours," Gillan adds. "Besides, if we ring the alarm bells too early, we'll miss our chance of uncovering Calder's role in all this."

"Here, proceed with caution," Arlo advises. "Don't let your dislike for General Calder cloud your judgment. Consider that Kallion could have infiltrated Aqua8. You said the guards by the device were wearing some kind of emblem. We could be dealing with a ring of conspirators."

"Operation Neptune," I whisper.

"What?" Gillan and Arlo look at me.

"It's just something I heard Kallion say to Duke when I followed them to the Red Earth site," I say, and I tell them about the conversation I overheard on the mountain slopes.

Arlo chuckles. "Well, I really must say Naya, you don't lack in audacity or resourcefulness. Didn't I tell you, Gillan? Now whatever this Operation Neptune might be, it would support our theory of a planned strike."

"And something bigger than just the privatization of Red Earth," Gillan says.

"Did you follow them into the cable car station?" Arlo asks. I nod.

"And you're certain they didn't get onto one of the cabins? They just vanished?"

"Like the earth swallowed them up."

"How uncanny," Arlo mutters.

"No, no, Arlo." Gillan leaps across the room, snatches up a paper map and unrolls it on the table. "Naya's onto something, look. I've noticed that on the charts, the Mortlake energy indicator jumps in location from time to time. Sometimes it appears higher up on the mountain, there; sometimes lower down, in this spot. And that's not all. I've stationed myself at the Red Earth site whenever I could. A certain amount of containers with Red Earth go missing when they pass the cable car station below Mortlake. About every fourth or fifth one. Kallion must have found a way to divert them from their monitored route to a secret location."

"You're suggesting that he has set up a secret stronghold?" Arlo glances at the points that Gillan marked on the map. "What would be its purpose?"

Gillan glances at me.

"All I know is that Duke's taking something," I say. "I saw him injecting himself with some blue liquid after training. I think it's making him swim faster."

Gillan draws in a sharp breath. "That would explain a few things. He's been kind of aggressive in the past few months."

Arlo raises an eyebrow. "More than usual?"

"You didn't think it possible?" Gillan asks, smiling.

Arlo paces the room, in thought. "Artificial stimulants such as you describe don't exist anymore. They could be created — with a significant amount of energy."

"You're saying Kallion is running a whole secret operation so that his son can beat me at a swim race?"

"It certainly wouldn't be his first sign of insanity," Arlo says. "But no, I suspect this all ties into a bigger plan. In order to create this stimulant, or serum, Kallion would need new machinery, a lab . . . which could be linked to his secret stronghold near the cable car station."

"You're saying he's set up a secret laboratory somewhere in the mountains? Arlo, how certain of this are you?" Gillan looks at him expectantly.

"Well, it would explain Duke's unusual behavior. Any newly developed drug has unknown side effects."

"Trust Kallion to test it on his own son," Gillan says grimly. "But Arlo, how does this tie in with Operation Neptune?"

"Difficult to say, without knowing what the serum is," Arlo replies. "We'd need to obtain a sample first."

"That's impossible," Gillan says. "Duke keeps his stuff stowed in his lockers or on him at all times."

"Couldn't a simple spot check—" Arlo begins, but Gillan shakes his head.

"Duke's a Junior Cadet. Even the staff's access to his lockers is closely monitored. I don't think I can get anywhere near it."

"Maybe you can't," I say, "but I can. Duke drives me to Aqua8 three times a week for cadet training. I've got no problem getting close to him."

"You're close enough as it is," Gillan says tersely. "I've noticed the way he looks at you."

I feel my face flushing. So Gillan does care about me. More than he let on. But I can't let that stop me from doing what I have to do.

"Gillan, I'm on the Barracuda team. It's the perfect opportunity."

Arlo gives a nod. "Duke's guard would be down around Naya. This may be our only chance."

"Why are you agreeing with her?" Gillan snaps at him. "I didn't save her in the Valley to drop her into Duke's clutches."

"And you aren't," Arlo assures him. "Naya has proven her ingenuity more than once. I think we can trust her to accomplish this task."

A scowl crosses Gillan's face. "We don't even know exactly how much time we've got. Maybe this is all wrong. Maybe we should just take out Kallion *and* Calder before either of them can make a move."

"No!" Arlo looks alarmed. "You know better than anyone what the consequences would be, should such a plan fail."

"Gillan." I step in front of him, so he's looking at me, not Arlo. "You asked for my help. So let me help."

He doesn't answer. His jaw is set and his brows are knitted.

"It's settled then," Arlo decides. He turns to me. "Emmerson, who drove you here, can be your contact. If you have information, signal him, not Gillan. The two of you should not be seen anywhere near each other after the incident at Breakers Cove, just in case."

"I'll get the Aqua8 members from our inner circle involved," Gillan says. "Any chance we can grab that syringe, we will."

Arlo clears his throat. "Your focus should be on that device. And the strange symbol you saw on it. If there is a coup brewing, it would help to know their secret way of recognizing each other."

"It was some kind of circular symbol, but I haven't been able to get close enough." Gillan smirks at me. "My last attempt triggered a variant hunt."

"Be careful," Arlo says.

"What happens to you if you're caught . . . being an Elite and all?" I ask.

"A more expensive bullet," Gillan replies.

"Gillan!" Arlo exclaims shocked. "That isn't funny."

"I know. It's not," Gillan says.

Arlo's eyes drift to the Governor's mansion and over to the sea. The waves are sparkling orange in the setting sun. "I think it's high time we got Naya back, before she's missed. By the way, the two of you should give some thought to the Iron Teens Finals. After all you will be competing against each other."

"It will be a Barracuda victory," Gillan says. "Anything less could endanger Naya's stay on Ararat."

"What are you talking about?" I blurt out. "You can't just throw the race because of me! People will notice. Besides . . . they can't expect me to win!"

"They don't," Arlo assures me, " . . . but tensions are running high in the council. It would be better not to leave anything to chance."

I stare at him. Are they both missing the obvious? "But Arlo, look at us. Gillan's way stronger than I am. And taller. And he's Ararat's undefeated champion. Who's ever gonna buy that *I* beat *him*?"

Gillan smiles. "It would be unusual. But it wouldn't be unprecedented."

I think back to the victory plaques that I saw in the competition swim hall: Aidan Fynn's name was up there. Followed by Alexis Janson's.

"Coach Janson won the Irons fifteen years ago," Gillan explains. "The other contestant was the captain of the Barracudas. A boy, uh, a bit like Duke, I guess, just with less of a temper. Janson beat him by a whole body length."

"The race in 228," I whisper. "The year that Aidan drowned."

Arlo clears his throat. "Actually, here's what is most curious: Aidan didn't drown. He asphyxiated. I was at the Cape Harmony Research Institute when they did the autopsy. There was no water in his lungs."

I turn to him, a frisson of fear running through my body. Was I right? Was Aidan a variant?

"Didn't people notice?" I ask.

"It would have been obvious to very few," Arlo replies. "Some members of the institute, the medics on site—if they paid attention, and Alexis, of course, who pulled him out of the pool."

"Wait, Coach Janson pulled him out of the pool herself?" I ask, surprised.

"Yes. Didn't she tell you?" Arlo asks.

"No, she left that bit out. She told me that it was Aidan's girlfriend who tried to rescue him."

Arlo sighs. "That's also true. She and Aidan were competing team captains, but they didn't let team rivalries come between their affection for one another. In any case, I will inform her of your plan for this year's Finals to ensure that she won't try some rogue attempt of her own to keep you safe."

I give him a curious look. Aren't Gillan and Janson working together?

Arlo walks with us past the walls of books and into the vast entrance hall and out the front door. "By the way, talking of rogue action, do we need to worry about any future sabotage attempts on the part of Miss Queen?"

I raise my brows. Arlo doesn't seem to miss a thing. "I don't think so," I reply. "Duke knows, so Jessica won't try again."

Gillan tenses at the mention of Duke's name.

I give him a pleading look. I so badly wish we weren't parting like this. With Gillan angry and me unable to tell him how I feel. But an EV immediately pulls up in front of the house, with crew-cut Emmerson inside.

"Ah, there's your chauffeur," Arlo remarks. "I shall see you on the day of the race, Naya. I will be attending on Gillan's behalf, of course, but I will be keeping an eye out for you as well."

"Thank you," I whisper.

"Visitor departing. Rhidian Cho . . ." the control panel by the door drones in its melancholy voice.

I don't look back as I walk down the steps, away from the house. Then I'm in the EV, driving down the hill slope with Emmerson who still doesn't speak a word.

CHAPTER 20

— Aqua8's Finest —

"You heard about Ararat's new 'De-weed the Beach' campaign? Think they'll weed out DeLora, too?" Jessica's voice carries throughout the halls.

"Yeah, they might confuse her hair with a mess of seaweed," Sloane replies.

I duck out of the way of Jessica, Mia, and Sloane van Buren, who are walking down the hallway. Since Jessica and I had our falling out, the three of them have been hanging out together at lunch time, joined by Peterson and his sidekicks. And that's not all. Jessica's sabotage attempt was like a go-ahead for people in school to voice their true opinions about me. I even heard one of the teachers complain to Principal Preen in the hall about the school's reputation deteriorating because of FRS strays. Arlo wasn't kidding when he said that tensions on Ararat are running high.

To top it all off, with Duke and Jessica's break up, our group has completely come apart. Kayla is spending more time with Marlo and Zeke, and I can't join them without Zeke thinking that I'm "checking out his moves." As for Duke, he's missing more classes than he's attending. His scowl has become permanently ingrained on his face. And I thought stealing that serum off him was going to be easy: flirt a little and grab the syringe. Instead I haven't spoken to him in almost three weeks, not even on our drives to Aqua8. I lean against the wall opposite a gigantic, framed photograph of Principal Preen and close my eyes. How am I ever going to make this work?

"Everything OK?" I open my eyes and there's Duke, standing right in front of me.

"Uh . . . yeah . . . sure!" I pretend to search for something in my bag, letting a strand of my hair fall over my eyes, like Jessica does when she's flirting.

"Cool." He turns to walk off.

"Actually no, that's a lie," I let slip out. "I'm miserable. Jessica's not speaking to me. And she stole my e-pad after dinner and deleted my physics assignment. I stayed up half the night redoing it and then Janson snapped at me, because I was 0.8 of a second behind my usual time."

Duke's face turns red at the mention of Jessica. "That idiotic, air-headed shopping bot! I'm not letting her ruin the Barracudas' chances. Not on my watch!"

"Uh . . ." I part my lips slightly, in the dumb way that Mia does, because she thinks it makes her mouth look kissable. "I meant . . . it'd be nice to get a break from her."

Duke isn't listening. "I just don't get it. Here we are finally with a real shot at the title, and she's playing right into Gallagher's hands. You oughta . . . you oughta slap her!" He struts off.

I slump against the wall. I can't believe I blew this. Duke leered at me for months and now I can barely get him to notice my existence. On the wall opposite, the photograph of Principal Preen seems to be observing me with disapproval. I roll my eyes at it and trudge off to math.

By the third class of the day, it comes to me: my lack of success has nothing to do with me. Duke's in worse shape than ever. His face is pale, his forehead clammy, and he's got this expression, like he's expecting something terrible to happen. I've observed that he gets like this just before he pulls one of his disappearing acts. I want to throw caution to the wind and just ask him about the injections. Maybe that would be better anyway, maybe our whole plan is overly dramatic. But as I wait for him after class to go to Aqua8, he doesn't show. I glance at the remaining EVs in the parking lot, wondering who I can beg a lift from, when tires screech and Duke pulls up in front of me.

"We're gonna be late—" I begin.

"I know, I know . . . get in!" Duke shouts. I jump into the EV and he steps on the gas. I'm flung back into my seat. With a hollow feeling in my stomach, I resign myself to the fact that we will soon be at Calder's mercy—which is pretty bad, because Calder doesn't have any mercy. I cling to the edge of my seat.

The EV tips on two wheels as Duke turns into the road that leads to the base. I suppress a scream. We almost flip over but no matter how fast the EV goes, the dashboard clock is moving faster. Duke skids into the parking lot and we leap through the gate and across the compound.

As we enter the training hall, changed into our Aqua8 wet-suits, there is absolute silence. The other cadets are standing motionless in a line, eyes dead ahead.

"Halt, Cadets." Calder's voice echoes through the loudspeaker. "Training starts at fifteen thirty sharp. It is now fifteen thirty-three. A few seconds can make the difference between life and death. Cadet Kallion, you owe me 180 seconds. You will pay for them in punishment lengths. That's 180 lengths. Fall in!"

I almost wonder whether she has forgotten about me when she shouts, "As for you, Cadet DeLora, I see you going from strength to strength. You've already shown your talent for failure and now you add laziness to your glowing record. Ninety lengths for you—you've done so many, they're starting to lose their bite. Fall in!"

I line up beside Duke and the other cadets, a sick feeling in my stomach. Ninety pool lengths? I will drown before I finish those. But I have a hunch that if I show any sign of weakness now, Calder will make our regular training session harder, too. So I clench my teeth and follow the others into the swimming pool.

"Keep swimming! Move it!" Major Hope shouts four hours later. I turn and begin my fiftieth length. Duke and I are the only ones left in the gloomy, barrel-roofed hall. The salt stings my eyes worse than ever today. I manage seventy-five lengths then cling on to the pool rim, barely able to keep my chin above water. My breath is coming in short, rasping bursts.

Major Hope shouts, "No stopping during this exerce—"

Shreeek!

I clasp my hands over my ears as Calder's voice interrupts him. "Cadet DeLora, you have already failed me once today. If you do not complete this simple exercise, I will make it a weekly task. Now move!"

I clench my teeth and continue swimming. The clock in the training hall shows 20:30 by the time I finish. My legs feel like jelly as I drag myself to the locker rooms. Duke is finishing his lengths in the semidarkness under the supervision of Major Hope. He managed to do nearly twice the amount I did in almost the same time. I walk out onto the parking lot and wait for him there.

"Ever felt like you're turning into a jellyfish?" Duke huffs when he finally appears.

"Least you don't have a scuttlefish waiting for you at home." I bite my lip, realizing what I said. "Sorry, I didn't mean—"

He grins. "Scuttlefish?"

"You know, a cross between a cuttlefish and something that's out to scuttle your buzz."

Duke laughs. "Oh right! Yeah, normally I'd have that *scuttlefish* over at my house. Or we'd go out for dinner, at the Golden Ark. You know the sort of thing: candlelight, wine, lobster."

"Actually, I don't know. I've never been out for a romantic dinner before."

"We've gotta change that. We'll go this Saturday night, OK?" Duke shoots me a wolfish grin and I want to bite my tongue.

"I don't think that would be fair on Jess—" I break off. What am I doing? This is my chance. It happened so naturally that I almost said no.

"Hey, doesn't have to be a date." Duke grins. "Just two teammates, hanging out. Where's the harm in that?"

I give him a small smile. "OK, yeah, I guess."

"Saturday at eight?"

"Sounds good."

I suppress the nervous thump of my heart. I did it—now I just have to get through the actual date that isn't a date.

*

"Uh, Jim, would it be OK, if I . . . went out this evening?" I ask while he's in the garden, recalibrating the garden bot.

He shoots me a curious smile. "Of course, Naya. I'd been wondering when you'd ask. I assume it's with that special someone from Marlo's birthday party?"

"Yes," I lie.

"Oooooh, how wonderful!" Mrs. Queen sweeps through the terrace door in a white-and-yellow dress. "Finding the perfect partner is so important. Their social credentials must be impeccable, of course."

I roll my eyes. Oh, no, where did she come from?

She continues, "Check if his parents are members of the Aeon Club. And remember, a good husband, two children max, that's the golden standard of our society. What did you say the name of the young man was?"

"Uh, I—"

"She didn't, Adelia dear," Jim comes to my rescue. "And I think Naya would very much appreciate it if we didn't ask."

Mrs. Queen stifles a look of disappointment. "Have you decided what you're wearing yet, Naya?"

"It's not an actual dat—" I begin.

"Oh, but you can't possibly go like this. Come with me." Her slender, white fingers grasp my hand. "Now, besides your outfit, we must also consider comportment. Don't drink from your finger bowl, that's for cleaning your fingertips after eating crustacea. And please remember, if you have a headache, fresh air doesn't help, painkillers do. I've had a complaint from the school—"

I shoot a desperate glance at Jim who suppresses a laugh while Mrs. Queen drags me away to her boudoir.

A few hours later I'm standing in the Queen's entrance hall in a horrible pale-pink dress that Mrs. Queen picked out. My hair is twisted into a bun that looks like something seagulls might nest in. What will Jim and Mrs. Queen say if they realize I'm going out with Jessica's boyfriend? Well, ex-boyfriend. If Jessica comes back from Sloane's before Duke arrives, she'll throw a fit for sure. I'm so nervous, I'd be chewing my nails, if Mrs. Queen hadn't insisted that I wear these horrid, long, fake pink nails. But when Duke's car finally pulls up in front of the Queen house, Jim has rushed back to work, to oversee some emergency, and Mrs. Queen is out in the back garden stopping the recalibrated garden bot from mowing zig-zags into her pristine lawn.

"Hey, gorgeous!" Duke greets me with a ravenous look. "You look stunning. Let's get out of here before the oldsters rock up and kill the vibe."

He opens the passenger door for me, putting a hand on my arm to guide me in. Then he gets into the driver's seat and shoots me another grin as he turns the key in the ignition. "Ready for our first date?" He hits the gas and we speed out of the driveway, amid a shower of gravel. What have I got myself into?

The Golden Ark is decorated in red and gold and is a little more intimate than the Aeon Club. Many couples are seated at the tables. Candlelight gleams off the silverware. A low murmur of discreet conversation eddies in the background. Duke keys the names "Kallion" and "DeLora" into a screen in the entrance, then leads me to table three. As I follow him across the room, I notice Arlo Quinn sitting across from us, talking to an elegant woman with white hair. He gives me a discreet nod. I nod back surprised. How did he know that we would be here? Has he been monitoring the reservations?

Duke pulls the seat out for me, then hangs his jacket on the back of his chair and sits down. His jacket is the only thing he has with him tonight. No bag. The syringe must be in his jacket pocket—if he even has it on him. But having observed him for the past three weeks I'm fairly sure that he carries it with him wherever he goes.

"Hey, Naya. Are you OK? You look kinda worried." Duke opens the top button on his black silk shirt and pulls at his tie so that it hangs at a jaunty angle.

I wrap my arms around me. "Yes . . . just cold. Can I borrow your jacket?"

"Seems hot in here to me. He-he, must be the company." He keeps his jacket on his chair and scrolls through the drinks list. "Ah, here's the vintage champagne that Dad always orders. A bottle of that will get you warmed up."

I give him my best flirty smile. "You're right, it will."

I skim over the menu displayed on our server bot, staring at the unfamiliar words. What does any of this mean? I click on three random things, one starter, one main course and one dessert. I'm so nervous, I won't be able to eat a bite anyway.

Across from us Arlo is now toasting the elegant white-haired woman with a glass of red wine.

"So what do you think of the Golden Ark? Romantic enough for you?" Duke asks.

I raise my brows. "I thought we were here as teammates?"

"If all my teammates looked like you, I'd have to hand in my captaincy of the Barracudas. Winning races would be the last thing on my mind." Duke leers at the neckline of my far-too-revealing dress.

The server bot brings a bottle of champagne and the starters. I cringe at the plate in front of me, which contains some horrible-looking, grayish jelly in shells.

"Oysters?" Duke gives me a grin. "Nice choice."

Not really. And why is he commenting on my food now?

Duke raises a glass. "To our first date."

I raise mine. "To our first nondate." I take a sip and put down my glass. Duke has already downed his. He grabs the bottle from the silver cooler by the table and pours himself another.

"What's with this 'nondate' stuff? You're not worried about Jessica, are you?"

"Well, we share the same house. And, I mean, we're friends, I guess."

Duke frowns. "Forget about it! She tried to sabotage you. She's crazy. Nuts. Demented. Besides, we broke up. She's got nothing to do with this and you owe her nothing."

Duke breaks off as the server bot brings out the main course. I stare at the shrimp tails sticking out of the salad in front of me. They look like some weird vegetable that's seen better days. I pick up my knife and fork, but they almost slip because of the fake nails that Mrs. Queen made me wear. How are you meant to eat with these? My fingers are like crab pincers.

By the time I've managed to take my first bite, Duke is already finishing up. At least it's given me time to think about how I'm gonna get to his jacket. I reach across the table, deliberately knocking my hand against his champagne glass, so that it spills into his lap.

"Oceans! I'm so sorry . . ." I leap up with him.

"It's . . . uh . . . it's OK." He dries himself off with the napkin.

"I'll . . . just . . . be right back." He hurries away in the direction of the bathroom.

I wait until he's out of view then quickly dig a hand into one of the side pockets of his jacket. Empty. I reach into the other side pocket . . .

"Miss DeLora." I jerk back my hand as the restaurant manager appears at my side. "Is everything all right?" He glances at the overturned champagne flute on the damp, white table cloth.

I give him a shy smile. "Yes. I spilled some champagne."

"Don't worry, Miss DeLora, we'll clean this up." In a second I'm surrounded by a gray-haired waiter and a whirring cleaning bot. I stand aside while they set the table anew. Gingerly I reach for the inside pocket of Duke's jacket. And there it is, the slender cylinder of the syringe. If I can just . . .

"Good, thank you."

I back away from Duke's chair as he suddenly returns. The restaurant manager and the waiter leave and we sit down again. Duke gives me his wolfish grin and pours himself a fresh glass of champagne.

"Drink up, Naya! This is the best champagne on Ararat."

I take a sip. I like the way the bubbles feel but my head is already beginning to spin.

"Will you come to the Water Festival with me?" Duke stares at me from across the table.

"Duke, I . . . I can't do that."

"Why not? Who else would you go with?"

"I don't know. I wasn't gonna go at all."

"Then why won't you go with me?"

"Jess . . ." I say. "I mean, you guys just broke up."

"OK, OK, I get that." He nods. "How about this then, Naya? You be my girlfriend. I won't tell anyone if you won't. It'll be our secret. What do you think? Huh?"

"I think you should try to patch things up with Jess."

"I already told you, we're through." His eyes are bloodshot and the muscles in his neck begin to tense. "Some date, HUH? Why did I even BOTHER!" It looks like he's about to break the glass in his hand. I draw a sharp breath—and then a crazy idea jumps to my mind. If he breaks the glass, he'll have to go to the bathroom again and I can get the syringe.

"Sounds kind of defeatist," I say. "Since when is it a Barracuda thing to give up? Do you think that's what GG would do?"

SMASH!

The glass goes to pieces. Champagne soaks the newly laid table cloth and blood drips from Duke's hand. He's stills squeezing the broken remains of the glass, but he doesn't even notice. For a moment I think he's gonna punch me. Then he launches himself from his chair, yanking the table cloth halfway off the table.

"Mr. Kallion!" Arlo appears at our table. "Are you well? Shall I call a medic?"

"Huh?" Duke gives him a vacant stare while the restaurant staff gather around us.

The manager clears his throat. "Perhaps a little bit of fresh air would do you good if you are feeling faint, Mr. Kallion?"

"I'm not feeling faint, you old porpoise. Get me more champagne!" Duke growls.

"I'm afraid I must insist, Mr. Kallion." The manager holds up Duke's jacket to him and waves over the security guards. "Pass on my regards and apologies to your father."

Duke gruffly flings on his jacket and follows the two guards outside.

I stare down at the messy table. Way to go. Now I've caused a public disturbance and I didn't get the syringe. As I dig a hand through my hair, I notice that I've lost one of Mrs. Queen's fake fingernails. I look around for it on the floor, but it's not there. Oh well, she'll just have to deal with it.

*

Over the following weeks, I barely see Jim and Mrs. Queen. Aqua8 training intensifies so much that I suspect Gillan might have been right, and that I was drafted into Junior Cadets to be kept busy. I'm doing punishment length after punishment length and can't focus on anything else.

Duke is twice as cautious as before, always locking his bag away, never loitering in the EV parking lot or between classes. I can't interpret the looks he gives me. They're halfway between longing and loathing. I wonder whether he noticed anything during the dinner. But how could he have? On the way to Aqua8 he acts no different than before. Maybe it's *me* who's losing my nerve.

My worries deepen with every day that we get closer to the Summer Solstice and the Finals, which are taking place the day before. May's almost over and I haven't been able to exchange a single word with Gillan. Did he find out what the device below the Governor's mansion does? Is Mom safe? What if our calculations were wrong? What if the Operation Neptune agents blow the FRS flood barrier earlier than we anticipated? These gray, gloomy thoughts loom over me like a dark monster eating up my joy. I might as well stop swimming all together. What does it matter if they send me to labor camp if Mom and all my friends are gonna die?

Calder's emotionless voice becomes an eerie soundtrack for my dreams. Her words "Cadet DeLora, you have failed this exercise" run over and over in a loop in my mind. They're a constant reminder that I am powerless to help Gillan.

In swim training I've started to adopt the same mechanical approach as for Aqua8: stroke, after stroke, after stroke.

"Naya DeLora, bench!" Janson calls out on the last Monday of the month.

"What happened, was my technique bad?" I ask as I hoist myself out of the pool.

"Your technique is fine. It's your race time that I'm worried about." Janson sits down on the Barracudas' bench next to me. "Where's that one length head start that you had over the others in the butterfly singles? You used to swim like it was second nature."

"Guess it would be better if killing was my second nature." I bite my lip. I completely forgot that school conversations are recorded. "I didn't mean . . ."

"Don't worry. I know exactly what you meant," Janson says grimly. She puts a hand on my shoulder. "Hang in there, Naya."

She stands up and blows her whistle. "Soraya, lead the cool down."

Once the class has finished, I shower off and slink away to the parking lot. The week continues in its usual blur of school, Junior Cadet training, and the short drive home, after which I barely manage to eat, then crash into bed, muscles aching. Come Wednesday, my head molds into the soft pillows, but I'm lost in a gray world of violence and killing. Through it all runs Calder's voice, icy, insidious, inescapable: "Finish him! Strike to the throat! KILL!"

I don't have the strength to pick up my e-pad and start my homework.

"Naya?" I look up and see Jessica in the doorway. "Peaches!"

The starlight above me turns from blue to a soft, orange hue.

"Mood lighting," she explains. "You looked kinda down so I changed the color to sunset." She jumps onto my bed and grabs my e-pad.

A tank of 15 pascals is 23 feet deep in the water. It sinks at a speed of 2.5 feet a minute for 30 minutes. How many pascals is it when it reaches its goal?

"Hydrostatics . . . ooh, you haven't even started." She starts tapping around, filling in the blanks.

"Go away, Jess," I whisper. The last thing I need is for her to write in the wrong answers, but I'm too tired to stop her.

"Naya." Jessica puts down the e-pad. "Is it true that they'd have sent you to labor camp if you hadn't won the race?"

"That's what they said they would do," I whisper.

She looks down at the e-pad and stays silent for a while. "You know, it's probably a bit late to say this, but I'm really sorry for what I did. I asked Daddy what goes on down there and . . . and it sounds really horrible. I was so jealous and silly. I thought you were stealing Duke away. And Daddy, too. And suddenly it was like your life was so much better than mine. But the stuff they're making you do at Aqua8 . . . you gotta have saltbrains to be jealous of that, right?"

"A little." I manage a small smile.

"And Duke . . . that was silly, too. I mean, he's more cracked than I thought you were when you first arrived here." Jessica pauses. "He told me what you said by the way. That he and I should get back together. I guess you probably won't ever forgive me, but if you can . . ." She holds out a hand. "Friends?"

I push myself off the bed to look at her. "Jess, I never meant to take your Dad away. Or Duke or any of your friends." Then I take her hand and nod. "Friends."

Jessica gives me a hug. "You know, having a sister is actually kind of nice." She blushes and picks up my e-pad. "Now, ssshhh . . . I've got a whole hydrostatics paper to take care of."

*

The next sessions of Aqua8 are brutal. Even Duke ends up with fifty punishment lengths. When Major Hope finally allows us to finish, I feel as though I'm sleepwalking. I keep one hand on the wall while I drag myself along the dark hallway. Halfway to the lockers I see a slim figure in a wetsuit walking toward me. I catch a glimpse of a white symbol on its chest, like an inverted trident. Am I hallucinating? I blink. When I open my eyes again, the figure's gone.

Did I just see an agent of Operation Neptune? No, that can't be. They wouldn't just be walking around Aqua8 headquarters. I shower and get changed, wondering if I should give Emmerson the agreed signal. But what's the point of risking a meeting when I don't have the syringe yet? Besides, Gillan might have seen the symbol himself by now.

That Friday Duke isn't at swim class. Jessica and I exchange a worried glance. We're less than two weeks from the Finals.

"Where's Kallion?" Coach Janson asks. "He better not think that he can copy Gallagher and skip class just because the Barracudas are on a winning streak!"

"He said he's overworked," Marlo says.

"Great, I feel like I'm teaching a class full of invalids," Janson exclaims. "Queen, take over as captain. Naya with me, let's get you ready for the Finals."

Janson has a point. If Aqua8 training continues at this rate, I won't make it to the Finals. I wonder if that's been Calder's plan all along.

*

Scrrrrchhh!

Calder's voice comes over the loudspeaker in a high-pitched squawk of static as we line up in her gloomy lair that afternoon.

"Attention. Night combat weapons training. Mission objective: retrieve weapons and ammunition and neutralize the enemy with silent force. Mission arena: marine. Remember, aim for the live targets. Punishment lengths will be added for stabbing the dummies. Commence exercise!"

The huge hall is plunged into darkness. I tighten my grip on the plastic knife in my hand. Flipping down my night vision goggles, I slip into the pool. I swim through the water without making a sound. The nearest combatant is standing with his back to the pool, armed with a knife and stun baton. Two packs of tranquilizer darts are lying at his feet, just outside his field of vision. What's Calder's catch this time? I search for combatants in the water, but the pool is unnervingly silent.

I dive then resurface just behind the combatant that I spied. I reach for the ammunition pack.

Brrrrrrr!

The pack emits a loud, whirring noise. The combatant spins around. He's got the advantage, with me in the water. I grab his foot and tug. While he flies onto his back, I haul myself out of the pool. My knife is in my hand as I hurl myself at him and plant my knee onto his chest, pinning him down. A spotlight beam snaps on from the control room and illuminates us.

"Finish him! Strike to the throat. Now!" A note of excitement flickers in Calder's voice.

The knife wavers in my hand. Even though it's a stupid plastic weapon, I hesitate. Suddenly the combatant flips me over and stabs me beneath the ribs. He twists the plastic knife to make it hurt more then flashes me a cruel smile and kicks his boot into my stomach twice. I double over, the wind knocked out of me.

"CADET DELORA!" Calder shouts. "This is what happens if you don't finish off your adversary. You pause at a crucial moment like this, you are not only throwing away your own life, you are jeopardizing the life of every single officer in your unit."

The guy above me pulls back his boot for another kick. At that moment a door slams open.

"Lights on!" a shout rings out.

I blink in the sudden brightness. Everyone around me stops where they are.

"Attention, attention," Calder calls out over the loudspeaker. "Whoever turned on the light report to me immediately for punishment lengths."

"No, I'm not here for your punishment lengths, Calder." Janson coolly strides across the room in khaki cargo pants and a black T-shirt. The briskness of her walk makes her hair fly.

"This is a secret operation." Calder's voice echoes over the loudspeaker. "You do not have military clearance. Remove yourself from this facility at once."

"You're doing night weapons combat training, mission area: marine, Junior Cadet level, there's nothing secret about it," Janson calls back. "Now quit snapping at me from your little tower and talk to me face to face."

There's no reply from the control room. The Aqua8 combatants around me tense as if they're awaiting attack orders, then the metal doors into the training hall swish open and Calder's gigantic figure sweeps in. Her expression is dark enough to kill as she strides past the soldiers who snap to attention. She stops no more than two feet from Janson. And as I look at the two of them, Calder seething, a thirst for vengeance in her eyes, and Janson in her military-style clothes, her expression set, I know: that most promising officer, who Calder keeps fuming about, who got kicked out of Aqua8, was Janson.

"Tread carefully, Coach," Calder hisses. "You're trespassing on military property—"

"What are you doing to Duke?" Janson interrupts. "Why is he missing classes?"

Calder looks at her surprised. "Duke Kallion's sloppiness has nothing to do with Aqua8. It's you whose standards are lax."

"Really?" Janson asks. "Because here's what I think: I think you're running this boy past his breaking point. And if that's the case, you'll have me to reckon with."

"Janson, are you threatening me?" Calder steps closer to her.

A shiver runs down my spine.

Janson doesn't back down an inch. "There's a rule. Junior Cadets have to be able to keep up with their academic studies.

If they can't, I will bring the matter before the principal, who has the power to remove a student from the Junior Cadet force." She glances at me, still hunched on the floor. "And that goes for ALL my students."

Calder's fingers twitch and her eyes flicker to the stun baton on the belt of the combatant next to me. "Don't cite regulations to me. I'm not the one incapable of following orders."

"Good, then we should have no problem." Janson turns and struts out.

"You better hope that you don't find yourself back under my command, *Captain*!" Calder calls after her. "I'd have you keel-hauled for this kind of act."

The door thuds after Janson walks out. While I get up, my knees shaky, I wonder whether the rumors that the A8C boys were talking about are true. Did Janson really sink Calder's flagship? And if she did, how did she get away with it? One thing's for sure: she's way overqualified for a swim coach.

CHAPTER 21

— The Finals —

As June 20 draws near, the Finals are all that everyone's talking about. Even the teachers are swept up in the excitement. Miss Li is distributing light revision exercises and Dr. Planck is watching "water-related learning clips" with us. I almost wish that we had a little bit of homework, to take my mind off all the anxiety that is building up in my chest. It's only just dawned on me that I'll be swimming against Gillan in front of the whole school. What if—and I know that it makes no sense—they can see how I feel about him? The thought of just the two of us on the starting blocks, with everyone watching, terrifies me.

"Hey, Naya!" Duke blocks my way in the hallway on the day before the race, just as Gillan passes. "Now that they finally lifted the curfew, wanna join the beach party we're throwing after we WIN?"

"You betcha!" I smile. That party might be my one—my last chance—at grabbing the syringe. The Water Festival is only a day away. My stomach twists itself into a knot as I walk to the swim hall. How will this last practice turn out? I dread the thought of a prematch between me and Gillan, but when I enter the hall it doesn't look like we're doing our usual practice. Two guys from the Rays and the Seals are dropping blue hoops into the pool at random intervals. Some of the other students have started lining up in two rows behind the black and the red starting blocks, regardless of their team.

"OK, listen up! I don't want anybody straining muscles this close to the big day, so we'll have a game of Fivers instead," Coach Janson calls. "You know how it goes. Five hoops at the bottom of the pool. First to retrieve three is the winner. The team with the most victors wins."

Soraya and Elijah, who are first in line, nod at each other and step onto the starting blocks.

"Ready, take your marks, GO!" Janson finishes with a sharp blast on her whistle. I join the left file and lean to the side to see what's going on.

"Man, I miss eighth grade." Marlo smiles. "We used to do stuff like this all the time."

Soraya climbs out of the pool with three hoops in her hand. She tosses them back in for Theo and Peterson. Peterson wins and is quickly joined by Ayumi and Torres, giving one point to us and three points to the other team. But all at once the cries and shouts of friendly rivalry die down. I step to the side and see Gillan and Duke standing at the starting blocks. Somehow they ended up next to each other. Janson looks as though she's contemplating asking another student to swap places, but that would kind of ruin the game.

"Ready, take your marks, GO!" She blows the whistle.

Gillan and Duke hit the water together. When they resurface, they each have not one but two hoops looped around their wrist. In a frenzy, they scan the bottom of the pool then, at the same time, they dive for the deciding hoop, disappearing in a splash of water. The students around me hold their breath and crane their necks to see who comes up first, but the surface of the pool stays disturbingly calm.

"Are they trying to set a freediving record?" Marlo says next to me.

"Duke's never ever freedived for more than a minute." Jessica sounds anxious.

Coach Janson strides along the edge of the pool until she's level with their blurry outlines. She looks like she's gonna dive in herself. Then water erupts as Gillan and Duke break the surface. Gillan is bleeding from his arm, but he has the third hoop safely in one hand. With the other he's fending off Duke who's attempting to push him under.

Janson's blast on her whistle is so sharp, it makes my ears go numb. "Kallion! Gallagher! Enough! Poolside now!"

They haul themselves out of the water. Gillan is clutching his arm. There's blood welling out from under his splayed fingers.

"Have both of you completely lost your minds!" Janson snaps at them. "Gillan — "

"Coach . . . he bit me," Gillan says.

Janson stares at the blood that's now running down his arm. "Seven seas! You look like you got mauled by a shark! Kallion, what's wrong with you?"

She ushers them outside. Through the glass windows of the swim hall, I watch her burst into an angry rant. But although I strain my ears, I can't hear a word. Gillan and Duke both look confused. Eventually, Janson stops shouting and Gillan strides off toward the nurse's office while Duke heads to the locker rooms. Janson steps back inside.

"Class dismissed," she calls out. "Shower off, go home, and Goldstein, get a cleaning bot to wipe up that blood before we get some prissy hygiene complaint from the principal."

I'm shaking as I walk to the locker rooms. There was so much blood . . . I hope Gillan's OK. How could Duke have possibly bitten him so badly? I let the water splash over my face in the shower. I hate this pretending! I want to run to Gillan and ask him how he's feeling. I'm so tired of always being on the wrong side.

I dry off, get changed, and cross the lawn to the EV parking lot when I'm grabbed by the arm.

"Gillan!" I stare at him in shock. "What are you doing? We can't — "

"It doesn't matter." Gillan pulls me closer to the wall. "I don't want you to follow Duke anymore, OK? Something's wrong. He wasn't himself today in the water."

"I know he's not himself!" I hiss back. "That's the whole point. But if I don't do something now, it'll be too late."

"No." Gillan holds my gaze. "He's . . . dangerous. I don't want you anywhere near him!"

"But — "

"Naya, look!" Gillan rips the fresh, white bandage off his upper arm. I gasp. There are two sets of deep circular gashes, one inside the other, from a double set of razor-sharp teeth. They don't look human at all.

"Oceans!" I exclaim.

"Naya, he's not normal," Gillan urges me. "I need you to stay away. Promise me."

"OK," I whisper.

He gives me one more look then turns and hurries away.

*

The next day the anticipation of the race numbs all my other thoughts.

"Just think, if you win the Iron Teens Naya, no one can send you away from Ararat, like ever," Jessica chimes as we arrive at school. She spins into the driveway signposted Staff Parking. "Normally students are like totally not allowed to park here, but today you're not a student. You're an Iron Teens competitor. And it's less walking from the staff parking lot to the swim hall. You should take every advantage over GG you can get."

I doubt that walking five yards less than Gillan will help me win the race, but I don't want to tell her that. Jessica's been trying really hard to be nice to me in the last few weeks.

Another vehicle pulls up two bays down from us. "Ladies!" Duke ostentatiously pulls off the unbuttoned shirt that he's wearing over his T-shirt and flexes his shoulder muscles. "Hot day!"

I want to look away, but something glints bluish in his front pocket. Was that a syringe? Duke leaps out of his EV, his shirt clasped in his hand and slams the door. And then I see it again. That's definitely it!

I hold my breath. I know I promised Gillan not to do anything, but if Duke's growing animal teeth, isn't that all the more reason to find out what's going on? And after the race—with everyone distracted—I'll have a better chance of grabbing the syringe than at the beach party.

Duke opens the trunk, pulls out his sports bag, and stows his shirt in the back of the EV.

"Let's go!" he calls out. "Victory awaits."

I enter the swim hall into a roar of noise. The spectator stands are overflowing. It's like all of Ararat is here. A big wreath with Eden Academy Swim Finals emblazoned on it hangs from the railing and a microphone and podium have been set up. Beneath the spectator stands the team captains and some council members are huddled around Principal Preen. As I walk past, Governor Proctor emerges from their midst.

"Ah, here she is. The new sensational swimming . . . uh, sensation." He looks relieved to have gotten away from Preen. "Good luck today, Miss DeLora. Pardon me, I should be up there . . ." With an apologetic smile he points to the seats of honor by the wreath. Two ladies are already sitting there. Mrs. Proctor and Mrs. Preen, presumably.

Principal Preen hurries to join them and taps the microphone by his seat. "Ladies and gentlemen, I need not tell you what an important day this is for Eden. Today we will see all of the virtues that we on Ararat hold so dear: courage, willpower, technical skill, the desire to win"— a burst of applause follows from the parents in the stands and Preen gives a vainglorious smile, — "and never in my time as principal of this fine educational establishment has the competition been so close going into the Finals. There has never been a greater call for everyone to demonstrate their absolute best. But, in the end, there can only be one winning team. So I urge all competitors to swim like they have never swum before. To swim like their lives depended on it. Ladies and gentlemen, I give you the Eden Academy Finals."

The crowd breaks into applause again.

Janson turns to Coach Almeida. "Switch on the scoreboard and double-check that the starting blocks are clean. I want to have a prerace talk with our Iron Teens champs." She waves me and Gillan over. "You're both staying with me. I don't want a repetition of the Midterms. We still don't know what happened there."

We stride past the spectator stands when the double wings of the main entrance fly open and General Calder marches in, flanked by two officers. She stops in front of us and pulls a pout at Gillan. "Lieutenant Gallagher. Our ranking officer. I trust you will uphold the reputation of Aqua8's finest today? And Cadet DeLora. Let's see if all those punishment lengths did you some good. After all, you're full of surprises. I hear you qualified for the Iron Teens, an astounding ten days before the beginning of the tournament?" Her eyes wander to Coach Janson while she says it.

I shift nervously. Is Calder fishing for information, or did she find out somehow that Janson broke the law, trying to keep me out of the Irons?

Janson looks at her unperturbed. "In terms of rapid ascensions that's not the only thing that's astounding on Ararat, General."

Calder pouts more, if that's even possible.

"Coach, shouldn't we be getting ready for the race?" Gillan asks.

Calder and Janson stare each other down for another moment then Janson walks off with me and Gillan. I exchange a concerned glance with Gillan.

"Don't worry," Janson says. "She can't actually have me keelhauled. She'd need a bigger boat first."

"Keelhauled?" Gillan raises an eyebrow. "Should I be looking forward to hearing that story or sending you a Galileo Tecc security detail?"

"You should be focusing on your race," Janson fires at him then hides a smile.

Seriously, how can they be cracking jokes at a time like this?

We walk over to the team benches. "Naya, start warming up," Janson says, then loud enough for the surrounding students and coaches to hear, she adds, "Gillan, you might want to think about swapping in a sub for your freestyle singles. You don't want to strain your injured shoulder before the Irons."

"Why?" Gillan gives me a cocky smile. "I'm only swimming against this shrimp."

"Your choice," Janson tells him. "Get to your starting block then. You and Kallion are up first."

While they pull off their charade for the cameras and bystanders, I fight back the suffocating feeling in my throat. I can't even ask Gillan if his arm actually hurts. He and Duke dive into the pool on Coach Almeida's whistle. They're neck to neck for the first lap then Duke shoots ahead. It must be the serum that's making him faster. My heart pounds. If Duke wins now and Gillan throws the Irons, won't that arouse suspicion? Calder's already on alert and only waiting for us to trip up.

Around me, the whole Barracuda team are on their feet in anticipation.

"He's gonna break GG's record!" Kayla squeaks.

Gillan and Duke flipturn. In the middle of the final length Gillan suddenly zooms past Duke with almost superhuman speed.

SEAL VICTORY: GILLAN GALLAGHER flashes up on the scoreboard. A one-point bonus gets added, for a new time record. Duke howls in rage. I sigh with relief—and at a glance from Mia, quickly change it into a groan.

Gillan uses the stairs, rather than hauling himself out of the pool, and calls over a medic as he walks to the Seals' bench. The medic jabs a needle into his arm. I bite my lip. Gillan's doesn't look like he's acting much. He's a shade paler than usual and seems a bit dazed.

"Look at Mr. Perfect pulling a show because I nearly beat him!" Duke slams himself onto the Barracudas' bench while the singles races continue.

Jessica wins her freedive, Mia loses her breaststroke, and I ace my butterfly, bringing the score after the singles to thirty-five points for the Barracudas and thirty-four points for the Seals with only the relay and the Iron Teens to go. The Sharks and Rays are in third and fourth place with thirty-one and twenty-two points and no more chance of catching up.

I glance at Gillan as we line up behind the starting blocks in our groups of four. Should I hold back on my butterfly lap? He avoids my gaze, but he's got more color in his face again. The injection must have helped.

I decide to give it my all in the butterfly and luckily so. When I hit the touchpad, Alba Williams and I are level. She swam faster than I've ever seen. Gillan and Duke enter the pool in sync, but this time Gillan takes an early lead. Although Duke churns up the water like a speedboat, he can't do more than match Gillan's pace. The audience are on their feet. This is the spectacle they were hoping for. Gillan and Duke are still tied in the final length. They slam their hands against the touchpad simultaneously.

SEAL VICTORY: RELAY TEAM

Duke pulls himself out of the pool shaking with anger. "How is he doing this?" He turns his bloodshot eyes to Gillan.

BLUE OUT

"He's been holding back the whole time," Zeke hisses through gnashed teeth.

Duke grabs me by the arms. "Naya, in the Iron Teens, finish him! Tear him to shreds, make him bleed!"

"Duke, stop shaking her around," Kayla says. "She's not a bottle of shampoo."

"Sorry." Duke lets go of me.

"I'll try my best," I promise, glancing at Gillan. He looks like he's about to faint. The medic is back by the Seals bench.

What if Gillan really isn't well? I think of Aidan Fynn. What if he *actually* died of overexertion? Can it happen to anyone? Gillan and I don't look at each other as we walk to our starting blocks after the thirty minute interval.

We step onto the blocks in sync and wait for Coach Almeida to call, "Ready, take your marks, GO!"

The FWEET of his whistle rings out and we hit the water. I chase Gillan in a smooth breaststroke. Already the gap between us is closer than it ever has been. I push myself to swim faster. I have to put in my absolute best to make this look credible. Neither of us takes a long breathe-up before the freedive. The shouts of the audience are silenced as the water closes over my head. I risk a quick glance at Gillan.

"GO!" he mouths to me. I kick out and pass him.

The audience gasps, surprised, as I surface first. I complete my second lap of freediving and hurl myself into butterfly. Water splashes around me. Without the anxiety, without the fear of losing, I'm breathing fast, but freely. For once my legs feel normal. As I flipturn for the freestyle I've got a solid head start over Gillan. I can hear the audience shout, "Barracudas!" and it spurs me on. In the final length I hear water splashing behind me and I know that Gillan is catching up as much as he dares. I leap ahead and thump my palm against the touchpad. Then I tear off my goggles and blink at the flashing scoreboard.

BARRACUDA VICTORY: NAYA DELORA

I catch a glimpse of Gillan, clutching his arm and swimming for the stairs while my team pulls me out of the pool and into a group hug.

"We won! We won!" Jessica is jumping up and down.

"BARRACUDAS!" Duke, Zeke, and Marlo lift me up and carry me to the podium.

Preen's voice comes over the microphone. "Ladies and gentlemen, what an exciting race day . . ."

The rest of his speech is drowned out by the Barracudas' shouting. I'm lost in a blur of whoops and victory cries until suddenly I'm on the podium and Governor Proctor hands me a small golden cup with Iron Teens, 243 PI engraved.

Preen shouts into the microphone. ". . . but today we not only have a new champion for the Iron Teens but we also have a new winning team. Duke Kallion, captain of the Barracudas, please step to the podium and accept the Eden Academy Swim Tournament Cup."

As all eyes turn to Duke, I scan the rest of the hall. Some of the swimmers are already leaving. Gillan is talking to Calder and Proctor. Quietly, I follow Soraya and Ayumi to the locker rooms. I shower off in a hurry, get dressed, stow my things in my locker, along with my newly won trophy, and rush outside to the teachers' parking lot. If I want to grab the syringe, now is the moment. Duke's EV is still where he left it. I pull open the trunk and snatch up his shirt. Finally! I take the syringe from the chest pocket where he stowed it when a white cloth with an odd chemical smell is pressed over my mouth.

"Ghmpf!"

Someone grabs my arms. The Eden parking lot distorts into a smudge of gray, green, and sky-blue and I feel as though I'm falling into an endless abyss.

CHAPTER 22

— *The Scourge of Ararat* —

The veil of blackness lifts. I blink. A distorted, gray room swims into focus. I want to lift my chin, but my head feels heavy. My arm stops short as I try to move it. Anxious, I look down. There are leather bindings on my arms and legs, strapping me to a medical reclining chair. Duke is standing, with his back to me, by a wall of machines with flashing lights. He hasn't noticed that I'm awake yet. I slowly turn my head. What is this place?

There are lab tables with glass vials, petri dishes, and miscellaneous apparatuses. To my left I see a water tank. It's half-full. Streaks of blood are smeared against the glass above the water level. A shiver runs down my back. My eyes dart to the only exit I can see: a tunnel entrance leading uphill, reflected in the glass of the water tank. Then I spot a second entrance on the upper gallery level, which is made up of two metal walkways running parallel below a rocky ceiling. I glance back at the machines that cover the wall where Duke is standing. They are white, with numerous buttons, levers, wheels and display screens. The other walls are bare rock. There are no windows, only a stone cave ceiling high above me, crisscrossed with pipes of varying diameters. We must be in some kind of underground lab.

Then it hits me: the cable car station. This is the secret laboratory that Duke and Douglas disappeared to when I followed them up the mountain. The one that Gillan and Arlo talked about where Kallion manufactures the serum Duke's taking. The tunnel must lead up to Mortlake, which means . . . great, my only way out of here is through Douglas Kallion's office!

I tug at the leather straps, but they hold tight. Duke turns around to me and a smile appears on his face.

"So, I was right. You were trying to steal the serum off me."

"How did you know?" I ask.

He grins. "One of your fake nails fell into the pocket of my dinner jacket."

I grit my teeth. Mrs. Queen and her stupid fashion obsession! "Duke, why—?"

He picks up a syringe loaded with a clear liquid from one of the lab tables. "You did such a bad job of it. I'm thinking maybe deep down you wanted me to find out. So that we can be together." He gives me a wolfish smile. "Why did you want the serum anyway?"

I remain silent.

He approaches, holding the syringe upright, a thumb poised on the plunger. "Doesn't matter. Whatever the reason, it's all good. Soon you'll understand. And then we can be together. Always."

What does he mean, "together"? I struggle against the straps. "Duke, no. Please!" All I know is that I want him to keep that syringe far away from me. "It's the blue liquid that's controlling you."

He starts dabbing my arm with a piece of cotton wool. "The blue liquid is making me who I'm meant to be. It's speeding up the evolutionary process. Soon I'll be indestructible. Invincible. Master of the element of water." The veins in his face and neck are blue and bulging.

The evolutionary process? It dawns on me. "Wait . . . you're trying to become a variant?"

"Not *trying*!" he exclaims. "I *am* becoming a variant."

I stare at him. It's so obvious all of a sudden. His swimming, the mood swings, the superhuman speed. "Duke, this is insane," I whisper.

"True, the withdrawal symptoms suck," Duke agrees. "But you've seen what the serum can do. When I've finally become what I'm supposed to be, I will be able to transform at will. I will be the best of the best. And Gallagher's gonna be squished like an ant by a giant."

I picture the gashes on Gillan's arm and cringe. Duke's teeth must have been transformed when he bit him. "You're crazy!"

I shout. "If you think you can cheat the natural way of things, you're wrong!"

"The natural way of things is the survival of the fittest. And the fittest are the ones able to adapt. Like me." Duke's eyes are fixed unblinkingly on mine.

I clench my fists. "I'm never gonna let you hurt Gillan."

Duke's knuckles turn white. "Oh, is that how things are?" he hisses. "You and the golden boy?" For a moment I hope he's gonna break the syringe, but he grabs my arm instead.

"Well, that's gonna change, too. And you're gonna be by *my* side. Consider yourself lucky. Just three injections with the new improved formula. You won't have to go through what I went through."

The cold point of the needle pricks my skin.

"I wouldn't do that if I were you!" a voice rings out from the upper metal walkway.

We both freeze and turn to the lab-coated figure. I expected Douglas Kallion. But it isn't. It's Jim Queen.

"No!" My insides twist. Jim. The only father I ever had. "You can't . . . How could you . . ."

Footfalls clang on metal as Jim slowly descends the stairs of the gallery. He ignores me completely and takes the syringe from Duke's hand, placing it in his lab coat pocket. "This injection is very powerful," he says. "The compound of metallic elements and stem cells in the serum is designed to transform the human body. But only the human body. If at any point it were injected into a real genetic variant, it might prove lethal."

I freeze. Jim knows? How can that be?

Duke is staring at me, dumbfounded. "Naya . . . is a variant?"

"Well, I can't be sure. Not until I've run certain tests." Triumph gleams in Jim's eyes. "But I think she might be a true variant. A born variant. You see, according to my research there are two types of variant. Those who are born as variants and the second type, who have the gene in a dormant state and in whom it can become active at a later date, typically in adolescence. It was the latter type that gave me the idea that the variant process could be engineered artificially. The serum I've designed creates the requisite genetic mutation that transforms any human subject into a variant."

I can't believe what he's saying. "It was you all along," I whisper. "Not Kallion. You."

"Kallion played his part, sure enough," Jim says, with a cautious look at Duke.

"H-how did you know about me?" I ask.

"Oh, I suspected from the moment Jessica told me about the race on the volleyball beach. An FRS-girl beating one of Ararat's best swimmers . . . that screamed variant to me. Which is why, of course, I used all my influence to make sure that we became your host family. The chance to observe a natural born variant first hand was one that I simply couldn't afford to miss."

"So that's what I was to you all this time." The tears are burning in my eyes. "Just a . . . a specimen. Something to be observed and monitored?"

"Don't take it personally, Naya. I did what had to be done. Thankfully Calder played right into my hands. She has spent the past few years making everyone on Ararat believe that variants are sea monsters, the Aquatic Other, lurking in the depths of the ocean. So you see, I was quite certain that no one else would notice your abilities. You can imagine how upset I was when Preen had you put forward for the Iron Teens—the one race that might give you away. And then Jessica tried to sabotage you . . . it almost ruined everything."

"You didn't tell her?" I ask.

"No." Jim glances at the instruments on the lab table. "*I* would never endanger my own flesh and blood. But I will do what I must to aid the human race. To advance scientific knowledge."

"To advance your own interests, you mean," I snap back at him. "Don't tell me you're going to use that serum for the good of humanity."

"But that's where you are wrong, Naya!" A manic gaze appears in Jim's eyes. "Once this drug is perfected, a new world order will arise. A world of beauty and strength. The weaknesses and corruption of the old world will fall away like a bad dream. And I will be the savior of the human race, a savior who has bestowed upon all of humanity a divine gift. Mastery of the

Waters." He laughs in triumph. "And for this, Naya, for this, I shall be worshipped as a god."

"You're insane," I shout. "Nobody's gonna worship a madman."

"Those who join my cause will live," Jim continues coldly. "Those who do not will die. Swallowed up by the sea. That is the simple choice people will have. It is the same choice that every god has given their worshippers since man dragged himself out of the primeval swamp and bowed down in veneration of its first idol." He laughs. "And you, Naya, are going to help me perfect this new drug. With the genetic input of a born variant, I will finally have the missing piece of the puzzle."

My eyes wander to the water tank and it dawns on me that that must be what it's for: experiments on variants! I tear at my bonds. "Over my dead body!"

Jim smiles. "Well, there is a lot that can be done by way of experimentation before we get to that final, inevitable stage."

"NO!" Duke throws himself between me and Jim. "I won't let you harm her!"

"Quiet!" Jim barks. "We have more important things to focus on. Operation Neptune is about to begin. Your father's waiting for your help with the final preparations."

"I'm not going anywhere. You told me I would be a variant by the time of the Water Festival." Duke turns his bloodshot eyes to Jim. "I'm not. And this stuff's making me sick. Give me one of the new injections."

"That's not possible," Jim says. "After the course of injections you've already taken, the dosage would be too high. The effects of an overdose could be catastrophic."

"I SAID" — Duke sweeps his hand across the steel counter, sending a collection of beakers and petri dishes crashing to the floor — "GIVE ME" — he pushes over a metal cabinet — "THE SERUM!" He stares at Jim, breathing heavily, his skin unnaturally red.

Jim calls into a walkie-talkie, "Get me a security team down here. NOW!"

The word *security* snaps Duke out of it. He stares at the mess of broken glass on the floor and wipes a trembling hand over his face. "No, no. It's OK. I'd better go. Dad will be expecting me."

He crouches down and starts gathering up the glass shards. "Don't worry, Mr. Queen, I'll get this cleaned up in no time."

Two guards clatter down the stairs from the upper gallery.

Jim spins around. "There you are. Kindly escort Mr. Kallion from the facility."

While Jim's back is turned, I see Duke quickly slip three unbroken vials of the clear liquid into his sleeve. For a moment, I have the crazy urge to tell Jim, to prevent Duke from over-dosing on variant serum. But who knows what Jim will do to Duke then. So I say nothing as Duke is led out of the lab, through the Mortlake tunnel, by the two guards.

"Naya, Naya." Jim turns to me with a chuckle. "Too clever for your own good. I've got to admit, I'm feeling more than a little proud, as your foster father. You and Duke spared me quite an ordeal. I've been wondering how to prize you out of the clutches of the Elites. They've been drawn to you like moths to a flame. The swimming sensation from the shelter. Imagine how disappointed they would be if they knew the truth."

I grit my teeth. "You won't get away with this. My friends will come looking for me."

"Oh, Naya." Jim laughs heartily. "After tomorrow night no one will come looking for you. I have a little surprise prepared. A surprise that ensures that the ruling families on Ararat will either be on my side or dead." He brushes my damp hair from my forehead in an almost concerned manner. "Unfortunately the production of this variant serum requires a lot energy. More than the local Elites have been willing to assign me. So, certain steps had to be taken for a change in leadership. And a neces-sary population reduction."

I feel the pit of my stomach turn to ice. Population reduc-tion? "You exploded the flood barrier of the Valley!" I exclaim tearing at my bonds. "It was you! People died because of you! They all . . ." A wave of sobs rakes my body, making my throat too tight to shout.

"I told you before, what I do is for the good of humanity," Jim says.

"And what if the serum doesn't work? What then?" I glare at him through a veil of tears. "You'd kill all those people, use up all the resources—for *nothing*?"

Jim shrugs. "In the unlikely event that this were to happen, I'll move on. Just like I did before. You didn't really think that my family and I ended up here by accident, did you?" He smiles. "But I don't think a relocation will be necessary. Ararat has resources enough. And the populace will thank me in the end. At least, those that survive will. But none of this need worry you. You will be safely out of harm's away. Kallion will be Governor. And Ararat's resources will be mine. To complete my experiments. With your help, of course, Naya. Which reminds me . . ."

Jim speaks into his walkie-talkie again. "Send down a tech team."

A moment passes, then the metal door at the end of the room opens. A man and a woman dressed in white lab coats walk in. Jim waves them over to a lab table and gives them instructions. They begin to prepare a clear liquid that they load into a syringe. When they're ready the man walks over. I can do nothing but watch as he pushes the needle into my arm with a stone-faced expression. My head thumps as the liquid enters my blood. Nausea overtakes me. The door opens again and a team of men in black battle gear enter. Then the room blurs and I close my eyes to stop the headache. I can still hear Jim talking.

"We have a problem, Kallion can't be trusted."

"Which one?" a rough voice asks.

"Both," Jim answers.

The rough voice speaks again but the words meld into each other.

"No, Captain." That's Jim again. "Nothing allowed . . . jeopardize Operation Neptune. Not . . . close to success."

My head drops and everything goes grayish.

"Nightfall. Take . . . girl . . . *Atlantean*."

Footsteps echo. I'm floating two feet above the ground. There is a whoosh and my stomach lurches as I'm carried upwards. One moment there is a wall in front of me, the next it is gone. I float on. Where are we? Mortlake? What does that mean,

THE SCOURGE OF ARARAT

anyway, the Lake of the Dead? All this machinery, these dials and controls . . . I've been here before . . . the cable car . . . Douglas and Duke . . . But they are not here now . . . I hear strange voices. I feel sick as I try to listen. It's too dark to see anything.

A soft breeze brushes my face and a black figure surrounded by a greenish glow walks toward me. I catch a glyph on its chest—an upside-down trident. I've seen this before. Where? But I can't fight anymore. It's the last thing I remember as the world goes black.

CHAPTER 23

— The Atlantean —

I awake with a dull ache in my head. It feels like someone has hit me with a heavy metal object. Around me there's an odd creaking, and the whole ground is shifting to-and-fro. Suppressing a feeling of sickness, I force my eyes open. I flinch in the light of a lantern giving off a dim glow. It's swinging from the ceiling like a pendulum. Opposite me affixed to a wood-paneled wall is a desk and on top of the desk sits a compass along with all kinds of nautical charts and instruments. A porthole window to my side faces a dim ocean, where a dusky sky meets a churning sea. I must be in the cabin of a ship! But a strange ship, made of wood. The creaking is the masts and sails swaying in the wind and the nauseous, rolling motion is the waves pushing us back and forth as we lie at anchor here. But where is here? I can't see any land outside, only the gray horizon. It's early morning or late evening, I can't tell. My best guess is that the night has passed and a new day is dawning.

I shift my arms. They are tied to the armrests of a wooden chair. Trying to shake the dizziness, I glance back at the nautical instruments. They're nothing like anything I've ever seen: bulky, large, and made of metal; like they're new and old at the same time. The ceiling creaks louder and I hear footsteps on deck. They're followed by a distant murmur of voices. I try to catch what they are saying, but the voices are too low and covered by the gentle hum of an electric generator somewhere in the bowels of the ship. What was Jim saying to his team in the hidden lab? Something about a problem, Atlantean . . . My head hurts as I try to remember. Operation Neptune! Wait, he's planning on taking over Ararat. With Douglas Kallion. To get control of the resources. And he wants to kill the Elite leaders. Tomorrow. But tomorrow is today! Suddenly wide awake,

I tear at the ropes. Whatever Jim is planning is happening tonight — I have to get out of here. NOW!

I fling my weight back into the chair, trying to lift it off the floor, but it won't move. Either it's fixed down or weighs a ton. I twist and turn my wrists. There has to be a way . . .

As I struggle to get free, the cord around my left wrist keeps catching on something. I lean forward and see an old nail sticking out just below the armrest. I stop my frenzied struggling and move my arm back and forth and make the cord scratch against the nail every time it passes. Blood trickles down my hand from the friction. I watch the rope getting thinner. Finally it snaps and falls to the floor. I tear at the knots around my other wrist and legs and prize them open. I leap up and rush to the cabin door and try the heavy brass handle. Locked. Obviously. If I try to kick the door open the whole ship will hear me — and I'll probably hurt my leg.

I scan the cabin for another way out. The porthole. I rush over to it. It isn't very large, but maybe I can squeeze through. I flick down the latch on the brass frame and pull it open. Carefully, I stick my head outside. I can see land to my left. A row of dark hilltops. More than ten feet below me the rough sea splashes against the hull. Droplets of water fly up into my face as the ship tilts in the storm. The whitecaps are almost as high as on the day I tried to swim to the FRS to see Mom. I clutch my necklace. I can't leave it behind — but if I survived ninety punishment lengths at Aqua8 wearing it, I can also do this.

Only, where do I go after I reach the shore? I look at the barren, rocky cliffs. How far along the coast of Cape Harmony are we? The hills all look the same in the scant light of dawn. I strain my eyes and spot a set of pillars holding the cable car wire on a distant mountain top. That would make this the western side of Cape Harmony. We must be just north of the Aqua8 base and Ararat Heights, about three or four miles from Ararat Harbor. The flood barriers will be raised in this weather, but if I manage to swim south, past them, I will get to Breakers Cove, just below Gillan's house. If I can make my way up the hill and tell him what happened, maybe we can stop Jim together. I just hope that I won't trigger another variant hunt when I pass the military base.

With my heart racing, I push my arms out of the porthole, brushing my fingers along the hull to find something to hold onto. Above me, the masts rise into the sky like skeleton trees, the sails furled. I find a rigging rope hanging off the railing and cling onto it. Then I wriggle myself further out, until I can sit in the ledge. I'm about to pull my legs out when I hear a loud creak of footsteps right above me.

I grab tighter onto the rope and hold my breath. A second pair of footsteps joins the first. Suddenly they stop. Has whoever's up there on deck noticed me? I hardly dare move. At that moment a voice rings out.

"Let's ready the other little boats. We're gonna need them to carry the people aboard."

The man has a foreign accent. I wonder if he's from a different place, like Jim? I prick up my ears and continue listening.

"What do you mean?" A rougher voice replies. "We only need the one boat."

"For a crew o' fifty? That's gonna sink the wee boat, that is."

"What fifty, bone'ead? The boss ain't gonna wait around for the whole crew if things go south."

"Oooh, I catch your meaning," the foreign-sounding voice says. "If the plan's gonna go wrong the boss's gonna run down the hills, taking nothing with him but the shirt he's wearing — but the plan ain't gonna go wrong, my friend."

"I'm not sure, mate," the rough voice replies. "I betcha, come midnight, we'll see a bright red flare and Jimmy-boy running down that hill right there with his dame and daughter like he's being chased by some monster tidal wave. Betcha all the money in my pocket."

"I'll take that bet."

I draw a sharp breath. Jim's crew are lying in wait, ready to escape. If Operation Neptune fails, Jim will double-cross the Kallions, ditch them, and move on to a different place — to drain it of its resources, just like he's done before.

"Hey," the foreign voice says at that moment, "let's go check on the girl."

I almost fall out of the window from fright.

"No need, my friend," the other man replies. "She's sleepin' real tight."

"You sure?"

"Plenty sure. That drug they gave her could've knocked out a whale. Betcha all the money in my pocket."

"Hey, your pants don' have no pockets!"

I stifle a laugh, despite my nervousness. On deck a clatter and a grunt echo, as if the two men have started fighting. I wait a moment for their footfalls to disappear into the distance then pull myself all the way out of the porthole. Pushing my legs against the hull, I jump away from the ship and into the water. The cold waves swallow me up. I let the momentum of the fall carry me down, then swim away from the ship, putting as much distance between me and Jim's crew as I can. When I surface and look back, I can just about make out the golden letters of the word *Atlantean* on the broad stern in the dim light. Is it me, or is it getting darker? I kick out and swim toward Ararat, spewing water as a wave splashes over my head.

Around me, the sounds of the sea are dull. I can't hear or feel the water, like I do without my trident necklace, only the current getting stronger and my arms tiring. The clouds turn darker and darker. Where did a storm like this come from, in the calm season? It was bright and sunny only yesterday. Even though I'm used to unexpected Blue Outs, the sudden vehemence of it unnerves me. Ahead looms the dark structure of the Aqua8 flood barrier with its watchtowers. A single star blinks above me. Then it hits me! It's not morning. It's evening. The man said I'd been given a drug that could've knocked out a whale. . . . I lost a whole night and day. The Water Festival is only a few hours away.

I tell myself not to panic. If I swim faster now, I'll tire myself out before I reach Breakers Cove. I have to keep a consistent pace. Rough waves splash into my face each time I surface. I keep my eyes on the shore, searching for the flood barrier protecting Ararat Harbor, but I can't see it. The next time I dive there's a shadow moving below me. Slim and so fast it's gone before I can see it clearly. Unnerved, I resurface.

BLUE OUT

What was that? I dive again, my senses prickling with the feeling of being watched. Again there's movement, this time on my right. Then I see a sharp outline of a backfin, contrasted gray against the water. A shark! It takes all my self-composure not to lunge toward the shore. I'm swimming near the surface, at dusk, its prime hunting time. If I start thrashing around, it will only attack more quickly. I dive deeper—and almost scream as a second, dark shape appears beside me. It's circling me, like sharks do with their prey before they attack. Then another swims by below me. It's as if they're drawn to me.

Wait . . . my hand. The blood. No, no, no, no! I propel myself to the surface. I know that's the worst thing to do, but I can't hold my breath any longer. Water splashes and I draw in a few panicked gasps, then immediately dive back under. The shapes are moving around me fast, so close, I can see their razor-sharp teeth. Suddenly, one breaks off its circles and zooms toward me. Its open mouth gapes at me. I have about a second to register that I'm gonna die in a very nasty way. Then a second shadow appears and whips its tail at the jaw of the first. The two are fighting each other. Fighting over who gets to eat me! I curl into a ball. The reverse currents brush my body as the sharks whirl around me. I feel a forceful push from behind, like one of them has crashed into me. I almost shout out. There is a tug around my waist and something starts propelling me forward, carrying me toward the shore. The water is rushing around me so forcefully I can't see. All I catch is a glimpse of a shark's tail to my right. This can't be . . . It's like one of them has started dragging me away, as its personal prey. Sharks don't do that. The others are giving chase, following the scent of my blood. My lungs are screaming for air. I try to surface, but the tug around my waist is firm. My head is pounding when finally I'm pushed up out of the water and onto the shore at the base of the cliffs. I quickly pull my legs up behind me. Alive . . . I'm alive. Gasping, I turn to the water. I don't know what I expect to see, but definitely not Gillan. He's in the sea in front of me, like the sharks don't scare him at all. But my heart freezes over as I see his eyes. They're pitch black, just like in my dream. Instinctively, I inch away.

"Naya, it's OK . . . don't be scared." He stretches out his arm toward me.

Where his waist meets the waterline, his skin looks grayish, smooth, almost like . . . like the gray skin of a shark. I gasp. "Gillan, you're a . . . a . . ."

A small smile crosses his lips. "Don't tell anyone."

I laugh. "I'd be pretty stupid to!"

He looks at me fully, his eyes taking in mine and I realize that he knows what I am. That he's probably suspected for some time. That's why he looked out for me, showed me everything, trusted me.

Gillan, a variant, like me. No wonder he's so different from anyone I've ever known. In this moment he looks more beautiful than ever before. I feel myself drawn to him. A feeling that's almost too intense to bear.

"How did you find me?" I whisper.

Gently, he reaches toward me and turns my wrist, revealing the wound. "Same way I found you in the Valley—the blood."

He holds my gaze. Slowly we move toward each other. The sea splashes against the cliffs in the wind. The water sparkles in the last rays of daylight. His hand brushes my cheek, warm against my cold skin. And his soft lips press against mine. It's as if my heart is going to burn through my chest. We're together. We're meant to be together. As he looks at me, his eyes deep and dark, I realize that ever since that night he saved me in the Valley, there has been a bond between us. A bond that I could sense before I ever understood its meaning. A bond that runs as deep within us as the waves of the ocean.

But like a breeze brushing over the sea, the moment ends, as if a spell has been broken.

"We need to get to Ararat before the storm." Gillan takes my hand.

"Gillan, wait." I hold him back. "It's happening tonight! At the Water Festival. Jim and Douglas are gonna kill the leading Elites."

Gillan stares at me. "A mass assassination? You're sure?"

"That's what Operation Neptune is," I say. "I just don't how they'll do it."

Gillan's breath catches in his throat. "The underwater devices . . . We have to get back to the house. And Arlo."

Gently he pulls me into the water. I recoil, with a glance at my bleeding wrist.

"It's OK. I won't let anything harm you." Gillan wraps his arms around me: strong and protective. He pulls me under the waves and we shoot forwards, him in his transformed state. The water rushes around us. He's swimming faster than I did as a mermaid. We surface a couple of times, and the shining, glimmering lights from the houses on Ararat are to our left. Then we reach the small cove beneath Gillan's house.

Dusk is turning to night as we climb up the narrow forest path. I shiver in the cold breeze. In the distance, a bank of black storm clouds is closing in from the sea.

"There's something unusual about this storm," I say.

"I know, it gives me the shivers, too," Gillan replies. "Come." He leads me through a basement entrance, half hidden by vines and shrubs, and partially obscured by the upper terrace of the house. No visitor announcement rings out as we step inside. In the hall, Gillan stops to pick up a white towel from a table. As he rubs his hair dry I notice that he isn't wearing his earring. Of course not. The earring must suppress his powers, like my trident necklace suppresses mine.

"Here." Gillan holds out a bathrobe to me. "There's a shower through there. Head up the stairs at the end of the hallway when you're done." He pauses, for a moment, as if he wants to say something more then turns and disappears through another door.

I quickly shower, glad to be out of my wet clothes, and cuddle into the white bathrobe with the initials GG embroidered on it. It's fluffy and a little too big for me. As I walk up the stairs, I find Gillan waiting for me in a sitting room, wearing a black tracksuit. Together we walk up another level, to the living room that overlooks the harbor. The lights are on, a clock reads 9:30 and a tall figure in a tuxedo is pacing the room with anxious steps.

"Look what I found floating around the ocean," Gillan calls out good humoredly.

"Gillan!" Arlo spins around. "What took you so long? The festival's starting, and—" He breaks off at the sight of me. "Naya! Seven seas! How did you get here? Where have you been?"

"Good question." Gillan turns to me. "I found her about to get eaten by hungry sharks."

"Jim kidnapped me," I exclaim. "I was escaping from his ship. The *Atlantean*—"

Arlo looks at me curiously. "Am I to deduce that Jim Queen is not the concerned foster father he pretends to be? He's had half of Ararat looking for you."

My heart stings as I picture Jim, with his fatherly smile, imploring people to find me before I get hurt—just so that he can recapture me.

"He's created a variant serum that enables people to transform at will. Duke's been taking it. That's why he was suddenly swimming as well as Gillan. Because he's now also—" I break off, realizing I was about to say that Gillan is a variant.

"It's OK," Gillan says. "Arlo knows."

"Oh." I look at Gillan, relieved.

"As I believe are you?" Arlo studies me with new curiosity.

I look down and grasp my trident necklace. "You knew all along?"

"Suspected," Arlo says. "A sudden, unexplained swim talent in adolescence . . . it's not the first time. Indications were that you carried the variant gene like Aidan. You've had us quite worried. We weren't sure if you were aware of your own abilities. Or if they had fully developed. Of course, when the council first mentioned you, Gillan and I had no clue who you were. Gillan had a near heart attack when he saw you in the hall and recognized you as the girl that he had rescued from the Valley. At that point he realized that you probably didn't know what was going on. And that he didn't have much time . . ."

"I thought you were going to report me." I give Gillan an apologetic smile. "You rushed off so quickly."

Gillan smiles back. "I went to the swim hall, to tell Coach Janson to keep you out of the Irons."

"Then Janson knows you're a variant, too?" I ask.

"Not exactly. She only knows what she surmised through my strange swimming abilities and Aidan's death," Gillan says. "We keep our conversations cryptic for both our safety. Janson's position is a little more precarious, as you may have noticed. Not that this stopped her from altering my swim times when my transformations first began to have a noticeable effect on my performance in class."

"But why the Irons?" I ask.

"Extreme stress can have adverse, even lethal, effects on the body in the early stages of development," Arlo explains. "The human body is not used to breathing underwater. Variants are at their most vulnerable until they learn to adapt. We knew that you would be all right in the singles races. The Iron Teens were a different matter. They are designed to push you to your limits and indications are that the fast switching between the styles can trigger a transformation. Gillan tried to warn you not to demonstrate your freediving skills . . . but his Aqua8 duties intervened."

"And I botched the rest," I say.

"This was in no way your fault." Arlo looks at me. "You could not know any of what was going on. In fact you've handled the situation incredibly well. Remember, we know very little about variants. The government banned all research and kept it classified. Whatever information I scraped together at the research institute, in secret, took me months to collect."

"Jim seemed to know quite a bit," I say. "He told me that I'm different. That I've had my powers from birth."

Arlo raises a curious brow and pulls over an armchair. "Why don't you start from the beginning?"

I sink into the soft, comfortable cushions. How nice to be able to sit in a chair without being tied to it! I recount what happened to me after the Finals. As I describe how I followed Duke, Gillan interrupts with an, "I told you—!" but Arlo holds up his hand to silence him.

"How did school security miss this?" he asks.

"The parking lot surveillance is more than shifty," Gillan replies. "Preen's already reported it twice, but someone on the council kept classing it as *nonpriority*."

"Douglas, no doubt, so as to help Duke leave at lunch times. A glitch in surveillance would have made Duke's absences appear less frequent." Arlo nods to me and I continue. When I get to the part about Jim and how he wanted to experiment on me, they both stare at me in shock.

"Naya, I'm glad you got out of the clutches of that madman!" Arlo exclaims. "If we save Ararat tonight, it will be, to a large part, thanks to you. But we must lose no more time." He turns to Gillan. "The other device that you went looking for this evening —is it the same as the one beneath the Governor's mansion?"

"An exact duplicate," Gillan confirms. Noticing my confused look he adds. "Arlo and I discovered yesterday that Douglas installed a second device on this side of the harbor. I went to examine it. That's when I found you. Or rather, the sharks that were drawn to you . . ."

"Stay focused," Arlo tells him. "Was there anything else you noticed about the device?"

"Just that it was emitting this kind of hum," Gillan says. "Like some continuous, electrical circuit. I think that anyone who tries to defuse it will have to break the circuit and then—"

"—it'd go off." Arlo nods grimly. "I suspected as much from the photos you took last week of the device below the Governor's mansion."

"So they are bombs?" I ask.

"No, no." Arlo shakes his head. "A bomb would be simple, mundane. This is complex, extraordinary, subtle." He spreads his arms out. "Two devices, one on either side of the bay. Both capable of generating an electric beam of the exact same ionic density and wavelength. Trajectory primed to intersect at the midpoint of the firing arc. A modified Tesla coil. An electronic pulse whose energy source, rather than being atmospheric, is thalassospheric. The energy conversion coefficient would of course be nothing short of—"

He breaks off and looks at me and Gillan. "You don't have the faintest idea what I'm talking about, do you?" He tuts, strides over to the bookshelves and grabs one of the old tomes. "Really, what do they teach you in physics these days?" He quickly flicks through the pages and puts the book down on the table.

I stare in fascination at the engraving of a huge ball of electricity spinning in the air, fed by crackling rays emitted from two standing copper coils positioned either side of it. A thin beam streaks out from the center of the ball toward some distant target.

"Do you see now?" Arlo asks excitedly. "A weapon that harnesses the power of the sea. Fire and water combining to wreak destruction. The beam can be directed at any target within five hundred yards of the two devices. Controlled, precision-guided destruction. Jim Queen is a genius."

"But an evil genius," Gillan says. "So what kind of damage can this thing do?"

"Ordinarily its effect would be limited," Arlo replies, "but today is the Water Festival. Water will be flowing everywhere."

Understanding dawns on Gillan's face. "A direct pulse at the water and anyone in contact with it will be electrocuted: the Governor, the guests . . . and tonight the leading families and all those in positions of power will be assembled on the upper garden terrace, close to the Governor." He pauses. "But Arlo, how does Queen intend to get the guests *into* the water? The fountains and water displays are contained in basins."

"There I'm afraid I'm out of my depth," Arlo says.

In the distance, thunder rumbles ominously. From Gillan's house we have an all too clear view of the approaching storm. "Maybe they'll cancel the festival," I say hopefully. "This weather looks pretty bad."

"No, no, they can't cancel," Arlo replies. "The very point of the Water Festival is to demonstrate humanity's prevailing over the forces of nature. If the Governor called it off, all of Ararat would lose confidence in him as a leader." He taps a finger to his ear and points up. "And have you noticed how the sirens and the lighthouse beam are off? The flood barrier of the harbor isn't raised either. They're trying to pretend that there is no storm."

"What do Queen and Kallion need in order to set this device off?" Gillan asks.

"Your photos showed no built-in timer." Arlo paces around the room, deep in thought. "Which means it's remote controlled.

But whoever has the detonator will need to be within range. Most likely Queen or Kallion will carry it on their person at the festival."

"Then we need to go to the festival and steal it," Gillan decides.

"That's far too risky." Arlo shakes his head. "What if my speculations are wrong?"

Gillan glances at the Governor's mansion. The lights are already on, illuminating the building and vast garden. "We have no other option. We're out of time."

"You could be walking into instant death," Arlo says. "We have no way of determining the timing of the attack—"

"Midnight," I exclaim. "The crew on the *Atlantean* said something about Jim fleeing the scene come midnight."

Gillan gives Arlo a determined look. "We're going."

Arlo sighs. "You're too much like your father for your own good. Very well, but I will accompany you."

Gillan begins to protest. Arlo cuts him off. "Somebody needs to warn Governor Proctor. He may not be able to arrest ruling council members without proof, but he has to be informed that something is afoot. He has to keep his bodyguards close. Besides, Douglas may have given the detonator to Duke, which means there are three people that we need to shadow."

"Fine," Gillan consents. "Once we get there, you will follow Jim, while Naya and I keep an eye on the Kallions. We will use my parents' watches and bracelet for communication. They have built-in transmitters that send off a light signal to their partner devices. If any of us find out who carries the detonator, we alert one another."

"What about the people in the FRS?" I whisper. "The flood barrier is rigged with explosives. If there's an attack tonight . . ." My voice trails off.

"Naya is right," Gillan says darkly. "If Jim and Douglas want as much energy to themselves as possible, they'll target Ararat and the FRS at the same time. It's the perfect opportunity. With the chaos at the Governor's mansion, no one will have time to send rescue teams to the FRS. The destruction would be catastrophic."

"I need to go!" I jump up from my chair. "I have to warn my mom."

"No." Arlo puts a hand on my arm. "You wouldn't get within five hundred feet of the guards. As a standing member of the council I am authorized to give flood evacuation directives as required. I will go."

"But . . ." I falter.

"I'll make sure your mom is safe," Arlo promises.

Gillan gives him a concerned look. "Arlo, a full-scale evacuation takes hours. If we can't stop Operation Neptune and the flood barrier breaks during this storm, the whole lower plain will be swept away . . ."

". . . and thousands of innocent lives lost," Arlo says. "Which is exactly why I have to go."

Gillan draws a shaky breath.

Arlo puts a hand on his shoulder. "Gillan, it really is our best chance."

"Take some Aqua8 members with you," Gillan says. "Send Lieutenant Williams and two others to defuse the explosives on the flood barrier. Keep the rest close to you. Kallion might have positioned some of his men down there."

"Don't worry about me," Arlo says. "Just focus on stopping the attack. You'll have the element of surprise on your side. Jim and Douglas think that Naya is safely stowed away on the *Atlantean*. Your arrival will unsettle them. They might make a mistake that they would not have otherwise made." He glances at the clock. "Now, the festival starts in less than an hour. Which means you two should get ready."

"Uh . . ." I hug the fluffy white bathrobe around me. "I . . . have nothing to wear."

Arlo and Gillan exchange a knowing smile.

"Just give me one second," Gillan says and disappears. A moment later he's back, holding a hanger with a bright red-and-gold dress. The dress falls elegantly and is embroidered in what the Elites call the Eurasian style.

I gasp. "Gillan, that's so beautiful. Where did you get it?"

"Well, part of me was hoping that we'd go to the ball together," Gillan admits with a small smile.

Arlo turns to go. "I will leave you to it. Gillan, if you don't have the detonator at ten minutes to midnight, get out of there."

"OK," Gillan says but his jaw is set and I wonder if he really means it.

"Aren't you worried about us being seen together?" I whisper to him as Arlo leaves.

"After tonight it won't matter," Gillan says. "We either stop Operation Neptune together, now, or things will change for the worse, either way." He hands me the dress. "Red—like the Barracudas."

As I take it, I notice that there is a skintight shortie jumpsuit attached to the same hanger.

"A combination my parents invented," Gillan explains. "In case there's a fight at a formal event. The dress will completely conceal the jumpsuit. There's a matching thigh strap to hold a knife—and we'll take a couple of gadgets along to keep track of Jim, Douglas, and Duke now that Arlo won't be there to help us."

I nod, but my hands are shaking with nervousness.

Gillan puts a hand on my cheek. "Naya, we'll make it. We'll stop them."

I look into his eyes. They're deep blue, calm like the ocean waves. And I know that Gillan will do everything he can to keep us all safe.

CHAPTER 24

— The Water Festival —

Gillan offers me his hand and I let him pull me out of the black motor car that drove us up to the Governor's mansion. A cool, crisp wind is blowing, fluttering through my red-and-gold dress. Gillan didn't say how he knew my size and I didn't ask. My heart is beating anxiously. Here I am, up on Ararat, about to save the Elite leaders, while my mother, my friends, everyone I've grown up with, might drown in the FRS. I am leaving the fate of the ones I love in the hands of Aqua8, while I am trying to save the people who despise us, the people who wouldn't care if we died. The thought churns up so many emotions that I feel sick. I clutch Gillan's hand tighter.

Arm in arm, we walk up the winding path to the Governor's mansion, lit by dim lights between the hedges and flowers. Gillan looks incredibly handsome in his black dinner jacket and bow tie and his hair styled back. We stride toward the house as if we were in a different time. A romantic couple, going to a glamorous celebration. Is this what Gillan's parents lived like? The jittery thrill is painfully suppressed by the tension in my chest. Tonight, we are not here to party. Tonight, there's no saying that either of us will survive the evening.

I feel for the thigh holster with the knife, concealed by the soft, red, silk fabric of my dress. Then I double-check the golden bracelet on my arm. The button next to the green gem is deactivated, neither the red nor the blue light lit. Gillan leans over and whispers in my ear, "Remember the signal: blue light for Kallion, red light for Queen, both lights for Duke."

We step through a marble entrance into a hall bursting with light and color. In the center, beneath a huge crystal chandelier, stands a marble fountain shaped like a wedding cake. The water brims over the top tier, cascading downward in golden waves. A chain of men and women holding hands are dancing around it, laughing.

The women are dressed in long sequined ball gowns, mostly in blue or silver, and many of the men are wearing velvet suits in shades of green and blue. They remind me of peacocks, vainly strutting around. I must stand out in my Eurasian dress, a solitary flame surrounded by an ocean of water. Gillan squeezes my hand, and we enter the room, merging in with the chatter of voices, the opulent swirl of waltzing couples, and the pop of champagne corks.

"Naya?" A voice calls from near the entrance. Jim stands there, staring at me as if I were the spirit of the Aquatic Other, risen from the ocean depths. Mrs. Queen is beside him, a cold smile on her face. She looks like an ice queen in her long silver dress—but an ice queen who has accidentally swallowed an ice cube. Gillan gives me a small smile. Our entrance has certainly had its effect.

"Mr. Queen." Gillan stretches out his hand. "Good evening."

"Gillan Gallagher." Jim puts on a frown of pretend concern. "I take it that you are the one who abducted Naya from us this evening?" He continues to hold Gillan's hand—a little tighter than necessary. "You should have stopped by our house first. You had us all worried. We sent out a search party."

"Oh, did you now?" Gillan asks bemused. "How . . . excessive. But I must disappoint you, I had nothing to do with Naya's disappearance. She showed up at my house of her own accord. Modern days . . . modern ladies . . ." He turns to me with a wide grin. "Makes us men feel quite—inept sometimes, doesn't it?"

Jim forces a laugh but he looks as if he'd like to land a punch on Gillan's face. "Well, what a relief to see you well, Naya." His eyes narrow at me. His glare asks how could I have escaped. "Quite brave of you, heading out into the night like that."

"Ooh, lighten up, Foster Daddy!" Gillan claps Jim on the shoulder and pulls him into a hug. "Don't you worry, old man, Naya's in 'safe' hands! Get it?" He winks at him.

"Get off me!" Jim pushes him away, dumbfounded.

I suppress a smile. I bet that Gillan just planted a tracker on Jim.

"Yes . . . you're right . . ." Gillan clears his throat. "You'll have to excuse me, I have some important business to attend to with the Governor." He swaggers off toward Governor Proctor, who is standing by the champagne bar dressed in a golden velvet suit, eating a shrimp that's about to fall onto his blue sash.

Jim and Mrs. Queen glare at me. I shrug and smile at them innocently, then disappear into the crowd.

As soon as I'm at one of the canapé tables, I pick a chocolate-coated strawberry from a glass dish and make a show of chewing it carefully. It's delicious—but my real attention is on the mirror behind the buffet. I'm watching Jim as he angrily talks to Mrs. Queen then turns on his heels and marches out of the room. This is my cue. Quickly, I activate the earpiece that Gillan gave me and follow Jim out of the reception hall.

The dazzling party lights subside as I enter a dimly lit hallway. I cast a quick look around. Jim is already out of view. Flattening myself against the wall, I open my handbag and take out a monitoring device that's linked to the tracker that Gillan planted on Jim. A glossy screen lights up with a floor plan of the villa, showing Jim's location as a yellow dot in a nearby room. As I approach, a noise of static crackles through my earpiece, followed by Jim's voice.

"What's the girl doing here . . . supposed to be on the ship . . . unconscious! Go get Kallion. We need to talk, NOW!"

The sound of footsteps follows but all I can hear is my own blood pumping faster. I've got to get out of sight. I pull open a door in the hallway and slip into the room adjacent to the one where Jim is. The monitoring device shows it as Governor Proctor's study. Soft lights illuminate a deep and luxurious armchair upholstered in dark green leather and a huge gold-framed portrait of Arcadius Proctor. Beside it is a golden statue of some important-looking person, with a scroll in its outstretched arm. The inscription says: Rufus Channing, First Governor of Ararat Heights, (49 AI—25 PI). Next to it a desk is standing against the wall. There's a glass monitor on it, showing paragraphs of green text. Strewn around it are wreaths of . . . garlic? Why does the Governor need those? I move toward the screen and read the headlines:

THE VARIANT MENACE: How to Protect Yourself from the Aquatic Other.

I skim the lines.

Garlic is said to keep away the denizens of the deep . . . successfully applied against Vampires, a type of giant, blood-sucking, humanoid moth . . . Avoid at all costs journeying forth on open water during the full moon, for this is when the powers of the marine marauders wax strong . . .

I suppress a snigger. This is hilarious. Proctor is completely paranoid. But the next bit is actually interesting.

Unknown sources tell of a curious metal, reputed to sap variant powers. Though it remains a mystery where —

The closing sound of a door in my earpiece makes me jump. "What is it now, Queen?" Kallion's voice rings out amid fizzes and crackles. "I th-th-to—"

I tap the earpiece then notice that Jim's dot has shifted to the far end of the adjacent room. He must have moved out of range. I crack open the door and slip back into the deserted hall, hurrying along until I can hear Kallion's voice again.

". . . so the girl gave you the slip? Your Operation Neptune is clearly proceeding as smoothly as your artificial variant experiments. We should cancel the operation."

"We'll do nothing of the sort," Jim replies. "The girl knows nothing. Just have our men keep an eye on her, so she doesn't slip away again when this is over. I need her to perfect the new serum." There's a crackle of static. "*Crsh—Sh-sh—*the only thing that's endangering our plan is your son. He can't control his temper. He smashed up half my lab."

"Leave my son out of this!" Douglas Kallion snaps. "It's your drug that's making him lose control . . . *sh-sh*—this whole operation is compromised. Gallagher is talking to Proctor right now."

"Well then, get your son to do something useful for once!" Jim replies. "Have him take care of the situation."

Kallion mutters something inaudible.

"Do you have the detonator?" Jim asks.

"Quit patronizing me!" Kallion hisses. "It's in my jacket pocket. Along with the ear plugs."

I hit the blue button. Blue for Kallion. But why do they need ear plugs?

Jim continues, "Make sure you wear them before you launch the attack —"

Kallion interrupts, "Will you finally let me know what they're for?"

"I don't know," Jim replies. "She refused to tell. She told me to leave that up to —"

She, who?

"Yeeeeh!"

A loud squeal from behind me nearly makes me drop the monitor. I spin around.

Jessica is standing there, beaming with excitement. "Naya!" She squeezes me into a hug. "What are you doing here?"

"I . . . I was looking for the bathroom . . ." I say.

Jessica rolls her eyes. "No. *Here*! Daddy told me you'd run away from Ararat." Her eyes fall on the monitor in my hand and her voice rises another octave. "Oceans alive, is that a CELL PHONE?"

I swear she could shatter glass at that pitch. "NO!" I quickly stuff the device in my bag. "It's just an Aqua8 training monitor. A pedometer, it measures how many steps I've walked today."

"Eugh—walking." Jessica's face drops into a scowl. Then she grabs my arm excitedly. "Come on, the Governor's about to start his speech. And the water display begins right after . . ." She pulls me out of the hallway and through the main reception room. "The preparations were like so much fun . . . Mom was the party planner . . . she and I worked all day . . . it's impossible to make an octopus out of crepe paper . . ."

I'm pretty sure she's suffering withdrawal symptoms from not having talked to anyone for the last two days.

"Do you like my new shoes . . . eugh, are you wearing ballerinas? So untrendy . . ." She drags me out the back of the house into the garden. It looks gorgeous, a maze of illuminated water basins with fountains, all spouting water. They're lit in different neon colors. In their midst, a large, oblong pool runs across the whole upper terrace and a rushing noise fills the air, of waterfalls streaming down the terraced levels of the garden. On our right, a semicircular infinity pool overlooks the cliff's edge and cascades down into the ocean. A statue of a gigantic human figure rises from the pool, half its body emerging powerfully from the water, arms outstretched to the sky. It sends out a very obvious message: the ultimate triumph of the Elites over the sea.

Just in front of the semicircular pool there's a raised platform. The Governor is standing on top of it, his back to the sea and the gathering storm. As he speaks, his posture is reminiscent of the statue of Rufus Channing that I saw in his study.

"Ladies and gentlemen, tonight, our victory, our domination over the elements . . ."

In the distance behind him, lightning strikes.

My eyes wander to a weird contraption beside the podium. It is made almost completely out of glass, with a series of bronze cogs running down the middle. The cogs are turning as water flows from a chamber on one side of the device to its counterpart on the other side. What is this weird thing? I watch the levers that are scooping up the remaining water in the right-hand chamber and transferring it to the left-hand chamber, which is almost full. It dawns on me. This is a clock — a clock powered by water. Doubtless it will mark the coming of midnight — and of whatever is about to happen.

I scan the crowd for Gillan. Did he get my signal about Douglas Kallion?

"Whoa, chilly." Jessica shivers, glancing at the tops of the trees along the garden fence that have started to bend in the gathering wind. Some of the ladies have draped shawls over their shoulders. It's as if the weather is in thrall to tonight's events.

"Duke!" Jessica waves at him in the crowd. "Duke, you gotta see who's here!"

"Jess, don't," I hiss, but Duke has already turned around. He looks straight at me, the color draining from his face and he pushes through the crowd toward us.

"Ouch!" A woman exclaims, as he knocks an elbow into her back.

"Naya! You shouldn't be here," Duke growls at me.

"What, Duke, that's so mean!" Jessica exclaims. "Just because she's from the FRS doesn't mean she can't celebrate with us. She's one of us now!"

"You've no idea what you're talking about!" Duke grabs my arm and drags me away, out of earshot. I try to pull away but his fingers are digging into my arm. "Naya, there's not much time." His gaze flickers between me and Jessica. "You need to go. NOW."

"I'm not going anywhere. I'm gonna stop whatever is happening tonight."

"You can't!" Duke looks at me, pale.

"I will at least try."

"NO!" his grip tightens. "Listen to me—"

"You're hurting my arm!" I say through gnashed teeth.

"Evening, Duke." I feel a gentle tug around my waist as Gillan wraps his arm around me. Duke's hand falls away.

At that moment the whole courtyard erupts with clapping. Governor Proctor has finished his speech. The fountains around us woosh upwards briefly, higher than before. People start to move around and chatter. Gillan offers me his arm and we walk along the oblong pool toward the dais. General Calder takes the floor, her black dress shimmers purple and blue in the light, like tar.

Gillan taps his jacket pocket. "Got it," he whispers to me. "Let's get out of here."

He's drowned out by an ear-splitting noise, a high-pitched, grotesque mockery of a song. I double over and clap my hands over my ears. Gillan crouches down beside me, with a look on his face that asks, what on earth is that? The water displays around us are going frantic, the fountains shooting up higher and higher. There's a person by the controls, but his hand is frozen on the switch, as if he's spellbound. And somehow, so is everyone else. The noise that nearly brought me and Gillan to our knees has everyone else rooted to the spot. They're completely entranced, their gazes fixed on the podium, as if they're unable to take their eyes off Calder.

"What are they doing?" I whisper to Gillan.

Gillan looks up at General Calder, who is still standing on the dais like a singer, her lips moving in some wordless chant. Is it her making that noise? The trees are bending under the force of the wind that whips around us, now mixed with cold drops of rain that splatter onto my face and bare arms. I glance at the guests, expecting them to flee the onslaught of the storm, but they remain where they are despite the downpour that turns their clothes sodden.

"It's so beautiful," a woman next to us murmurs.

"They're in some sort of trance—like she's bewitched them," Gillan says.

I look down at my feet, which are soaked. The water from the fountains is overflowing the basins. It's flooded the upper terrace of the garden and is still rising.

The conversation that I overheard between Douglas Kallion and Jim comes to my mind. Kallion had said the detonator was in his pocket—along with the ear plugs. Ear plugs. That's why he needed them. This is all part of the plan. The part that neither Jim nor Douglas knew about. Jim had said she refused to tell. And now I know who *she* is. I glance up at the stage.

"Her voice," I whisper to Gillan. "Calder's enchanting them with her voice."

"How's that possible?" Gillan asks.

"I don't know, but Gillan—the water!"

The leading Elites on the upper terrace with the Governor are all ankle deep in the water from the overflowing fountains. Entranced by Calder. If the electric beam hit the Governor's mansion now, every single person would be killed.

Gillan grabs my arm to pull me out of the water. Just at that moment shadows in my peripheral vision start moving. It's barely perceivable, like the ripple of a wave, disturbing the absolute stillness that surrounds us. Shapes of black-clad figures are emerging from the cover of the trees around the house. On their chests is the white symbol of the inverted trident. Operation Neptune. Spearguns at the ready, they advance in a semicircle, stationing themselves between the crowd and the house.

Gillan cuts a wry grimace. "I think our situation just got a little more complicated."

At that moment Douglas Kallion breaks away from the rest of the black-clad figures and leaps onto the stage. He casts one apprehensive look at Calder, as if he's wondering how exactly she is doing this, then he looks down at the crowd with a gleeful sneer.

"Ladies and gentlemen," he calls out to the uncomprehending guests, "prepare for this evening's surprise highlight!"

Behind him, the gong strikes the first chime of midnight. Douglas reaches for his jacket pocket. A look of confusion appears on his face. He searches his inside pockets maniacally, left, right . . .

"Looking for this, Kallion!" Gillan holds up the detonator.

Douglas freezes—along with the rest of the Operation Neptune agents. They look around, confused. Only Calder stays completely composed on stage, still singing her eerie tune. If we're gonna do something, it has to be now!

With one quick motion I reach for Gillan's shoulder holster and pull out the combigun he carries. It's a ten-yard shot, but I barely pause to take aim before I pull the trigger. The dart is already whizzing through the air as the black-clad figures swivel their guns toward us. Calder spins around and catches one glance at me and Gillan before the missile hits. Her arm flies to her chest and her voice breaks. She pulls out the black dart. Then her body goes rigid. The whole dais shakes as she drops backward and lies still, like a beached whale.

At once the crowd stirs from its collective trance. Confused voices ring out as people look around.

The Operation Neptune force aim their spearguns and yell, "Everybody stand back!" but the guests scatter in panic. And total mayhem breaks out. The Operation Neptune agents start firing their spearguns indiscriminately into the crowd while, around me, the cries and screams of people fleeing in all directions mingle with the noise of the storm. The Governor leaps onto the dais shouting, "VARIANTS! VARIANTS! Guards, Aqua8—to me, to me!" At once, four men in green velvet suits splosh through the water and leap onto the dais around him.

"Out of the water!" Gillan shouts. "Everyone out of the water. NOW!"

Terrified, the guests jump onto nearby flowerbeds, marble steps, and the stone walls that separate the different sections of the garden. I try to find Douglas in all the havoc when I see the red dot of a gun's laser sight dance on Gillan's chest. "Gillan!" I call out to him, but at that moment Duke's voice roars through the night.

"GALLAGHER!"

He flings himself at Gillan like a berserker, knocking him clean off his feet. The sniper shot, aimed at Gillan's heart, hits the house wall instead, as the detonator flies from Gillan's hand. I leap after it, but an Operation Neptune agent jumps in my way, lashing out at me with the butt of his speargun. I duck under his attack and dig my knee into his stomach then smash an elbow against his temple. Finally, all the Aqua8 training is paying off! A harpoon flies past my ear and embeds itself in the back of a man making a break for the house. He crumples into a heap. I dive past him, reaching for the detonator, but a fleeing guest kicks it away. More harpoons whizz through the air.

Some guests have started to fight back, rushing at the Operation Neptune agents. Bodies already fill the floor, harpoon shafts sticking out of silvery dresses and green tuxedos. I make another move for the detonator when I see Jessica, frozen to the spot, as a black-clad man wielding a knife leaps at her. I jump between them, grabbing my knife from its thigh holster, and dig it into the man's side just below his ribs. It slices through his body armor. Warm blood runs over my hand as the man collapses to the ground in front of me. With a quick tug I tear off my dress to reveal the skintight shortie jumpsuit underneath. Jessica is still standing there, immobile, staring aghast at the knife in my hand.

"Naya?" she whispers dully.

I grab her arm and pull her with me. "Come on, inside." I push her into the reception room and cast a hurried glance back. In the garden Gillan and Duke are fighting. Duke is throwing wild punches, shouting like a maniac. Gillan barely manages to block. The combigun that I handed back to him, after I stunned Calder, is lying in the grass between them. Then Duke deals him a powerful kick that sends him flying. I wince as Gillan sinks into the grass, groaning. Duke hurls himself across the garden and snatches up a small metal object. The detonator! Duke stands in front of the oblong pool, ready to push the button. I punch a fist into the face of a Neptune guy who rushes at me and grab his speargun. As I take aim, Gillan runs at Duke and knocks him full force into the pool. A beam of bluish-white light arcs across the sky and hits the courtyard, dead center.

"NO!" I scream.

Duke set off the detonator. A sheet of crackling electricity runs across the flooded upper garden terrace in a pulse wave. All those still standing in the water, twitch frantically then fall down and lie still. Above us, a red flare bursts into the night sky: Jim's signal that the plan has failed. The crew of the *Atlantean* will be readying the ship for his escape—but I don't care. All I see is Gillan, lying facedown in the water of the oblong pool, motionless.

I sprint toward him. Just as I reach the edge of the pool, a massive plume of water explodes from the middle of it. A shape rises from the water. The head and upper body are covered in shiny, reddish scales and resemble a grotesque mix between a barracuda and a human. Razor-sharp teeth line its maw. It's the most hideous thing I've ever seen! With horror, I realize that it's Duke. The serum overdose must have turned him into some abnormal version of a variant. Screams fill the air as the guests take in the monstrosity standing before them. One voice stands out above the others.

"VARIANT!" the Governor shouts. "VA . . . VARIANT! VARIANT!" He's pointing his arm in horror, his worst fears realized.

Gillan stirs in the water.

He's alive! "Gillan!" I grab his arm and pull him out of the pool. He slumps into my arms, dripping wet.

"Naya, what is that . . . thing?" he whispers.

"D . . . Duke," I say. "He overdosed on the variant serum. The electricity must have made him transform . . ."

The giant head spins around to us. Its eyes linger on Gillan.

"Naya, get out of here." Gillan pushes me aside. He gets up, raising his fists but he's thrown backward by a punch from Duke's giant, scaly arm. Gillan rolls and scrambles to his feet. Duke leaps onto the pool rim with a *thud*. He and Gillan fight their way through the garden, dodging between the fountains. Gillan does his best to keep Duke away from the guests, but Duke shrugs off his attacks. A few more steps carry them to the infinity pool on the cliff's edge. A silver-haired figure detaches itself from the crowd and runs for the house.

"Naya," Gillan calls out. "Kallion! Get Kallion! He's getting away."

Duke takes advantage of this moment of distraction and throws out both fists, flying at Gillan with a shout of rage. The force lifts them both up into the air. With a roar Duke slams onto the outer edge of the pool. Time seems to freeze as he twists around and plummets over the edge of the cliff, dragging Gillan with him.

"GILLAN!!!"

My scream is so loud it deafens me. I sprint to the edge, where the cliffs fall away in a sheer drop to the sea below. There's no sign of Gillan. Or Duke. Just the dark waves splashing white against the jagged rocks.

CHAPTER 25

— *The Heart of Mortlake* —

He's gone. I can't believe he's gone. The sound of fighting and the cries of guests ring dully in my mind. I stare down at the raging sea. A roaring buzz fills my ears as if the ocean were around me, drowning out all other noise. Again and again the waves break on the rocks, get washed back, pulled to the depths of the ocean. And with every crash the despair and the pain that grip me grow worse.

The world has come to a standstill. All I can picture is that last moment of the fight. Gillan calling out to me, Duke hurling himself at him. But the memory of Gillan's last words snaps me awake: Kallion! Get Kallion! I turn and run, snatching up the combigun that he dropped. I will stop Douglas Kallion if it's the last thing I do.

As I pass the dais I see Calder, no longer tranquilized, a speargun in her hand. It's trained on me. I skid to a stop—but before she can pull the trigger, someone kicks the gun out of her hand.

"Oh no you don't!" Janson fires a stun dart at Calder's neck.

Calder manages to throw her one unbelieving glance that quickly transforms into a glare of hatred before she sags back to the ground, unconscious a second time in one evening.

"Go get him, Naya!" Janson shouts to me while fighters from both sides rush at her. I give her a quick nod and run.

Kallion's already out of sight as I sprint into the house. A Neptune operative runs at me. Without stopping, I shoot him with the combigun and run through the reception hall. Out of the corner of my eye, I see Jessica's purse lying on the ballroom floor. No trace of Jess. I hope she's OK, but I don't have time to worry about her now. I sprint outside, onto a gravel yard. Three black SUVs are parked immediately outside the entrance.

The driver's door of the first one is open and two guards in bulletproof vests are lying on the ground. As I look past them, I see red taillights moving along the driveway.

I run to the SUV. One of the dead guys has some company logo on his sleeve that has been blacked out. They're Operation Neptune agents posing as the Governor's private security guards. Kallion must have killed them as he escaped. Apparently Jim's orders were to let nobody through, not even his business partner. I holster my combigun but as I'm about to swing myself into the first SUV someone grabs me from behind. I find myself looking up into the face of one of the guards that had been lying on the ground. Not-so-dead after all!

I throw back my elbow and twist forward, flinging him over my shoulder. He falls to the ground. Holding his arm in a lock, I plant my knee on his chest and jab three punches to his temple. He stays down, unconscious.

I get into the vehicle, but when I turn the key the engine doesn't start. Instead, a blue screen flips out of the dashboard with a whirr. *"Zephyrus company vehicle: identity verification required,"* an electronic voice drones and a thumb reader appears on the blue screen.

I glance at the guard that I just took out. Jumping out of the SUV, I grab his arms and drag him to the passenger door. Good thing he's not one of those six-foot-tall, bulky Aqua8 guys. I hoist him up and plonk him on the passenger seat then rush around and climb back into the driver's seat. I turn the key again, grab the guard's hand and press his thumb to the reader.

"Agent Chang. Security clearance acknowledged. Have a nice drive," the electronic voice sings in super polite tones and the vehicle engine springs to life with a soft whine.

I release the handbrake. Determined, I push down on the right pedal. The SUV violently jerks backward, smashing into the car behind. Oops! Do I care? I move the gearshift down a few notches and press my foot down again, this time bashing into the vehicle in front. With satisfaction, I watch as the front car's rear bumper breaks, hanging loose beneath a dented trunk. Good! Having cleared a path, I swerve to the right and drive off in a shower of gravel.

Although the driveway leads away from the Governor's mansion in a dead-straight line, I somehow still end up on the lawn. Whoa! The steering on this thing is really different to EVs. The tires tear up the carefully tended turf. The next moment I'm spinning left, knocking down a majestic, marble statue. Oh well, the Governor can blame that one on the variants!

I turn out of the driveway and swerve onto the main road, tires screeching. Through the black night, the red taillights of Kallion's car are winding their way up the serpentine track that leads away from the coast and up the hill to Mortlake Industries. Dark rocks rise up ahead of me as I push down on the gas pedal in pursuit. The car skitters as I hit the mountain track. I grip the steering wheel but on the fifth bend I almost crash. I slam on the brakes. Next to me, Agent Chang's head knocks against the windshield.

"Please correct your driving, Agent Chang," the super polite electronic voice announces. *"Multiple road conduct violations registered."*

I grimace. Kallion's car has disappeared into the night. He must be halfway to Mortlake by now. The engine squeals as I push down on the gas.

"Agent Chang, please change gear."

The steering wheel judders in my hands. A repetitive thud accompanies my driving as Agent Chang's head bounces against the side window. The car jolts over a rock. Suddenly, there is a sharp movement to my right. My arm shoots up in a block. Seems that last bounce has woken my passenger. His nostrils flare as he pulls back his left arm for a flat palmed attack to my throat. I block again, knocking his arm aside then, keeping my left hand on the wheel, I rip the combigun from my thigh holster, and stun Agent Chang. He slumps against the passenger door. I press the button to open it and push him out.

"No more road conduct violations for you today, Agent Chang," I say.

The combigun emits a dull *bzzhooo* . . . and flashes red. No more stun darts left. Only bullets now. Just as well. I wasn't planning on stunning Kallion.

A black shape looms on the road in front of me. I slam on the brakes. Just in time. Kallion's SUV is parked across the mountain track. The front and back bumper are almost touching the jagged rocks to either side of the path. He's completely blocked my way. But where is he? I jump out of the car and strain my eyes, staring into the darkness beyond the twin beams of the headlights. Then I see him. A dark shape above me, scrambling up the hillside behind the dancing beam of a flashlight. I jump over the rocks and run after him. If he thinks he's getting away, he's wrong. I can get up this hill faster than him!

It's lucky that I can see in the dark even with my necklace on, because the night sky is full of storm clouds that hide the light of the moon. I hasten over the uneven ground. Kallion's dancing light flickers and disappears. He's too low on the mountain to be at Mortlake, but I didn't think that he was heading there, anyway. My lungs are burning as I leap the last few yards across the rocks. The little plateau of the cable car station is familiar even at night. Loose rocks and broken branches of shrubs crunch softly under my feet as I make my way toward it. The control room is empty, just like when I followed Douglas and Duke up here.

I start tapping and pressing the concrete walls. The entrance to Jim's lab must be here, somewhere. I remember the artificially lit room, full of machinery, with the rock ceiling and cool night air on my face as they carried me out, drugged. We were underground, hidden away, inside the mountain.

The west wall somehow looks thicker than the rest. I run my hand along its smooth surface then glance at the dull glow of light that emanates from the instrument console. What if there's a lever or button placed among the other buttons that operate the cable car? Hidden in plain sight? I push an unlabeled green button. A loud whirring noise rings out from the direction of the embarkation platform. That starts the cable car. I press it again, but nothing happens. There must be a different button to turn it off. As I step closer to the control panel I feel something squishy under my shoe. I crouch down to check. Uggh! An ear plug. Kallion's ear plug! Double Uggh!

So now I know he's been at the controls. With a sudden idea I glance up at the underside of the console. A black button! I press it. At once, a swooshing noise echoes from the west wall. Where the thick, concrete wall was, there is now a pair of metal doors. I run up to them and see a single button with an arrow pointing down. A hidden elevator.

I call it and step into the cabin that appears. Again there's only one button. UG. I press it. The elevator moves downward and comes to a gentle stop. I draw my gun and step out. I'm in a tunnel, a stone passageway that slopes downward. I follow it, scurrying through the pools of light cast by a row of lamps positioned at regularly spaced intervals. My shoes slip on a smooth surface and I notice that the floor of the tunnel has changed from stone to glass. Peering down I see a conveyor belt carrying containers of Red Earth. A robotic arm lifts them through a trapdoor in the mountain and carries them to a series of funnels, where the Red Earth is sucked out into copper pipes that run up the wall and disappear into the ceiling. The empty containers continue on the conveyor belt and are moved out through a trapdoor. So this is how Jim and Douglas are stealing the Red Earth. Gillan was right. I wish that I could tell him, but he's at the bottom of a cliff. All because of Duke and Douglas!

Burning with pain and anger, I clutch my gun and walk further down the hall. There's a door and next to it an electronic panel for fingerprint verification. But I don't need it, the door is already wide open. I walk inside. I'm on a steel metal walkway — the same one that Jim stood on when he suddenly appeared in the lab. A similar metal walkway runs along the opposite wall. Both have stairs that culminate in a single staircase, which leads to the ground level.

Above me, the ceiling is low and covered in a network of metal pipes. I take a cautious step across the metal grid. A pile of crates and the reclining chair that Duke tied me to are directly beneath me. The sinister water tank with the blood-smeared sides is underneath the other metal walkway and is now filled with a liquid that shines in an unnatural, fluorescent orange. Above it, suspended from a metal chain is a steel cage. It was probably used to lower variants or people into the tank for experimentation. I shiver.

I glance at the huge bank of machines that covers the entire wall behind me. Kallion is standing by the controls, on the ground floor, pressing buttons.

"Seismic device armed and ready to fire," an electronic voice announces.

I grab my gun and point it directly at Kallion. "Stop!"

He spins around.

"Step away from the controls," I shout.

Kallion gives me a snarled smile but doesn't move. "Are you really going to shoot me? What if I hit the detonation button before your tranquilizer dart takes effect?"

I keep my gun on him. "This isn't set to stun."

"I should have known." He gives an evil laugh. "Same risk. You kill me, I hit the button . . ." His hand hovers over the controls. "And imagine if you miss and hit the control panel instead. You'll make an even bigger mess."

I grit my teeth.

Kallion's smile widens. "That's right. You wouldn't want to risk the lives of the people on Ararat on a bad shot would you? You see, while Queen was bragging about his perfect path to glory and divinity, I developed a plan of my own that actually works." He takes a few steps along the wall with the controls.

"Stay where you are!" I move along the metal walkway to keep him in my gun sights. Which of the buttons on the instrument panel sets off the bomb? Which one is he trying to reach?

Kallion continues, "I modified the seismic bomb that Jim attached to the underwater devices with a superconductor that picks up charge from the electric pulse weapon. When the weapon was fired, the discharge was absorbed by the bomb's superconductor, which is now primed. It can't be set off by a remote control detonator, but—fortunately—it can be, from this lab. On the push of a button, it will bring down half the hillside, the Governor's mansion along with it. Do you follow me? The technical details are probably too much for your simple mind."

"I follow all right. You're all crazy. You, Jim, and Calder. All playing each other in your deranged bid for power."

He takes another step. I walk along the metal walkway, mirroring his steps, trying to keep a clear shot.

"But I'm the one who's winning," Kallion gloats. "There will be no more of that ineffectual figurehead, Proctor, who jumps at his own shadow. The tsunami wave, triggered by the seismic shock I'm about to set off, will destroy the tidal power installations and the transmission stations connecting the wind turbines to the town and crack the photovoltaic panels of the solar power plants. Conveniently leaving me in charge of the sole energy resource."

"You're out of your mind. Mortlake's coal-fired power plant and oil rigs won't survive the wave either. You'll leave Ararat without any means of survival."

Kallion chuckles. "Alas, my poor power station, my beloved oil rigs! It's a good thing then that I will control a practically inexhaustible supply of Red Earth and the means to transform it into energy. So who do you think gets to be the new Governor? The squabbling remnant of the Elite leaders? Or the guy who says when the lights get turned on?" He takes a quick step forward.

"That's far enough, Kallion." I raise the gun and point it at his head. A few more steps and I won't have a clear shot anymore. The metal floor of the walkway will be in the way. I move further along, to my left.

Kallion barely pays attention. He switches to a playful tone. "On a separate note, the security in this lab is formidable. I knew Queen's paranoia would come in useful one day. His constant fear of being crossed or double-crossed. Anybody who isn't carrying a security badge when they enter is in for a nasty surprise." Kallion lifts a black card with an upside-down trident hanging from his lapel. "I brought mine, Naya—where's yours?" His eyes wander to the left of my head. "Such a shame."

I spin around—too late. An oddly shaped white gun on a metal arm swivels toward me and a jet of smoke shoots into my face. Then the whole room turns upside down.

*

Brrrr—Shhh—
When I come to, it's to a heavy metallic clank. My head is

swimming. Groggy, I scramble onto my knees and pat around for my gun, but it's not there.

"Detonation in T-minus eight minutes and counting," an electronic voice announces.

I fight back the wave of fear that comes over me. The bomb. Kallion has set off the timer. I have to stop him.

Through the metal grid of the walkway I catch a flash of silver. My gun is lying on the crates below. It must have fallen when I was knocked out.

I scan the lab for Kallion. He's at the end of the room, by a huge green screen that has flipped out of the bank of machines, below the large control panel. The screen is showing a countdown clock and a spinning red diagram of the seismic device.

I clamber to my feet, wondering if I have some kind of resilience to these drugs. I'm sure this one wasn't meant to take me out for just a few minutes.

I squint at the screen below the countdown clock. It's displaying a graph labeled Red Earth Levels on which green squares are spinning around and aligning neatly. It must be showing the energy required for preparing the weapon launch. Hang on . . . this whole lab is being powered by Red Earth. When I walked through the tunnel that led me here I could see the earth being funneled in via copper pipes. I scan the lab and notice that affixed to the wall, at the far end of the other metal walkway, there is a large, steel box with the same copper tubes running into it. From the bottom of the box, more pipes emerge and run directly into the bank of machines. So this steel box is where the Red Earth is converted to power. If I can break it open, I can smash the power converter inside, and stop Kallion's seismic pulse weapon. But it looks like the box is hermetically sealed.

"Detonation in T-minus seven minutes and counting."

I glance around the lab for something heavy. It's then I notice the twin glass pipes emerging from the top of the steel box that are pushing green liquid into the box and sucking it out again at intervals. This liquid must also be connected with the Red Earth conversion process. If I can stop its flow . . . I trace the course of the twin pipes that run up the wall and across the

ceiling of the lab with my eyes. Where the cage hangs suspended above the water tank, almost flush with the stony ceiling,
there's a small red lever with the words Flow Control written
on it. It must be a manual override for the conversion liquid in
the event that there's a fault with the electronic control panel.
If I can reach it, maybe I can shut off the flow of Red Earth to
the converter and disable the destruct sequence.

I jump up and grab one of the gray pipes that run along the
ceiling of the lab. Hoisting my legs around it, I shimmy along,
ignoring the lurch of my stomach as I move away from the metal walkway, the lab floor now a fifteen foot drop below me. The
pipe leads me right to the center of the ceiling.

"Detonation in T-minus six minutes and counting."

I reach for the lever, but it's too far to the side of the pipe that
I'm clinging on to. Next to me is the cage for the water tank. I
stretch my hand out toward it. Not that I really want to touch
that, but if I can grab onto the bottom of it, I should be able to
get to the lever. The cage shifts as it takes my weight and emits
a dull clunking noise. Hanging on with both arms, I swing myself up and lift my legs to pull the lever toward me with my feet.
A dull thud rings out as I miss and hit a pipe. I swing again.

DONG!

Again I hit the pipe. My arms scream from the strain of my
body weight but this time I also feel my foot connect with the
lever. Just as it does, a metallic whirring noise rings out and the
cage jerks downward. Clinging on, I kick out in a frenzy, accidentally pushing the lever forward instead of pulling it toward
me. The cage rattles down toward the lab at high speed. A cry
escapes my mouth as the floor rushes toward me —

But the chain jams and yanks me up before I hit the ground.
Kallion walks toward me, a sneer on his face. The noise of me
kicking the pipes must have alerted him. I'm about to let go of
the cage and roll to the side when I see the pile of crates to my
right. Wait — didn't my gun fall onto those crates? With sudden
determination I swing back and forth, let go of the cage, and
leap onto the first crate. Using them as stepping stones, I jump
from the lowest to the highest. But Kallion has also seen the
gun. He kicks away the pile of crates under me just as I reach

for it. The crates crash down, pulling me with them. I break my fall and land on the floor in a push-up.

Kallion catches the falling gun with a manic grin. "Thank you, Miss DeLora."

I flip myself up and dive behind the fallen crates. Wooden splinters fly as Kallion shoots and misses. I run, using the crates for cover. Kallion shoots again. Bullets zing around me and sparks fly from the control panel, where a purple light starts flashing.

"Heating process activated."

I jackknife for the nearest cover, the water tank. Kallion fires, and with a crash the neon lamp above me shatters, glass shards raining down on my head. I cower against the tank, its walls hot against my back. The liquid inside it is boiling, changing color. Kallion's stray bullet must have set off the heating mechanism. But where is he? The liquid is bubbling and foaming so vigorously that I can't see through the tank.

BOOM!

"Alert: Energy overflow. Countdown modification. Detonation T-minus two minutes to T-minus four minutes. Cylinder failure, Red Earth converter."

I steal a glance at the Red Earth convertor on the walkway above. The steel casing has been blown apart, and the front panel is dangling on its hinges. Inside the case, three glass cylinders are now visible, with green liquid and Red Earth circulating in spiral tubes. The fourth cylinder has exploded, spitting a mixture of Red Earth and green liquid across the wall. Did I do this? When I hit the Red Earth lever with my foot to try and shut down the conversion process, I pushed it the wrong way —and must have increased the flow and caused the convertor to overload. The explosion of the cylinder blew off the lid of the box and delayed the countdown. Which means if I can get there and destroy the other cylinders, I can stop the seismic device from detonating.

I stick my head around the side of the water tank. A shot rings out, followed by a loud click. Kallion's out of bullets. I race for the stairs to the metal walkway. In passing, I notice an iron bar on the floor that has fallen off the metal cage and snatch it up.

That should break the cylinders.

Kallion catches up with me as I reach the stairs.

"AAAHH!!" I shout out as he grabs my ankle and I crash onto the metal grid. I kick at his hand and his face. He lets go. Scrambling up the rest of the steps, I race along the metal walkway. The cylinders are at the far end, but before I get halfway, Kallion yanks me back by the arm. I swing the metal bar at him, but he catches it midblow and tosses it aside. It clatters across the metal walkway.

"Detonation in T-minus two minutes and counting."

Kallion smiles. "Too late, Naya. You're too late. Soon destruction will rain down upon them. But you'll taste it first." His grin is scarily like Duke's. He grabs me and tries to wrestle me into a stranglehold, but I twist out of his grip and shove him against the railing. He slams into a panel. A light turns on.

Part of the metal walkway railing beside me swings out and an electronic voice says, *"Warning: cage loading area open."*

The bubbling water tank below has changed color from orange to purple. I cling on to the metal railing so as not to fall. Kallion uses my moment's distraction to kick me. I stumble back, and he punches me in the stomach. I double over. He follows up with another punch and a jab to the face which send me sprawling to the floor. I try to get up, but my ears are buzzing and my eyes don't seem to focus.

The electronic voice continues, *"Confirm name of test subject, please."*

"Here, let me help you with that." Kallion grabs my hair and yanks me to my feet. My head is screaming in agony, I can feel his hot breath rasping in my ear. "You never were good enough, were you, Naya?" he taunts. "Just another piece of FRS trash. Totally expendable." He drags me toward the water tank.

Anger explodes inside me like a storm wave. I stamp down sharply on his foot. His hold loosens for a second and I wriggle free. Kallion tries to grab my arm, but I jump for one of the pipes running close to the ceiling. Hanging on with both hands, I swing back my legs and kick him in the chest with both feet. He lets out a surprised grunt as he's knocked backward toward the open section in the railing. For a moment he teeters on the edge, arms flailing. Then he screams and falls into the tank below. His scream is strangled as the purple, frothing liquid closes above him.

"So long, Kallion," I mutter.

The electronic voice responds, *"Name of test subject confirmed. Kallion, Solong."*

I wipe sweat off my forehead.

At that moment an alarm sounds from the control panel below and another voice says, *"Alert. Detonation imminent. Detonation imminent."*

I whip around. The countdown clock. It's registering fifteen seconds. I'll never make it down the stairs and to the console in time! Then I see the metal cage hanging fewer than ten feet away from the metal walkway, where it jammed. I take a diagonal run and jump through the open metal walkway railing, over the hissing water tank. The chain of the cage creaks as I cling onto it and swing with it toward the console. At the peak of its upswing, I jump off, land, roll forward and slam my palm down on the red button in front of me.

Nothing happens. Was I too late? Was that not the right button?

An electronic voice rings out, *"Detonation canceled. Detonation canceled."*

With an exhausted sigh, I sink to the floor.

"Red Earth Levels critical. Emergency. Evacuate."

I leap back to my feet as a deep rumble makes the whole lab shake. It feels like the floor beneath me is being torn apart. On the display screen, the squares showing the Red Earth Levels are lit up and flashing red. I spin around to the conversion cylinders up on the metal walkway. They are shaking, the green liquid swirling inside them. The overflow that I accidentally set in motion is becoming too strong. While I was fighting Kallion, this whole place built up enough energy to blow.

I need to get out now! Scrambling to my feet, I rush up the stairs to the metal walkway. Another tremor runs through the lab. Part of the ceiling comes crashing down, blocking off the tunnel entrance that runs uphill to Mortlake. I cover my head with my arms and run on while small rocks and dust rain down on me. The door ahead is the only way out now. I can only hope that the elevator that got me underground is still working with the whole building coming apart. More rocks dislodge themselves from the ceiling. The metal walkway breaks off behind me as they come crashing down. They hit the water tank, smashing it to pieces. I duck to avoid the explosion of boiling liquid and glass fragments. The metal walkway trembles under my feet as I hurl myself through the lab door, into the glass-floored tunnel. Below me, the Red Earth containers continue to pass by on their conveyor belt. I run for the elevator.

Gasping for breath, I hammer down on the silver button but the doors won't open. NO! I look up. There's a symbol above the button with the upward pointing arrow. It's a manufacturer logo. A double-winged diagram. And I have seen it before. In Jim's office. The drawing of the hang glider, the project he never developed! It can't be here by coincidence. I run a hand over it. At once the elevator control panel slides to the side revealing a keypad with letters. Enter Password. I try A-d-e-l-i-a. Nothing. J-e-s-s-i-c-a. Nothing. I try to think. What's important to Jim? His experiments. His company . . . Wait, what was the name of his terminated project? I-k-a-r-u-s. Still nothing. Rocks break off the ceiling and crash to the floor beside me. What if the password is a whole phrase? With trembling hands I type in: T-o d-e-f-y i-s t-o d-e-i-f-y.

Metallic wheels crunch as the wall next to the elevator slides aside, revealing a vertical tunnel with an iron ladder. Arlo was right, Jim is a genius. This whole secret escape route is mechanical rather than electrical so that a power cut doesn't affect it. I grab the rungs of the ladder and climb up.

At the top is a trapdoor. I push it open and step into a large chamber that must lie halfway up the hill, somewhere between the secret lab and the cable car. Lights jump on as soon as I enter, illuminating the walls and a floor of silver metal. Right in the center stands a full-scale version of Jim's model hang glider. Wow! He actually built it.

Over the low hum of a generator, a friendly female voice says, *"Welcome, Jim. Routine visit or emergency?"*

"Emergency. Emergency," I say quickly.

"Oh, sorry to hear that," the voice says calmly. *"Have a nice flight."*

The wall in front of me rolls to the side and I'm staring out at the night sky, cool wind rushing in. I walk up to the hang glider. I've no idea how to fly this, but as I approach it, I notice an inbuilt glass screen with flying instructions.

"Prepare for takeoff," the polite voice announces. I strap myself into the ropes that hang from the light metal structure, until I'm suspended safely beneath the big sail-like wings. As I close the last clip the voice says, *"Takeoff commencing."*

Before I can so much as blink, a propulsion system blasts me out into the night sky. The headwind sucks my breath away and then I'm soaring, high above the hills of Ararat. I can see the contours of the coast ahead and the mountains with the wind turbines to my right. On my left, the faint lights of houses are blinking. The wind is whipping through my hair, piercing my clothes while the mountain slope shoots past below me. It's amazing. I've never felt so free.

BOOM!

Over the whooshing and singing in my ears, the blast of a huge explosion rings out like canon fire. I look back and see a ball of flame shoot out of the open mountain wall. The night sky turns bright orange and an invisible force jolts me forward. Fire and burning rock fragments rain down on me. The glider shakes so much that I feel like I'm gonna fall out of the sky. I try to turn toward Ararat. I can see the lights of the first houses ahead, but the falling rock fragments are burning through the linen fabric of the glider, spattering it with holes that are smoldering around the edges. I glide lower to force a landing. The barren mountainside is behind me, the first scattered trees below me. I can make it! Then with a sudden burst, the whole right wing of the hang glider blazes up in flames. I tilt sideways, veering into circles. There's a terrible tearing sound as the tips of the fir trees rip through the linen sails of the left wing. Then I am falling through the darkness in a tangle of fabric and broken metal: spinning, twisting, turning.

CHAPTER 26

— New Beginnings —

I stare at a vast, white expanse. My head is cradled in something fluffy and soft, and for a moment, I get the crazy idea that I'm in the midst of the clouds, cocooned in cumulus. But then I realize that the cloud layer is a white ceiling and I'm lying in a bed. I want to sit up, but a dull throb runs through my right wrist and my head aches, so I just stay where I am, blinking in the sunny light. There are some flowers on the windowsill and outside, lush, green trees are swaying gently underneath a bright, blue sky. I turn my head and see Arlo sitting in an armchair on my right, looking at me through his glasses.

"Arlo . . ." I murmur.

"Good morning, Naya." He beams as he sees I'm awake.

I try to sit up, but my arm hurts as I put weight on it.

"Careful," Arlo says. "You took quite a fall."

"Where am I? What happened?" I ask.

"You're in Ararat Hospital," Arlo says mildly. "You've been asleep for two days. You were knocked unconscious when you landed in that curious aerial contraption you were flying. We found you in a heap of metal at the edge of the mountains. You are lucky to be alive. A concussion, a couple of burn marks, and a sprained wrist."

I touch a hand to my head as woozy images flash before my eyes. "Jim's hang glider . . . I escaped with it from the lab . . . after the . . . explosion . . . the bomb! Arlo, are the people OK?"

"Ararat's safe, Naya. Governor Proctor's safe. You stopped Kallion." Arlo smiles at me but something seems different about him.

Then it all comes back to me: the Water Festival, the electronic bomb, the melee at the Governor's mansion.

"Gillan . . ." I whisper. Like the shadows of a nightmare, the fight between him and Duke returns to my mind. The infinity pool . . . Duke transformed into a hideous monster . . . and Gillan falling. I look at Arlo, desperate for him to say that Gillan is all right and that everything is OK, but he gently shakes his head. And suddenly I'm crying, my whole body shaking, tears streaming down my cheeks. He's gone. How can he be gone after all we've been through? All the times he saved me. At Eden when I was angry with him he was still protecting me. And now I'll never see him again.

I feel a hand on my head as Arlo tries to comfort me. "All will be OK with time," he whispers.

But how can it, without Gillan? We had so little time together . . . We'd only just found each other. Without him, it's like a part of me is missing. We were one. I could feel it. As strongly as I can feel the whole life of the ocean around me when I'm in the sea. How can I explain that to anyone?

The door to the room opens and a doctor walks in. "Miss DeLora, you're awake," she says. "You may go."

I dry my eyes while the doctor turns in the doorway and walks off again. Arlo pulls a grimace. He picks up a bag and gets out a few things.

"I bought you some clothes." He puts a pair of joggers, a T-shirt, and some sneakers at the foot of my bed. "I hope they fit. I'll be outside when you're ready." He closes the door behind him as he leaves.

After months of Jessica's fashion, the clothes look really comfortable. I get dressed, fumbling a bit with the shoelaces. The bandage on my wrist is in the way, and I'm still feeling dizzy when I bend down. There's nothing to take with me as I leave the room. I sign out of the hospital at reception then follow Arlo to the exit.

The air is fresh and clear. I step across the parking lot, but at the sight of the shining rows of EVs I stop. "Arlo, where are we going?" I glance up the green hill slope, at the big villas. Is anyone even still living in the Queens' house?

"You're not going back to your deranged foster family if that's what you're wondering." Arlo turns around. "In fact, none of them are here anymore. Jim and Jessica have disappeared, most likely on the *Atlantean*, and Adelia, I'm afraid, was killed in the chaos that ensued when the electric pulse weapon struck."

I stand there confused. Where does that leave me?

Arlo reads my expression. "You're staying on Ararat. That's for certain. You've more than earned your place. The Governor has recognized you as a permanent member of our society. And he has awarded you a medal for your heroic actions at the Water Festival; for saving his life — and indeed most of Ararat."

I nod numbly. I should be relieved, but I feel entirely lost. What is there for me on Ararat without Gillan?

Arlo looks at me as if he's half guessing what I'm thinking. "You're coming home with me."

We get into his green EV. It whirrs a little as he starts it up. As we pull out of the parking lot, I realize that I haven't even thought about the FRS or the explosives set to blow the flood barrier.

"Arlo, what about the FRS? Are the people safe? Is my mom OK?"

Arlo nods. "Gillan's Aqua8 friends disabled the bombs fairly quickly. There were some Operation Neptune agents stationed at the fence, but we fought them off — along with some help from the residents. Two young men, called Neal and Ethan, proved particularly eager in the struggle," he adds with a twinkle in his eyes. "They asked after you and send their regards."

We crest the top of the hill, south of Ararat Harbor, and head toward a smaller house with gray stone walls. To my right, I recognize a single house perched high on the cliff edge above the harbor. Gillan's white mansion looks solitary and silent. I feel a lump in my throat as we drive past.

"What about my mom?" I ask Arlo. "How is she?"

Arlo pulls into a driveway bordered by trim, green hedges. "Why don't you ask her yourself?"

I look up and there she is, standing in the doorway, smiling at me.

"Mom!" I leap out of the EV, running toward her and throw myself into her arms.

"Naya, my darling, I missed you so much."

I'm swallowed in the waves of her long hair and her soft, knitted sweater.

"Arlo how is this possible? How can she be here?"

"Let's go inside first." Arlo leads us through a square hallway with walls paneled in dark red wood.

I vaguely register an electronic voice that chimes from somewhere near the entrance, *"New resident detected: Citizen ID 7121."*

Through an open door I see the living room with a stone fireplace and an orange shield above it, with the name QUINN picked out in green lettering. Double-winged doors lead onto a terrace with a view to the sea.

Arlo waves us over to a large leather sofa and plops himself down in an armchair then makes a pyramid of fingers on which he perches his chin.

"With the Queens gone, the Governing Council were planning to assign you to a new host family," he begins to explain. "Given recent discoveries about your uh . . . genetics, I knew I couldn't let you end up with just anyone. Unfortunately, my status as a bachelor precluded me from being granted the guardianship of a second minor. As you may know, our society encourages social bonding. And with Gillan still missing . . . not yet declared dead . . ." he falters. "In any case, the council wouldn't permit it. Once I had seen your mother nursing the wounded after the skirmish at the FRS, it occurred to me that her skills could be regarded as a scarce and invaluable asset to the hospital on Ararat. So I convinced the authorities of the advantages of a civil partnership between your mother and I. After all, their new Aqua8 champion needs a stable home."

I stare at Arlo. "You . . . you got married? So then she can stay with us? On Ararat!" I exclaim.

Arlo stutters, "The marriage is only official . . . Don't worry . . . I'm sorry we couldn't ask you . . ." But he doesn't get any further because I throw my arms around him and pull him into a hug. Arlo hugs me back, a little baffled.

Mom smiles.

"You must be hungry." Arlo puts an arm around me and leads us out onto the terrace where the table is already set for lunch.

When we're done Arlo picks up the plates. "I'll give you two a moment."

Mom puts her arms around me, then takes me upstairs and shows me my room, which overlooks the garden. There's a dark wooden bed in it with blue sheets and a small desk in front of the window. It's much smaller than my bedroom at the Queens' but more cozy. Mom's bedroom is right next to it. We go there and sit and chat for a long while. New clothes are laid out on an armchair. It looks like Arlo has already taken care of all the essentials. On Mom's dressing table sits the golden conch, no longer concealed in its box. I look at it and think of the sound of the waves and the stories Mom used to tell me.

"Jim says that I'm a born variant. One in whom the gene was active since birth . . ." I say while Mom strokes my hair out of my face. "He was a variant, too, wasn't he? My father?"

She nods.

"Is that why he left?"

Mom sighs. "Your father was different from anyone I ever knew. He belonged to the sea in a way that I couldn't comprehend. There are others, like him, living out in the ocean. They look to him for guidance. He couldn't stay, because they needed him. But he left me this conch to call him if ever I found myself in danger."

I look at her, surprised. "Why didn't you use it when the Valley flooded?"

"Because I had tried before. When Hurricane Nero hit the mainland and everyone thought that it would wipe out Cape Harmony and the Valley next. I sent out calls to your father four times in those days. But he didn't return. I don't know why."

"Did you know that I was like him?" I ask.

She smiles and shakes her head. "And neither did he. He left you the necklace, just in case. To keep you safe."

We sit a while longer in silence, but as the sun sinks lower on the horizon, I slip from her room. Even though I'm so happy to see her, I need a moment to myself. The weight of Gillan being gone is ever present. I cuddle up in my new bed and fall into a dreamless sleep.

The next morning I wake to a soft clatter of plates. I walk downstairs and find Mom in the kitchen making porridge and fruit for breakfast, like she used to when we lived in the Valley. I sit with her and we chat for a while until Arlo returns from the Governor's mansion.

"Curious news. My visit to Governor Proctor certainly paid off," he greets me. "But let us get all the official things out of the way first." He leads me into his study and sets down a thumb print reader in front of me. "This is for your credit account registration. The Governor has awarded you a not-too-shabby monetary reward to accompany your medal of honor. A little something to get you started as a permanent resident of Ararat."

I press my thumb to the reader. There's a *beep* and a little inbuilt screen pulls up a picture of my face. Next to it I read: Naya DeLora, Citizen ID 7121, 30,000 credits. I tap the confirm button and the machine beeps again: Registration complete.

"There, now you have full access to your finances. We will sort out your EV license in the next few days," Arlo says happily. "School won't begin until late August, but in light of recent events General Calder has requested that all Junior Cadets attend an intensive training course over the summer."

"Calder," I exclaim louder than intended. "Wasn't she arrested for treason?"

Arlo raises a bushy eyebrow. "Should she have been? So far only Alexis suggested as much. From what I've gathered not a single person can remember how the fighting broke out or where the Operation Neptune insurgents came from. Only that there was total chaos, no one knowing which side they were on."

"Calder was definitely on the Neptune side!"

Arlo looks at me, worried. "She claims that Kallion had bewitched her, same as everyone else."

"What? No, she was doing the bewitching. Didn't people notice when they woke from their trance?"

Arlo shakes his head. "I'm afraid not. According to Goldstein and Donovan, all they remember is Calder getting on stage. Then they heard beautiful music. Enchanting . . . quite peaceful . . .

hard to describe. When it stopped, fighting had broken out. General Calder assembled the attending Aqua8 members and apprehended the Operation Neptune insurgents. She claims she saved the Governor and the guests and that she would have done so sooner, had Alexis not stunned her twice."

"Once," I correct, "the first time was me."

"Oh." Arlo looks surprised. "Well, I'd keep that to myself."

"I can't! Calder was in on the whole plan. She tried to kill me. And there's something weird about her . . . She bewitched everyone with her song. And the stun dart barely had any effect on her. We need to tell Governor Proctor."

"Remember, proceed with caution when accusing high-ranking members of our society. If we go against the head of Aqua8, we need support. Is there anyone who can corroborate this?"

Gillan. If he were here. I ignore the painful sting in my chest.

"Only Coach Janson."

Arlo sighs. "That won't convince the council. The word of an ex-captain who was thrown out of Aqua8 for insubordination won't hold against the venerable head of our military. Alexis had a close brush with the authorities the first time she stood up against Calder, and has been under close government surveillance since, for her 'rebellious tendencies.' You see, even if you are born on Ararat, it is not generally advisable to fire harpoons into the dinghy of your military superior." He raises his brow in fatherly exasperation and adds, "Even so, Alexis does have an unhealthy tendency to ignore the fact that she has a noose around her neck, which is threatening to pull tight the minute she sets a *toe* out of line."

The way in which he emphasizes the word *toe* reveals that he knew about her covering the fifteen meter marker on my first day at Eden.

"Will she be OK?" I ask.

"Fortunately, Governor Proctor is a vain man," Arlo says. "The Water Festival exposed more than one of his weaknesses. He asserted that, as the head of the military, General Calder should not have allowed Kallion to bewitch us all in the first place. Since she failed to do her duty, she has only herself to blame for the events that ensued."

I grimace. Calder can't have been happy about that. I'm surprised she didn't try to arrest me, too. She saw me fire the combigun at her. I guess she can't mention that to anyone though. Not without me telling everyone that it was her song that bewitched the crowd. But now she knows I'm against her. A shudder runs down my spine as I think of Junior Cadet summer training. What if she just kills me on the military base and claims it was an accident? How could Gillan be so cocky around her, so unafraid? If only he were here with me. The feeling of loss in my chest threatens to grow into an all-consuming pit of despair.

I go out onto the terrace. The sea is calm, a perfect red and gold all the way to the horizon. There's only a soft breeze that blows through my hair. I stand there, taking in the morning sunlight. The sky's as golden as it was when Gillan and I went out on the boat. I look over at the Governor's mansion and the cliffs. The water around the rocks looks peaceful now, like no storm ever disturbed it. I can feel my heart ache in my chest. It's hard to believe that these are the same cliffs that Gillan plummeted down. Arlo's soft footsteps patter across the terrace behind me.

"He's really gone, isn't he?" I ask, my eyes on the sea.

Arlo stands beside me. "He is gone," he says then he holds out his fist and opens it, revealing Gillan's shark's-tooth shaped earring. "But I don't think he's dead."

The Blue Out Trilogy will continue with:

Riptide

About the Author

Thanks so much for reading our novel—we hope you loved it! We'd like to introduce ourselves … we're Miranda Storm Yes, there's actually four of us. Wow! Right? Our names are Kai Knight, Evan V. Francis, Skyrah Archer and Ira Kiourti. Some of us have chosen artist names, some are using our real names, and we all have our areas of expertise.

Kai's our sports enthusiast—a kung fu black belt, scuba diver and rock climber—who loves developing plot twists and action scenes. Evan's our star at adding comedic elements to dialogue and action, and he is fascinated by the power of books to bring imaginary worlds to life. Skyrah's our expert at developing characters and their background stories—which is no surprise given she's also an actor—and she has a hidden passion for military stories. Last but not least, Ira's our logician, philosopher, and stargazer, who loves the sea and is on a quest for consistency and meaning. We'd also like to give a shout out to Nadia Whyte, who's been helping us with her feedback along the way. Nadia loves travelling. She thinks reading is a good idea, no matter where, and she has a not-so-hidden passion for sci-fi and fantasy. A special thanks goes out to Kelly Urgan, who fell in love with the story right away—we couldn't have asked for a better copy editor!

Our story starts on a sunny summer afternoon when the four of us sat together in a sleepy Athens taverna and came up with the concept of Blue Out and the character of Naya DeLora. Over the next four years we laughed, struggled and conspired to bring this story to you. So many things inspired us; our connection to Greece and its deep blue seas united us and it runs deeply within this novel. Our greatest joy is sharing this world and all its characters with you. We've had a blast bringing them to life and we hope you enjoy reading about them just as much as we loved writing them!

Printed in Great Britain
by Amazon

11213544R00181